OYA BAYDAR was born in 1940. She studied sociology and philosophy at Istanbul University and in 1965 became a member of the Turkish Labour Party. She worked as a journalist but after the 1980 military coup was arrested for her writing and forced into exile in Western Europe. In 1981–2 she lived in Moscow and was in Frankfurt in 1989 at the fall of the Berlin Wall. In 1992 she returned to Turkey. Since then she has published six novels, a short story collection and other works of fiction and non-fiction, and her work has been translated into a number of languages, including German, French, Greek and English. She has won many literary awards in Turkey for her fiction, including the Orhan Kemal Novel Award.

THE LOST WORD

The Lost Word

OYA BAYDAR

Translated by Stephanie Ateş

PETER OWEN PUBLISHERS
London and Chicago

PETER OWEN PUBLISHERS
20 Holland Park Avenue, London W11 3QU

Peter Owen books are distributed in the USA and Canada by
Independent Publishers Group/Trafalgar Square
814 North Franklin Street, Chicago, IL 60610, USA

Translated from the Turkish *Kayıp Söz*
English translation first published in Great Britain by
Peter Owen Publishers 2011

ISBN 978-0-7206-1347-6

A catalogue record for this book is available from the British Library.

Printed and bound in Great Britain by
CPI Group (UK) Ltd, Croydon, CR0 4YY

This project has been funded with support from the European Commission.
This publication reflects the views only of the author, and the Commission
cannot be held responsible for any use which may be made of the information
contained therein.

Education and Culture DG
Culture Programme

ONE

'Do They Kill Children with Tiny Bullets, Mummy?'

I was looking for a word and I heard a voice.

I was in pursuit of the word. The word that I had used roughly, spent recklessly, blown into bubbles of soap and used up: that first sentence that would begin the story, carry it along and conclude it. The sentence that somehow could never be put down in words, that merged into the nebulous lightness of thought just as I thought I had got hold of it . . . The missing word . . .

I heard that voice; I forgot the word and followed the voice.

The man who plays with words, the acrobat of language, the word wizard . . .

Empty words of praise attached like labels to his name, laying siege to his identity. To the trite question 'Is there anything in the pipeline, master?' asked by his admiring, well-meaning and somewhat simple readers, the enthusiastic, ambitious art and literature correspondents and the critics, the arbiters of one's writing and fate, the curt answer given with an icy, insincere smile, a slight twitch of a muscle: 'There are a few things started. They are coming along. You'll see them in the near future.'

Yet there is only emptiness inside him – 'the frightening barren emptiness stretching to eternity of mirrors facing each other without reflection'.

Exhausted from striving for days and nights to produce the awaited great work from this polished, hollow sentence that he has heard somewhere . . . Thrashing around in the web of 'code name: love' relations that leave behind only the bitter taste of regret. The comebacks, each one of them a small-scale defeat: returning home with the feeling of bleak emptiness and suffocation only to escape again; to his wife always there, always loving, always restrained and always distant; to literary circles, pretending not to see their smirks of 'We know your past' hidden behind displays of praise and friendship; to his old comrades with the fear of not knowing where he will find them, in what mood and in what sphere. Roads, countries, towns, hotels, seas, ports and people: all just for the sake of living. With that feeling of emptiness and pointlessness clinging inside him . . .

He was in pursuit of a word, the word he had lost. He heard a voice. A voice that broke from the hum of the city reverberating in the far distance and bored into the desolate darkness of the night like a drill; that passed beyond time and space and broke on the shores of sleep and sleeplessness like surging waters, like the wind.

Did I hear it?

You hear the hum, the whisper, the shout, the talk, the music, the sounds and silence of nature, but you do not hear the scream. The scream closes in on you, envelops you and surrounds you, and adding a sixth sense to the five it becomes a single sense and pierces your cells. He recognizes it from the scream emitted by his wife when she was giving birth to their son, from the last inhuman scream of a man knifed beside him one night, and from the scream resounding to the world uttered by a woman in a black burqa – which war, which conflict, where, he does not remember – tearing at her burqa and baring her bosom before throwing herself over her dead son. The scream overcomes the voice and silences it. You don't hear the scream. It envelops you, surrounds you, drags you after it and engulfs you. The scream . . .

The passengers of the Anatolian coaches departing after midnight; common folk with their characteristic faces, clothes and smells. The sham, shabby order and the lively bustling disorder of the large city coach terminals attempting to emulate the slickly run airports. Monotone announcements with wrongly stressed words whose ends stretch like chewing-gum: 'Your attention please, passengers. Your coach is about to leave from Platform 17.' The small kebab shops, the vendors of dried fruit and nuts, booths, people selling scratch cards, stalls overflowing with religious books, booths stocking cassettes and CDs, halva and puddings; toilets smelling of urine, their floors always suspiciously wet, reservoirs broken, basins blocked. The coolness of June nights making one shiver slightly, the yellow melancholy diffused from dull, dim lights, the waiting-rooms gradually becoming deserted, and the platforms falling silent.

He has to wait more than half an hour before his coach is due to depart. He tries to kill time watching passengers bustling around, those coming to see people off, children begging, selling chewing-gum or tissues at the late hour, those gathered in front of the stalls selling cassettes or dried fruit and nuts. While drinking – in truth he had had a little too much to drink as usual – in the bar of a recently rediscovered trendy hotel that he used to visit frequently he suddenly had the thought that he could not bear to spend another night in the tedious city. He decided to cancel the two minor appointments for the following day and return to Istanbul that night by coach.

While buying a bottle of mineral water and a packet of cigarettes from the Başkent Büfesi – the chain of kiosks named for the capital city – in the corner by one of the large glass-panelled doors opening on to the platforms, he notices that he keeps repeating, 'Başkent Büfesi, Başkent Büfesi' like a jingle. Sometimes a word, a sentence or a line would get stuck in his mind like a broken record, especially if he has been drinking. As he thought about the meaning of the phrase repeating in his head he wonders why it's called a capital city. Do such cities change over the years? If so, how do they change? Why have I . . . why do we have a lifetime? And what is a lifetime? At least say a 'youthtime'. Could one produce an article from that inane question?

For how many generations have we been repeating the conundrums of our meaningless lives like a jingle without being able to answer them or resolve them? Especially this word 'conundrum' that we use everywhere. One uses words like these so that people consider one intellectual. There's nothing to write about here. I've got nothing to write about either. In any case, what sort of things did I ever produce? Come on, be honest, at least to yourself. But let's not be too harsh. Even if I'm not as great as I think I am I'm not a nobody. Damn it! I'm confused and I'm pissed. My head is like a terrible barren emptiness stretching to an eternity of mirrors facing each other without reflection. I really mustn't drink so much. My brain is like mush. If only the coach would arrive and I could find my seat, get my head down and fall asleep. If only I could lean my head back against the headrest smelling of sweat and fall into a deep sleep, to revive the memory of the days of youth and innocence when air travel was incompatible with our miserable student budget and frugal lifestyle, our horizons, surroundings and revolutionary principles. It would cost a month's basic wage for a plane ticket!

If he hadn't noticed the woman with the odd hat sitting outside on one of the benches near Platform 8 while he was waiting for his change in front of Başkent Büfesi he would not have headed in that direction. As he stashes his bottle of mineral water in one of the outside pockets of his small travelling bag the wide-brimmed, light-coloured hat catches his eye once more. He has always been drawn by the fascination of objects and walks towards Platform 8.

The woman is short, plump and elderly. She must be more than seventy. She is wearing pale, worn trousers that end just below the knee. Would you call them Bermuda shorts? On her head is a wide-brimmed old straw hat with a green ribbon and her hands are covered with white gloves. She could be a retired teacher who has settled in Bodrum or somewhere similar or the wife of an elderly bureaucrat spending half the year at a summerhouse by the sea. She reminds him a bit of his mother. These sorts of women paint fabric, tie-dye and sketch when they are not playing rummy. They also dabble in art and literature. Most of them are know-alls, insufferable women with the air of a pedagogue. They are women who believe in the certainty of their own convictions, who preface their remarks with 'We are the daughters of the generation of the Republic.' When they see a woman covering her head with a scarf they see red and lament, 'Even Atatürk could not make these people see sense!' – refining their vowels like teachers, officers' wives and friends of my mother. Perhaps I do the poor woman an injustice because she physically resembles my mother and because of the revulsion I feel towards my parents and that self-opinionated elitist circle.

The elderly lady is talking incessantly. He looks around to see whom she is addressing, but there is no one.

'Isn't that right, sir?' she asks in a voice with a foreign intonation, strangely accented but refined.

Has she recognized me, I wonder? She has recognized me. She has. God knows she has probably even attended my book-signing sessions. A warm sense of pride and self-satisfaction fleetingly passes through him, the pleasure of the gratification of fame, of being spotted and being considered important. However, he still plays the part of the man who is a little weary of and indifferent to fame, who is beyond this type of worldly gratification and who has had his fill of praise. He does not answer and pretends not to have comprehended that the question is directed towards him. Anyway he does not want to talk to anyone. If only the coach would pull up at the platform and he could put his head down and sleep. He remembers the days when, partly for love and partly for the revolution, he travelled back and forth between Istanbul and Ankara in cheap overnight coaches with their long bonnets. Those were the days of youth, the days of immaturity and innocence. Good days.

It is clear that the woman is determined, that she will persist until she gets an answer. He is angry with himself. Why on earth had he been drawn by a shabby hat and headed in that direction? Ever since a keen young critic referred to me as a 'writer who can perceive the magic of objects and put it into words' I feel I have to appear interested in objects. There you have it – a dowdy woman's hat! Why did I rush over here looking for trouble?

'You were there, too. We were in Warsaw. No, I think it was Budapest. When we were put on the boats the child was with me. We were escaping across the Danube. I did not want to leave the city, but they made me. I'm telling you, as I was boarding the boat the child was with me. You saw him. Tell them you saw him. They'll believe you.'

Should he reply? He is light-headed, befuddled, his thoughts scattered. When he drinks alone he loses it completely. There are, in fact, plenty of old friends and a lot of new acquaintances in this city. He could call one of them if he wanted, and they could go for a drink. If he were to get in touch with any of the new friends they would be only too pleased to be seen with the author Ömer Eren. The old ones, you never know – they might have written me off or perhaps they would be happy if I called them. One can't tell. I have many acquaintances but no friends left. I have used them all up, or I've buried them. Literally, I really have buried most of them, the best ones.

The voice of the strange woman interrupts his thoughts. 'They might not believe you either, but tell them all the same.'

It is obvious that the woman is batty. He racks his brains. Who was evacuated from Hungary across the Danube in 1956? He had listened to such stories from old folk. Damn it! I can't remember a thing. My memory is deteriorating by the day. I mustn't drink so much. I must listen to what my wife tells me, I mustn't go over the limit. Elif always keeps to the limit. The limit? What and whose limit? Elif's? Why?

'Just tell them what you saw. That's enough,' the woman repeats beseechingly. 'Tell them, sir.'

Tell them what I saw? Did I see anything? Had I seen anything? Had I told them what I'd seen? Would I have told them even if I had seen anything?

He doesn't say anything. He must get away from here. He must escape from this woman.

'They said the child was going to follow. I waited years, but he did not come. How could a tiny child travel those roads alone! When the Wall fell, the Hungarian daughter-in-law hid all the papers and the silver candlesticks, too. Well, perhaps the silver candlesticks stayed in Pest. One shouldn't put the blame on her. Isn't that right, sir?'

She gets up and walks towards him, Ömer Eren. He tries to escape, but the woman pulls at his sleeve. He shakes her off. 'I wasn't there. I don't know. I don't know anything,' he says as he tries to escape sideways like a crab.

She says, 'Everyone says, "I wasn't there", and "I don't know". In that case, who was there? Who knows, and who does remember what happened? Who took the child off the boat? Could it have been the daughter-in-law? She had begun to work for the others after my son was suspended for being a traitor. She, too, could very easily have hidden the silver candlesticks. I did not want to leave the east. I was going to wait there. I wasn't going to leave the child. He could have found me there. He could have found me. The child doesn't know these parts at all. He wouldn't be able to find anyone here.'

The woman returns to her place muttering. He can no longer hear or understand what she's saying. He is relieved that he's got rid of the madwoman. Without hurrying, he walks slowly over to the next platform so that she doesn't notice and follow him. 'The suspended son, the lost child, the river, the Hungarian daughter-in-law, candlesticks and the rest, the east, the Wall . . .' Words blown about in the air and swept along with people in the whirlwind of the age. What has all this got to do with this overweight ordinary old woman? Why shouldn't it have something to do with her? No one carries what they have experienced on their bodies, on their clothes or on their faces. They carry it in their hearts, their memories and their eccentricities.

The words of the strange woman are lost and become inaudible amid the shouts, cries, the chanting of familiar marches and the general commotion. At first he doesn't understand where the uproar is coming from.

He looks over to where the noise is emanating. A coach, with a large flag hung at the front and its windows adorned with paper flags displaying the star and crescent, is pulling up at Platform 3. It has a banner stretched the length of one side on which is written, 'Our soldier is the greatest soldier'. Thirty or forty boys walk in step towards the bus carrying young men on their shoulders, youths like themselves. Flushed with excitement, their serious faces with wispy moustaches look quite tense under the dim yellow lights. Mesmerized by their voices they make the sign of the wolf's head with hands raised and eyes almost popping out of their sockets. It is one of the familiar send-off ceremonies for soldiers that everyone is used to. Everything damned normal in the everyday flow of life. Everything moves in a frightening circle of desperation and absurdity that causes more and more pain.

A night coach terminal – they used to call them bus stations; a woman who had escaped across the Danube by barge and is still on the run – who knows why and where to – was it the Second World War or the Hungarian Uprising? And the boy? Was there really a boy? Here other boys are yelling with all their might: boys rending their throats and the night with cries of 'Love or leave', 'Death to the leader of the separatists', 'The flag will not be lowered', 'Our homeland will not be divided' and 'Our soldiers are the greatest soldiers.' Children of another place, another time and another cause . . . Child actors who take parts in all the tragedies played out on the world's stage but who always remain extras.

What am I doing here? I'm tired, I'm exhausted and I'm drunk. What's more, I've lost the word. I cannot write any longer. I don't like myself. I'm at war with myself. And now the idea of going to Istanbul by coach doesn't seem that great. It is as repugnant to his tired spirit as it is to his body that is well into its fifties. A drunken decision made on a bad night drinking alone. Suppose I go back to the hotel and zonk out . . . Then tomorrow I'll return to Istanbul like a lamb on the first plane with a free seat. There's no need to catch the first plane. What urgent business do I have? What is there waiting for me in Istanbul apart from Elif? In any case, she's busy with her experiments, her students and those scientific articles that she writes for foreign journals. Waiting is the job of unemployed people, and Elif is always up to her eyes in work.

He did not hear the gunshot, and if he did hear it it had not registered. However, the scream became a bullet of sound and hit him with full force in the chest. An anonymous stark-naked scream, without identity and without substance broke from the hills of Çankaya, from the vineyards of Seyran and from the Citadel, from slopes and ridges. It enveloped the lofty districts of the capital girded with the state's arrogance; its boring civil-servant districts of ties and suits; its shanties decorating the naked hills with poplars, oleasters and pear trees, its slums inexorably edging into the city, its slopes climbing to the Citadel, its avenues, streets, bus stops and stations and its midnight coach station. It spread over the city and struck the heart of whoever was in its path and echoed all around. It reached the strange old woman and Ömer.

He was caught up in the vortex of the sound. How long did he turn in that vortex? How did he get out? Was he able to get out? The woman had crept up to him. Or had he moved towards the woman? He heard her whisper, 'They killed the child.' And inside his head the scream turned into a voice and the voice into words and the words into meaning. The child! They've killed the child!

Between Platform 2 and Platform 3 and in the middle of the deathly silence that suddenly falls on the coach station a young woman is lying on the ground. The blood flowing between her legs leaves ever-widening circular stains on her long printed cotton skirt. She is very young, almost a child. Her face, lit by the wan lights, is a bluish-white. In the middle of this nightmare she is too beautiful to be true. As she turns her head to the swarthy youth kneeling in front of her, she tries to smile. Then her face contorts with pain, her lips move and she tries to say something – and perhaps she does. The young man gently puts his hand under the girl's head. He pulls off the headscarf with the crocheted border that covers her forehead and hair and drapes it round his neck; he winds her thick corn-coloured hair around his fingers. With one hand he continues stroking the girl's stomach and, inclining his face to hers, whispers something, words of love.

The time-stopping absolute silence, that moment of consternation and indecision experienced in another dimension must, in fact, have lasted just a few moments. Two of the youths, who had been making a commotion a few minutes before, shouting slogans, waving flags of crescents as well as Turkish flags, are running away, and no one is pursuing them. The coach station's night travellers, those being sent off on military service and those seeing them off, approach very slowly, in circles, moving in time to the silence like the final scene in a tragic ballet. Then a burst of sound, shouts, disjointed sentences, questions, oaths, curses and complaints. The young man kneeling beside the girl who has been shot whispers, 'You've shot her. You've killed the child! You've killed the child!' as though he has spent all his voice in that first cry that pierced his throat.

The words become a voice and they echo, You've killed the child. You've killed him! *We zarok kuşt! We zarok kuşt!*'

Then the commotion. The screams, 'Someone's been shot! Come and help!' The shouts of 'Help!' The hum that makes one's head throb. 'Is there an ambulance? Is there a doctor?' The bustling men arriving with a stretcher, the paper flags trailing on the ground, the bewildered security men. A voice rising from among the dispersing crowds, 'Martyrs do not die. The homeland will not be divided.' The brothers trying to gather the people running away and continue the commotion from where they left off, as though nothing had happened. The accursed murder by a gun fired in the air for the sake of a cause that they do not even understand. The childish innocence of the unknown murderer who pulled the trigger. The desperation in the eyes of the youth who clings to the stretcher as they carry away the girl hit by a stray bullet, and the suffering engraved on his face. And the bloodcurdling words of the strange woman who is insensible to what is going on around her and who does not leave Ömer's side.

'They put pressure on me, but I didn't become a collaborator. And I knew who killed the child, but I didn't tell them. I persuaded myself that he hadn't died. And it wasn't the Hungarian daughter-in-law who had hidden the candlesticks. There, I'm confessing to you. I saw who shot the child and who stole the candlesticks, too. It was one of our lot.'

With anger, desperation and bewilderment he grabs the woman by the shoulders and shakes her. 'What child, which child, madwoman? Who did you see?'

'Take your hands off me. The people who shoot are all the same and the people who get shot, too. I didn't speak then. I didn't give anyone away. The child is always the same, the same child. You shot him. I saw you.'

He pushes the strange woman roughly and runs after the people departing with the stretcher.

He hears the woman shouting after him, 'Where are these boats going to? Tell me if you know, sir. Where was I going to get off? Which port? I won't tell anyone it was you who shot the child. Where does this river flow?'

A dirty cover has been thrown over the wounded girl, her eyes are closed and her face and body contract and shake simultaneously. She moans continuously like a sick kitten. From time to time the moans change to stifled sobs. Ömer puts his hand on the back of the boy who is trying to hold one end of the stretcher and says, 'I'm a doctor.' There is no point in being honest and saying, 'I'm a writer.' Who will take any notice of a writer? Right now only a doctor is important.

They leave the stretcher on the ground. He puts his hand on the patient's forehead. It's like ice. To make out he's a doctor he tries to take the wounded girl's pulse. She moans, and he takes fright and gives up. The siren of the ambulance is heard in the distance. The security guard arrives with the chief police officer.

'Did you see the incident?'

'Yes, I did. I don't know who shot her, but it must have been one of that group sending off new recruits. Two people ran away. Yes, I'm a witness.' Identification, address . . . 'Yes, I'll stop by the police station tomorrow.'

The face of the youth beside the wounded girl is the colour of pus. He seems completely drained of blood. He struggles to find his identity card. For a moment Ömer is frightened that the boy does not have one, that they will take him away and that he will get into trouble. If necessary I'll intervene. I'll explain who I am, and I'll protect the boy. He sees a few tears trickling down the youth's cheeks and getting lost in the stubble on his face.

'She'll be all right', he says, 'She'll be all right. Don't worry.'

While the police are trying to take statements the wounded girl carries on bleeding profusely.

'The child has gone. The child was our life,' the youth keeps repeating. He does not care about anything beyond that.

This is when Ömer realizes that the wounded woman was pregnant.

'Just wait and see. Don't worry. Perhaps they'll be able to save the child, too.'

An image of the clotted blood oozing from between the girls legs, spreading on her skirt and over the concrete platform appears before his eyes. He doesn't believe his own words either.

The noise of the siren gets closer and closer.

'Where are they going to take her?' asks the young man in a fearful, suspicious voice.

'To the hospital.'

'We don't have any money,' he whispers. His voice is desperate, pathetic and sad. 'And if they are after us . . . they won't let us live. And what's more . . .'

It is then that Ömer notices the strong eastern accent in the boy's voice. He remembers the Kurdish cry for help. He looks at his face carefully for the first time. He sees the loneliness, fear, hopelessness and the look of a cornered, wounded animal. He guesses that they are on the run. They are running away from someone. What a good thing the policeman trying to get the statements signed did not hear what he said.

The ambulance arrives and stops just in front of them. As he helps to lift the stretcher he says, 'Don't be afraid. I'll come with you, and we'll sort out the hospital and everything. I know a hospital where there are doctors who are acquaintances of mine. Don't worry. If there are any other problems we'll see to them.'

He speaks with the confidence and the power of being Ömer Eren. The youth looks at his face with mistrustful, suspicious and anxious eyes that question why he is doing this.

The night is dark and the sky an inky blue. The moon sheds no light. The lights of the city obscure the stars. Over there, in the distance, is the Citadel. The giant flag on top of the Citadel is illuminated by a bluish light and is waving gently. To drown out the noise of the ambulance's siren that grates on the nerves and wrenches the heart Ömer shouts, 'Where did you come from? And where were you heading for?'

Just then the wounded woman screams in pain. Blood trickles on to the ground from the side of the stretcher. He cannot hear the answer. Perhaps no one has responded.

Looking lovingly at the laboratory animals with their pink eyes and hairless pink tails in the little cages Elif remembered a little sadly and with a longing for the days of her youth how she had cried when she killed her first mouse. It was thirty years ago – perhaps even longer. They were my first dead mice, my first murder.

She used to enter the laboratory at the crack of dawn before anyone had started work to finish the studies for her doctorate that she had begun with great hope, enthusiasm and determination. Her lecturers used to say jokingly that she would be the first Turkish girl to get a Nobel Prize. Why not! I'll get it, you'll see.

It could not be said that she was modest. As the not especially beautiful middle daughter of a middle-class low-income teacher's family with three children, she had discovered at an early age that the way to break out of the narrow family circle, to excel and escape from a inevitable and dreary future and to gain recognition and respect was to achieve success. She was ambitious. Her ambition fed her determination, and her studiousness made up for anything she lacked in talent, ability or intelligence. She did not want to resemble her mother and to live like her aunts and neighbours. She hated being cooped up in rooms and kitchens and houses permeated by the smell of the workaday lives of ordinary people, mending clothes, making food and giving tea parties. Even when she was a little girl she had not played mothers and fathers; she had not liked toy furniture or kitchen sets, and she had not shown much interest in dolls. She adored soft furry animals: teddy bears, rabbits, cats, dogs and mice. If they had been alive, of course, that would have been better, but she was not allowed to keep animals in the house. She had cried bitterly when the timid hazelmouse that she had fed with nuts, dried fruit, breadcrumbs and morsels of cheese without telling anyone – not even her siblings – had been caught in a trap baited by the cheese that her father had smeared with poison. Her father had had to swear to her that he had let the mouse go and not killed it.

As she dons her lab gloves she remembers the agonized, numbed look of her dear little mouse caught in the trap. How strange! So many years have passed, and it's still a vivid memory. She opens the cage on the large table and takes out one of the test animals, holding it with two fingers. Trying not to hurt it, she places it on the table covered with sterile paper. Now let's put you to sleep and see what's happened inside! When she realizes that she is trying to avoid looking the mouse in the eye a sad smile passes over her face. It is good that I recall my emotions when I cried over my first dead mouse. She feels compassionate and sensitive, and she is pleased about it. She stabs a needle into the nape of the mouse's neck. There's a faint desperate 'eek' that she still hasn't got used to after all this time and that she cannot pretend not to hear: the mouse's feeble dying scream. The animal goes into spasm, and its paws quiver a few times. She feels the tiny body go limp between her fingers. And that's it. After all these experiments who knows how many little dead souls I have left behind. Suddenly she begins to weep quietly. And she is surprised at her tears. Is it because she has killed the mouse? She takes a curious delight in the warm drops trickling down her cheeks.

It had not been easy for her to get used to killing laboratory animals. 'To obtain results one needs to be fairly brutal,' her tutor used to say. 'Think of the thing in your hand not as a living being but as a piece of cloth. Think how many children's, how many people's and how many animals' lives you can save in killing one test animal!'

Elif wanted to obtain results, to succeed. She had thought about and approved of what her tutor had said and had been convinced. All the same, there was a side to this work that disturbed her. Can one consider a living thing a piece of cloth? Thousands of souls in return for one soul, thousands of lives in return for one life. And who was going to account for that one soul, that one life? Does the principle 'for the benefit of the majority' render all murder justifiable? Perhaps it was the increasing weight of these issues that gradually distanced Professor Elif Eren from the lab work that she had at one time passionately loved. It steered her to the philosophy and ethics of science and to ponder on ethical issues involved in genetics. She had also matured enough no longer to dream of a Nobel Prize.

As she examines the piece of brain that she has taken from the small white mound of fur under the microscope linked to the computer, she tries to free her mind from the sound of the telephone that continually rings somewhere in her mind and concentrate on her work – in other words, the dead mouse. The effort is useless. Everything she does and thinks comes back to the phone that rang towards dawn and to the strident metallic sound continuously jangling in her brain. The sound of the phone persists like some horrible background music that she cannot silence.

Towards dawn she awoke in a sweat from a confused dream in which she was trying to escape from an arrow of fire stuck in the middle of a misty, foggy road along which she was walking. In her drowsiness she had not grasped at first what was happening, and when she realized that the arrow of fire was the telephone ringing she became agitated. Since her childhood she had learnt through bitter experience that knocks on doors after midnight and before dawn and midnight telephone calls brought bad news. In her childhood memory, the death of her father was a midnight telephone call coming from a small, remote Anatolian town. Her father, a harmless teacher, had been posted there having incurred the wrath of the ruling party. In the days of the military coup, they had come for her husband in the early hours of the morning, kicking the door until it almost broke and barging into the bedroom with their heavy weapons. At the time she was three and a half months pregnant. She had silently watched Ömer being taken away with a look of contempt on her face, trying to protect her stomach with her hands – they could have harmed the child if they had pushed her around. The pain of her son – or should one say his going and disappearing – was the ring of a phone after midnight piercing their deep sleep, a call from the hospital. 'Is Deniz Eren a relative? His condition is serious. Come straight away.' They had informed her by phone at dawn, too, about the laboratory fire, which had, in only minutes, turned to ashes the months of effort she had expended on the important experiment and destroyed her beloved test animals. Elif was afraid of midnight telephone calls and knocks on doors at dawn.

She had reached for the phone in a state of panic with the thud of accelerating heartbeats, and when she heard Ömer's voice her agitation had mounted. Something bad must have happened. He's a night bird; he doesn't wake up at this hour. Sometimes he works until morning, writing continuously while he drinks. Perhaps he's drunk, too drunk to realize that I would be asleep at this hour, perhaps even worse . . .

'Is something wrong, dear? Why are you calling at this hour? Are you all right?' She tries not to sound anxious.

'I'm fine, fine. Nothing's the matter. I was planning to return tomorrow, but it didn't work out. I'll tell you later. I'll be travelling for a while; I'm going east. I'll be delayed, and I just wanted to let you know.'

Now what was that all about? At the crack of dawn . . . He hadn't told her when he was coming, so why should he let her know that he would be delayed? Perhaps he had simply wanted to hear her voice. Or was he checking up on her? Was she still there – not just in body but emotionally for him? Was she waiting for her husband with tireless patience?

What is left of love? What can be left after thirty years? The fear of not finding what was left where it was left, the anxiety of the insidious power of separations that gnaw at relationships and the worry of losing a person. The cosy habit, the sense of security, that begins where the fire of the passion of the flesh begins to wane and the attraction of the unattainable is lost. A sort of comfort, the feeling of someone being there for you. A bond that both are still afraid of losing.

'You're going east? What a coincidence! I'm going west next week, to Denmark. There's a symposium on the philosophical and ethical dimensions of gene technology.'

'Me to the east and you to the west . . . We are gradually drifting apart!'

Did Ömer say these words, or did I imagine them? It's true we've been together seldom during the last few years. Our work and hobbies are very different, and, like it or not, our social circles differ as well. However, I never thought that our paths could separate after we'd shared so many experiences. After all, we have so much behind us. So much what? Youth for a start. Our passionate effort that transformed pain and hardship into the hope of good days to come; a shared belief that we held the key to a bright future not only for the people of this country but for mankind in general, and the revolutionary dream that fired our blood and burnt our hearts. We were excited, innocent children who had not yet learnt that fire burnt. And we played happily, leaping into the heart of the fire. That wasn't all. There were the shared delights, pleasures, happiness and joy, mutual friends and mutual victories, the smells, the pain experienced together, as well as successes. There were the fiascos and the defeats. And that . . . that defeat we can't discuss, that we don't mention because we fear that if we were to break our silence even once the bond between us would be irreparably broken. Defeat? No, complicity.

'And while you're there, will you go and see him, too?'

She understands what her husband wants to say but is still upset by his words. 'We are gradually drifting apart,' she repeats. Then, 'Who am I going to see?' – just to hurt him.

'The boy . . . Are you going to visit the boy?'

She feels anguish as she hears the insecure, humble, begging tone in his voice and his inability to say the boy's name. Are men more fragile, more vulnerable than women when it comes to such matters? Can mothers endure pain better? Is it the physiology of fertility reflected in the brain? Ömer never got used to it. He never forgave himself or the boy or life itself. And what about me? Have I been able to get used to it while still being 'me'? Have I been able to accept it?

She sits down at the computer. For a moment she becomes engrossed in the magic of the colourful images on the screen. She remembers the kaleidoscope that she never tired of playing with as a little girl. The cardboard telescope that made flowers of paradise bloom, fairytale butterflies fly about and spilt multicoloured stars from the sky when she put it to her eye and turned it. It was her favourite childhood toy. She did not know the word kaleidoscope but used to call the magic cardboard pipe, a 'fairytale telescope'. One day she had not been able to resist removing the transparent mica at the end of the cardboard tube from its casing with a knife. She wanted to see those wonderful colours and shapes without the aid of the instrument and to touch the stars and flowers. And she was also curious about the workings of the toy.

As she admires the multicoloured complex patterns reflected on the computer screen, she remembers with regret the coloured paper and pieces of glass that fell on the ground from the kaleidoscope. Never try to analyse the truth behind beauty. Heavenly images can be created from detritus. Just look, enjoy and take pleasure in them. Is it always crucial to know the truth behind an illusion? Is it possible to turn on its head the impulse that the search for truth is crucial? What in these days of virtual reality is the meaning of such questions? She must examine such conundrums in the paper she is going to present at the science ethics congress. It could be useful for enlivening her talk and exploring the link between reality and the virtual world and between the virtual world and ethics.

She makes a note of the formulas of the images reflected on the screen and of her own interpretation. All the reactions of the mouse's brain cells match her hypothesis. At present the experiment is progressing successfully. How many more mice will be needed? Then will it be the turn for cats? And what about research on people? I must take the students to the lab for today's lesson. Let them see for themselves how a hypothesis is verified step by step. That is, if any of them are interested. She knows that most of the students enrolled in the department out of necessity because their marks were not good enough for the subjects they really wanted to study. What good is basic science in this day and age? Especially in Turkey. That is why she is pleased that everything is going well with the experiment, and step by step her theory is being proved – even though she doesn't always feel like giving lectures. She is happy, too, with the images and the figures that she sees on the screen. This may not result in a Nobel Prize but a lesser award, a European Woman Scientist award, for example. So why am I crying? Surely not because I killed a mouse.

She thinks about his question, 'Are you going to visit the boy?' For months this issue has played on her mind, since the day she was invited to present the paper at the symposium in Copenhagen. Relatively speaking, Copenhagen is just a stone's throw from Norway. Naturally she can go to see the boy. What is strange is Ömer asking this on the phone. What was behind it? Was it a mere reminder or suggestion, or was it a request? It is the first time he has mentioned the boy for a long time. Has the memory faded, or doesn't it hurt as much as before? How much time does a person need for pain to turn to sadness? She remembers the words of a favourite author, 'Because sadness is the projection of pain.' My pain has slowly turned to sadness. It doesn't burn as before, but it is more profound. And this is what I can't bear: everything ending, passing, getting accustomed to it, and it becoming ordinary . . . How did Ömer survive? How did he bear his pain? We have never talked about it. We refrained from talking about it, and we avoided the subject. We did not share our mutual pain. If the source is the same, if it hits two people with the same arrow, pain cannot be shared – or at least it doesn't lessen with sharing. You said, 'Me to the east and you to the west' in a broken, bitter tone. If you keep going straight to the east and I keep going to the west, perhaps one day, my love, we might meet on a small remote island.

A small remote island; her lost son's island. She doesn't not know if that tiny spot on the northern map is a real piece of land or a part of a nightmare from which she can never wake up. If she forgets it she thinks she will be able to overcome the pain. Nevertheless she strives not to forget – because this would mean forgetting the boy, too.

The island was a small point as big as the head of a pin on the tourist map. They had read the map with difficulty because the light in the car was insufficient on that December day when darkness fell at four in the afternoon. They had left Bergen and were travelling towards the north of Norway. The places that were marked with 'overnight facilities' symbols on the map were closed, and not a soul was in sight. The keeper who offered bed and breakfast at the lighthouse where they had stopped as a last resort had explained in English, German, Norwegian and sign language that they were not open on Christmas Eve and that he was going to have Christmas dinner with his family in the village. He had said that there was a small island fifteen kilometres further north and that they should try there. 'We are little more than a smoke away from the North Pole,' Ömer had said with his usual nonchalance. 'Let's put our foot down so that we reach this Devil's Island before it's pitch dark.'

They had been on the road since morning. The boy was only small; he was tired and hungry and, after grizzling for a while, had fallen asleep on the back seat.

'At least he's an easy, adaptable child – or we'd be in trouble!'

'My son takes after his father. Am I complaining?' Ömer replied.

She had thought: He's right. It was my idea to go north in the middle of winter. But, still, we did the right thing. We'll return to Turkey in the summer, and we might not get the chance to see these places again.

Her contract with the Genetics Research Institute in Denmark where she had been working for the past two years was going to finish at the end of term. And the short-term grant given to Ömer by the International PEN's fund for writers under threat or suppression in their own country had been stopped. Now they wanted to return home. 'Yes, we know that everything will be very difficult, but it's our homeland. Our roots, our friends, our struggle is there. We can still do something there. We can still be useful. We are foreigners here. No one needs us.' This is the sort of answer they gave when they were asked why they wanted to return to Turkey. And, what was more, Turkey was slowly changing. The darkness of September 1980 had begun to lift at the edges. The same old folk song was on their lips: 'Don't give up hope for your country.' The song that Ömer sometimes sang as 'Don't give up hope for man.'

They hadn't yet given up hope for life, the world, their country and mankind. We were young. Flames hadn't yet begun to envelop the smouldering world. Even if bastions were falling one by one, we thought that they fell down because they hadn't been well built, that too much sand had been mixed with the cement. We believed that stronger ones would be built in their place.

Was the weather especially clement that year, or was the climate of this region protected from Arctic winds by the surrounding mountains always this mild? 'It's because of the Gulf Stream,' Ömer had said. 'The warm current tempers the cold of the Norwegian coast.' On one side of the road there was an inland sea without a wave like a smooth lake and on the other side were rocks covered with moss and stumpy deep-green reed-like plants. While travelling on the little car ferries that used a winch system to cross the twenty or twenty-five metres between the small islands, they thought to themselves: What an adventure! They tried not to show each other that they were a little concerned, wondering where the road would end.

Where the road ended – and the road really did end at the sea – there was a makeshift quay at which was moored a small boat resembling a miniature steamer with its funnel, wheelhouse, cabin and ship's rail. A woman wrapped in woollen shawls carrying two heavy baskets, one on each arm, was standing at the edge of the quay observing the boat. They paused for a moment without knowing what to do and then realized that they had to leave the car there. A man with a pipe in his mouth beckoned as though to say, 'Hurry up.' The woman with the baskets jumped on to the boat. They went back to the car to fetch the child and their travelling bags. The boy had woken up and was looking around with anxious eyes. His father undid the seatbelt in the back and took his son in his arms.

'There, we're going to the Devil's Island in the book. You can tell your friends about it when you get back.'

'You don't get back from the Devil's Island,' said the child in a sleepy but certain voice. 'And, in any case, I don't have any friends to tell.'

She remembers that just then a sharp pain shot through the middle of her chest, an irrational bad feeling. Was it the child's loneliness or his anxiety – even in his father's arms – that affected her like this? Then she heard Ömer's laugh, his jokes that made the child laugh as well, a return to the familiar happy course of things . . .

On the boat no one was asking for tickets or directing passengers. It was just them, the woman with the baskets and two others. The island was immediately opposite. They could make out one or two dim lights and an imposing fortress meeting the sky in the twilight, like a castle of wicked giants in fairytales. Ömer continued the game with his son:

'There, I told you! That is the Devil's Castle.'

The boy had shaken off his tiredness and the drowsiness of sleep and joined in.

'Daddy, tomorrow morning let's go and see the Devil. And when I draw my sword, then . . .'

When they set foot on land there was no one around. The boat's captain and the couple of travellers had vanished in a trice. Then they saw the woman with the baskets. It was as though she hadn't got off the boat but had suddenly appeared from the sea or – in some strange way – had always been there, while the woman they had seen on the opposite shore was her ghost.

'Hotel? Bed and breakfast?'

They try to get help from the woman with the baskets in half-sentences by utilizing the few words they know of Danish, English and German. The woman points to the road stretching along the coast.

'At the end, at the very end.'

That much they understand. They walk in front of the houses that line the length of the road, each one a different colour – yellow, pink, green and lavender – with light filtering from behind their short-lace-curtained windows, with not a soul in sight. Leaving the cafés and the bistros behind them, with doors open and lights on, tables and counters empty, at the end of the road they arrive at the door of a white wooden cottage with the single German word 'Gasthaus' written on it.

'Why in German?'

'We'll have to ask.'

The door is open, and lights are on in the entrance and in the corridor as well. They enter rather diffidently. 'Is anyone there?' They call out first in German and then in the few Nordic words they know. No one answers, and no one comes to greet them. They open the door facing them at the end of the corridor. It's a large homely kitchen. The wooden chairs arranged round the large table in the middle show that the place is also used as a dining-room. The stove is burning, and the room is warm and cosy. They only notice that they have been cold when they feel the heat of the room and their faces scorched by the flames from the logs burning in the stove. After all, it is the end of December and we are in the north! On the table there is an appetising cheese platter and a round cake. 'Cake!' shouts the boy with excitement.

It is then that they see an old man sitting in a rocking-chair next to the stove in the corner with a hand-knitted woollen blanket on his knees.

'Everyone has gone,' he says in German. 'They've all gone to church – to the service. I cannot walk very far. In any case, if I could, I would rather go to the bar than the church.'

His language is formal and bookish, strictly observing the complicated grammatical rules of German. He laughs, making a funny hiccupping noise. 'The rooms are upstairs, and the keys are in the doors. You can stay where you like because there are no other guests. If you are hungry that's too bad. There's cheese, coffee and cake . . . That's all.'

'You speak excellent German.'

'I was German once upon a time. Language is the country that a person has lost.'

' Language is a person's country,' repeats Ömer in German.

'His lost country!' insists the old man. Then with his right arm extended in a Nazi salute he continues in a cynical high-pitched and tremulous voice, 'Deutschland, Deutschland über alles . . .'

He utters an expletive that sounds like a bit like 'fuck'. It is obviously a swear word.

'Stand to attention, ladies and gentlemen. Here you have the unknown deserter. Deutschland, Deutschland über alles! The only way not to be an unknown soldier is to be an unknown deserter.' He laughs again in the same strange way. 'There are memorials to the unknown soldier in all the countries of the world, but for some reason there is not a single memorial to the unknown deserter.'

'Which war?' asks Ömer, feigning interest. He recalls the Unknown Soldier Memorial at Potsdamm in Berlin and that it was made by a Turkish sculptor. He had heard that someone, possibly a neo-Nazi, had destroyed it.

'That's not significant. Wars never end. I'm the deserter of all the wars in the world.'

As they emerge from the kitchen to find a room and rest for a while or at least put the child to bed, the old man calls after them, 'The rooms are chilly. Light the fire to warm the place up so that the child doesn't get cold. Perhaps they'll bring you something to drink when they return from the service. If anyone comes back, that is. Do you have anything to drink on you? Alcohol? I mean alcohol.'

Ömer opens his case and holds out the brandy bottle that they have brought along for emergencies.

'There are glasses over there in the cupboard,' says the man without getting up. 'Cut a piece of cake for the boy while you're at it.'

Ömer takes three small glasses from the worm-eaten wooden cupboard and fills them with brandy. The three of them drain their glasses in one go. He leaves the bottle on the coffee table next to the man.

'We'll be off early in the morning. We're going further north.'

'They come, stay one night and then leave early.
I don't know where they go when they leave. Is there any place to flee?
There's nowhere else to go other than to yourself.
The violence of the age will find you everywhere.
Everyone's last refuge is their own island.
I've been here for a thousand years; unknown and a deserter.'

Even with their lack of German they realize that the old man is murmuring lines of verse.

'I've been here for a thousand years; unknown and a deserter,' repeats the man.

'That sounds like a poem,' says Ömer.

'Yes, it is. A poem that thousands of people read once upon a time. This is because I'm a poet deserter or a deserting poet.'

Without feeling the need to pour the remaining drink into a glass, he empties the brandy dregs straight into his mouth from the bottle.

Was the island real? Or was it a mirage, a nightmare? That piece of land, that island of invisible occupants surrounded by a sea as calm as a man-made lake in a season when the storms in the North Sea are at their wildest, where not a single soul wandered its streets, where no one seemed to live in the pink, indigo-blue, pale-green and candy-yellow houses with the light filtering through the windows, where no one was to be seen other than the ghost of a village woman carrying baskets and a thousand-year-old deserter whose legs could not carry him; the imposing fortress with the open sea extending to eternity and the freezing wind that made one shudder when one climbed the ruined ramparts; the room with its wooden ceilings where they tried to get warm by huddling together in bed in a small guesthouse where no one greeted them, showed them their rooms nor gave them their keys. The old man, the unknown deserter . . . Were they actually real?

When they awoke in the morning the sea and the sky were a deep blue. The man had fallen asleep in the rocking-chair where he had sat all night. Perhaps he had passed out. The bottle of spirits on the small table beside him was empty. There was fresh coffee in a pot on the stove, hot milk in a jug and buns, a cheese platter, salted fish and the cake from the previous evening on the kitchen counter. They had breakfast while they waited for someone to offer them a bill. The child liked the milk and cake, Ömer the salted fish and sweet sauce and Elif appreciated the coffee. The old man was in a deep sleep. Still there was no one else around. They left some money on the counter and left. Everything was normal and ordinary on the island, now stripped of its creepy and mysterious darkness and clothed in a blue light. The boat that was to take them to the opposite shore was tied to the quay. The woman with the baskets on her arms was there once more. There was no one on the road, at the quay or in the square.

'Who would awake at the crack of dawn on Christmas morning!' said Ömer, feeling a need to rationalize the strange quiet.

The child wanted to go up to the Devil's fortress and see the Devil in his castle.

'Look, there's no one in the village. Even the Devil has gone on Christmas holiday.'

'Perhaps everyone has gone to the castle to wish the Devil a merry Christmas,' said the boy. 'Even if you don't let me, I'll come here when I'm grown up and meet the Devil.'

'All right. You do that. Now let's get aboard this boat before it's too late and cross to the other side. Let's see if our car is in its place.'

Elif held the little boy's small hand tightly. The child had not worn his gloves, and his hands were like ice and his tiny nose red with the cold. She put her arms round her son with a surging wave of love that felt as though it would pierce her breast.

Now, in the laboratory with a dull ache in her breast and a dead white mouse in the palm of her hand, she is thinking about that small, remote island back then. The island of the unknown deserter and crazy old poet. The island of her fugitive son . . .

When I said on the phone, 'I'm going east', Elif had said, 'And I'm going west.' She did not ask where and why. As usual she did not say, 'I've missed you. You've been away a long time', or any similar sentiment. There was neither disappointment in her voice, nor anger, nor reproach. At most there was apprehension at not being able to understand why I was calling at the crack of dawn.

Even when I went on about us drifting apart her voice didn't change. She has bottled it up, I know; she doesn't easily show her feelings. Yet I had wanted to tell her something quite different. Those words were a lament for what we had lost; the mortification I felt about us taking separate paths. I had to express this somehow. It was the reaction to the effects of time that dulled, gnawed at and ruined everything. I felt I needed to express reproach, regret, but I couldn't find the right words.

Ömer still loved his wife, after all those years. To be able to convince his circle of friends that he was far removed from the behaviour of the average male he had convinced himself that he loved his wife of thirty years as much as ever. Ömer Eren, surrounded by a host of admirers, most of them women, at book-promotion launches, openings of exhibitions and at meetings where he was expected to make an appearance, at celebrations and in places frequented by intellectuals, had to love his wife as much as ever to prove that he hadn't changed, and that his heart and his soul were as they had been in the days of faith and innocence. He needed to prove that despite being a famous, widely read author – being termed a 'best-selling author' made his blood boil – he was atypical of his sex in terms of his behaviour. So often when a man becomes rich or famous the first thing he does is divorce his wife. Other relationships, other women, other men, long separations, taking refuge in a small seaside town off the beaten track with the excuse that he was writing a book, those surreptitious holidays, retreats . . . They were like the garnish for the main course that came to the table after the hors d'oeuvre and the appetizers. Even though he didn't much care to contemplate on such matters, whenever he did the image of a roasted turkey on a large platter appeared before his eyes – a turkey, the essential part of the New Year table, decorated with a tasty garnish that enhanced its appeal and savour.

He is enveloped by an ominous feeling, a dark fog. What an appalling metaphor. I, who am considered a master of language, Ömer Eren who thinks that he is endowed with the power of the word . . . I'm nothing. The French call it *médiocre*; in other words, average, indifferent, lacking in originality. 'Hackneyed sayings and clichés, a bit of nostalgic sauce, a pinch of revolutionary spice, plenty of love and as much melancholy as it takes. The works of the famous writer, Ömer Eren . . .' Was that smart-arse critic who wrote thus wrong? While some among us rejected the past and denigrated their former beliefs, cursing the gods that at one time they worshipped, I put such subjects into my writing and transmuted words into fame and money.

Lately, as the emptiness loomed and the fear rose within him that he could no longer write well or would never be able to write as well again, his dissatisfaction with himself grew, too. Drink was one escape. Taking refuge in book-signing days, talks, meetings and travelling from town to town was another. Was it the andropause or whatever they call it? A midlife crisis? The panic that there is little time left to live, the anxiety of having wasted past years, the sadness of knowing that there is no going back to those years . . .

Elif tacked those years together day by day, step by step, leaf by leaf and she reminded me that those years really had been lived. My wife ties me to a past that I have left behind and that I miss all the more. I should not have said to her, 'We are gradually drifting apart.' I should have said, 'Let's not part again.'

The question 'Will you see him, too?', like him saying 'We are gradually drifting apart', was his way of expressing the rebellion that he felt against the love, passion and sexual excitement that had been eroded by time; against Elif taking refuge in her never-ending experiments, her beloved mice, her successful scientific studies and in her acceptance of her husband's distance, his absence and his affairs; against the loss of his passion, love, immature excitement and hope and the reality that they would not be returning to that beautiful country of their youth again. He had wanted to hurt his wife. He did not know why, but perhaps it was because he was hurting very much somewhere deep inside.

He was almost smug when he said, 'I'm going to the east, to the south-east.' He had implied intellectual bragging, of being ready to pay the price and make a sacrifice for his art, together with a degree of western arrogance. He had expected his wife to ask him what he was going to be doing in those parts. She had not asked. He wanted her to ask because he had things to to tell her. If he were to say them, it would relieve him and give him peace of mind. A forgotten tale whose remembrance would be good for his heart and soul . . .

'Once upon a time, when we were eighteen or nineteen, we went with the revolutionary train to build a bridge over the Zap River. At that time this whole country was ours, from Edirne to Ardahan, you know, like the poem that we learnt in childhood. We had grown up, and we no longer believed in the "villages that were ours even if we didn't go and see them" of our primary-school books. We had begun to understand that no place would be ours if we didn't visit it or if we didn't build bridges. We didn't yet know that it wasn't enough to construct bridges of good intention, that it was necessary to pass to the other side, and that the bridges that we had built were not strong enough and not wide enough. But we would learn. In our twenties we were burning revolutionary fires on the Nurhak mountains, in the Söke plains and the surrounding towns in the Çukurova countryside. The east was on our agenda, like a song of the people sung first in a timid and cautious and then in a loud voice. Those who lived there were our people – our shame because we left them destitute, our source of pride because they resisted oppression, and in whose name we went to prison for using the word "Kurd", thus salving our conscience. They were a part of our hopes and our revolution, and they were partners in our liberation. They spoke our language with harsh, clipped accents evoking the craggy mountains. We knew deep inside that they spoke another language; but, still, they were our people; they were us. They were enigmatic, and they were not very open; we sensed they had secrets. We tried to respect these and to share their suffering. We were revolutionaries; our enemies and friends were the same. Our grievances concerned the military police, the state, the landowners and the bosses, as well as imperialism in general. We felt wronged, downtrodden and rebellious. If we felt it once, they felt it three times over. If you went to gaol and "if you were the three K, then you were in trouble", our old comrades-in-arms used to say. "*Kürt–Kızılbaş–Komunist*" – you really were in trouble. If we were in a bad way the Kurds were three times worse off, so we felt inadequate. We used to sing the folk songs of the east together, read their epic stories and attempt to comprehend the things they could not say. But we were always inadequate and fell short.'

If Elif had asked, he would have liked to tell her a tale of remembrance like this. If he were to write, this is what he would have liked to write. Writing is the best thing. To write what he really wanted to say and leave to one side the worry of who would read it and who would be interested. In these postmodern times, when poverty, oppression, rebellion, revolution, the workers, peasants, ordinary people, flesh and bone, people with real feelings were subjects considered old-fashioned, stretched and sagging – 'Are you still singing the same old tune, buddy?' – he wanted to remind people about people – and to tell about people and their lives.

I would like to, but do I have the courage? Am I ready not to disappear but to be ignored? Am I ready to have no one around me – for my publisher's polite warnings, for my career that for fifteen years I have been building brick by brick to be reduced to nothing, to hear the words, 'Yes, he was quite famous at one time. People used to read him a lot, but then he aspired to probe deeper and returned to topics that were history and got stuck on anachronistic revolutionary discourse and a dated humanism. Well, of course, no one reads him any more. A pity.' I've run out of words. I've worn out the words using them again and again; I've worn them down and emptied their contents. The shell of a word that has lost its soul rots.

Ömer Eren knows that he cannot write as he used to. He realizes the emptiness of the sentences that appear on the computer screen, their meaninglessness and that they are just black consecutive symbols. Does a person lose the word when the voice inside him is silent, or does it happen when the feeling of pointlessness brings the writer to the place where the word ends?

When he begins to muse how, step by step, he has lost his voice and how the gushing spring that fed the word has dried up, he feels caught in a trap. The only way he knows how to get out of it is to take refuge in alcohol and in the halo of his undeserved reputation. In the years when he excelled with his first novel and surprised the literati, a famous critic had called him 'the writer endowed with the word'. Had he betrayed the magical word he had been endowed with, or had he been betrayed by the word? He doesn't know.

Now he is looking out of the window of the vehicle that has been stopped for the second time in the last hour, amazed at how he set out on these roads and why he is on this coach. Making an effort to appear indifferent and at ease, he asks an elderly passenger in local dress sitting anxiously beside him, 'Is it always like this or is it because of the events of the past few days?' The answer is flat and short. 'It's always like this, but it's got worse recently.'

The heavily armed and intimidating men in camouflage uniform and masks who barge in without leave are checking identity cards, lightly prodding the passengers with their guns. There is a tense silence on the coach that will break at any moment. Is it the fear of getting used to fear – or of showing it? By now he has learnt that they are going to take some people off the vehicle. Cases, bundles, cardboard boxes tied up with string and sacks will then be thrown down, opened and strewn around. Sacks of onions and potatoes – why do people insist on carrying onions and potatoes from one place to another? – jars of honey, packets of *lokum* – made by small-town confectioners, underwear, packets of pills, tins of cheese, embroidered linen from a trousseau, artificial flowers, long johns and more will be scattered around. Then the things that have been picked through and strewn around will be gathered up in grave silence. Faces will reflect the shame of displayed underwear, the paucity of the bundles. How many of those taken off the coach will get back on again? Who will end up next to an empty seat? The driver will doubtless grasp the gearstick with the imprecation 'God give me strength!' He will begin humming a Kurdish air and put his foot down on the accelerator. The coach will start moving off again with sighs, curses muttered in hoarse voices and oaths hissed between the teeth. The curses will be in Kurdish and the oaths in Turkish, and the rebellion smothered by fear will be entirely human.

'The bridge we built over the Zap River has been destroyed,' said one of Ömer's old friends who frequently came here on business. He works it out: thirty-seven years . . . No, it can't be. Was it so long ago, so far back in time? It can't be. A tiredness of thirty-seven years descends on him. As the coach travels along the winding road with rocky mountains on one side and a deep valley on the other, he looks intently around. In vain . . . After all these years, he would not be able to pick out the location of the bridge. When they stop for a tea break he addresses the driver. 'You're young, but perhaps you've heard about it from older people. Years ago youngsters from Istanbul and Ankara came and built a bridge over the Zap River with friends from the area. We carried the stones and mixed the cement together. Is the bridge still standing? I have heard that it had been destroyed.'

'I have heard about it. I know of it,' says the driver. 'My uncle worked on the bridge. There was Deniz Gezmiş, too. I know about it from what he told me, *abi*. Would such a bridge still be standing here after all these years, in this day and age? It was mined years ago. Some say it was the military and some say it was guerrillas. If you ask me, it was the Zap River itself that demolished it. It's stronger than all of them. In fact, the bridge's abutments are still standing. I'll point them out to you as we pass.'

Was Deniz really there on the Zap Bridge expedition? If he had been I would have remembered. Perhaps he just stopped by. In those days Deniz wasn't in a position to stay long in one place. Even if he hadn't been to the river heroes are ubiquitous. People need epics and heroes.

Without turning round the driver shouts, 'Zap Bridge!' as they pass through a rocky gorge. He slows the bus down to a crawl. All that remains of the bridge are the ruined stone abutments. Ömer remembers that he has seen such ruins on both sides of the river all along the road. It was as though our bridge was further along and on the opposite bank was a village clinging to the rocky slope. No it wasn't here; it must be further along. It doesn't matter where it was exactly. The good thing is that there are people who still remember it, who know of it. 'Thanks,' he calls out to the driver.

Let them remember the bridge as being here. It is important that someone remembers. Legends shouldn't be forgotten, the spell shouldn't be broken, and doubts should not arise.

The Zap River flows a murky grey. It's as if there is less water these days. Calm in appearance but seething beneath, it has forgotten the fury of the winter months during these hot June days. It's the same as it's always been – just the same. The cliffs rising on either side of the gorge and the grey slopes are the same, too. At the hour when daylight falls and the sun disappears behind the high mountains, the road stretching away, the sky, hills and river are girded in the same yellow-grey. And now, just at this moment, in their bareness, wildness, starkness and isolation they are all incredibly beautiful. Too beautiful to compete with the blue of the sea, the green of forest and meadows, the white of snowy peaks or the red purple of the setting sun. Or so it seems to me. Even though we look with our eyes, we behold through the glasses of our longings, our beliefs and our dreams. That is how we were when we believed that we would establish the union of the revolution and the brotherhood of the people with a makeshift bridge. The bridge was the symbol of hands held out by young people from the west uniting with the hands of the east. The good thing was believing in it and in the hope this belief created.

The depression of knowing that the poignant sadness of 'I travelled these roads years ago', the despair of 'The bridges that I built have been completely destroyed' and the fruitless, hopeless fatigue of Sisyphus as he carried the rock to the peak will never turn to hope.

He looks at the remains of the bridge. Even if it isn't here it is good that someone still remembers it. A lad from the east, who perhaps had not even begun to talk when Deniz was hanged, knows Deniz Gezmiş. It is necessary to die young for memories to be appealing and for heroes to remain immortal!

Ömer Eren is going to the east. To the most eastern part of the east. The title of his last book was *For the Light Rises in the East*. It was a phrase borrowed from the Bible, from the faith of the western world. It rose rapidly on the bestseller list, and literary circles and thinkers praised it to the skies. He admits to himself that when choosing the title he had looked for a reference that could be translated into English and French. We take our bearings from the west and write about the east. We are eastern Orientalists. He finds his play on words clever. He must use it in an article. With a heavy heart he remembers the Argentinian Solanas's film, *South* or *El Sur*. Solanas, too, was in exile in Europe in the 1980s. They had met at the showing in Paris of his film *Tangos* that told of Argentinian political exiles. Solanas was filming *El Sur* at the time; the film in which three old men play tangos on their bandonéons on a street corner in Argentina in front of the Lost Dreams café amid the mists and smoke. Whether dream or reality nobody knows. His film tells of people in love, rebelling, betraying, resisting and defeated, and people embracing hope and life. Their *ka'bah* is the south: the place where wars and freedom begin and where hopes of revolution are hidden. Patagonia, with its ice, freezing winds, and air of desolation and isolation, a refuge for fugitives, a grave for prisoners who do not return . . . The melancholy tango of Maria seeking her lover who has died while being tortured . . . 'South: the land of our hope, our glorious dream, silently dying comrades. South: the final stop of our love, our never-ending road.' Her lover murdered, the very young Maria is going south to carry on the fight on a truck travelling along the never-ending roads of the pampas, perched next to the driver like a silent bundle of sorrow.

Ömer Eren goes east murmuring Maria's song, 'South: the country of our loneliness, the final stop of our hopes, our never-ending road . . .', breathing in the air that has grown heavy with the smell of human breath and sweat in the coach that travels between the yellow-grey hills, cleaving the yellow-grey light. He asks himself yet again why he is on this road. He goes along singing Maria's ballad in his own language. 'East: the last stop of our conscience, the refuge of our defeat. East, land of the eternal struggle . . .'

'East: the distant land where our fathers – civil servants and soldiers – did their compulsory service. The land of migration where officer families living in outposts and garrisons deployed all along the borders think that the howling of jackals is an enemy raid; where children hide under their bedcovers in fear; where the snow does not melt in the north and where scorpions scorch in the heat in the south; the land of those magical, suspect languages – Kurdish, Zazaki, Armenian, Syriac, Arabic and Georgian – the distinctive spicy food that has the taste of bulgur and is consumed with homemade *rakı*; where the impoverished smugglers, the brave and innocent old-time bandits, the *Mehmetciks*, and the guerrillas are killed in minefields or in battle – so many killed, continuously being killed – the land of rebellions, deportations, wars and migrations. That distant land that has become more than a region or a climate in whose mirror we test our fears, our enmities, our friendships and our beliefs in life and man; and not being able to stand the stress we prefer to forget and accuse instead of being accused. A fountain in which we hope to wash clean our wounded, frayed, enlightened consciences. The last refuge in which to hide our fear and tiredness, to dress the wounds of defeat after the working class that was buried beneath the debris of the times deserted us – or was it we who deserted them?'

He must write this down. He must write it in more lyrical language, with deeper thoughts and an infinitely large heart but sincerely and with genuine feeling. He must write it looking into his own heart and finding the word once more. He must not mind who reads it, how well it sells or who condemns it, and he must take the risk of losing his reputation and becoming nothing. He must write the story of real people, not the east desired by the west that is bored with itself, satiated but which has failed to achieve happiness; the west that looks for peace in mysticism, in the deserts, at the tops of mountains, in Buddhist temples and Hindu shrines. Not the unnatural fiction that the literature market operating according to supply and demand requires, the stories without people, the fairytales of the well-to-do, sick and tired, wealthy westerners sitting on their pots of money who leave everything behind and find happiness in poor lands.

He knows that he has to question frankly, without fear, the reason for his losing the word and the fact that he has not been able to write for some time. He feels that the query 'Who would be interested in our story apart from a few dinosaurs?' lurks behind his fear of his reputation sinking, of not being on the bestseller list and losing his readers and is a trick, a self-deception. He recalls the German war correspondent committing suicide, leaving a note saying, 'I have not a single line left to write.' Had he not been able to write because of the suffering he had witnessed, or was it simply because he had dried up?

Now, making his way in a decrepit old coach in a yellow-grey light between soldiers minesweeping in the eerie high mountain passes, their lives entrusted to the mercy of their commander, the militants in the mountain and to the Devil, too, he is seized with doubt that he will be able to find the word – the true words that he wants to say – and that he will be able to tell the real story that he wants to tell. He is not quite sure of the virtue of the path he has taken in pursuing a scream that cleaved the night, that he will be able to find what he is looking for – or that he even knows what he is looking for. He almost regrets setting off on the journey. He feels like a drink. Damn it! I always used to be prepared. Well, I was taken unawares. Homemade *rakı* and similar delights – they are all left behind, past memories.

There is no sign of alcohol on the shelves or the counters of the make-shift shops that line both sides of the road where they stop for a break. The shops sell anything and everything from vegetables to wheat, cheese to soft drinks and hardware to prayer mats. He doesn't have the courage to ask. But still he consults the driver.

'*Abi*, there isn't any. Don't even bother looking for it! You can't find it round here. Oh . . . if you want white stuff, I mean powder, that's easy to find. It's all over the place. The military police know where it is and so do the guerrillas. If you need some . . .'

'I don't do white stuff or powder. I want a drink for . . . You know, my throat. Also my gums are all inflamed. I expect I'm developing a cold. That's why I'm looking for alcohol.'

The driver doesn't seem to have swallowed the line. He grins in a friendly manner. Ömer is sorry that he has told a fib, buys a bottle of water and returns to the coach. In this place where he has come in pursuit of a scream he is as foreign and as nervous as a tourist. 'Being the other one of those we have otherized . . .' That's a good phrase; I must make a note of it. Now and then he finds good phrases and notes them down. But they are all empty words; not one of them is the word he is seeking. Perhaps all that I have written until now was just words . . . empty words, nonsense.

As he looks for his notebook in the many pockets of his hunting vest he remembers his mobile phone. Much of the time there is no signal out in the countryside. Particularly in the gorges and when they go between the mountains they are out of signal range and service. Just as these parts are out of our personal service area . . . There is a tiny envelope icon on the screen. You have a message. The first text is from Elif: 'I'll be seeing the boy.' He doesn't even look at the messages from his publisher, his editor and from the International PEN or from a society to which he has promised to give a talk. He returns again and again to his wife's message: 'I'll be seeing the boy.' Ordinary words: the burden, the poison and the pain of which both of them know well.

The disturbing woman at the coach station had whispered that they killed the child. The whisper had turned into the young man's scream that had pierced the night and the cowardly, furtive tranquillity of oblivion. 'They've killed the child! *Zarok kuştin!*'

Which child? Had he decided at that instant to remember the child? No, it was later, it was while waiting for news of the woman being operated on, leaning against the wall smoking cigarette after cigarette with the young man in the stuffy corridor of the emergency ward half lit by a dim light, where patients lay on broken benches and where their relatives with worried, anxious faces looked round hopefully each time a door opened . . .

This matter should have ended after he had made sure that the seriously wounded patient was operated on immediately by giving his own name and using the name of a professor he knew and after he had completed the hospital admission procedure and left some money as well. At most, he should have given his mobile number and as a conscientious, responsible citizen gone on his way. This was the natural thing to do – and it was also in keeping with his character. However, there he was pacing up and down in the hospital corridor with Mahmut – he had finally learnt that the young man's name was Mahmut – whose face was overcast with fatigue and suffering, waiting for the outcome of the surgery.

Mahmut looked in his mid-twenties: he had a fine, swarthy, open face in spite of his stubble, and he was handsome despite his dishevelled appearance. He was also silent, scared and alien. When speaking he looked not at one's face but at a point beyond, like people who are guilty or shy. It was quite obvious that he was from the east, but he did not have a strong eastern accent that would make him difficult to understand apart from a shortening of the long A's and the slightly guttural G's and also the emphasized separation of syllables. It took Ömer some time to understand that the youth's silence, his evasive glances and his ill-at-ease manner stemmed from insecurity.

'Why are you doing this, *abi*?' In his voice there was suspicion mixed with gratitude and surprise.

Ömer had not been able to say, 'Because of that scream . . . because of the child.' Instead he had said in a forced tone that defied credibility, 'What else could I have done? How could I have left you like that?'

'You're not a doctor.'

'You're right. I'm not a doctor. I just said that at the time so that I could get into the ambulance with you. In fact I'm a writer. Perhaps you have heard of me. My books are read a lot.'

Why would he have heard of you? Again that empty boasting. As if the whole of Turkey from east to west reads you! As if they are obliged to! As he took a card from his wallet and held it out he added sheepishly, 'Very occasionally articles appear in the papers about me. For that reason perhaps . . .'

'I haven't read a paper for a long time. I'm sorry.'

The boy had begun to use the formal mode of address. Was it from respect or was it because the more they spoke the more distant, the more alien he seemed?

'You've got a problem. That's evident. If it's something I can solve . . . There's no need to be suspicious. Anything can happen to one at your age. I'm not an agent or anything. Don't worry.'

'No, of course not, *hocam*. Don't take it like that. I – I mean we – we're desperate. We're in dire straits.'

The words, freed from the clutches of fear and doubt, suddenly spewed out. Ömer looked carefully at the youth's face and saw the despair, fear and loneliness that he had seen in the features of his son.

'Sometimes we are all desperate. I have a son your age. When I last saw him he looked as desperate and helpless as you.'

When I last saw you there was the suffering in your eyes of a shot animal. And when I first saw you, I had just come out of prison. Those were the days when it was more difficult being outside than inside. When I thought about those who were executed, those who had died from torture and those who had been given life imprisonment, mine was an insignificant thing, too embarrassing to even mention. I had been given eighteen months for a disparaging article that I had written before the September coup for one of the hundreds of left-wing magazines that were around at the time. A third of the sentence had been dropped, and I had spent a year in gaol and been released. When I left, you were in your mother's womb and when I found you you were six months old. You regarded me as a stranger. I could see you asking where on earth has this stranger sprung from? In your eyes there were questions, fears and doubts. Holding my son in my arms was a unique, incomparable feeling that I had never experienced before, neither in the joy of the first kiss nor the pleasure of orgasm, nor in the awe, the elation one feels standing before a work of art or a natural wonder. My life blood, a life entrusted to me and that belonged to me, tiny and helpless against this terrible world! I always loved your mother, and I loved her still more because she gave birth to you. We named you Deniz to commemorate others named Deniz. It was not that you should carry the flag that they hoisted on the gallows to the future, as you assumed when you rebelled against us after you grew up. It was to the memory of the friendship and brotherhood of the rebellious days of our youth that were full of hope; and we gave it with a melancholic loyalty and romanticism afraid of breaking the ties with our lost youth. But I always called you 'Son', just as I said 'Cat' to the cat. I created a special name from the common name to express that you were the one and only.

When Ömer had last seen his son there was the same defeated, helpless, crazy look in his eyes: Mahmut's look.

He had said, 'Don't go. Stay. There's nowhere to run, Son.' He had fixed his eyes on the ground. He could not look at his son's clumsy body that had got prematurely fat, the swellings, the bruises that had still not gone down, his face disfigured by the deep scars of stitches and surgery.

'I can't do it, Dad. I can't stay here, on the border of hell or right in the middle of it, and with Bjørn! Besides, with this body, with this face!'

'Everything will pass. It will all get better. It's not important. Bjørn would be happier here with us. Your mother needs you, too.' Afterwards, he had added shyly, 'I do as well.'

'No one here needs me – neither you nor Mother. Mother's happy with her experiments, her guinea pigs, her scientific meetings, her lessons and her students, as you are with your books, your articles, your social life, your friends and your admirers. I have nothing here. Here I, I'm not . . .' – he can't find the word he seeks. 'Here I'm a loser. This place scares me.'

He had wanted to embrace his son, not with love but with pity, with desperation. 'You're not the only one to lose. We have lost together. The truth is that in a sense we are all losers. Perhaps . . . I don't know, we can begin . . .'

My words sound like trite dialogue from a bad television soap opera. But my sentiments are not contrived. They just come out like this. Perhaps the humdrum conversations of humdrum people in those soaps we despise are the most sincere, the most natural way of communicating. It is that incurable intellectual malaise: one despises everything. One speaks differently. One makes comments that sound significant, and one tends to pontificate so that one seems elite and superior.

'Let's not dream, Dad. We can't start anything again. I can't be reborn, and I can't be the son of your dreams. I can't pretend what's happened never happened. I saw Ulla scattered in pieces, and I saw the tarmac soak up the blood that spurted in every direction. It hasn't been four months since then. I'm no stranger to blood and violence, as you know. After all, you sent me into the middle of battle to be a war correspondent. There was a great deal of blood in those deserts and in the battlefields. However, it was a foreign place – abroad – and the people who died, were burnt and in fragments were not my wife, child, relative or friend; they were merely the subjects of the photos that I took; they were objectified. Despite that, I could not stand taking pictures of suffering for long. I hated the work. Just think about it: blood is flowing, people are dying and I'm trying to depict the most striking suffering, violence and death in the pictures I take. The more violence, the more blood I show, the more successful I'm considered. I took hundreds, perhaps thousands of photos. I received praise, and I won your approval. Then I understood that I couldn't do it, I couldn't continue, and I ran away from there. I'm talking too much. What I mean to say is that I, who couldn't stand the suffering and the blood of strangers that I didn't even know, watched the woman I loved, the mother of my son, being killed in front of my eyes. If we had brought Bjørn here for you to see perhaps he, too, would have been blown to smithereens like Ulla. This land frightens me. Please understand.'

He had not been able to find anything to say. He was assailed by a sharp pain, a deep feeling of guilt. He had said, 'What can I say? You are right, but, still, despite this terrible thing . . . here is more . . .'

Deniz had interrupted his father angrily and aggressively. 'Here's what, Dad? Were you going to say here's safe? Were you going to say peaceful – or what were you going to say? What happened happened here, in your legendary city that you write about in your novels. I'd brought my wife to meet you and to show her my country. You know you were dying for us to come. For a moment, even I hoped that perhaps here, here in a village or on an island, I could start a new, peaceful life without blood and lies. Then . . . and then . . . Look . . .' He stroked the deep wounds and cuts on his face. 'You can't even look at my face! You're right. I was never an Adonis, but I wasn't hideous either. Start afresh. Well? Even if I did begin all over again, how could I bring back Ulla? She was the one person who really loved me without making demands, without wanting me to be important, successful or handsome. She wanted me and loved me as I was. With her I found peace for the first time. It was my wife who made me feel that I didn't have to lie and to pretend to be someone I wasn't. She was the stupid, little northern village girl whom you despised, whom you ignored and whom you did not think suitable – not for me but for yourselves. A corpse without a grave or a grave without a corpse.'

The words 'a corpse without a grave' stuck in Ömer's heart like a lump. 'Violence doesn't just strike here. There's violence everywhere. The world's ablaze, Son. The Middle East and Iraq are in flames. You saw those places with your own eyes. Where can we be safe? There's nowhere to run.'

'Here, we are much closer to the fires. The flames are licking the borders. Don't you feel the heat? In this country it's as though the fires, the bombs and the bullets are in the very people themselves. Ready to explode, to burst into flames at any moment ... Bjørn and I are much safer on our island than we are here. He will grow up there in the middle of nature and the sea, content, without anyone pushing him around, despising him and expecting him to bring the sky to their feet. I ... I am not Deniz there either. I am the good foreigner from far away. I don't have to account for myself to anyone. I don't have to be a hero or a scholar. I don't have to be anyone other than myself. There I'm no one or everyone. I'm like everyone else. That makes me happy. Although you're angry, Dad, can you understand?'

He did understand. He was amazed that Deniz could explain his feeling of defeat, his fears, and his need for refuge so openly and eloquently.

'I understand in my mind, but it is difficult for me to accept it in my heart. Son, do you know what it means to have a son?'

'I have a son, too, so, yes, I know. I want to protect him. I don't want him to be a loser. No, I don't want him to be a loser. Do you remember the old man in the Gasthaus? You know, that old German who said, "I'm the unknown deserter"? I was young then, but I didn't forget the island or that man. Many years later when I returned I tried to explain with the little Norwegian I had and in sign language that years ago when I was small we had come to the island, stayed in that guesthouse where there was an old man and that he had sat in the rocking-chair and given me cake. They knew him, of course. He had died a few years before. He had taken his own life. He was all alone and had no heirs or relatives. He had left the guesthouse to Ulla's family who had worked with him for ages, and now they run it. Anyway, that's how I met Ulla.'

'Is that so? I didn't know.'

'Of course you didn't know. You never asked, so how could you? You weren't interested in how I lived – just in my achievements. When she learnt that I had taken refuge there Mother just said, "The Devil's Island? What fate!" Well, anyway ... They had kept the old man's room just as it was. They gave it to me. Mother has every right to be astonished. Indeed, what fate! What a coincidence really. There was some writing on the wall in German in a coloured pencil. "Running away from war is easier than running away from life. I'm finally beating the odds." It was signed "the unknown deserter".'

Suppressing the reluctance in his heart he had looked at his son's face.

He had seen a tired, defeated, frightened look. If only he could hug him, embrace him and never let him go, eradicate that look in his eyes. If only he could look after him and rescue him. If only he could prevent him from being the unknown deserter of life on a forgotten tiny island in the North Sea.

'Let me go home as soon as possible. I mustn't keep Bjørn waiting any longer, he's missed me a lot. I can't leave Ulla's family alone either. I have a responsibility. After all, it was I who brought their daughter to her death.'

'It's not your fault. It could have been anywhere in the world. Terrorism is everywhere. In Spain, in New York, in Iraq, in India, in London, in the Lebanon, everywhere . . . It's a terrible coincidence that a suicide bomber should panic and pull the pin just as you were passing. You weren't especially picked out. What I mean to say is . . .'

'That's the worst thing. You don't have to be chosen as a target. Everyone can be a target at any moment. I know that terror prowls everywhere. You're right. It could have been elsewhere. That's true. However, it happened here.'

It happened here; in this beguiling, magical city, the unchanging backdrop of Ömer's novels and narratives where the tragedy of man has been lived out in its various forms intensely for thousands of years; in the Istanbul of tourist brochures and travel guides – with Ömer Eren's words, 'Epics and poems should be written of this city; not history.'

Deniz had wanted to take his wife around the city where he was born and in which he had grown up, to show off his city and to share the memories of his childhood and youth. However, Ulla had insisted on looking round Sultanahmet, the Grand Bazaar and St Sophia first. It was written in the Norwegian guidebook on Istanbul that one should see this area first of all, 'to understand fully the spirit of the east and to get to know Byzantium and Islam'. From the Grand Bazaar she had bought herself a beaded sequined belt with silver tassels, for her grandfather a Meerschaum pipe, for her grandmother a colourful, flowery shawl, for Bjørn a toy camel decorated with bells, blue beads and ribbons and a huge blue charm to ward off the evil eye. She had been as happy as a child with her purchases. She had immediately put the belt round her waist and hugged Bjørn's camel to her bosom. Walking cheerfully along, their arms wrapped round each other, to Sultanahmet from Nuruosmaniye they had arrived in front of St Sophia. They had decided to wander round Sultanahmet Square and Sultanahmet mosque – a disappointment to Ulla who had thought it would be a really bright blue because in the book it was called the 'Blue Mosque'

– and leave St Sophia to last. There was no particular reason for choosing this route. Perhaps it was because a large group of tourists was standing in front of St Sophia at the time. Perhaps it was because Ulla heard the irresistible call of death waiting for her in front of the flowerbeds of bright red blooms at the edge of the park. 'How beautiful the flowers are,' she murmured in admiration. 'They're tulips. When I was a child Grandpa used to read me a story about a little Dutch girl. It was a picture book, and a little girl in clogs used to wander around the tulip fields picking flowers of different colours for her mother.' Then she had leapt up joyfully. Darling Ulla was like that. One moment she would be like a still, calm lake without a ripple, and suddenly she would surge like a turbulent sea. 'I must take some close-ups of them straight away. When we get home I'll draw some tulips on either side of our door, and I'll paint them yellow, red and white like these. But hang on. First take a picture of me in front of them.' Then she had dashed off like a chubby, mischievous child, and while she was hurrying towards the park she had paused, turned round to look at her husband who was watching her with a smile. 'Take a good photo! Make sure the tulips and I look beautiful. We'll show it to Grandpa and Grandma and Bjørn. Let them see how lovely your city is!'

Deniz had seen her for the last time in a frame of a photograph, just as she had wished, in her long blue dress holding the toy camel clasped to her bosom, with the colourful silvery belt with the beaded edges that she had wound round her waist, her long bright blonde hair and the deep red tulips behind. He had pressed the shutter. But had he pressed it? Had he been able to depress the button? He doesn't know; he doesn't remember. However, the photograph of Ulla smiling in front of tulips the colour of blood with Sultanahmet mosque in the background, the skirts of her dress blowing in the breeze and the toy camel that she hugged to her bosom like a child is etched in his mind and remains there never to be erased. Then an explosion deafening ears and senses, screams and smoke, and blood splattering the red tulips, and all around legs, arms, shoes and a toy camel scattered amid the blood, smoke and screams . . . First, the searing pain he feels in his face, hands and body and then the swirling and tumbling into a deep, dark bottomless well. Then . . .

When he regained consciousness in an intensive care unit he could not make sense of the thin rubber tubes that encircled his wounded body like a spider's web and were attached with sticking plaster to needles stuck into his hands and trailed from his nose and his mouth. He had not spoken at all. He had not said anything when he came round from the anaesthetic after each operation or during the days while lying with his head, face, arm and fingers wrapped in thick bandages in the hospital in which he had remained for weeks. When they came for the routine questioning to shed light on the incident, a single sentence had come from his lips. 'There were red tulips, and Ulla stood in front of the tulips.'

When he said to his son, 'Stay, don't go,' Ömer realized that his request was as hopeless as it was cruel. For Deniz Istanbul was now a grave where Ulla's scattered, fragmented body and her blood showered on the tulips, the streets and the city remained. He had shown respect for his son's grief and felt it deep inside and had not made the suggestion again.

When the day of parting arrived, Deniz had not wanted them to come to the airport to see him off. His mother was worried about her son's health. He still had a bad limp, and perhaps he would require further operations. The burns on his face had healed, but the scars were too deep to fade without cosmetic surgery. He felt uncomfortable under Elif's gaze and had said to his mother to comfort her and to make her think he was recovering and not too bothered about his appearance, 'It'll pass. It'll all pass in good time. The longer I stay here, the deeper my wounds get. They don't heal. I've missed my son a great deal. I can't leave Bjørn alone any longer. I know he's well looked after but he needs me.' He hadn't talked much. He hadn't opened up his heart, and he hadn't shared his grief. Not to offend her, he had taken a bite of his favourite food that Elif had prepared so carefully, and he had talked a little about his island, and then he had fallen silent until the hour of separation had arrived.

Mother, father and son had tried to suppress the grief within them and lodged in their throats like a lump of metal with pleasantries such as 'You used to like this food' and 'You used to love this *börek*.' Deniz had told them about herring fishing, the best way to salt fish, that although they went to the castle almost every day they hadn't met the Devil, that they had painted the Gasthaus bright yellow and that the ghostly woman with baskets on her arms was still alive – although perhaps it was her daughter– that the island was as deserted and peaceful as always and that visitors who came for a few days stayed at the Gasthaus. As a formality he had said, 'If you happen to be in the area, come and stay. You'll have a feeling of *déjà vu*. And you can see Bjørn, too.'

Then it was time to leave, and he repeated that he didn't want them to come to the airport. He had gone off limping, dragging his clumsy body with his heavy pack on his back and his head bent, not looking back. From the balcony they had watched him get into the taxi that came to the door. Elif had, for custom's sake, poured a bowl of water after him so that he could go and come back with ease, like water. The child that we had condemned to the Devil's Island because he hadn't been equal to the dreams that we had failed to realize, the enthusiasm that had abandoned us and our hopes that had been left in the past; and because he had not taken revenge for our disappointments and our defeat in the battle we expected him to fight in our name. The son that we had left alone and almost abandoned because he did not want to be a hero, because he had refused to compete and had been crushed under the cruelty of the age, and because he had not the strength to contend with life; because he was not ambitious enough, capable or strong.

He always remembers his son like that, as he saw him that last day. Whenever he thinks of him, he remembers him slowly going off – lost, alone, tired and defeated. And that look in his eyes: Mahmut's look.

'When I last saw him he had the same look that you have.'

'And what was that, *hocam*?'

'Grief-stricken, defeated and desperate.'

'Like an animal that has been shot? Like a guerrilla who has surrendered with the barrel of a gun thrust against his mouth and an army boot pressing on his chest? Your son, the sons of people like you, wouldn't look like that though!'

He is upset by Mahmut's words. He doesn't answer. The left corner of his lip twitches slightly. He had not had that dreadful tic for a long time. Or was it going to start up again? The doctors had said that too much alcohol could weaken muscle control. I really must take more care of myself. He is angry with Mahmut. They believe they are the only ones who are downtrodden and wronged. So our son wouldn't look like that, wouldn't be left helpless! Is it only you lot who suffer? That talk of being victimized even in this hospital corridor, in this peculiar situation! Well-worn ideas learnt by heart, the familiar attitude of tarring everyone with the same brush, hanging everyone with the same rope. His anger mounts. Whatever you do is futile. They never trust you. And after all I've done to defend their rights. I almost got into trouble over the issue of them using their mother tongue and because I wrote articles on the unsolved murders in the east. If it hadn't been for the European Union, the reaction of the non-government organizations, the concern for what Europe would say, because of the lawsuits against me, they might have convicted me.

He tries to appear calm. 'Everyone has their own suffering, their own setbacks,' he says. 'A moment comes when we are all afraid, we are all desperate. Turk, Kurd, French, Arab, whatever nationality, it makes no difference. Today everyone is oppressed. Everyone is a tyrant, and everyone is a victim.' His anger, resentment and weariness are reflected in his voice.

'I didn't say that. I don't know, I'd thought your son was one who had made it. I mean, had a good job, had studied and all that. Forgive me, but it's usually like that. I mean big, important men's sons . . .'

The boy's honest, worried manner and the anxiety he feels that what he has said may have been misunderstood softens his heart. The boy is right: it is like that. Our children do make it. Most of them succeed – or that is what people think. What is the fallacy 'We are all in the same boat' other than a brilliant deception? Wouldn't I have talked like that in my youth, in those happy, hopeful days when we thought we were fighting for the revolution and for the people? Suddenly he feels depressed. It is dawn, and the sun is rising. What am I doing here at this hour? What am I doing in this hospital corridor? For what am I paying the price, giving alms?

The team who performed the operation appear at the end of the surgery corridor in their blue-green gowns. Telling him to wait, he jumps up before the youth and walks towards them. He hopes that one of the team will recognize him and give him information.

'I was going to ask about the condition of the wounded woman who's been operated on. I . . .'

Nobody pays attention. They carry on walking and talking among themselves.

'I'm the writer, Ömer Eren. I wanted to learn . . .'

One young man among the gowned doctors turns him.'If you are asking about the woman hit by a bullet, she'll survive.'

'And what about the child? The child . . .'

'The bullet lodged in the foetus. It was a boy. A pity. Most want boys . . . So you're Ömer Eren? Pleased to meet you. I started one of your books. This could be a good subject for a story for you.'

Without wasting much time and with rapid steps he catches up with his colleagues. He doesn't appear to have been impressed at meeting the writer. Perhaps he is arrogant or just very tired, thinks Ömer. He said he'd started one of my books. He didn't say he'd read it, the bastard! Perhaps he doesn't like what I write. Who knows? In fact he probably doesn't read.

This generation isn't in the habit of reading. It's likely that he's one of those who buys a book because it's fashionable and puts it to one side.

Mahmut suddenly appears beside him looking somewhat green and without making eye-to-eye contact. Ömer says to him as though he's repeating a line that he has learnt by heart in a language he doesn't know, 'Congratulations. Your wife has been saved. The doctor said that the baby in her womb had protected her. But they weren't able to save the child.'

Why had he lied saying the baby had protected her?' The doctor hadn't said anything of the sort. Perhaps I made it up so that he wouldn't be so upset about losing the child and that he would find comfort thinking that if it hadn't been for the foetus his wife would have died. He doesn't tell Mahmut that it was a boy. The stray bullet, the son shot in the mother's womb. The young doctor had said, 'This could be a good subject for a story for you.' Was it a clumsy compliment or was he being sarcastic?

Mahmut takes two steps back and crouches against the corridor wall. He presses his chin on his chest, folds his arms round his knees, making himself into a ball as though he wants to grow small and vanish. He murmurs something in Kurdish to himself; like a lament, a plaint. Then he lifts his head. 'The child wasn't going to be like us. His destiny wasn't going to be like Zelal's or mine. He wasn't going to take to the mountains. He wasn't going to fight, and he wasn't going to be sacrificed to the organization or to the code of honour. The child was going to be educated and live a decent life. We were going to get lost in the big city. No one would be able to pick up our trail: not the state, the organization, her father, nor her agha. The child would have been free, and he would have been without fear. His name would have been Hevi – Hope.'

Rocking slightly where he crouches he continues his quiet, muffled lament. The tears trickling down his cheeks thread their way between the stubble and gather on his chin. 'This would be a good story for you!' Is that right? Who has the right to write the story of suffering when they can't relieve the pain? They've killed the child. Hevi's dead. Now what's the point of running away? What is there to save now? *Zarok kuştin. Hevî mir, êdî hewceyî reve nake?*'

He lapses into Kurdish. Perhaps he's repeating the same things for himself, for his heart and for his memory in his mother tongue. As he speaks in his own language his suffering stops being a narrative and becomes his own property. It becomes himself. He no longer needs words. Pain escapes words and settles in his heart for ever.

'Why and who are you running from, Son?'

He realizes that he has said 'Son' to the young man and is astonished at himself. I used to say 'Son' only to Deniz!

'From death,' he says as though spitting through his teeth. 'From the military, the military police, the organization, the state and from tradition . . . From everything, everything that you know about our parts, because they all bring death.'

'Where are your parts?'

'They are burnt villages, ambushed hamlets, mines, unsolved murders and codes of honour, and they are the mountains – especially the mountains. They are all death.'

Now the boy speaks with the typical accent of an eastern mountain villager. He has returned to his mountains, thinks Ömer. His suffering has taken him back to his native self. He doesn't shun himself any longer or his language . . .

'Where was your village?'

He gives its name. Then, again as though he is lamenting for the dead, he says, 'Our village was burnt down. Our aghas took to the mountains. I was still a child, aged eight or nine. We abandoned our animals, pastures, fields and our two-roomed house; we left it all behind. The old, the disabled, families and our belongings, on our backs, on carts, on an old tractor, the black-nosed puppy in my arms . . . I screamed the place down and wouldn't leave it even though my dad beat me. When we came down the hill to the plain and looked back, our village, home and barns were all in flames.'

It's as though he is someone else when he speaks with that broad south-eastern accent. The pain has pierced his silence; words flow like water gushing from a burst pipe. For him there's no longer any point in being silent and trying not to give himself away or hiding behind a digni-fied, sceptical resistance. There is no longer anything left to lose. He wants to speak, and it is as though he can't stop speaking. Like breaking down under torture, thinks Ömer. The moment you break down you start blurt-ing out both what is asked and what is not.

'We came to the city and took shelter with my uncle by the stream. We settled in a tent and then we made a shack from sheets of tin. Later I went to school. "This son of mine, my young son, my last son, will study," my father used to say. "I'm not going to sacrifice him to the mountains or to the state." However, the mountains completely surrounded the city, and they beckoned. The teachers taught us in Turkish. To begin with, we didn't understand what they said and asked what it was in Kurdish. Some of them said kindly that Kurdish wasn't allowed and that in any case there wasn't such a language. As children we were astonished that the language we spoke didn't exist. Some of them used to cane us, and we learnt Turkish with a good beating. In the senior class they taught us history – about Atatürk mainly. We used to bemoan the fact that the Kurds had no Alparslan, no Fatih and, especially, no Atatürk and that all the great men were Turkish. Were Kurds stupid? Were the Kurds cowardly? Didn't they have heroes? Didn't they have great men? We took it to heart, and we felt downtrodden, and because they used to say Kurds have tails we used to check to see if we really did have them. As we grew up we looked to the mountains and listened to the mountains rather than to what our teacher told us. We no longer checked our tails. To spite those without tails we began to wish that our tails really did grow. Wherever we went we were completely surrounded by mountains. And even if there weren't any we would create them. The mountains were ours, and we understood their language. We didn't have any heroes. Well, that was all right! Yet we didn't even have our paltry honour, our name or our dignity. At the slightest mistake they said we had no honour. And, well, if you were stubborn and tried to defend yourself then you were deemed thoroughly dishonourable. In the mountains we were no longer going to be without honour. We would be heroes, and we'd gain a reputation. We didn't have a future, so we'd establish our own. We listened to the voice of the mountains, and we took to the mountains. Then . . . and then . . .' He falls silent.

'Then? Then what happened, my little man?' Ömer is lost in the voice tunnels of his own words. My little man . . . my little man . . . my little man . . . A poem that filters through from the depths of his memory, a piece of music, a vague feeling, a recollection.

'Dear little man, you are afraid,' says the Pilot to the Little Prince who going to meet the snake in the desert. The Little Prince tells him that he will be more frightened that night and that the Pilot should not come then. But he says, 'I shall not leave you, my little man,' even though the Little Prince says that he will suffer if he does, as it will look as though he's dying.

Why did he say 'my little man'? What similarity has Mahmut to the child in the story who came to the world from his own little planet that was big enough only for a single rose bush to make friends and to get to know the world? There was nothing about him that resembled the Little Prince. But, yes, there was his loneliness, his sadness and his passion for his rose and the longing he felt for his mountains that were a distant planet. The night the Little Prince got the snake to bite him so that he could escape from his body that prevented him from flying to his planet, had the Pilot stayed with the child? He can't remember. He recalls that he hadn't been able to persuade him to stay on the earth and prevent him from flying off to be reunited with his rose and his lamb and the sunsets waiting for him on his planet.

He repeats 'my little man' with a sentimentality that he is slightly ashamed of but that he can't suppress. 'Then, my little man?'

'Then I saw and understood there is blood and tyranny in the mountains, too. There's no future other than death. The more I saw and experienced, the less I believed in what I had formerly believed and became disoriented. I began to ask and question what it meant to live a decent life and what it meant to die and to kill. We had broken away and escaped; Zelal from the code of honour and I from the mountains. We had never seen the sea, but even so we longed for it. My father used to say that the sea softens people and the mountains harden and make them more harsh. Zelal and I set off towards the sea. We wanted to reach it. We were going to have a child, and he was Hevi or Hope. He would have a good life. He would live like a proper person. Then . . . Then what else can there be! There is nothing more.'

'There is something more. There has to be. New Hevis and new Hopes will be born. Zelal has been saved, as you see. You will reach your sea. As soon as Zelal gets better I'll take you to your sea. That's a promise!'

'Thanks,' says Mahmut. He pulls himself together. He leaves his native land and language and emerges from his depths, changing once again into his masked-ball costume, discarded for an instant with the intensity of suffering. 'Thanks, *abi*, but we can't run away any longer. Wherever we go the mountains will always follow us. But thanks again.' He takes a piece of paper and a pencil out of the pocket of his shirt stuck to his body with sweat and grime, and he scribbles something on it. 'If one day you should ever happen to pass through our area, near my parents, tell my father I am well and that I ask for his blessing. He made so many sacrifices for me. He paid for special schooling for me, and I won a place at university. Tell my father not to write me off because I took to the mountains and didn't study at university. Tell him it wasn't because I wasted my time and didn't work. It's a complicated story, and if we are reunited one day I'll tell him. Don't say anything about Zelal and the child. If the child hadn't died we were going to go and kiss his hand once everything had settled down. But now there's no need. And I'm going to give you another name, too. Can you do all this? I mean, I don't know if you will. In any case, why should you bother?'

'Tell me anyway, and if it's something I can do . . .'

'If something happens to me, if they track Zelal down, they won't let her live. There's only one person I know of who might help her. She's from our region, a chemist, and she works for women's organizations. She's a woman of the world who knows no fear. She comes from a large family, the daughter of a clan leader, and she commands great respect. She is the only person who can take Zelal under her wing in my absence. I'm writing down the address of the pharmacy and other details. If necessary, if I should ask for help, please call her. Make sure she protects Zelal.'

Ömer wonders if it was the unborn child that bonded these two young people to each other. Their hopes seem to have died together with the child. The young man looks as though he is ready to leave the woman he loves and return to the mountain he has fled. Perhaps it's from despair, suffering, hopelessness . . . Perhaps it's just from being young. Who knows.

He feels there is something to this story that he cannot quite grasp or figure out. The stories of people who belong to another world that he is not familiar with, one he doesn't know, different loves, hopes and fears. He knows that if he decides to write these stories he will always be a stranger to them. He won't be able to tell them even if everyone thinks he tells them well, that he and those people will know that he couldn't tell them or get anywhere near the other side.

'Don't attempt to go anywhere. Just stay here.' The fatigue and stress of the strange sleepless night descends on him. He had said to Deniz, too, in the same way, the same voice, the same desperation, 'Don't go. Stay.'

The boy is silent.

'There's no place to run, Son.' He looks straight into the youth's eyes.

This time the young man doesn't avert his gaze. 'That's true. When you are dreaming about the sea as you lie with your arms around the one you love in the hidden valleys between the mountains or in the shelter of caves or in groves, it feels as though there is somewhere, that it is possible. But when you come down to the plain you realize that there is nowhere to flee. If there is, we don't know about it. When we come down here, we lose our way completely, and we lose all hope.'

Voices in the corridors and on the stairs; cleaners wiping the floors with long-handled mops; the smell of disinfectant, bedpans and commodes being emptied; nurses noisily opening doors, janitors in blue jackets, sleepy-faced doctors on night duty and the relatives of patients who have managed to slip in early unnoticed; the morning bustle of a hospital.

Ömer leans against the corridor wall. He feels the coolness of the wall on his back. He is so tired. His mouth is dry and furred. He thinks about crouching down like Mahmut, but he can't. We city people can't sit cross-legged either. I must write something about body language in different regions and classes. He looks for his phone in the many pockets of his hunting vest. As always, he finds it in the last pocket. He dials his home number, and the phone rings for a long time. Clearly Elif hasn't woken up. Well, never mind. It's time she did. A sleepy 'Hello' from the other end . . . 'Good morning, dear' . . . 'I'm going east' . . . 'Me to the east and you to the west. We are gradually drifting apart' . . . 'While you're there, will you be going to see him, too?' . . . 'The child?'

The unanswered, rueful question that hangs on soundwaves.

TWO

The Child Waiting for Princess Ulla

The little boy is playing among the ruins of the old castle. He is absorbed in building houses with the stones he picks up from the ground. Deniz is watching his son. The sun setting over the ocean drives shafts of light that change from yellow to orange, pink to purple, over the ruined towers of the Devil's Castle. Then a milky-grey twilight . . . The season of white nights . . .

Deniz likes this place. This feeling of timelessness, the sound of the waves that break white against the rocks without disturbing the silence, the mystery of the ruined castle, the solitude, the lack of people, the feeling of being cut off from the world and from time. He and Bjørn come a lot. 'I was just a little older than you when I first came here,' he explains to his son in his broken Norwegian. 'My father said that this place was the Devil's Castle. I wanted to see the Devil, so I . . . How do you say it? You know when you repeat "I want, I want", keep on wanting the same old thing?'

'It's called insisting. See, I know better than you. So did you see the Devil, Daddy? And was his castle fallen down like this back then?'

'Yes, it has always been like this. Devils like ruined castles. My parents were in a hurry to get back to the opposite shore to continue the journey. They didn't let me climb up. So I promised myself that when I grew up I would come here and meet the Devil.'

'And you kept your promise and came back, didn't you, Daddy?'

'Yes, I kept my promise.'

The child wants his father to recount yet again the beautiful story he never tires of hearing.

'Come on, Daddy. Tell me. The Devil had shut the beautiful Princess in his castle. The Princess used to cry at night. Come on, Daddy.'

'The Princess used to cry at night and her tears would mingle with the waves of the sea, and the fish would read her tears like letters. And then one day a fish that was caught in my net brought me news of her. He said that when the full moon hung at the top of the highest tower of the castle the Princess was going to throw herself out of the tower window.'

At this point of the story that he has heard hundreds, maybe thousands of times the limpid blue eyes of the child become wide with excitement and fright. 'Then just as the Princess leaps out, you come to her rescue.'

'Yes, I pull alongside the rocks beneath the castle in Uncle Jan's fishing boat. Just as she is about to fall on to the rocks and get smashed to pieces, I catch her in my arms.'

'Her hair is very long, the colour of my hair. Her eyes are just like my eyes.'

'Yes, her eyes are just like yours.'

'And her name is ...'

'And her name is Ulla.'

'Then you sail out to sea and escape from the Devil. You bring Ulla to the Gasthaus. You love each other very much. Then you get married, and I come along. Then ...'

When they reach this point in the story a terrible feeling that is a mixture of longing, grief and despair engulfs Deniz. However, the child doesn't notice. He has opened his deep blue eyes wide and is waiting for the end of the story that he knows by heart.

'Then you are born. We name you Bjørn. Princess Ulla is so beautiful and so good that the Devil is in love with her, too. He can't forget her. He disguises himself as a bad man with weapons and bombs and takes her away from us. He wants to shut her up once more in his castle.'

'In that tower there, doesn't he, Daddy?' The child points with his tiny hand to the remains of the tower in the middle of the ruins.

'Yes, right there.'

'But my mother ... Tell me, Daddy, what does my mother do then?'

'Princess Ulla doesn't ... what's that word, you know, when you put up your hands as if to say "All right, I give up"?'

'Surrender. You say "doesn't surrender". You asked this when you were telling me the story before. Why don't you learn, Daddy?'

'Yes, well, Princess Ulla doesn't surrender to the Devil. She reaches up to the sky and catches a star. And jumping from one star to another ...'

'And there it is, Daddy! Look, over there!'

The child points to the evening star that can just be discerned in the sky which is beginning to turn from milk-grey to grey.

'Yes, over there, Son.'

'And what about the Devil?'

The child has got carried away with the excitement of the story and has nestled into his father's lap with a childish frisson of fear so that he can enjoy even more the pleasure of being frightened.

Deniz strokes his son's blond locks. 'And the Devil can't stand the pain of losing the Princess. He goes to the east far, far away.'

'He won't come here ever again, will he?'

'No, don't be afraid. He can't come here.'

'Is the east really very far away, Daddy?'

'It's far, very far.'

'My grandma, Bestemor, said that you came from the east. She said there are wars in the east and bad men who don't pray and who cut people's throats. Did you go to the east to find the Devil and kill him?'

He doesn't know what to say. He is not happy with this. A child should not be told such things. The child's grandmother is right – from her point of view. She thinks she has sacrificed her daughter to the cruel violence of the east, to the savages who live there. On this tiny little island that is far even from the west, let alone the east, how can one expect a poor village woman to think otherwise? Nevertheless he gets angry. 'The east was the land of good people and delightful stories. Then devils came from the west, and they destroyed those good people, the beautiful countries and lovely stories. They destroyed them, wiped them out with bombs and weapons.'

He is angry with himself, but he can't stop. What am I saying to the boy? Indirect ideological arguments with his grandmother . . . Goddamnit! 'Do you remember where the sun sets, Bjørn?'

The boy points to where a faint pale pink on the horizon resists the twilight.

'Well done. That's right! Now turn your back to that side. There, you're looking straight at the east. The sun rises over there.'

'Then everyone who comes to this island comes from the east, because when I look straight ahead there's the quay.'

Deniz laughs. So does the boy, and they both brighten up. The boy hugs his father affectionately.

'I told Bestemor, "Even if my father does come from the east he's not bad. He's very, very, very good." And she said to me, "Your father is different. He is a good foreigner." What does foreigner mean, Daddy?'

'It is someone who has come to this island from abroad, from another place, not of this island.'

'Are there bad foreigners, too?'

'There are bad foreigners, and there are also bad local people. Come on. Let's pick up our things and go home.'

As father and son walk down through the ruins of the castle towards the village Deniz thinks about the message left on the Gasthaus's telephone. 'Deniz, dear, it's Elif. I'm in Copenhagen for a meeting. If you are free I would like to come and see you. Call me on my mobile.'

A cold, unfeeling message . . . She cannot say 'Mother' any more; certainly she hasn't said 'Mother' for a long time. And affectionate terms of endearment and pet names have long been forgotten. 'Deniz, dear, it's Elif. Deniz, dear . . .' My mother says 'dear' when addressing people she doesn't much like, people she looks down on or with whom she feels uncomfortable. In her language 'dear' is a treacherous word that masks a lack of love and puts distance between people. So I've become 'dear', have I? There's no point in postponing my call. I can leave a very short message on her mobile saying, 'We are better off like this. Let's not complicate life.' Yes, that's the right thing to do. It's much better for everyone. So it's 'dear' now, is it? So distant, so foreign . . .

He used to play games with his mother when he was small. He recalls them with a sharp pain. His favourite game was the stray kitten and its master. These were cherished moments in the mornings when he could climb into the big bed where his mother and father slept together and, purring like a cat, bury his head in his mother's bosom, feeling her warmth, her closeness; when mother embraced child and stroked him gently like a kitten. Moments of happiness when his mother scratched him on the neck, behind his ears, under his tiny feet, when he never complained even if she tickled him, never said, 'Stop! Don't do that!' He used to be 'Tiny Kitten', 'dear little cat' and his mother's 'kitty', 'his mother's little mouse'. He didn't remember his mother ever calling him Deniz when he was little. Then a light slap on the kitten's bottom. 'Come on. I've got to get up and go to work. The kitten should go to the kitchen and drink his milk.'

'Take me to work with you, Mummy.'

'I can't, because my workplace is full of mice. Cats aren't allowed there.'

Once she had taken him to that magical place. Elif was going to call in at the laboratory and pick up something she had forgotten. From there they were going to the cinema together to see the film *ET*; another one of those rare happy occasions: going somewhere with his mother!

'Stay still. Mind you don't harm the mice, Kitten.'

'Why do you keep mice here, Mummy Cat?'

'For my experiments.'

'What's an experiment?'

'Well, for instance, to find a new medicine that will save the lives of sick children or to do something to stop their pain. We first give that medicine to animals. If it's good for them, if it's harmless, it can then be given to people. In other words, we experiment on animals.'

'Why are there mostly mice here?'

'The structure of mice is close to that of people. That's why.'

'But don't mice feel pain?'

Elif was silent. Deniz still remembers that silence.

Then she said, 'When you grow up and study, you will become a famous scientist and do experiments. You will find things that will be good for people. My tiny kitten son will be a great, great scientist.'

'But I won't hurt mice. I'm a good kitten, and mice are my friends. You know how you always say that even cats and dogs can be friends. And when the boys at kindergarten make fun of me and beat me you tell me that I should treat them well and try to tell them nicely that what they are doing is wrong.'

'That's true. You're right, Kitten. Nevertheless, please stay away from the test animals until I'm finished. After all, you never know what cats might do!'

Whenever he recalls his childhood and thinks of his mother he feels a vague pain, like a scratch in the middle of his chest, a feeling of guilt, inadequacy and inferiority. Her voice is still in his ear. 'Don't sulk. I didn't say your school report was bad, but your biology and chemistry could have been better. You could have had ten instead of nine for your physics if you had paid more attention to the exam questions.'

He remembers pulling his report roughly out of his mother's hand saying, 'I'm no Einstein and don't intend to be!' and shutting himself in his room seething with anger and rebellion. To hurt his mother, he shouted, 'Carry on killing your mice!'

On the whole, his father didn't get involved. He used to say, 'Don't stifle the boy. Let him be. He has his whole future in front of him. Besides, even if he isn't first in the class he's not a bad student. I wasn't a model student at school either. One never knows what a person will be in the future, what they will develop an interest in or whether they will be successful. All that matters is that they're a good person, someone who is interested in the world and someone who takes responsibility for people and for living things.'

The pain of the scratch in his chest gets more intense. That hateful feeling that he has known since his childhood, the feeling of being beaten without being able to defend himself, of suddenly being left stark naked in the middle of a crowd ... The pathos of the dog that begs for affection as it gets beaten or the test animal whose brain is cut open while still alive ... Guilt, remorse, helplessness, the wish to die ... But I'm neither guilty nor repentant.

Deniz wants to hug his son who is skipping happily along in front of him. He wants to be washed and purified with him, to take refuge in innocence. He doesn't dare. He is afraid of passing on that indefinable, horrible feeling to his son. Bjørn must never know that feeling – and he never will. He will capture the real meaning of happiness. He will be glad to be himself. He will spend his life surrounded by nature, peaceful, calm, contented with himself and full of self-respect, knowing that this is the one and only meaning of life.

I shall protect him from violence. I will not allow him to be a tyrant or victim. Nobody will be able to impose their values on him or ask him to conquer the skies. Perhaps he will be a kind-hearted jolly fisherman. Perhaps he will run a small guesthouse with customers who come only in the season of the white nights. I will not allow anyone to mistreat Bjørn or to force him into anything he doesn't want to do. I must leave Elif a message saying, 'Don't come.' Perhaps the best thing is not to answer at all.

Words, sentences and conversations that filter through the intricate maze of his memory and prick his insides like a pin, deepening his restlessness and suffocation: to carry the name of Deniz like a true Deniz ... To be worthy of that name ... They died for their beliefs ... Even if the world should change, basic human values do not ... Man cannot remain indifferent to his times, to his society. He should not ... What do you think is the meaning of life? Should I be hanged like your Deniz to win your favour, Dad? This is basically the question of what life means for a human being ... Pigs are happy, too, but I prefer to die fighting for human rights, justice and freedom rather than live happily like pigs ... And have your son die, too? My son will be a scientist ... You have everything, you have been given every opportunity to excel ... You can go to the best schools abroad if you like ... To be worthy ... Of what, of whom? As you don't seem to be good for anything, well, go to Iraq and take photographs of human suffering. I've fixed up a war correspondent's job for you in Iraq . . . Wars are evil. People die in wars . . . It would be good for you to see how the world really is . . . Those named Deniz . . . The gallows . . . The domains of science, laboratories . . . A little ambition is good. It forces one to get ahead in the race . . . Well, what do you want to do in life? The happiness of pigs . . . To sleep, to sleep for ever . . . With that village girl, on that island where you've buried yourself alive . . . The meaning of life? And what is that? The eternal fugitive, the eternal loser . . . Don't go. Let's try to start all over again . . . As a child you struggled even to learn to ride a bike. That stupid psychologist who said your IQ was close to that of a genius should see you now . . . I don't want to be a genius. I want to be a nobody . . . Leave me alone. I want to sleep . . . Your values, your value, my value . . . Don't go, Son . . . To lose a child . . . What is love? Ulla loved me. She was the only one who loved me . . . Am I invisible? The girls who come to class in the mornings kiss all the boys, but they don't even see me . . . I'm lonely, so lonely . . . I'm very, very, very well . . . Everything I told you was a lie . . . Everything I told you was true . . . I'm frightened, Mum . . . I'm frightened, Dad . . . I'm frightened, Ulla . . . The unknown deserter . . . The unknown deserter of life . . .

I must get hold of Elif without delay; send a message to her mobile.

He remembers that he doesn't have a mobile. A mobile means a link with the world. Wherever you are, they will find you. I'll use Jan's phone when he gets back from fishing. There's no need for that. I'll call from the Gasthaus. A very short message: 'You don't have to come, I'm fine.'

The child walking along in front of him disappears among the rocks. He is playing his usual game of hide-and-seek, but this evening Deniz panics; he is anxious about his son. 'Bjørn,' he calls. 'Bjørn, please come out. I'm not playing.'

To lose Bjørn . . . The last time we saw each other, Dad, you asked me if I knew what it was to lose a son. You were suffering; you were sad. Even I noticed. You know, you always say I'm insensitive. For a moment I even thought of doing the things you wanted me to do, being what you wished me to be and trying again. However, hadn't you considered the risk of losing your son when you sent me off to become a war correspondent? When I could stand it no longer and came back, and you sneered at me saying scornfully, 'Didn't that job work out either?' When you lamented the fact that I couldn't be like others named Deniz?

'Come on, Bjørn. Come out. Look, it's late. Daddy is going home now.'

The child comes out laughing from behind the rock where he has been hiding. 'I frightened Daddy, I frightened Daddy!'

'Don't frighten me again. Daddy doesn't have any other sons. And, besides, we are as hungry as wolves. Let's go straight home and have dinner. Let's see what Bestemor has prepared for us.'

The child points to the boat approaching the quay in the slowly darkening sea. 'Look. Our boat has arrived. Let's go and see if there are any passengers.'

This is another game: Bjørn's game of waiting for the mysterious strangers he imagines will disembark from the boat that links the island to the mainland. Deniz knows that the child is really waiting for Princess Ulla. In the fairytale world they have invented Ulla may miss them very much, come down from her star and come back to earth one day. The boat either returns empty from its last run, especially in the winter months when it gets dark early, or a few belated villagers get off the boat. Very seldom there are one or two strangers who cannot face continuing their journey and prefer to spend the night on the island. There are more arrivals in the summer months, especially at this time. They stay at the Gasthaus. The child is not content with these. 'Why doesn't anybody come to us, Daddy?' he asks. His high-pitched frail voice quavers with disappointment, loneliness and sadness.

'Our island is far away. Not everybody is brave enough to come here. That's why.'

'Then how did you come, Daddy? Are you very brave? You weren't afraid of pirates or the Devil, were you?'

'No I wasn't afraid, Son.'

How can I tell him I was afraid; that I was a skein of fear that rolled to these parts; that I'm here because I was afraid?

Actually, how did I come here? How can I tell him about my cowardice, my weariness, my desertion? How can I explain to him that I am a deserter of life? The old man had written on the wall of the Gasthaus just before he committed suicide, 'Fleeing from war was easier than fleeing from life.' He had signed it 'the unknown deserter'. Not the unknown soldier but the unknown deserter, the deserter of life . . .

The child runs towards the quay. The woman with the baskets disembarks first, then two students from the island, perhaps returning home from examinations. Then . . . Bjørn stops dead in his tracks. The boat has another passenger, a foreigner – finally a real foreigner!

As Deniz approaches the quay to fetch the child he realizes in the twilight that the passenger is a woman. The woman in jeans and a light-coloured T-shirt has slung a large bag over her shoulder and is walking with deliberation towards the jetty.

I know that walk and that bag from somewhere, just as I know the woman with the baskets from afar without even seeing her face. For a split second – that infinitely tiny, short and yet infinitely long moment that is filled with everything a person is: all that he has experienced, felt and thought – he wonders what he should do.

It's too late. Passing the little boy standing perfectly still as though he is still enchanted and without paying any attention to him or even noticing his presence, the woman walks resolutely towards Deniz. The yellow lights of the quay make her face look pallid and its lines deeper. There is that insincere smile hovering on her lips; the one that Deniz knows so well, that he is wary of and which he doesn't like.

He doesn't know, he cannot sense that the smile is a mask for Elif's insecurity, her fears and anxiety. He doesn't know that the woman's heart is pounding madly and that her jaw hurts from clenching her teeth so hard; how many sleepless nights the decision to come here has cost her and with what great effort she controls her desire to run back.

'The woman with the baskets hasn't changed at all in twenty years,' says Elif in a casual, natural voice, as though they had been speaking only a little while ago and had had a long chat. 'This must be a real Devil's Island where zombies live. So how are you?'

He notices that her voice trembles, her cold smile disappears and that her face becomes sad.

'Mother!' he says amazed and hesitantly.

'Well, how are you,' she asked in the casual tone they use in television serials. Good question. How am I? Yes, indeed, how am I on this Devil's Island where zombies live?

The woman with the baskets hasn't changed in twenty years. That much is true. Is it always the same woman, or is it her daughter? Deniz is astonished now that he was never curious about this. Small wooden houses in pastel candy colours, a quay with piles of fishing nets on both sides, a miniature ship with a bridge and a funnel linking the island to the mainland, women with baskets on their arms, pot-bellied bearded fishermen, steep cliffs above and the ruins of the old castle . . . That's the sort of place this is, not really worth thinking about, where people quietly live their natural, straightforward, uneventful lives and die in the same natural way. Just as it should be, just as I want it to be . . . So that means I'm fine.

He wonders what dragged him back to the Devil's Island of his child-hood after all those years. Was it fate? Nonsense! What is fate other than the steps we take or the paths we choose? Perhaps it would be better to call it coincidence. Yes, just a coincidence. When he joined his father's close friend – the famous war correspondent and a prominent member of the press – and went to Iraq, he did not know he would reach the small island in the North Sea in such a circuitous way.

It would be more accurate to say that he was sent to Iraq rather than that he went there. It was his father's idea that war photography would be a suitable job for him. It was not his own choice. Ömer had said to his friend, 'Let's send Deniz to Iraq with you. I'll take care of the bureaucracy – visa, accreditation and the rest. It will be a new beginning for him. He will learn about the job from you. Deniz is a good photographer. I have faith in my son.'

He knew his father was lying, that after those dreadful days that he didn't want to remember his father no longer had any faith in him; and, what was worse, he had every reason not to. Deniz was embarrassed and reluctant, but he could not refuse to go. He had nothing to lose anyway.

They were the days when his indifference and lethargy turned into failure, failure turned into hopelessness, hopelessness into fear and fear into shame. He was all alone, incompetent and desperate. He had built himself a dream world. In that world he was successful, brilliant and the best. He was all that his mother wanted and all that his father expected him to be. He left everyone behind, ran like a thoroughbred, took the lead and reached the summit amid applause. This fictitious world where dreams mingled with lies and where the borders between the two were undefined was his only refuge. He had friends in that world, phantom friends. They loved him; they admired him. He went on trips with them, imaginary trips that he had never taken, never made. He had a small pretty girlfriend in that world with whom he walked hand in hand, whose warm lips he felt on his own, someone who loved him, who took him seriously, who didn't mock him or look down on him. The girlfriend that had never existed, that lived nowhere except in his dreams . . .

If there hadn't been the others to whom he had to endear himself and ingratiate himself, and if he hadn't been surrounded by people expecting him to conquer the world, there wouldn't have been any lies. The lies were innocent, the expression and manifestation of dreams. In the land of wakeful dreams, as he went from one joy to another, from one love to another, from one success to another with a childish smile on his face that gave him a somewhat idiotic expression, his step was as light as a feather and his heart a cloudless deep-blue sky. Then one day, when he realized from the blows of arrogant kings and princes holding the scales of right and wrong, true and false, that he was forced to return to this cruel world, that he was nothing but a dreamer lost in his dream world; and that the curtain had finally come down at the end of the play, he put on indifference, insensitivity and silence as protective armour. Nothing could pierce his armour, reach his heart or affect him any more.

When the day came to face up to the truth, and he said in an icy voice, 'All the achievements I told you about were nothing but lies', he was surprised to see that they didn't believe him. They in turn were amazed at how calm, distant and indifferent he could be. He didn't object when his mother insisted that he saw a psychologist. He didn't even feel the need to withdraw into his shell. In any case it was empty; it was an endless, bottomless, black hole that swallowed all emotion, pain and joy. Didn't I really feel anything, or was I just suppressing my feelings? No, I didn't feel anything. I was empty inside.

The last psychologist from whom his mother expected miracles had told him, 'This is your safety valve, your defence mechanism. You wouldn't be able to endure it if you felt anything. This is how you protect yourself. Your instinct for survival still fights back. That is good.'

To live; to live like the weeds, trees, flowers, a field mouse, a cat, a tortoise or a fish . . . To be a harmonious part of nature, of life and the universe . . . He knew that this philosophy of life was not one he had chosen but one he had accepted. And he was trying to live it on a razor's edge as though it had been his own choice. Still all alone, without letting on to anyone . . .

Like the wounded, defeated soldier of a routed army he returned home from the foreign university town where they had sent him. What was home? My mother, my father, the cat, houseplants, shelves full of unread books. And what hurt him most was their never asking for an explanation. It was their smothering him in a circle of understanding and care instead of accusing him and being angry that he found disturbing and embarrassing. He wasn't the good-for-nothing son who had disappointed them but the defeated sick child. His mother, who always criticized, always wanted more, always expected success, was now quiet and looked at his face with thoughtful moist eyes. His father acted as if nothing had happened; as though his son, who had been studying abroad for years, had successfully completed his education and returned home and was now looking for a job. He had struck bottom. As a family they were all part of a big lie. They were like actors who were trying to play their parts well in a badly written play.

Deniz had felt relieved when Ömer said in a light-hearted jocular voice that wasn't at all convincing, 'All right, we understand. You won't get the Nobel Prize, but at least you can testify to the suffering of this world with your camera.' His words carried all the sadness, disillusionment and betrayal that weighed on his heart. Perhaps these weren't his father's exact words. No, he wasn't that cruel, but, well, it was something along those lines. Whichever way you looked at it, it said that he had been discarded. A new unbearable load that he immediately threw into his black hole and discarded. He couldn't bring himself to say, 'I don't want to testify to the sufferings of this world. Pain cannot be witnessed. It can only be fought – and I'm not ready for such a fight. I'm not ready for any fight.' For a moment he even imagined that he could return to his dream world and succeed, that he could become an internationally famous war photographer. A very short moment that was shattered into pieces and disintegrated when reality struck . . . Hadn't his mother said, 'If there's nothing you can do, go and be a human shield?' No, no, mothers didn't say such things; Mother Cat would never say that. No, she hadn't said anything like that, but I know as surely as if I had heard it with my own ears that the thought went through her mind.

Triumph or death . . . Aim for triumph even if there is death at the end. They were willing to have a dead son rather than one who had not been successful. For them, a child who had been sacrificed for what they regarded as the right causes – science, the revolution, peace, whatever they might be – was not considered lost; whereas in their eyes and their hearts I am the lost son.

He is exaggerating, and deep down he knows it. He is freed from humiliation, his feeling of guilt and shame by exaggeration. Blaming others turns his humiliation into anger, his guilt into victimization and his shame into self-confidence.

In those days when we were still in shorts we were not lost. We were their hopes as we were dragged to private crammer academies and made to study without pause or sleep for entrance examinations to the most select schools; trained like racehorses to be the most successful in the most prestigious establishments. 'A lot of work has gone into children like you, and you have to make it worth while. You are privileged children, especially in a society such as ours,' Elif used to say. She would give examples of her own students, talk about children who were successful in spite of being under-privileged, for whom no effort had been made but who had studied and been successful under very difficult conditions, and she would praise them enviously. He remembers how depressed these oft-repeated words made him feel even as a child.

Of course he hadn't wanted to become a nobody, as his mother expressed it. Who would? However, he hadn't quite understood what being a nobody meant. It would have been good if what they called 'success' had come naturally, but he neither had the will nor the strength to compete for it. He had studied very hard and memorized everything to get the high marks necessary to make his parents happy and win their favour. However, they always scorned his efforts and wanted better school reports. Even the teachers at school said they expected more from the son of Elif and Ömer Eren. He was unable to understand this at the beginning; then he found it unjust and cruel and rebelled against it.

Elif used to say, 'Too much ambition is not a good thing. However, its absence makes one lazy and passive, distances one from success.' I had no ambition, no passion. I never wanted to be better than others. Perhaps because I knew I couldn't, or perhaps I didn't want to force myself, I didn't have the power. I had no desire to be the best. What I wanted most was to be loved. I wanted to have friends who loved me and girls who showed me attention. I wanted to live my one and only little life quietly, full of love and happiness.

It was the beginning of the war when, armed with the most expensive state-of-the-art photographic equipment, he set out towards the hell that was Iraq. Beside the professional correspondents using much simpler cameras he felt embarrassed about the expensive kit that had been his father's present. They were expecting Baghdad to be bombed soon. For some it was war, for others an assault; for Deniz it was hell. The world hadn't yet become inured to the war in Iraq. There was still hope that the fire could be extinguished, that the madness could be stopped. From around the world thousands of voices rose, shouting, 'No to the assault on Iraq!' 'No to the war in Iraq!' There were young people who had come from many European countries to defend Baghdad, if only symbolically, to be human shields in hospitals, kindergartens, schools and oil refineries. If when he went to interview them he hadn't met the bleary-eyed, Norwegian albino youth who knew English so well he would have been somewhere else now. Was it coincidence or fate?

To make news, he had first spoken to a very young English girl. However, he had realized that they weren't on the same wavelength and his interview wasn't getting anywhere. They were standing at the door of the children's hospital in Baghdad, its walls riddled with bullet holes, its windows broken and three wounded children to each bed. It lacked the most essential medicines, and surgery was performed without anaesthesia. He had noticed the albino youth sitting on the steps watching them with a weary and a somewhat cynical expression. He turned the camera towards him, approached him with the microphone and asked him what he was doing and what he was after in these foreign parts.

The boy said, 'It's simple. I'm here so that people don't get killed and the environment destroyed. I'm here to ease my conscience and, most importantly, because this is what feels right to me. Aren't you concerned about these things?'

'I'm a photographer. I'm training to become a war correspondent.'

'Which country are you from?'

'Turkey.'

'There are young people here from your country, too, and, from what I've heard the doves where you come from have stopped Turkey joining this dirty war.'

After turning off the microphone Deniz had mumbled rather sheepishly and inadequately, 'I went to the war protest meetings, too, but I'm not a member of any organization', remorseful for not having been at those meetings.

In the suffocating, tense nights of those days when Saddam's voice promised his people absolute victory while they fearfully waited for the bombing of Baghdad, he had found several occasions to talk to Olaf – that was the Norwegian boy's name – at length. Deniz was as impressed as he was astonished by Olaf's never-ending march triggered by a deep impulse – perhaps a kind of belief – that he called 'my conscience'. It had taken him from Eritrea, in the grip of famine, to the Sudan where starving children were abducted and forced to fight and die in the war; from Bosnia, where people were murdering each other for belonging to another race and religion, to Iraq, which was gradually turning into an inferno, and to who knows where else. Olaf didn't tell him all this as though he had sacrificed himself for a worthy cause or had accomplished important things. He talked about it as a simple, ordinary part in the flow of daily life, in the same tone as 'I went out with that girl', 'This is my favourite beer', 'It's good to see the world', 'I'm completely broke; I must make some money.' This was how Olaf lived; no heroism, no rhetoric about being a saviour; no sermons on noble causes, no bragging; this was his way of life. Deniz liked the simple straightforward, lively way Olaf talked. There was no trace of the oppressive atmosphere that, since his childhood, Deniz had always felt when he was with his parents' old friends; lengthy discussions about defeated soldiers, great causes and glorious revolutions, the unnatural and morbid longing for the past and the years of their youth, complaints about this awful world. He had begun to like Olaf. He seemed like a balm for the growing emptiness inside him, his feeling of futility and inferiority.

As he followed the famous war correspondent south towards the Persian Gulf, Deniz was rather upset to leave Olaf behind in Baghdad. Now he would feel completely alone in the desert. His camera was gradually becoming heavier and heavier, and so was everything that happened around him. In both mind and heart it was all too much for him, too heavy to bear. It was not his camera that was difficult to carry but the images caught on it.

There was no doubt that Ömer loved his only son as he handed him the very best camera and photographic equipment and sent him off to the middle of the war, to bloody, fiery, deadly deserts. I never doubted his love, but I found it difficult to understand. It wasn't an introverted love that warmed his heart and gave him happiness because I lived, I existed. It was an extroverted love, presented for the approval of others and nourished by the pride he would feel for my achievements. Baghdad and the Iraqi deserts: these were the places I had been sent to revive and nurture this love that I had injured and destroyed. No, my father had not wanted to sacrifice me. It wouldn't be fair to say that he thought of it like this. He just wanted to heal the wounds I had opened, to increase his love for his son and to be able to have faith in him again. I know that.

There was a lot of blood. I saw such a lot of blood, pain, fear and death. Blinded, enslaved, destitute, pathetic, humiliated people who had been made to squat next to walls, thrown behind barbed-wire fences, their heads covered with black sackcloth hoods reaching down to their chests . . . Mothers with their dead children in their arms, trying to make shrouds for them with their bloodstained black chadors and tattered clothes . . .

Dead cats, dogs, dead birds, dead trees, mixed with the stinking rubbish heaped in the streets . . . Burning cities, houses collapsing, ruined buildings, humble mud huts riddled with holes, ponds where corpses floated . . . I saw more than a human heart could endure, but I was completely empty inside. I just stared indifferently, without reaction. As the psychologist said, I threw this, too, into my bottomless black hole. Only those who hope, who have something to lose, are afraid. I wasn't afraid. I went right up to them to take photographs. I got much closer to the land of death than the most daring, most ambitious war correspondents. I smelt it in my nose, and I heard it in my ears. I kept on clicking to satisfy the crowds mesmerized by blood and violence, that never tired of watching the horror and the carnage they themselves had created and to satisfy the media that fed on the blood it offered those crowds. I transformed the suffering of mankind from reality into frozen images as I photographed devastated villages, towns in flames, people with bleeding wounds, shot children writhing in pain on the ground, babies burning up with high fever before they died from lack of care and medication, mothers opening their chadors and tearing at their breasts as they mourned their children, wounded soldiers around whom vultures flocked. I fitted the horrors of war, the collapse of humanity, into a tiny chip within my digital camera.

When he was working, he was as calm as if he were taking pictures of scenery, of birds, flowers or children. He was interested only in capturing the best pictures, in getting the best results. His emptiness, his lack of feeling, his indifference bordering on schizophrenia, his apathy and remoteness were thought to be courage. His skill was praised. His photographs were published – with the help of the famous television correspondent – on the front pages of newspapers and appeared on television screens over and over.

This time – once in a blue moon – he had been successful finally. When they reached a burning Baghdad, having passed through the desert, he had made contact by phone with Istanbul just before the foreign press were evacuated from the heavily bombed city. While he was speaking to his parents, he understood from their words and their voices and he felt in his heart that he had been forgiven. They were proud of their son. He could almost hear them talking to each other. 'Well, so what? Not everybody can become a scientist. Being a good war correspondent, a brilliant photographer, is better than nothing.' He waited in vain for them to say, 'The war is spreading. Things are getting serious. The region is very dangerous now. Come back straight away.' Even if they had said it, he might not have returned; he was so wrapped up in his work and the dazzling euphoria of success he probably wouldn't have gone home. However, they didn't say 'Come back'; they didn't summon him home. On the phone they expressed the hope that he would look after himself, and they wished him luck. 'Keep it up, Deniz. You're doing a great job. That's my boy!' said his father, and his mother said, 'Be careful, Kitten. Give us a ring whenever you get a chance.' It was the endearment 'Kitten' that upset him the most. Mother cats protect their young; they remove them from danger. He couldn't bear the solitude any longer. He wanted to cry. His loneliness stuck like a lump in his throat. He couldn't even manage to cry.

Attached to the American troops and protected by tanks, they passed through a poverty-stricken sacked village as they headed north. If he hadn't seen the prisoners surrounded by barbed wire and heavily armed American soldiers he wouldn't have jumped out of the jeep he had boarded with such difficulty. Was it the desire to capture a few good shots, or was it more that he was spurred on by success, love and admiration?

He later told himself hundreds, perhaps thousands of times that if he hadn't seen 'him' his life would have been quite different; he would have been in an entirely different place, on an entirely different road.

'Him' . . . The one with a black hood – or sack – pulled over his head, sitting under the sun with legs spread apart, the sleeve of his white tunic with yellow stripes stained red with blood flowing from his wounded right arm, torn plastic sandals on his bare feet . . . 'Him' clasping his small son close to his chest: that wounded captive father, human, victim . . .

In the days that followed, he would remember with lasting shame and pangs of remorse that he had thought as he clicked, 'Why shouldn't it be the Photo of the Year?' The man with the black hood over his head was clasping his son to his chest with his wounded arm while his dirty, dusty left hand was placed on the forehead of the poor boy half-conscious from fright or fever. It was as though all the love of the world was in that thin hand with its slender fingers; so soft, like a caress, afraid to hurt . . . His head was bent low; one couldn't see his lips moving, but his chin was touching the boy's black hair that was stuck to his forehead with dirt and sweat. He was obviously comforting his son with words of love from under that accursed black hood, the symbol of humiliation, defeat and possibly death that had been thrust over his head. Perhaps he was saying, 'Don't be afraid, this is only a game.' He had embraced his son closely with his heart and his wounded arm, as if trying to protect him from the world – as if this were possible – but also with the mad, hopeless grief of knowing he could do nothing. No fear, no tears in the child's half-closed eyes, on his face smeared with his father's blood; no reproach, no scream from his parted lips; a silence, making it obvious that he would never talk or weep again . . .

He kept snapping away, taking pictures from the same angle, sometimes zooming in, not thinking, not seeing. The prisoner's face was not visible. He was blind, dumb, alone and helpless under the terrifying hood. The image in flesh and blood of the victim made a caricature of the Pietà sculptures which are among the most treasured heritage of western culture, reducing them to absurdity. The Saviour, the sacrificed son lying in his mother's arms after being taken down from the Cross: the statue of the wounded father sentenced to death, the prisoner who cannot protect his child . . .

The man knew soon they would be tearing his small son from his breast and dragging him away. He didn't know what would happen to him, himself, whether he would be shot dead with a single bullet. He didn't know what crime they were supposed to have committed, why the troops had directed their guns at him and placed that black sack over his head. He had taken his son by the hand and they had been heading to Grandpa's house near by to get a small cup of sugar, if there was any. When they were stopped by troops with their terrifying weapons, their shouts in a language he didn't understand, their commands, perhaps their curses, he had no idea what they had done wrong. He had clasped his little son tightly, and the boy in terror had clung to his father in such a way that the soldiers had found it easier to throw them both behind the barbed wire rather than try to prise them apart.

For an instant Deniz thought he caught a glimpse of the captive father's face under a miraculous light through the thick black hood. He thought if there is only one human depiction, one image to last for the next thousand years, it should be the face of that Iraqi father and not Christ on the cross. Then, from the misty mysterious depths of his soul where heart meets brain, a forgotten image came up to the cold and clear level of his consciousness and adhered itself to his eye. Many years ago, when he was still a child, a team had come from the council to their neighbourhood to put down dogs and had poisoned a bitch with puppies. He remembered how the dying dog had dragged herself over to the men when she noticed them approaching her pups, how she had looked at them with imploring eyes and tried to lick the hands of her murderers as she begged them for mercy. Deniz had shouted, 'No! Don't kill them!' and had fallen to the ground, unconscious and foaming at the mouth. His mother had told him later that they had panicked, thinking he was having an epileptic fit.

While he continued to press the button on his camera as if in a trance, the indefinable grief in the hearts and the eyes of the captive father and the mother dog merged together like superimposed photographs and became one single picture. The image of the powerless father, his head covered with a sack and his small son whom he held hopelessly to his chest, was etched into Deniz's heart and his memory and remained there, just like the imploring look of the mother dog that licked her killers' hands to protect her puppies.

In the past few months he had taken scores of photographs without batting an eyelid – images that were unbearable to look at. He had thrown the whole lot into the black hole inside him. However, there was no room inside him for the suffering of the captive helpless father at death's door, with a black hood over his head, clasping his small son to his breast behind barbed wire. Perhaps his black hole was not as deep as he thought, or perhaps it was now full. He did not send those last photographs anywhere, did not show them to anyone or look at them again. He deleted them from the camera's memory card. He would have liked to delete them from his own memory, too, but he couldn't. He considered that taking pictures of cruelty was a form of collaboration with the tyrant. He felt that photographing the murders committed in front of his eyes instead of trying to stop them made him an accomplice to the crime. He believed that to perpetuate human grief by freezing it as photographs served to make it commonplace for ever. He became disgusted by and frightened of the news, photographs and television interviews that brought as much fame and money as the blood, death and devastation they showed. The more they laid bare the cruelty, the violence, the hopelessness, the desperation and the shame of human beings, the better . . . They wanted him to be successful, didn't they? Well, here was success! Was it possible to defeat the oppressors by telling about the suffering, by spreading the news and showing it? Was there no other way? He could find no answer other than to flee. Just as he had seized the opportunity of crossing to the other, the winning side, he had lost yet again. I couldn't make it this time either; I couldn't pay the price of success. I'm a coward; stupid and incompetent. I've lost again.

He knew there was another solution. He felt it deep inside; and that was to face violence, cruelty and pain instead of turning one's back on it. He wasn't strong enough to do it. He didn't believe in salvation. What he had seen during his time in Iraq had strengthened his belief that mankind could not be saved and that humanity would not triumph over evil, cruelty and war. He watched with some amazement, trying to understand his peers – girls and boys, northern, southern, Middle Eastern, European, American, Australian, Japanese, Turkish, blond, dark, all those young people – who voluntarily rushed to the centre of the fire, the blood and the cruelty for the sake of solidarity with life and humanity. They were all very different, but they all had something of Olaf in them. Even if they seemed to be there for others, they were actually there for themselves.

One day he was trying to photograph children in hospital; some without arms, others without legs, all wrapped in rags, lying on top of each other on beds with torn mattresses in a ward where the walls were riddled with bullet holes, bloodstains and dung beetles and cockroaches thriving on the dirt and blood. He came across a young French doctor from the organization Médecins Sans Frontières and asked her why she was in that hell. The answer was 'Because I feel responsible for what is going on here. Because I can't tolerate such a world. I don't want to collaborate with bandits, be an accomplice in crime.'

'You are only saving yourself, easing your conscience by feeling you are of use. That's all.'

'Your problem is solved if you can square your own conscience with that of humanity as a whole. I think I've been able to do that.'

'What power does conscience have? The winner is always the one who uses violence, the one who is strong. We see it all the time.'

'You are wrong. We win in the long run. Brute force will destroy itself. The world will change.'

'How?'

He felt that the young Frenchwoman with the dishevelled hair who had not slept properly for God knows how many nights had an answer. It was evident that she had not even had the opportunity to shower – the city water was cut off and she, too, had helped to carry a few jerry-cans of water to the hospital – and while looking after patients she had come close to being ill herself. If she didn't have an answer that she believed in, had faith in, then she wouldn't be able to carry out the job she was doing; she would not be able to bear it. Deniz was afraid of measuring himself on the scale of that answer. He had just asked himself, 'How?' He hadn't even asked the question aloud.

He gave his valuables to a child who was begging amid the ruins, and, not telling anyone, he left for Baghdad with very little money in his pockets. When he reached the city after risking all sorts of danger including death on the hazardous roads, most foreigners had already left. The young people who had come in solidarity, the teams of human shields, had scattered. Nobody was in a position to deal with them, and there was no work for them in a Baghdad on the verge of defeat. Some of them had given up; others had decided that passive resistance was pointless and had armed themselves to organize militant resistance. Deniz found Olaf in a hotel in which western correspondents were staying.

The young Norwegian was preparing to go back. He said, 'There is nothing more I can do round here. I'm a pacifist. I don't use weapons. And there is nothing here except weapons, violence and death. I'm going home now.'

Deniz had tagged along with Olaf, and together they had escaped from that region of chaos. After the desert, the blood, the turmoil and suffering what he needed was an oasis where he could rest his tired soul, a dark cave to which he could retreat like a wounded animal, a place where he could lick his wounds. This time, instead of hiding in a dream world and lies, he was going to take refuge in oblivion, in disappearing and becoming an anonymous stranger.

He came across the mysterious Devil's Island of his childhood by accident when he started working as a night porter at a small hotel run by a Turk who had come to Oslo to work years before. A photograph hanging on the wall by the stairs leading to the rooms on the upper floor: a sheer cliff pounded by the foamy waves with a ruined castle on top and a deep blue sky . . . A nebulous image stirring in his memory, a feeling of *déjà vu*, mists clearing from a corner . . . I know this place. Then another step forward: I want to go there.

While he was killing time staring at the wall in front of him during the long Nordic nights, this ordinary Norwegian scene, one of hundreds of islands, thousands of cliffs along the coast of the North Sea, became a dream that slowly turned into an obsession. His dreams were illuminated by a fleeting memory that surfaced from the depths of his mind, a distant recollection of the island of which the little boy had said, 'I'll come back here when I grow up, and I'll meet the Devil.'

A refuge where no one would be able to find him and destroy his peace . . . A land where bombs don't explode, where its dead don't lie in scorched streets stinking of blood . . . A real island where he could live naturally, peacefully and simply just like the fish, the cats, the wind and the earth; a place where successful, grumpy, cruel or conceited grown-ups didn't point accusingly with their menacing fingers and give him condescending looks. I shall be happy there, and I shall be free. I shall be me.

He knew neither the name of the island nor its location. He wondered if the place had a name. It was so many years before. I was only a child – so how can I remember it? Candy-coloured dolls' houses with decorated Christmas trees visible through the windows, empty streets in the early twilight, a strange old man sitting in a rocking-chair, a woman with baskets on her arms who kept appearing and disappearing, the castle ruins on top of the cliffs, the Devil's Castle, the dark-blue sky, the toy ship that connected the island to the mainland . . .

I must call my mother. She will know. He wrestles with himself for a moment. If I call her, she will interrogate me again. She will ask why I abandoned my brilliant career as a war photographer and fled. There will be that condescending, accusing, hurt tone in her voice once more. He will ache inside. He will feel sad.

Still, he calls her with a deep longing in his heart that he doesn't want to admit even to himself; impatient and fearing to hear her voice . . . But, he tries not to show it. His tone on the phone is as calm and natural as if they had spoken only the day before.

'Hello, Mother. You know that island we went to when I was small, where we spent the night? You know, the one with the Devil's Castle? Do you remember where it was?'

'You are incredible, Deniz! Not a peep out of you for almost two months . . . Good thing you remembered that island. At least we know you're still alive!'

'Don't start straight away, Mother. I told Dad I had left Iraq and was in Norway.'

'So you think that's sufficient, do you?'

'Yes, Mother. I do. I don't think you need to know more. Anyway do you remember what the island was called and where it was?'

'I can't remember the name, but I can recall roughly where it was. What are you going to do there?'

He lies. 'I told my girlfriend about it, and she wants to go there during the holidays.'

He has no girlfriend; he is all alone. He knows it will make his mother happy to think that he is with a girl. My solitude has always hurt my mother. He feels guilty and sad. He pities both himself and his mother. The only way to eliminate this bad feeling is to enter a world where dreams and lies are intertwined.

'My girlfriend's gorgeous, Mother. You would love her if you saw her. Don't worry. Your son isn't alone any more. She works for the socialist newspaper here. I'll start working as a photographer next month.'

In a hurt voice Elif describes the location of the Devil's Island as far as she can recollect it. 'You'll find it. It's so quiet round there that anyone you ask will show you the way. As your girlfriend's Norwegian, you can ask as you go along. Have a good holiday!'

He senses the doubt in his mother's voice and hears the sadness that has returned just as the wounds were healing and when what happened has almost been forgotten.

'Thanks, Mother. Say hello to Dad. I'm all right. Don't worry about me. No, I don't need anything. I'm fine, just fine.'

He didn't need anything except a quiet, distant sanctuary – and an old vehicle to take him there; perhaps a motorbike . . . As long as it got him to the Devil's Island, there was no need for more . . . He wouldn't be going back anyway.

He recognized it as soon as he saw it from a distance. He was not surprised that his mother recalled the location so well after all those years. It made him angry. Professor Elif Eren, always unruffled, always clever and always right, never made a mistake! Please be wrong for once! Fail for a change! Stop making people feel like worms in front of you. Don't crush them and reduce them to the test animals you dissect!

When he got closer to the island and saw the boat tied to the pier his anger collided with the sweet reminiscence of the scent and warmth of his mother's bosom that rose up from the depths of his mind and dissipated. The woman with the baskets on her arms appeared through the mists of his memory and walked towards the boat. It was foggy and the Devil's Castle was barely visible, but Deniz knew it was there from the playful memories of his childhood. As he boarded the boat with the motor cycle he had bought for almost nothing from a man who sold second-hand, third-hand even fifth-hand vehicles, he remembered his father's words: 'We are going to the Devil's Island that was in the book your mother read to you.' A shadow passed over his heart, something like regret. 'Don't go. Stay,' he had said, 'There is no place to run to, Son.' His father's eyes were moist. They were more than moist; they were full of tears. They think that I don't notice, that I'm cold, unloving, whereas I notice everything. I feel and I understand, but I can do nothing. I become helpless. I shrug, pretend to be indifferent. I throw everything in the deep, bottomless pit within me – and I'm free of it.

When he reached the island, he walked his bike directly to the Gasthaus, without lingering at the square by the quay. Had he remembered where the little guesthouse was, or was there no choice other than the road that passed in front of the varicoloured wooden houses and continued east-wards towards the last inhabited part of the island? The house suddenly appeared in front of him next to the steep cliffs, where the road met the sea. Yes, this is the place. He remembers it now. He also remembers the strange old man sitting in the rocking-chair. He remembers that the room where they slept was cold, that his body and his heart grew warm as he lay between his parents. His father reached over to his mother and stroked her hands, and he felt happy as though it was he who was being stroked.

It was foggy that day but not dark. A milky-blue mist had settled over the island. The yellow house, stone-grey cliffs, silver sea . . . The serene and some-what sombre painting of a Nordic artist depicting shadows rather than light . . .

The front door of the Gasthaus that opened on to the road was closed. He knocked a few times, but no one answered. He remembered the door facing the sea. He had run out of that door and tried to climb the cliffs but had been scolded by his mother. He walked around the house to that side. Yes, the door was open, just as it had been all those years ago.

A plumpish girl with long blonde hair and blue eyes was leaning against the door frame observing the sea. First in English and then in broken Norwegian he asked whether there was a room free. The girl made a gesture as if to say 'Come inside.' He took his rucksack off the back of the motor-bike and followed her. From the few words he knew, he deduced that she was shouting, 'Grandpa, a stranger's arrived. He wants a room.' He thought that he might have seen the grandfather all those years ago, but, no, the man wasn't familiar. They went upstairs together. He seemed to remember the room with its large bed and wooden ceiling, overlooking the sea. He nodded with approval. 'Good,' said the man and smiled pleasantly.

'How much? How many kroner?'

At first he didn't understand the price the man told him. He always confused the tens with the hundreds in Norwegian. Still smiling, the man indicated the figure with the fingers of both hands.

'Fine. All right!'

'How many days will you be staying?'

'I don't know. Perhaps a very long time.'

A shadow seemed to pass over the man's face, a memory, a question. Then he smiled again. He opened the shutters of the room. He said something to the effect, 'The room is yours. Make yourself at home', and went out leaving the door open. The old wooden stairs creaked as he descended, and then there was silence.

Deniz lay on the bed and stared at the wooden panelling on the ceiling. A few minutes later he was asleep. He slept as though he hadn't slept for days, dog-tired, as though he had reached the end of life and the world.

It was almost evening when he awoke. A storm had blown up, and one of the shutters kept banging. He wasn't immediately alert. What is this place? What time is it? Why am I here?

The girl was standing motionless in a long white dress – perhaps her nightgown – barefoot and with her blond hair loose down to her waist in the open doorway under the wan yellow light from the corridor. She ran off quickly when she noticed that Deniz had woken up. The stairs creaked, and a door downstairs closed quietly. In the room only the sound of the wind and the shutter banging against the wall could be heard.

He got up, and as he washed his face he realized that he stank of sweat. He remembered that he hadn't changed his T-shirt the whole trip. He went downstairs to enquire where the shower was. In the room with the fireplace that was doubled up as a dining-room the girl was sitting in the old rocking-chair watching television and stroking a teddy bear in her lap.

'Excuse me. Where's the shower?' He mimed shampooing his hair with his hand to make himself understood.

The girl pointed upstairs as she continued to rock the chair. 'Upstairs, second door on the left, two doors before the room you're in. The second,' she repeated, wiggling two of her fingers. They were to continue this private game of charades in the days to come. It was a game they didn't give up even after Deniz began to learn Norwegian and make himself understood.

It was not that night but not long after his arrival on the island. Had he left his door ajar with a premonition intensified by desire? Was he expecting Ulla? He wasn't surprised when the girl appeared at his door in her long nightgown. The weight on his loins suddenly turned into an arrow of fire.

and rowdy on land, adopted the stranger who had come to share their lives. Ulla's grandparents liked him because he had drawn their granddaughter out of her solitude and her melancholy and rescued her from solitude. She had never known her father, and her mother had gone far away in a fishing boat when she was three years old. They were curious as to why the stranger had arrived on their island, but they never enquired or had any doubts about him. And he told them, 'I came here on a trip with my parents when I was very small. I hadn't been able to climb up to the ruined castle then, so I promised myself I would come back to see the Devil's Castle when I grew up. Now I've arrived!' He told them about the old German, the unknown deserter, whom he could hardly recall but whom he had heard about so often from his mother. They were surprised that he could remember; happy, too.

He was looking for a burrow, a shelter where he could hide like a wounded animal, but he found more than that. He had never belonged anywhere until then, and now he had found a place where he could belong. He loved the people, Ulla's grandparents, the fishermen, the villagers, the little wooden church's old priest who had known the unknown deserter, the young teacher who was curious about the Muslim religion and eastern culture, and Jan the Bear who was so proud of producing the best moonshine ...

I loved them all with a love that was without fear or obligation, because they accepted me, didn't expect me to be anything other than myself. They were happy with me; because when I was with them I didn't feel inferior. And perhaps it was also because, deep inside, I secretly enjoyed feeling superior to them. I don't know if love is the right word, but for the first time since my childhood I felt relaxed, at ease and happy. Mother would call it 'the happiness of pigs'. This island where people made do and were happy with small, simple things was a refuge far from the cruel adult world.

Their baby would be born in this sanctuary and grow up in safety. The flames of a world set on fire would not reach them; nobody would be able to hurt him or push him around. Their child would not have to share the fate of the one behind barbed wire in Iraq whose wounded captive father with the sack over his head had tried to protect him so frantically and hopelessly. He would not feel the weight of the world's suffering or humanity's sins. He would not have to account for them. Nobody would force him to settle this account or weigh down his conscience. He would be as natural as a beautiful animal, free as nature – and be himself.

Then Bjørn was born. It was three days after the Gasthaus's white-faced, blue-eyed Alaskan husky gave birth to two beautiful puppies; the day that the fishermen had succeeded in rescuing baby whales beached on the shores of the island and floating them back out to sea. When the grandfather, Ulla's Bestefar, who was anxiously waiting at the door of the delivery room heard the baby's first cry, the cry of life, he shouted with joy, 'There! Another baby has been rescued today!' He was even happier when he found out it was a boy. He said, 'Let his name be Bjørn', without consulting anyone. It was then that Deniz realized they hadn't thought of a name for the infant. Bjørn was a good name – so why not? In that language, the bear was the symbol of strength, of nature. Why not?

Bjørn came with the spring, when the dwarf snowdrops of the north were beginning to bloom, seagulls were sitting on their eggs and wolves were happily suckling their cubs. The days were growing longer, the darkness was getting shorter, and the sun was preparing to visit the north. Ulla pressed her son to her huge breasts and nursed him. Deniz carefully took his son in his arms and cuddled him as though he were the world's most precious object; afraid of hurting him, looking at him as though he had seen a miraculous creature. Both felt the joy of having a living thing that belonged only to them, one they would love and who would love them back.

'So how are you?' asked my strange mother who wore masks on her face and over her heart to conceal her feelings and who tried to hide the trembling in her voice behind her brisk impersonal tone. Good question! How am I, really? How am I on this small, remote, solitary island, one among thousands of Norwegian islands, big and small, facing the North Sea; Ulla's island, Ulla, who was scattered into pieces with the happiness of red tulips reflected in her eyes?

Elif is looking at the stranger in front of her, as though she is trying to recognize him, afraid of recognizing him, hoping she is wrong . . . If only the stranger would say, 'You are mistaken' or 'You must have mistaken me for someone else' or 'I don't understand your language' and then turn around and go. But there he stands with an astonished, questioning look shadowed by sadness; a look that had already settled in his eyes when he was a small infant.

Is this my son? This thick-set ageing Norwegian villager with a long beard who looks like a fisherman. Is he my son? This is a nightmare that has dragged on! A nightmare that I haven't been able to wake up from for years, one I can't forget, that follows me and adheres to my heart, my mind, my emotions . . . 'Will you be seeing the boy, too?' you asked during your phone call at dawn. Well, the boy is standing in front of me. No, I won't tell you everything. I'll say his poor health is not in evidence. I'll say he's fine; he's happy. And perhaps he is.

My son, our son, is standing in front of me, and I can't put my arms around him and breathe in his smell, feel his warmth. I love him like an animal loves her young, so naturally, so sensually and instinctively it's more than I can bear. However, I can't express it in words. I can't show it. The son we lost is standing in front of me, and I can't bring him back to life – to our life, to the place where he should be. I can't even reach him.

Deniz hugs his mother. He feels her trembling in his arms. Then the little boy, his eyes wide with excitement, approaches them with a strange crab-like walk. Stroking the boy's straw-coloured hair that shines under the wan yellow lights, and trying to make his voice sound as natural as possible, Deniz says, 'This is Bjørn, Mother.' Then in Norwegian, 'This lady is my mother, Bjørn.'

The child stares at the woman with eyes full of wonder and surprise. 'What did you say to her, Daddy? How did you speak like that?'

'I introduced you to her. I spoke Turkish.'

'Doesn't she speak our language? Is she a foreigner, too?'

'Yes, she's a foreigner as well – but a good foreigner. She doesn't know our language. Why should she?'

'Yes, but how will I speak to her?'

'Grandsons and grandmothers get along in any language.'

As they walk along the road with the sea on one side and the row of pastel-coloured houses on the other, Elif says, 'It's been more than twenty years since we came here. Who would have guessed?'

Who would have guessed that we . . . That we what? That we would lose our son? Does the word 'lose' fit here? 'Bury'? No, no . . .

The little boy with curly hair the colour of straw and huge blue eyes pulls her by the hand and tries to tell her something.

'He says that he was waiting for Princess Ulla, but, all the same, he's happy that you came.'

'And who is Princess Ulla? Is she the heroine of a fairytale? Do children still read classic children's stories here? That's nice!' She pulls herself together. 'Oh, I'm sorry! I didn't remember. I'm so sorry.'

'There's no need to apologize, Mother.'

There is a need to apologize. Elif knows there is, even if nobody else does. She must apologize for her lack of love and understanding, for her self-absorption. I would have understood if he had just said 'Ulla'. I didn't understand because I couldn't think of her as a princess; she was far from resembling the beautiful princesses in fairytales. When we met for the first time I was full of such strange feelings that I didn't know what to do, how to act. She was a plump Nordic girl, far from elegant, with straw-coloured hair and eyes that were a lighter blue than the boy's, almost grey. When I put my hand on her shoulder out of politeness – instead of hugging and kissing her – I realized that she was trembling. We were at the door of our apartment in Bebek. We hadn't gone out to the airport to meet out son and daughter-in-law. I had watched them from the balcony as they emerged from a taxi and crossed the road to the apartment building, both walking with the same awkward turkey-like gait. I saw their their unfashionable casual clothes, their old rucksacks and their neglected appearance. I didn't open the door before the bell rang. I took my time, partly out of anger – a reaction – but also because I didn't know how to act.

Instead of hugging and kissing, Elif settles for a distant touch, a pat on the shoulder, and she feels the girl trembling like a trapped rabbit, a mouse petrified with fear. The girl is trembling with emotion, the fear of not being able to please, of being disliked. She is overwhelmed by the magnificent door of the apartment and the entrance with its marble floors, brass decorations and house plants; and she is frightened of the reaction that will be shown by the famous writer Ömer Eren and the respected woman of science Professor Elif Eren. She feels alone and powerless in this world of assured adults, in this foreign country to which Deniz has dragged her. The expression on her homely doll's face shows that she is about to burst into tears at any moment.

Elif feels the girl's fear, panic and loneliness at the tips of her fingers. When I take them into my hand laboratory animals tremble like this, too, from helplessness and the fear of death. And I end their tremors with a death blow, a thin needle or sometimes with a scalpel that doesn't kill immediately, and the tremors continue for minutes. That subtle feeling of guilt hits her every time; that imminent death smell, the senseless regret . . . They say one gets used to it, that it becomes a routine procedure, like swatting flies, but I haven't been able to get used to it. I still carry on though. I kill them lovingly, gently stroking the soft fur of my dear little animals, without letting on to anyone, even to myself.

She suddenly hugs the girl and kisses her on both cheeks. She is surprised at what she has done.

Ulla dissolves into tears. She shakes with small sobs as they trickle down her cheeks. 'Sorry, sorry,' she repeats in the little English she knows.

Apologetically Deniz says, 'She's exhausted from the journey with all the excitement . . . Ulla has been extremely tense. It'll pass when she's rested.' Elif notices that her son is pale, too. With his careless growth of beard, his cheekbones pink with excitement and his lustreless eyes that seem to have sunk with the weight he's gained, his is a familiar face from far away and long ago. A bad caricature of her son's comely fine features . . .

If the poor girl hadn't trembled like that at their first meeting Elif wouldn't have felt so guilty. After all, she is the most innocent among us, she thought to herself. Two scarred children who have escaped the cruel world of adults and taken refuge in each other, awkward, vulnerable, craving love and recognition . . . That was why Elif's heart melted and she wanted to console them, take them under her wing. The reason for her excessive sentimentality was the heart-rending ill-defined remorse she felt when she asked herself if she hadn't played a part in what had happened. Yet her affection and her understanding had lasted only for a short time. The anger she felt towards her son for his lack of courage and success, for causing them so many disappointments and making them feel they had lost him, got the upper hand. He had disappeared into another world, condemned himself to a life of misery, buried himself alive and turned down the bright future they had prepared for him. Ulla's presence – and now also a child – was tightening the chains on his shackles, making the situation irresolvable.

That day as they tried to talk to each other half in English, half in German and through Deniz's efforts to translate, the poor girl, who was obviously not a great conversationalist, stretched her linguistic abilities to the limit and asked the question redolent of so many second-rate domestic film dramas.

'Do you think I've ruined your son's life?'

Ömer, fearing his wife would say something callous, quickly intervened. 'No,' he replied. 'On the contrary, we must thank you. Our son was going through a difficult period. You were there for him.' Did he really think that, or was it just a trite sentiment uttered to save the situation, to ease the tension?

Elif couldn't help saying, 'Wasn't it too soon to have a baby? Have you considered how difficult it might be to raise a child, especially in the tiny community in which you live?'

'It depends what you expect from a child,' Deniz responded. 'What a child means to the parents. Are they an object for the realization of their ambitions, for the satisfaction of their own egos? Or do you want to create a person whose happiness will bring joy, whose values and choices will be respected?'

The sarcastic tone in his voice, the ill-concealed revenge and bitterness, did not escape anyone, even Ulla who didn't understand what had been said.

Sensing that something was going awry, she regarded her husband with fearful eyes. 'Bjørn is already two years old,' she said. 'It's not at all difficult. He gives us joy and happiness.'

'He is a very easy child, and we don't pressurize him or force him in any way. He gets on very well with his grandmother, too. He won't upset her while we're away, I'm sure of that.'

'I wish you had brought him along so that we could have seen him.'

'It would have been difficult. You aren't used to children, Mother. And also you've lots of work.'

They closed the subject and talked about things in general. Then they sat down at the table. The home help, who was a good cook, had been told to make not only Turkish dishes but ones their Norwegian daughter-in-law would like, including fish. It was observed, however, that Ulla did not touch any of the dishes that had been prepared with so much care, and she was deemed the girl with no table manners.

On the one hand, there was that deep feeling of pity in Elif; the desire to hold them close and say, 'If this is the way things have turned out, don't worry about it. Let it be! Live the way you want to live. Don't stress yourself. Don't be so tense. We don't demand anything from you any longer. Just be happy – that's enough.' On the other hand, there was anger and sadness; her inability to accept the biggest defeat of her life . . . And the question that nags at her mind; the hollowness and insincerity of the words 'Just be happy – that's enough', said with doubt, the relative meaning of happiness . . . And knowing deep inside that the kind of life that Deniz calls happiness is defeat and escapism . . .

One day, when he was very small – he was extremely frail, unimpressive and much smaller than his peers but always smiling – the children playing in the playground had refused to include him in their game and had pushed him around saying, 'You're too small. You're tiny. You can't play with us.' He stood in the middle of the sandpit watching them play, with an expression on his face that was far too sad for a child. And when occasionally their ball rolled towards him he would half-heartedly pick it up and throw it back to them. He looked so dejected but so good-natured and so ready to do anything to be liked and accepted that she ran to him and embraced him tightly. Then she had noticed that tears were running down his cheeks, yet he still had that strange smile on his face. What had gone wrong? What was missing right from the beginning that we never even noticed? Why didn't he defend himself, resort to violence or fight? We had always interpreted this positively. We were happy to think we had a well-adjusted, peace-loving child.

As they walk along the coast towards the Gasthaus at the end of the road, Elif asks herself the same question. On this Nordic island, previously recalled as the location of an interesting trip twenty years ago but which has now turned into a nightmare place, the question becomes even more crucial. What went wrong?

The wooden house suddenly appears in front of them where the road ends and the steep cliffs rear up on both sides. She remembers this from their first visit. They had seen the white house just when they had given up hope, thinking they had lost their way, that there was no hotel there.

'Do you remember the Gasthaus, Mother?'

'How could I forget? Of course I do. If I'm not mistaken it used to be white.'

'We painted it yellow. Ulla used to say white looked too bleak.'

In the endless twilight of the white nights, the building rises a bright yellow against the grey and dark-blue sea. She notices a sign illuminated by neon lights above the front door. The word Gasthaus has been decorated with colourful designs of fish, mermaids and flowers, evoking children's pictures. A cheerful, whimsical, childish eccentricity amid the grey gloom of the North Sea and the formidable steep cliffs against which the house rests.

'It was Ulla who painted the sign and the garden walls. She enjoyed making such pictures – fish, mermaids, fairies, happy dancing children . . . Inside are other pictures that she did. You wouldn't like them. They are naïve paintings. But she really enjoyed creating them.'

'It's true that I don't like naïve art, but these are very interesting. They contrast beautifully with the lack of colour of the surroundings, the harsh weather and the stillness. We do a similar style of painting in Turkey. Bright-coloured mermaids, roses and so on are drawn and painted on glass. They remind me of that.'

The little village girl who yearned for vibrant colours, flowers, joy and life . . . She feels the same emotions as she did when she noticed the girl trembling like a test animal that smells death. She realizes that in a few minutes she will meet the girl's family. How is it possible that I had not thought of this? At least I could have prepared myself. What to say, how to act . . .

'Does Ulla's mother live at the Gasthaus?'

'She doesn't have a mother or a father. It's as if they never existed. She has a grandmother and a grandfather – *bestemor* and *bestefar* in Norwegian . . . This is also their home. They will be very surprised to see you. They are not prepared for this.'

'Are they angry at you, because of . . . what happened to their daughter, I mean granddaughter?'

'Because of Ulla's death? I don't know. It wasn't my fault. It was a terrible misfortune. They understand that. We hardly ever talk about it. They find solace in Bjørn. But perhaps deep in their hearts they do blame me for taking Ulla there. Actually I blame myself, too. It was a mistake to go away from here, to leave this sanctuary. She was afraid of travelling to another country, of leaving her island. She never wanted to make that journey, but she came because of me. I will never forgive myself.'

Elif thinks: They lost their daughter, their granddaughter and I lost my son. So we're quits. I don't know whose grief is deeper. How does one measure grief? I don't know that either.

THREE

With Whose Bullet Was I Shot?

Mahmut remained standing until Ömer Eren had walked slowly to the end of the intensive care department corridor and disappeared down the stairs beyond the glass door. He gazed after him for a long time, trying to gather his thoughts, to understand what had happened that night. His mind was in utter confusion, in turmoil. Nothing fitted into place. For instance, that writer . . . There was something strange about the man that Mahmut couldn't figure out. There was his sudden appearance beside them when the gun went off and Zelal fell to the ground. Then his accompanying them to the hospital and taking care of everything without asking who they were or what had happened. His voice trembling when he said 'Son' and his eyes misting over, ready to cry at any moment. It was all very strange. Let us say that it's because he's a really decent person. If it had been simple kindness he would have brought them to the hospital where he knew some doctors and the set-up, handed over some money and gone off. Why should the man care? What is more, it's obvious that we are in trouble. We are fugitives. We have come down from the mountain, we've got blood on our hands and we are illegal. This much is quite obvious. The man sensed this, he understood, yet he wasn't afraid; he didn't walk away. A strange man, somebody well known. If he hadn't been a famous writer I would have said he was a secret agent sent to tail us.

As he crouched from fatigue in the corridor, he felt embarrassed by his thoughts. He felt a pang of sadness. The mountain makes one suspicious. It turns people into enemies. You start being afraid of the slightest thing; you doubt even your comrades. His father used to say, 'People are scorched and hardened by the mountains, softened and mellowed by the plains.' Not that he disliked the mountains. Where I come from, the mountains are like our ancestors, our saints. Each one has its ghosts and spirits, its names that don't exist on maps or atlases. People speak to the mountains and pour out their hearts; they plead with them and seek refuge there, and sometimes they curse them for claiming our sons and daughters. My father didn't say those things because he disliked the mountains but because he was wise and knowledgeable and he wanted his children to have a better life. Perhaps it was because he had lost hope that people could live on this land like human beings, without fear or hunger. Perhaps it was so that his children would be saved.

Mahmut has crouched down in the hospital corridor with his back against the wall, his eyes closed, weary from exhaustion and lack of sleep. However, his mind is still crystal clear and he is thinking of the mountain tale he and Zelal lived together. Their love story that is nothing like the ones in novels, television serials or in the films he hasn't seen or watched . . . A legend that befits those told by the *dengbej* on long winter nights . . . One day in the future will they also tell the legend of Mamudo and Zalal? The heroic epics of the *dengbej* always end in glory, but the love stories are usually sad. Wicked characters come between those who love but only death unites lovers. He shudders. Ours will be a happy ending. All will be well. It doesn't matter if it doesn't become a legend or tale, if the *dengbej* don't tell our story, as long as my Zelal recovers and she loves me.

He thinks about their coming down the mountain to the plain, to the city, to be among people. Then . . . He returns to the moment he does not want to remember but which never leaves his mind, to that moment when he is filled with a horrible feeling that sticks to him like tar. The more he tries to chase it away, the bigger and deeper it gets. The moment that is the end and the beginning. He doesn't know if it is the end or the beginning.

He goes whirling into a dark tunnel with a searing, intense pain in his left shoulder; he doesn't know if it is a knife wound or the bite of a poisonous snake or a scorpion. He remembers his own voice, his scream and that he whirls out into daylight from that endless dark tunnel. Then he begins to roll down a hill. If he wants, he can make one last effort to cling to a bush or rock, to stay where he is or call for help. He doesn't. He lets himself go. He no longer feels any pain. His body feels as though it is made of sponge, rubber and rags instead of blood, flesh and bone. His mind is alert, quicker and clearer than usual. He wonders if they will shoot at him. He feels like a stranger observing the event from outside, like a television cameraman – once foreign television people came to the camp; that was where he saw them – as if he is watching an action film. He feels no fear, just curiosity.

The bleeding from his shoulder gets worse as he continues to roll down. The blood smears the grass and the rocks. If they want to catch him, they can track him down from the trail of blood. If only he could stop for a moment and stand up, tear a piece off the *shutik* around his waist or, if that didn't work, from his other clothes and wrap it tightly around the bullet wound to reduce the bleeding. But he can't stop; he mustn't. He has to roll all the way down to the dwarf oak trees and from there reach the depths of the woods and hide his tracks.

He knows these parts like the palm of his hand. He is familiar with every nook and cranny, every possible hiding place. The meadows, pastures and playgrounds of his childhood; the secret places of passion, innocent escapades of precocious village youths . . . Hillsides that were once green, then burnt black and which are becoming green once more . . . Who can stop the life that bursts from nature? Who can destroy for ever the seeds that hide in the depths of the earth? And who can prevent them from sprouting and cracking the soil, staying alive in defiance of death?

Even though the fighting is carrying on above, it is clear that it is gradually dying down. The shots are becoming less frequent, and the noise of the guns is quieter, further away. The only sounds in that odd moment of silence between the bouts of gunfire are the flapping wings of the frightened thrushes and the monotonous humming of the wasps that seem to have confused night and day. Today the operation lasted a long time, late into the day. This is not very common. Sometimes you fight as a duty; sometimes it is a matter of life and death. You are wound up to kill in order not to get killed. And at other times you fight with fury and passion, for the cause, for victory. That was how it was this time. New recruits who had just joined and had been sent fresh to the front – many of them still children, some of them young female guerrillas – were fighting, their belief in the leadership, the organization and the cause still intact. These people offer their lives, and their faith is as hard as a rock. They don't retreat, run or surrender even if they know they will be killed. Death is a part of the saga. It is not the end, it is merely the prologue for becoming the hero of legends. They are so young, so far removed from death and have so little to cling to in life that they are afraid of pain, but they are not afraid of death. That is the reason why the conflict has lasted so long.

And how about me? What did I do? Did I run? That horrible sticky pitch-black feeling . . . No, I didn't run; I was shot. Shot! It wasn't my first combat so why should I panic and run? If I were to run, I would have done so long ago, when I had all those chances. I didn't run. I was shot. Had he not stopped himself at the last minute he would have shouted at the top of his voice: 'I was shot! Shot!'

The soldiers use the north and we the south face of the mountain when retreating. As though they have come to a tacit agreement, weapons are silent as the soldiers return to their barracks and the guerrillas to the mountains, the survival instinct prevails, and life overcomes death. They say that once the operation is over and both sides have begun to retreat, soldiers and guerrillas who happen to meet on the road do not draw weapons on each other. Perhaps it is just a rumour, but, still, it makes one feel better.

No one is firing at him. He lies face down and hangs on to the bushes and thistles with his good arm. He digs his fingernails into the soil and looks up for an instant to the top of the hill. No, there is no one following me. Didn't anyone see me rolling down? Is everyone trying to save themselves? Did they see me tumbling down the hill like a stone and take me for dead, or is it something else? Whose bullet shot me? This is the question that hurts more than his wounds and gnaws at his insides and settles heavily on the stones, the rocks and his heart. I was caught in the crossfire. Had I thought of defecting, had it crossed my mind even for a moment? No ... Yes ... Yes! No. I don't know. I was at the front, not from heroism, just an error in calculation ... I shouldn't have crept up so far. Why did I do it? Was I the bravest? Or was I running towards the soldiers? No, I don't know.

He doesn't know, and he doesn't want to know. He hopes he was hit by a soldier's bullet. The idea of being shot with a *heval* bullet is as good as committing a sin. It was an enemy bullet. It came from the opposite side. It must have winged me. Or is the bullet still lodged there? He feels his shoulder with his hand. He was wounded from behind. He shudders. I was facing the enemy, but I may have turned around for a moment when I realized I was a good way away from our group.

The enemy: a nameless, soulless, bodiless, faceless concept, a ghost. He can't bring himself to call soldiers 'the enemy'. My cousin Mamudo – he was also called Mahmut after our great-grandfather – my namesake and my soulmate ... He is in the military, and I am here. Hıdır of the Zahos is a soldier, and his cousin is with the guerrillas. This is why his heart ached whenever he placed a bullet in his rifle, every time he fired, especially at the beginning. Now are we supposed to call these *kekos* enemies? We must of course. We have to. Once you get used to saying the word 'enemy' they really will be enemies. Keep on saying it and you will learn the enemy by heart. You will shoot the ones you've learnt to call the enemy, hurt them, take revenge and become a great warrior, a hero. Mahmut senses the aggressive power of the word that hones the mind. He knows that a tongue can become a weapon. What he can't understand is why he has such difficulty in identifying the so-called enemy as such. When you come face to face with him, when you look him in the eye, you don't see the enemy; you see another human being. If you have a split second to think, even when you are pointing your guns at one another, you cannot understand why you are foes. Some people have sent soldiers to the mountains, and others have led the guerrillas to soldiers and village guards. Instead of having a smoke together, chatting about your loved ones and showing photographs to each other, you shoot and kill. Then the one who is faster and a better shot, whose hand doesn't tremble when pulling the trigger and who doesn't nurse sentimental ideas, is the one who stays alive.

He was the first to realize that gradually he was becoming a bad fighter, sometimes missing the target on purpose. What was worse, he was staying in the rear during combat. This was due to his inability to call the soldier the 'enemy' and his obsession with 'Is that my cousin facing me?' He was afraid that the *hevals* would realize this, too, and his group commander would know. He knew that he would be criticized for being soft and weak. He would have to deliver a self-criticism and try to make it up to them; nothing would be the same as before, and a doubt would always remain somewhere in the hearts of his comrades. What was worse, one could be tried as a traitor, a *caş*, a secret agent and then . . . In the camp, one snowy morning at dawn they had executed Seydo who had panicked and attempted to surrender in the middle of a battle, and they had made all the troops stand and watch as a lesson. Mahmut had pretended to look but he hadn't been able to. He had just seen the warm blood spreading on to the snow as it flowed from the chest of the boy who had fallen face down on the ground. Later, when they were carrying his still warm body towards the frozen rocks to hurl him into the darkness of the deep valley, he had noticed that the boy's feet had become purple and swollen from the cold. What hurt him most and tore his insides to shreds was not death but those purple feet.

And yet, as things stand, if I'm to be shot let me be shot with a soldier's bullet. The bullet of a soldier is preferable to that of the organization. If the former, you go as a martyr; if the latter, as a traitor. It is the same death, but the names are different.

To have studied at university, not to mention medical school if only for three terms, was a privilege that brought one safety at the beginning. It was rumoured that the leaders took the educated and the students under their wing. You felt well supported. However, some of the troops in the mountains, especially certain commanders, had no sympathy for those who had studied or for the students who came from the city. 'These people have problems in focusing, and they can't stand hardship. They tend to broadcast their concerns and lower the others' morale.' Such words were circulated in whispers and sometimes even out loud. You could sense what they thought about you from the attitude of the people who were close to the commanders. A few incidents in the camp had been enough for Mahmut to understand that he was being given the cold shoulder. He felt that they had taken him along on the last combat because they had to – and perhaps to test him as well.

I'm not a traitor. I have never been one. From time to time children would be taken from their villages against their will. However, no one brought me to the mountains by force Most of us were not obliged to come here. It was our choice. We felt in our hearts the sound, the poetry, the legend of the mountain. We combined them with the heroic stories we had acquired since childhood. We fortified the memory of our raided, evacuated, burnt villages with rebellion against our poverty, our oppression and rejection.

We followed the sad songs of comradeship that echoed over hill and dale:

> *Dur neçe heval*
> *Na na! Tu dur neçe!*

We dedicated our squalid, hopeless, futureless lives to legends of liberation, silently and without feeling the need for ponderous words. We were ready to believe and we believed. We were ready to fight and we fought.

His father used to say things like 'The future is not in the mountains. *Dahati ne li çiyanan e.* You can fight each other in the mountains. You kill and get killed, but you can't build a future with guns and weapons. You can't gain your rights in the mountains. If you study and have a good career you can save and enlighten both yourself and other Kurds.' Nobody forced me to take to the mountains. To the contrary, they always told me not to go. I was never coerced into joining the organization.

I believed my father. I thought I could do it. I thought I could save myself. The whole family collected rubbish to pay for my courses. My father, that great proud man who was a descendant of holy wise men, rummaged in bins. He always tied a scarf over his face, not to avoid the foul stench, but the shame of being recognized.

He had studied very hard. Only two students from the course had got into university that year. He had won a place at medical school, his first choice, too; what was more, at a university close by, in his region. People had looked down their noses at him, saying, 'You can't become a doctor in those provincial universities. At most you will learn how to dress wounds, and no one will give you a decent job. All you will be able to do is to help midwives and give injections in state-run health centres.' But the family was overjoyed. His father had patted him on the back, and his mother had thrown her arms around her son and wept. The neighbours had come to congratulate him and had been offered refreshments and sweets his mother had made out of nothing. My mother had always been a secret hoarder. She had produced the last of the five gold pieces that had been given at her wedding. They thought it had been spent long ago, but she had put it aside for a rainy day. They bought me a new pair of jeans, a good pair of trousers, some shirts and a pair of shoes. Their son was going to appear in public. No one should look at him askance; he should not feel wanting or ashamed. Everyone had believed things would work out, even Mahmut himself.

He had completed the third term and passed his examinations when he was disciplined for dancing on the campus at Nawroz and suspended for a term. Then the military officer at the campus, who had taken a dislike to him for some reason, had filed a complaint against him and the other members of the student culture club saying they had sung Kurdish songs and staged a silent liberation play. As a result, he was suspended for another two terms. Otherwise he would have continued his education and become a doctor. It didn't matter if it were in the state clinics or small-town health institutions; he would still be serving the people of this country. And what was wrong with a civil servant's salary. Your money was in the bank at the beginning of every month.

It didn't work out. He did not have the chance to carry on to the fourth term. If he had had the means or been able to find a part-time job he could have waited for the suspension to be lifted and continued from where he had left off, although it would have been difficult. He had no means, no job or money from his father. When he was handed the disciplinary order he became so distressed that an electric dart had passed through his brain and burst a blood vessel in his eye.

In our region, if you are in trouble, if lightning flashes through your brain and stress makes a blood vessel burst in your eye, the places you go to, the places you take refuge in, are the mountains that surround your land and your heart. To see a free horizon you look at the mountains, and then you climb them. You heed the mountains, and you listen to their sounds before singing a song in your language. At the beginning, when the mountains were merely mountains, there was no war, treason, guerrilla forces or Kurdish separatism. In our region, where all exits and doors are sealed, where all screams and voices are smothered, where your voice is silent however hard you scream and is never heard even if it does emerge, the mountains represent hope; they are liberty, the high podium from which you can make your voice heard, where your scream will echo.

Bleeding, he tumbles down the hill, surprised at the speed of thought and remembrance, with a pleasant drowsiness in his brain as though he has smoked grass.

The night their village was raided, the doors of the huts and barns were broken open with rifle butts and the people inside lined against the walls. His mother, grandmother and aunts were forced to lie face down on the ground while boots pressed on their necks and the house was searched. The grown men were taken from their homes – some in their underwear, some naked – and herded together in the village square amid Turkish-Kurdish curses, slaps and kicks. He was only a small boy cowering under the only window of their flat-roofed yellow-grey mudbrick house that stank of dung. He remembers – how could one forget? – seeing his old limping grandfather, his father in his long johns, his cousin and his big brother as they were frogmarched away. He remembers watching the armed men in snow masks and motley uniforms that blended into the night, as they goaded the grandfathers, fathers, uncles and brothers crawling along the ground with sticks and rifle butts. He remembers that some of his people were pushed and prodded into trucks amid shouts of 'Spawn of Armenians and Kurds!' 'Traitors!' 'Criminals!' and were taken away and that his father and grandfather were considered lucky to have returned home, even if bruised and broken. He also remembers that for three days his father didn't get out of bed, not from pain or sickness but from grief and shame, that for three days he lay facing the wall on the cushions in the corner.

'We must leave this place,' he said when he eventually got up. 'We must go far away to a place where houses are not raided at night. Don't anyone dare say to me that this is our homeland. What sort of a homeland is this? The guerrilla attacks, demanding food, shelter and sons to fight in the mountains; the state attacks and wants you to forsake yourself, your life, your honour. We must go to the city, a big city where nobody knows one another. It's too late for the others, but this poor boy must go to school, get an education and become a responsible member of society. The mountains are no longer safe. Death lurks there. Brother shoots brother in the mountains.'

The day the village was evacuated and burnt down and they were trying to reach the plain below with their loads on their backs, women and children, everyone totally wretched, when they stopped to look back something incredible happened, his father had wept; he went down on his knees facing the village, as if prostrating himself in prayer, and talked to himself as he cried. Seeing him like that, the women crouched next to him and bade farewell to the village, sobbing and wailing, '*Şin û şivan*', as if praying for the dead. He heard his father muttering, so that he wouldn't be heard by the soldiers accompanying the migrating group and hissing under his breath like a wounded animal, as though whistling through his teeth, '*Ma li serê çîyan mirin ne ji rezilbûyina li vir baştir bu?*' Wouldn't it have been better to die on the mountain rather than suffer this disgrace? The home of our ancestors is ablaze. What good is living if you're not strong enough to put out the fire in your homeland? '*Ger mirov ji boy tefandina şevata welat xwedi hêz ne be, jîyan çi re di be?*' They had cried together, silently this time, grandfather, grandmother, mother, daughter-in-law, grandchildren, everyone. Their homeland remained as the smell of burnt grass and dung in their nostrils, the colour of embers in their eyes, salty teardrops on their lips, pain in their hearts and longing in their minds. Burnt villages, burnt hills, burnt mountains . . . Was that all that was burnt?

He is not rolling any more. He slides down the steep slope on his behind putting his wounded shoulder forwards. Only the sound of the crushed grass and the rolling pebbles . . . And the silence . . . He can't decide whether he should consider it peaceful or ominous. And just in front – about 100–150 metres away – the dense clump of trees that looks like a tuft of hair on a bald head . . .

He slides in the opposite direction for a while to cover his tracks. He must go on a little more, a little further. There is a cave. He must leave some traces there. He tries to smear blood on the grass and the pebbles. His shoulder is bleeding badly. It won't stop. However, the bullet is not inside; it must have just winged him. He knew he would have been in a worse state if the bullet was lodged inside. After all, he had studied medicine. He had heard in secret conversations that this was why so many wounded fugitives confessed. What can you do if you are a badly wounded fugitive? You will knock at the door of the state. And if you don't want to stay in prison all your life you will surrender.

I can cope with this wound. The barking dog doesn't bite; a profusely bleeding wound doesn't kill. But if the bone is shattered that means trouble. He will go into the cave and leave a torn piece from his shirt and one or two bullets from his cartridge belt. He will bind up his shoulder and try to stop the bleeding, and then he will get up and make a dash for the woods.

He knows that all this is pointless; that if they want to they will find him wherever he goes. I wasn't anyone significant; just an ordinary fighter with the mountain troops, that's all. They wouldn't have let me get away if I had been someone special. Most of those executed were important comrades or just boys like Hıdır. So why do I keep thinking that it was our side that shot me? Who could tell where the bullet came from in all that confusion?

He reaches the entrance to the cave and with one last effort pulls himself inside. The cave is peaceful and cool. He is beginning to feel slightly drowsy. Although Mahmut thinks it comes gradually, sleep pounces on him. I must have lost a lot of blood. It isn't safe here. I mustn't fall asleep. I must reach the other side. There is an impenetrable area in the middle of the woods over there where thorny shrubs intertwine with dwarf oaks and birches. Neither the guerrillas nor the soldiers use that place. If you intend to hide, that wood is good and safe, but there is no escape out of it. Once you are surrounded, you are finished.

With one last effort he takes off his cartridge belt – many loops are empty – undoes his *shutik*, pulls off the shirt stuck to his body, and, winding his sash under his armpit and over his shoulder from the back, he binds the wound tightly. It is the first time he feels such intense pain. It is deeper than a flesh wound. It spreads to the bones. His collarbone is probably damaged; no, not damaged – completely shattered. Clearly he will be disabled for life. Luckily it's the left arm, he says to himself. He feels faint. I must get to those woods opposite. It's not safe here. They will hunt me down like a rabbit here. As he struggles to get up his head touches a warm soft pillow. He lets himself go. I must get to the woods . . . I must . . . I . . . must . . . get . . . In the damp coolness of the cave, his head on the soft warm pillow, he sees a myriad stars in the dark-blue sky. Stars colliding and falling like balls of fire . . .

*

You put your head in my lap and passed out. You slept. I couldn't make out your face. You were wounded and bleeding, your chest and your back were bare. When I ran my hand over your head and your chest; my fingers touched your thick, soft hair. I shivered and felt funny. No, I was never afraid of you. When I realized someone had entered the cave I retreated to the deepest, darkest corner. In the light that filtered in from outside I could see that you were wounded. It is in our tradition to help the injured. If a wretched, wounded man took refuge in our fields, neither my mother nor my second mother asked or considered which side he was on. Sometimes my father would ask, 'Who are his family?' My mother would stand up to him responding, 'Whether he is from the mountain or from the state army, he is still a human being, his mother's darling, so what does it matter?' And my second mother would back my mother up, saying, 'Your son is in the mountains, and two brave boys from my village are soldiers of the Turkish Republic – the TC – so what does it matter?'

The men who raped me, were they soldiers or guerrillas? I have no idea. It was getting dark. I had left the herd in the valley below, and I was looking for the lost black lamb among the rocks at the top. As I jumped from stone to stone and rock to rock I must have strayed quite far. Somebody grabbed me from behind. I couldn't see his face. They forced me down, pulled up my skirt, pulled off my trousers, tore off my knickers, parted my legs and raped me. The first time – I don't know how many they were and how many times – I shouted not from fright but from pain. I struggled, kicked, punched and tried to escape. The last one said, 'Don't be afraid.' I can't remember now if he spoke Turkish or Kurdish, but I understood that he told me not to be frightened. He caressed me all over if somewhat hurriedly; he kissed me, too; both before he entered me and while he was inside. He had a beard. He rubbed his beard on my face, my lips, my nipples, my belly and even my female parts, softly, caressingly. I realized that he didn't want to harm me. The pain between my legs was increasing. I was hurting and bleeding. I was wounded inside. But the fear in my heart had faded a little. Suddenly an arrow of fire shot between my legs, passed through my stomach and struck my nipples, then my throat and my lips. I released my fingers that were clutching the earth and the grass, and dug them into the back and the arms of the man on top of me. I didn't want to hurt him, just to hold him. I wanted him to stay where he was, not to get up and leave, to remain there like a protective shield. I didn't want him to throw my bleeding body to other bastards. Perhaps he understood: perhaps not. The others called him, not with words but with a whistle. He said something as he got up from me. I couldn't understand what language it was or what he said. My head felt numb. Then they hurriedly went away. I could see their rifles dangling under their armpits from where I lay. I was tired, but I wasn't entirely worn out; I was no longer afraid either. What worse could happen? I walked over to the spring close by, and I washed myself thoroughly all over. I felt purified, cleansed. I looked at my reflection in the water. How they would jeer at me as the raped and abused seed of a whore if they knew! Yet the iridescent reflection rippling in the water was still the same me. The stain on my honour had been washed clean away with the water. Could it be that my face was shining more than usual? I couldn't see myself in the shimmering mirror of the water; I saw with my inner eye. I had become prettier. I had grown and become more feminine. There was a midwife in the village who used to tell dirty stories to young brides and women, caress our budding nipples whenever she could and feel our private parts with her finger, saying, 'Let's see if you are a virgin.' She used to giggle as she told my mother, 'Look out for that daughter of yours. She's got the fire of a whore.' Even if she hadn't said it my mother always kept an eye on me in any case. I wasn't allowed to play mothers and fathers or get too friendly even with girls, let alone boys. It wasn't that she was afraid something would happen to me or that I would lose my virginity. She was frightened of the code of honour and wanted to protect me.

When you put your head in my lap and slept I could have got up quietly and run away, I didn't run away. While I was stroking your naked chest, that arrow of fire shot through my groin and rose to my stomach, my breasts, my nipples, my throat and my lips. I was enveloped by a sweet, sinful feeling. Do I really have the fire of a whore? Do I lead men on? Am I really a sinful slut, as people get my second mother to say instead of saying it themselves? Are they right?

Zelal remembers all this as she lies in the white bed of the whitewashed hospital ward with a severe pain in her stomach, the taste of pus in her throat and rust in her mouth. And she remembers that long road she used to walk along with the boys to school when she was a small child. They would pinch her, try to squeeze her breasts and pull down her pants. She would think of her mother and be afraid. She loved school, but sometimes because of this she did not want to go. She would insist that her brother took her. The road went through a mountain pasture covered with snow in winter and tall flowers and grass in spring and met a stream. At the point where the stream was at its shallowest and calmest, forgotten by the waterfalls and the foaming waters close by, there was a ramshackle wooden bridge with a rope for a rail. When the water rose, it left neither bridge nor stepping-stones. Once, as she was crossing the bridge with her mother and her brother, the rope they had been holding on to broke and she and her mother had fallen into the stream. Luckily the water wasn't high at the time, so they survived the accident with few injuries. Then she had also stayed in a room like this with white walls and white beds in the county clinic. There was another child in the next bed. His name was Süleyman. She will never forget him. They had amputated one of his legs and one of his arms at the hospital in the city. And now they had brought him to the clinic because his wounds would not heal. The boy's mother wept and cursed all day long. Zelal had cried her eyes out, terrified they would cut off her arm and leg as well. Her mother had tried to console her saying, 'He was a naughty boy. He walked where he shouldn't have and stepped on a mine. You have no business with mines and such things. Don't be afraid.'

Then one day they said to her, 'You are grown up now. You have almost reached the age of marriage. You cannot walk along those roads with boys, and it's out of the question that you go alone. There are boys at the school beginning to sprout moustaches, and there are male teachers. A girl who has started to have periods doesn't go to school.' She hadn't told anyone, not even her second mother, that the boys had already squeezed her breasts, pulled off her knickers and looked with curiosity at that particular place and laughed.

If it weren't for the walk along the road, school was fun. They taught in Turkish; reading and writing, Atatürk, the flag... Her favourite subject was arithmetic. Numbers fascinated her. How does 1 become 10 when you put a 0 next to it? How does 2 times 2 make 4? If you have 15 eggs and 5 of them are rotten, how can you know there are only 10 good eggs left without counting them one by one? During the four years she attended school she saw herself as a wizard who solved the riddle of magic signs. While the other children were still scratching their heads with their pencils and counting on their fingers, she could solve a problem in her head and give the answer right away. Once, the teacher had called her father to school. When the man didn't show up, the teacher made a point of going to the village. He told them, 'I'll look into the possibilities of sending her to a regional boarding-school or similar. She has a good mind. She is very different from the others. She might continue her education, become a teacher, go to university.' But her father didn't pay any attention to the teacher's words. 'You may be right, teacher *beg*, but my younger son was like her, too. You weren't here, but that time they came to the village, too. This gift from God comes from my grandfather. He used to make calculations for the whole clan even though he could hardly read or write. If I had the means, I would have sent the boy to school. The girl's grown up now. That's enough study-ing for her. An educated wife looks askance at her husband.'

When the teacher, his head bowed, walked slowly away down the slope with his stick, she had wanted to run after him and go away with him. She would have liked to learn about the magic of numbers and the spell of words, to discover the secret of how the same things could be said in different languages, to understand why Kurdish should not be spoken, to find out about the moon and the stars in the sky, and those distant far-off countries – and especially the seas – the teacher had told them about; how that incredibly huge, misshapen ball called the Earth kept on spinning for ever in space and where that endless space ended. Something else she wanted to know was why the language they spoke at home and in the village was forbidden at school, why they got a thrashing if they spoke Kurdish – no, her own teacher didn't get angry or punish them; he just said to them 'You have to learn Turkish.' However, the Principal – you know the type, hardly human – used to beat the hell out of those who spoke Kurdish. Why did people speak different languages? You could say 'mother' or '*yade*' or '*daye*' or 'mum', call a lamb 'lamb' or '*berx*'. They were the same; you understood the same thing. So why was it forbidden to say *daye* for mum and *berx* for lamb at school? She wanted to know this, to learn and teach what she knew to others like the teachers did. But these were things that could be learnt only in the city, at the big school, not the local school in the nearby village; she sensed that.

Happily they hadn't married her off when she was twelve or thirteen. It is not our tradition to marry off girls that early. And if a girl is beautiful and has many suitors, they wait for the bride price to go up. The daughters of *beys* and aghas are hard to get. My father's relatives were not *beys*, but we weren't that poor either. It seems they had plenty of property and cattle before the war. My great-grandfather was also a sheikh, a holy man. People used to come to kiss his hand, and bring him chickens, food or whatever they had stuffed into their bags. She can barely remember. They used to eat a lot of sweets. Sweets in colourful wrappings that smelt of lemons and strawberries, toffees wrapped up with fortune poems . . . They used to give them to other children, too. There would be a crowd around her, waiting for sweets. She remembers a long house with separate rooms opening on to the earthen courtyard, a large, crowded house where women and children, grandfathers and grandchildren, wives and second wives all lived together. Then she remembers leaving that house suddenly one day and moving to a hamlet. She remembers that they no longer ate sweets, they had no cattle except for a few goats and sheep, their sheikh grandfather died, her brothers left home one by one and her favourite brother, Mesut, disappeared and his name was mentioned only in whispers. She remembers her father as a good man, that he was always affectionate and never beat her mother, although he beat her second mother once, badly – but she deserved it because she had been disrespectful to my mother – that he never ever hit his daughter and used to caress her when she was very little – fathers didn't caress their daughters once they had grown – saying, '*Keça min ja çawşina xweşik!* My beautiful blue-eyed daughter!'

One day her father beat himself. You couldn't say that he beat his breast because he literally beat himself. The women and children in the house ran to hide in corners so as not to witness it. They were afraid that if they did they would be guilty of being eyewitnesses.

A man had arrived. It was obvious he had come from afar. He was empty-handed, but there was a cartridge belt and gun at his waist. Without looking at her face he had said to her, 'Call your father.' How did he know I was my father's daughter? She had run and summoned her father. Was it summer time? The weather was pleasant. Even so, the two men hadn't sat in front of the door or in the courtyard; they had retired to the privacy of the house. When the man had gone away they heard her father cry, 'The boy's gone. The boy's finished!'

'The boy's gone,' repeated her mother in a whisper. That was all. Then she began to pray silently for the soul of her dead son. Her lips, not her eyes, shed sorrow as they moved. The man left the way he had come, without looking around, not a real human being but like the evil messenger in stories. Then her father had come out of the room and had started to beat his head with his fists in the middle of the courtyard. He seemed to be beside himself, not knowing what he was doing. Then the women had run out of the courtyard so as not to see and not to show that they had seen him. Then her father had hurled whatever he could find on the floor; even the tiny puppy of the golden dog of which he was so fond. That night her mother learnt that her son had not died. She had sighed with relief and started to pray. She had promised God to fast and to offer a sacrifice. 'You scared me to death, husband! I thought my precious lamb was dead. He's alive, isn't he? And that's all that matters. I don't care if he's confessed, whether he's a soldier or a guerrilla as long as he's alive!'

'I can't stand this. There isn't treason in our code of honour. There aren't *caş*, there aren't traitors, in our household or in our family. I didn't tell him to go to the mountains. Whoever eats this shit has to bear the consequences. A traitor eh? A *caş*, eh? I'll shoot him with my own hands if he comes back. I won't spare him even if he's my own son. I can't stand it. I can't stand it! He should have died. At least he would've been a son, a martyr then. A *caş* – someone who's surrendered! I can't stand it. I can't take it. I can't bear it!'

She saw her father in floods of tears; she was astonished. She hadn't been able to understand what could be worse than death, why her father wished his son dead.

'Just look at you!' roared her mother. 'Look at you! A grown man wailing like a fox! Why are you hollering like that? Weren't your entire clan village guards? I mean, those that stayed in the village. Didn't they save themselves by being village guards? Didn't they all see some money in their pockets? Village guard or those who confess – don't they both serve the state? At least wait a bit. Let's wait and see if the news is accurate. Would it have been better to learn he was dead? Stop and listen for a moment, find out what really happened and why.'

'I wish he were dead! There isn't such a thing in the code of honour as betrayal. There aren't turncoats or traitors in our family. If he's a village warden, he stays a village warden. If he takes to the mountains, he stays in the mountains. Now we are all in deep trouble!'

Then her father had left. Nobody knew where he had gone. Her second mother worried, but her mother said, 'I know him. He goes crazy, and then he calms down. He'll be back, don't fret, girl. Have a few nights' rest.'

Zelal had sensed the bitter reproach in her mother's voice and the repressed sadness, and she felt really upset.

Her mother was right; her father returned in two days. He didn't say where he had been or whom he had seen. They pretended nothing had happened. Nobody had seen or heard anything. It was as though Mesut *Abi* had not surrendered. The children were cautioned not to say anything to anyone. They were threatened with being nailed to the ceiling by their ears if they let anything slip out.

And then one day towards winter her Mesut *Abi* dropped by. Three people came, three men, two of them fully armed. Her Mesut *Abi* had lost weight, but he looked very fit and handsome. He was full of airs and graces as though he had become a commander. Those who saw the armed men took flight and hid. Zelal didn't run away; she fixed her deep-blue eyes on the men. She couldn't go straight up to her brother. She had missed him very much and wanted to throw her arms around him. She took a step forward, timidly. Then she remembered her father's words the day he had cried: collaborator . . . *caş* . . . *caş* . . . traitor . . . She froze. Her Mesut *Abi* smiled; he always had a beautiful smile. Zelal was his favourite among his siblings and he was hers.

'You have become as tall as me. You are ready to become a bride, my girl!' he said and stroked her hair. She had never heard her brother speak Turkish before, and she felt awkward. 'Go and call Mother. Tell her Mesut is here and wants to kiss her hand.'

She didn't move. She didn't say, 'Your wish is my command, brother.' Instead, she said, 'My father has sworn to kill you on sight.' She regretted her words as soon as she uttered them. She was so frightened. She couldn't understand how those words had slipped out, how she had used such strong words.

'Is our father here?'

'No, he's gone to town.'

'Good. You say he'll kill me when he sees me, so we're all right.' His voice was sarcastic. He was obviously making fun of his father and his little sister. 'Go and tell my mother. This place is just a tiny hole with five or six houses! Where the hell is everyone?'

'Mother will be frightened when she sees armed men.'

'Come on, girl. Buck up, and call her. Don't make me go in there like this, or we'll turn the place upside down! Tell my mother, "He was passing by and came to kiss your hand." Come on, move! And give these brothers something to drink, some ayran, tea or whatever.'

When she went inside and called her mother, she didn't say '*Keke Mesut hatiye!* Mesut *Abi* is here!' but she called out, 'Your son is here!' Something had happened to her Mesut *Abi*. Even his voice had changed. He talked in a imperious manner as if he were giving orders. Something bad had happened to her Mesut *Abi*. She remembered how her father had been so upset, how he had been beside himself with grief when he learnt that his son had confessed. Perhaps Father was right, she thought. He is no longer loving and affectionate. Even his smile has changed. She couldn't tell whether he was showing off to the other men or whether he was afraid of them. He has become strange. There is something alien and cruel about him. And what is that fear in his eyes as he struts around defiantly? What is the reason for him turning his head from one side to the other? What is the reason for his restlessness? What does confessing mean? It must be something bad, like *caş* or bastard. She remembered; she had seen it on her way to school. They had killed a man and thrown his body on to the road. They had written *Caş* on his forehead in red paint. Her father had said '*Caş*' as he sobbed. '*Caş!*'

My mother rushed to the door without even pulling down her skirt that she had tucked into her waist. I ran up the hill towards the boulders, leaping between the adobe roofs like a goat so that I wouldn't have to see mother and son embracing, so that I didn't have to bring those men tea or anything. I amused myself counting, adding and subtracting the pebbles on the way. I wanted to forget my Mesut *Abi*. Whether my father shot him or not, either way it would still be devastating. He was as good as dead anyway. I felt in my heart the grief of my brother as well as that of my father. I was a child at the time.

You are sleeping with your head on my lap. Who are you? What kind of sleep is this? You are bleeding. In the village, they used to a say a wounded man should not sleep. There were always people being shot; by soldiers, by the guerrillas, because of vendettas or land disputes . . . They used to try to keep the wounded awake. They wouldn't let them lose consciousness. They used to call it the sleep of death. Is this your sleep of death? How were you shot? Who are you? It is almost dark in here; I can't quite see your face. I'm feeling with my fingertips to get an idea of what you look like. I'm stroking your hair. I don't want you to die. I don't want to remain here all by myself. I'm frightened.

When he woke up or came round, his head was still buried in that soft, warm pillow. Someone was gently stroking his hair as his mother used to do. At first he thought he was dreaming. He was in pain, his shoulder was killing him and there was no sensation in the fingers of his wounded arm. He tried to straighten up and work out where he was. The pain shot into his chest, making him moan. He made another attempt to get up. It was then that he saw the girl.

'*Tu birîndarî, tu ji ser hişê xewê, çû û kete xewê.* You are wounded. You passed out here, fell asleep,' says the girl in Kurdish. Her voice flows softly like limpid waters or snow melting in the spring.

It is then that Mahmut understands that he is where he shouldn't be. So I couldn't make it to the woods. I fell where I was. And what about this girl? He can't bring himself to ask if she is some sort of a sprite. If I do, she will think I'm afraid. He tries to get up, leaning on her for support.

'What are you doing here?'

'Whatever it is that you are doing, I'm doing the same.'

Well, just look at her! Mahmut adds a wry smile to his voice. 'So were you in the fighting, too?'

'No, I'm running away. I'm hiding.'

He is surprised at the reckless tone in the girl's voice. He can't work out whether it shows courage or merely indifference to her fate.

'How can you talk like that without knowing who or what I am? Aren't you afraid I might turn you in?'

'No. You're obviously a fugitive, too, and you're wounded. You won't harm me.'

'Where are you running to? Who are you running from? You'll be prey to wolves and vultures in these mountains and caves.'

'The wolves and vultures have long since eaten. They won't bother me.'

He doesn't understand what she means. His arm hurts, and he feels faint. I mustn't pass out, I mustn't faint, I mustn't stay in this cave. And as if that isn't enough this mysterious girl has sprung out of the blue. He can barely see the girl's face in the dim light of the cave as she tries to place her arm behind his head to keep it from coming in contact with the rock. Am I dead and in paradise? He slightly lowers his eyelids, deliberately . . .

'You are wounded,' she repeats, like the clear water that skims over pebbles. 'Are you from the mountain?' she asks. 'Many bullets were fired. There was a lot of shooting. I could hear it even from here.'

'Yes, I'm one of the *hevals*. I got shot and rolled down the hill.' He doesn't tell her the truth. He doesn't say I was running away from the mountain.

'I had a brother on the mountain.' Her voice is broken, sad and full of reproach. In spite of his pain, his exhaustion, his stricken heart, Mahmut notices the tremor in the girl's voice. Her brother must be dead, he thinks. He doesn't dwell on it.

'But he has come down from the mountain now. Perhaps you know him. His name is Mesut. Or have you confessed, too?'

'No,' he says, mustering as much force as he can into his voice. 'I haven't confessed, and I don't know your brother. Anyway on the mountain people are known by different names. Things like that aren't discussed openly.' His wound hurts even more. If only this girl would take a look at his shoulder, do something about his wound instead of talking.

'All right. We won't talk then. Here, drink some water. It'll be good for your wound and your soul.'

He takes a few gulps from the plastic bottle she holds out to him. A bottle of water with her . . . The girl has come prepared. Perhaps I have walked into a trap. Whose trap? He shudders. 'Take a look at my shoulder. It's bleeding badly.'

'It has been bleeding, but there's less blood now. You've had a close shave. The bullet grazed the bone, but it hasn't lodged in the flesh.'

'I tried to bandage it, but I couldn't. Could you bandage it again, tightly?'

'OK. First I'll wash it, then I'll bandage it with a clean piece of cloth.' She gently undoes the dirty bandage that has adhered to the injury and which is soaked with blood. She tries to clean the wound with a little water. Mahmut moans between his teeth, in pain.

'Stay still. Don't faint again. Your wound isn't that bad. What sort of a *heval* are you!'

'Oh yes. So you're an expert! I studied to become a doctor, so I know about wounds. This sort of injury can have complications.' Then he changes the subject and to put her on the spot he asks this mysterious impertinent girl in this cave in the middle of nowhere, 'You haven't yet told me who you're running away from. Is there someone you love or what? Are you eloping?'

He panics at his own question. Hell, why didn't I think of this before? Why did I assume the girl was alone? These people run away with their lovers. Who gives a damn about battles, operations, war, that we are dying and killing on the mountain?

'I'm running from our code of honour,' says the girl in a dry voice. She doesn't elaborate with any explanation, any details.

His constricted heart relaxes, feels lighter. So there is no imminent danger! He tries to make out the girl's face in the dim light of the cave. Dishevelled heads of wheat, snowdrops, wild roses, fresh thyme, chicory, cool springs, waterfalls . . . All the beauty he knows is reflected in her face. It merges with a milk-blue cloud and disappears. This time he really does faint.

How many days and nights did they spend in the cave? The girl who knew about numbers counted the rising and setting sun. One early morning just before dawn, at the darkest hour, they left the cave and took shelter in the most secluded part of the woods opposite.

Just as in the legends of the *dengbej* and the tales of the woman storyteller in the village, Zelal carried water from a secret magical spring that the mountain elves and forest fairies had created in the wood for the two lovers, Mahmut and Zelal. And with that healing water she cleansed his wound. She collected all sorts of plants, boiled and mashed them and spread the mixture as a poultice on his wound. Although it had started to heal his arm was still in a bad way, and he couldn't really use it. They giggled, saying one arm was enough to make love.

It was more than enough. It was that kind of love. It was Leyla and Mecnun, Tahir and Zühre, Yusuf and Züleyha. It was a legend, a folk tale . . . It was a fire that fed on confinement, grew with helplessness, in which they were bewitched with the intensity of their love and which burnt them in their passion. They were two innocent children, banished from hell for their innocence and yet banned from paradise and hurled on to earth for the sins of their ancestors. Their bodies were cleansed every time they made love, and as their bodies were cleansed their hearts grew big enough to embrace the whole world. They were free of evil, sin, blood and death. The bullets fired on mountaintops and distant slopes did not reach them. Flames from the bushes and burning fields kept their distance. Neither soldier nor guerrilla came their way. It was as though all roads had been closed or as if this side of the mountain had melted away and disappeared. Angels were watching over them, as they do all innocents, because such passion defeats sin, because in the eye of the creator, love purifies and cleanses both the innocent and the culpable. A legend, a miracle was happening and they were unaware of it. They did not know about miracles; they knew only each other's bodies, hearts and minds.

Then one day, in the lee of the green trees and bushes, Zelal told Mahmut about the seed that was growing in her womb, the life that was sprouting in her belly. She spoke in the tongue of holy books that fascinates and finds depth in its simplicity, as though saying, 'I know and I make known.' Mahmut remained silent for some time. Then he put his hand on the stomach of his beloved and wept.

During one of the clashes he had engaged in, his companions noticed that he wasn't fighting as furiously as formerly, and they had reported him. While he was offering self-criticism, they had said, 'Battle tolerates no softness or mercy. You must either kill or die. Be inspired by the example of our female fighters and our *hevals* who pull the trigger without turning a hair.'

War does not tolerate softness or mercy. Men don't cry. Well, he was crying. While Zelal brushed away his tears with her lips and tried to bandage his wound with a flood of words of love, he thought, I'm soft. If I wasn't I would have shot her here and now. If I weren't soft I wouldn't be able to bear the thought of her carrying the seed of the enemy in her womb. Then he rejoiced silently. What a good thing I'm soft, that I don't kill her, that I don't kill anyone.

Were they his words, or was it a divine force that had entered him and made him feel like this? He spoke with the voice of that force. 'The child is my child. The child is our child, yours and mine. For days now my seeds have been falling on to your soil. The child will sprout from that soil with those seeds. Whether soldier or guerrilla, he will not be a child of war. He is our child. We will take him far away from these mountains, and we shall reach the seas. He will be a child of peace.'

The code of honour did not penetrate the green sanctuary near the cool spring that gushed from the rock. Neither the laws of the state nor those of the mountains were recognized there. Zelal and Mahmut were in a dream where they ate wild fruit and plants and drank the healing waters of the holy river in Eden. They were the joyful tidings and the dream of a sorrowful world that had lost its innocence.

They realized it was time to wake up from that dream the day the military police arrived on reconnaissance. From their nest in the most secluded corner of their green shelter and without seeing anyone, they could hear the military police discover the cave which they had abandoned. The military police raided it, armed with heavy weapons. They moved cautiously. The green sanctuary was so inaccessible, so well hidden, that Zelal and Mahmut saw neither the large guns nor the wary steps of the men's clumsy boots. But they heard the sounds; they understood what was going on from the noise – familiar sounds they had known since their childhood.

'Military police don't come to fight,' said Mahmut. 'They must be after something else.'

'They're after me,' said the girl. '*Apê minan dû min xistine* . . . My uncle's family has sent them to look for me. They never give up. When my death penalty was pronounced my father didn't have the heart to kill me. He is an extraordinarily good man, my father. They shut me in the sheep pen.

They hung a rope from the ceiling and the noose was ready for my neck. I checked the rope, and it was strong. But would the roof of the pen take my weight? I wasn't sure. They couldn't risk doing it themselves. I don't know if they couldn't bring themselves to do it or whether they were afraid of the law. They told me to take care of it myself. I was the one to sin for taking my own life and that of the one in my womb. I said to myself, if this is your code of honour, if what you are doing is right, well, then do it yourselves like men. You'll get no help from me. Take the sin of two lives upon yourselves. Let's see which of you pulls the rope. It won't be me. My mother cried when the decision was taken, but she hadn't objected. What good would it have done anyway? My second mother said, "It's not right. You're not to blame. This is God's child. Your father weeps for you secretly, I know. It's your village warden uncle who insists, saying it is the code. Apparently he goes around saying, 'Can I be head village guard and not punish the whore? Can I be a guard and violate our code of honour? Impossible!' Your father wasn't defeated by the traditions; he was defeated by your uncle. I don't know how he heard, but your brother Mesut, too, sent word. Apparently he said, 'I won't let that whore live.'" They told me, "You have until morning. Make it quick. Do what you have to do", and off they went. It was way past midnight when the door opened and my father came in. I was so frightened my heart was in my mouth. I thought he would finish me off quickly to end his pain. I didn't hide. I came to the middle of the room and stood right under the noose. If I stood a little on tiptoe it would just about pass over my neck. My father was carrying a bag. He said, "Take this and leave immediately. Well, go on. Get a move on." I did. I took the bag he gave me and left. Life is sweet, especially when you are young, especially if you are carrying another life inside you. It was a strange night. There was a full moon, but it had gone behind the clouds so it was very dark. It was the work of God. The dogs were quiet as if they knew. Nobody made a sound, and there wasn't a soul about. Did everybody know I was going to fly the coop, or was it providence? I know the area well, and I've got a good sense of direction. I can find my way easily. I walked over rock and mountain for days, always getting further away. There was water in the bag, food, a little money and my identity card. My father was always proud of having got us identity cards. Just think; even the girls had them. I walked and walked and then I reached the cave.

'I was walking with another life in my stomach. I was feeling light-headed, my mind a blur. It was as though I was in a dream, walking on clouds as I skipped over stones and rocks, jumped over puddles and brooks. My bare feet hardly touched the ground. I didn't get tired or hungry. I hadn't even opened the bag of provisions. I had escaped death and had lost all fear. I steered clear of hamlets and grazing grounds. I walked towards the mountains, always the mountains. I saw fires in the distance. The winds from the east brought the smell of burnt grass and straw and charred trees. Sometimes, I heard gunshots in the distance. I walked along in deep thought, thinking about the life I carried in my womb, wondering what would happen to it, what life was all about, asking myself what had become of my life, of my mother's, my sister's. Never mind about us women. What about my father, my grandfather, my brother – what had they done with their lives? Mine was a walk in the opposite direction. I was walking up the mountains, whereas I should have been walking down to the city. My father had told me to bypass the town and head straight to the city. He had said, "The city will envelop you, you will be lost in the crowds. You will change, become unrecognizable, and perhaps you will escape." I walked in the opposite direction. I preferred the freedom of the mountains to being lost in the anonymous crowds of the city. Then I found you. Then I understood that I had been coming to you all along. It was all about meeting you.'

She had walked those roads thinking about the life in her womb. As she climbed over rocks and steep slopes, as she rested when tired in a hollow, under a tree, in the shadow of a boulder, her mind kept returning to the foetus in her belly. Perhaps she was unconsciously trying to get rid of it by walking so rapidly over such rough terrain. Pregnant women in the fields who wished to get rid of unwanted babies would carry abnormally heavy weights, leap over fires or reach out for ropes way above their heads. If that didn't work, the midwife would give them medicine or poke about inside them to make them miscarry. Zelal might have tried to do the same. If she wanted to live, she had to get rid of this thing growing inside her. She had to pluck out this bad seed that held her body prisoner if she wanted to reach that vast water of her dreams called the sea. However, she was scared and had not been able to do it. She was paralysed by the image of Mizgin who had died in the village; her face growing paler, her lips turning white, her eyes bulging as the blood trickled between her legs and her last long scream was etched for ever on the mirror of her mind.

She had been brooding over this when she saw the wounded stranger who had fainted at the entrance of the cave with his head against a rock. She was about to make up her mind. She was going to get rid of the encumbrance inside her. Then with empty womb, empty heart, free, she would reach the boundless open sea.

Towards the sea that her teacher had described to them at length with such passion and longing . . . He had told them the sea was nothing like the Botan Brook or the Zap river or the Uluçay. He had said, 'These streams and rivers are not even puddles compared to the sea. They're just lines of water.' So that the children might grasp the concept of the sea better he had asked with a faint hope if any of them had seen Lake Van but got no positive response.

Zelal had enquired how far from their village the nearest sea was.

The teacher had considered this for a while, scratched his head, made some calculations and had answered, 'If you calculate in a straight line as the crow flies, disregarding mountains and hills, it would be 600 to 700 kilometres. If you calculate it by road it would be much more than that.'

The girl who was good at numbers quickly calculated in her head: 350 times the road they walked to school every day. 'That is not very much, sir. It is like walking to school 350 times. And that equals 175 days there and back from school. We walk that many days every year anyway.'

The teacher looked at his little student not with pride and joy but with desperation and as though suffering. This was God's gift, a miracle. She heard her teacher murmur softly to himself, 'What's the point of such brains? If she had a thousand times the intelligence what good would it be? To hell with this world!' and shake his head.

From that day on Zelal thought constantly about the sea. They didn't have big maps at school. The teacher brought to class pages torn out of an old geography book or atlas. He had shown the children what a small area Turkey covered on that vast ball called the Earth. They wanted to see their village and were surprised when they couldn't. It did not exist either on the world map or on the map of Turkey. Even the county where the government was based wasn't there. So that they should have some idea, could understand, the teacher had said, 'Imagine me as the world. Turkey would be as large as my smallest fingernail.' How much of that fingernail would be their village? The children felt disappointed. Those huge mountains, the wild rivers that dragged people away with their rushing waters in the springtime, pastures and meadows, their village, their houses, their school: didn't they count for anything? What good is it if you're not even a dot on a map?

This issue had not bothered Zelal. Not that she didn't care but because she understood that if there had been a bigger map Turkey would have looked bigger; that their village – and even their houses – would be marked on a Turkey that had been drawn far larger. Instead of listening to the teacher it was the sea that she was obsessed with, that she could not stop thinking about, the dream that she became engrossed in during lessons. The sea that was very far away but still not further than a school year . . .

The vigorous evil seed that had resisted so much hardship and was growing inside her was hindering the life granted her when she was at death's door. It was preventing her from reaching the sea. Not even Mizgin's bloodless lips, the dark, dirty blood oozing from between her legs or her final blood-curdling scream was going to stop Zelal from getting rid of the thing inside her.

It was then that I saw you, as I was getting ready to dig about and empty my womb, to taste the freedom of life or death. You were wounded and bleeding. You had lost consciousness and fallen into a deep sleep, and I took your head to my bosom. I felt your warmth just below my stomach where the seed was sprouting. I imagined a vast sea; lukewarm, limpid, the colour of the sky . . . I made a wish, a vow; that if you, a stranger, were a good man and I took care of your wounds, you would take me and we would go and reach the sea together and become the sea. I calculated it was my ninety-sixth day. It would become more visible every day. Then I calculated by the moon in the sky; I had 184 lunar days to go. I told you, but it wasn't out of fright. Why should I be afraid? What did I have to lose? I told you because my love for you could endure no lies and because I believed myself innocent and clean. You stroked my stomach and cried. They were tears of love that came from your heart, not your eyes. I understood that.

You said, 'Perhaps everything, even the bad things, happened so that we would find each other.' I was just about to say that when you took the words out of my mouth. At that moment I believed that the child was a gift from heaven. Those who had raped me were not soldiers, guards or guerrillas; they were spirits who had assumed the form of the cruel male warrior so that we could find each other, possess each other. Spirits of the skies, the waters, the mountains . . .

You knew that, too. You said, 'The child is our child – not a child of war but of peace and hope.' The seed inside me that I had thought was evil bloomed that moment like the roses of paradise and became our hope. My child became your child because we loved him before he was born. We loved each other for the miracle of the unborn child, to bring the unborn Hevi into this world.

They watched the military police leave hurriedly after a half-hearted search. They didn't like to venture so far into the mountains to look for someone. They never knew who or what would emerge from a cave or from behind a boulder. It was obvious that they didn't want to linger in these dangerous parts. Although some of them headed for the woods they gave up halfway there and turned back.

'How many days have we been here?' asked Mahmut when the soldiers were gone and all was peaceful and quiet once again.

'Seventeen days,' said the girl who knew about numbers.

They had bonded as though they had been living close to each other for seventeen years. And yet they were as full of longing as if they had been together for just one day. They could not get enough of each other.

'How many days old is our beloved Hope?' asked Mahmut.

'He's completed his 103rd day,' answered Zelal.

They knew the time had come. They knew they had to wake up and return to the world, to bid farewell to the mountains and walk towards the open sea.

Two souls without refuge or shelter, two innocent children, carrying a third one within them like a lucky charm, descended to the land of hope to save Hevi from being consigned to the caves in the mountains, the barrenness of charred hillsides and the eerie solitude of deserted villages.

'Tell me a tale of escape; one that is not sad, where nobody dies, nobody cries. As you are a storyteller, tell me a good story, where lovers are united, brothers make peace and everybody lives happily ever after. Storyteller, tell me a beautiful tale of escape. Let fugitives reach their goal, let no children die, let lovers not part and let no one go hungry. Let there be hope and peace at the end. Tell me a good story with a happy ending.'

Had Zelal spoken these words to Ömer Eren when her fear had left her and she had found her voice, or had he written them himself as he gazed at the sadness in the girl's beautiful iridescent blue-green eyes?

When Zelal was transferred from intensive care to a standard room she had not said a word, had turned her face to the wall and been silent. Was it from weakness or was it anger, they couldn't tell. To begin with Mahmut also remained silent so that his beloved did not exert herself and get tired or upset. Afterwards he could not tolerate the silence and the pretence that nothing had happened. He was afraid that she had lost her mind and her memory, that she would not remember anything. It was more than that: he was terrified. He panicked. What if she had forgotten their passion, their love and their love-making? What if she didn't know him, if she could never again remember those fairytale days? He spoke to her. He told her again and again all that had happened. He told her at the risk of tiring her and causing her pain so that she would remember. But Zelal still said nothing. How much had she understood? He could not tell. He asked the doctors in fear and trembling. They said, 'It will be hard for her to get over the shock, but she will get better.' Then one day, when Ömer Eren was visiting, the girl turned her beautiful head towards the door. She pointed at the writer who was standing by the door with a bunch of flowers in his hand and asked in a brusque, unfriendly voice, '*Ew ki ye?* Who is he?'

'Ömer Eren, our famous writer. He's helping us,' said Mahmut.

'*Çima?*' asked the girl. Then she repeated it in Turkish so that the man standing at the door with flowers in his hand would understand. 'Why?'

Mahmut and Zelal looked at Ömer, and Ömer looked into his heart. Why?

'Can't a man help those who are in trouble?'

There was silence. The air in the hot hospital room, where the synthetic, light-coloured curtains could not keep out the sun, became even more oppressive.

'He can,' said Mahmut.

The girl turned her head the other way again and said nothing.

Ömer did not give up. He tried to pierce the girl's shell, her armour impervious to emotion.

'I know suffering and desperation, too. People need each other. Evil can come from people, but so can kindness. I was there when you were shot; I was waiting for my coach. Should I have boarded the coach and left? Is that what you would have done? You were suffering. I wanted to share it, to ease it. That's all.'

Was that really all? I might not have followed these people and missed my coach if it hadn't been for the pain of my son and the terrible memory of Ulla who had come from the North Sea to be blown to pieces in the middle of Istanbul. I would have pressed a few lira into the boy's hand, boarded my coach and gone my own way. But if you have ever once felt another's grief in your own heart as though it were your own grief and if you have felt responsible for it, it is only then that you understand what grief is. And after that you can never pass it by. If it hadn't been for the grief of my son I wouldn't be standing at the bedside of this obstinate, angry, suspicious Kurdish girl.

'It happened to someone very close, someone like my son . . . A bomb exploded as they were passing by, and his young wife – a foreigner who had come from far away – was blown to pieces. They couldn't even find all the body parts. She left a very small child behind.'

'Which group was it, *abi*? Did they find out? Did anyone claim responsibility?' Mahmut's voice reveals more than concern; he is worried, anxious.

'What does it matter? It was just one of those armed organizations that claim to be left-wing. Anyway one of their militants also died in the explosion – a young woman.'

'For a moment I was afraid it was one of us.'

Taking advantage of the boy's unguarded remark Ömer tried to make a point. 'It could have been one of yours; it could even have been you. Once you are involved in this business, once you seek salvation in violence and weapons are regarded as a solution . . .'

'There comes a moment when there is no escape except through weapons and death. If others kill, there's nothing for it but to kill, too. If they come at you and get the better of you, then you defend yourself with weapons.' It was the first time the girl had said so much.

Ömer wasn't expecting such words or such a harsh voice emanating from that slender body, that pallid, soft, beautiful face. He was surprised and disappointed. 'Blood does not get washed away with blood,' he said weakly. He was aware that these weren't his own words, his usual mode of expression. He had made an attempt to talk in a way the girl would understand – to talk down to her. As soon as he realized this he felt uncomfortable. It was an ill-conceived attempt at empathy . . . The pretence of talking in the other person's idiom for the sake of political correctness . . . And without really knowing the other person or getting a response . . . The endless futile endeavours of the western intellectual . . .

'If we have to talk in proverbs, they also say, "Only the wearer knows where the shoe pinches" or "Fire burns the place where it falls." It wasn't that person close to you, your son, who died but the foreign girl. If they had killed your son you would have born a grudge. You would have gone after them. You would have wanted to kill them,' she replied.

'All the same, our writer *abi* wouldn't have wanted a feud,' said Mahmut trying to soften Zelal's words. 'Feuds aren't for intellectuals. All those killings, all that blood over all those years . . . What has changed? We are trapped in our fears, our enmities. We kill each other while listening to the same songs, some in Turkish, some in Kurdish.'

'If you really want to help, take us somewhere far away where nobody will find us. Where we won't be subject to a code of honour, organization or the state . . . Take us to the sea,' she said in an abrupt tone of voice that did not suggest a polite request.

'I will do what I can. Just get well and fit enough to leave the hospital.'

'The doctor said it would be about ten days, *abi*.'

'If they let me go in ten days, it will be seventeen days in total. What day is it today?'

'Wednesday.'

'So it was Thursday when I came here. That means I will be discharged next Sunday or Monday at the latest. That's still a long time.'

Ömer counted on his fingers and was amazed. Without any hesitation to work it out, the girl had told them the day she was admitted to the hospital and the day she would be leaving.

'She's a very fast calculator,' said Mahmut proudly, laughing at Ömer's puzzled face. 'Ask her to do some mental arithmetic if you like. She'll work it out straight away. It's a gift from God.'

'No, don't tire her needlessly. Once things improve, we could start a business for you; say, a small shop in a summer resort by the sea. Zelal could take care of the accounts there.'

'Why are you doing all this? You are not family. You're not a relative. You aren't even Kurdish. Why?' asked the girl once again in the same sceptical, suspicious tone.

He searched for something to say but he couldn't find anything. 'Because I'm a storyteller. I write stories. Perhaps I will write your story one day.'

'Even if you are a storyteller, you are a storyteller of another world. You can't write our story. You can understand it in your mind, but you can't feel it in your heart. Even children won't listen to a story that doesn't come from the heart.'

She's a strange girl. Mahmut is naïve, but she is clever, sharp and uncompromising. She won't meet anyone halfway. She looks like a beautiful cat. Ömer realized that he had gone beyond pitying the girl and had started to feel a curious interest in her, even respect for her. 'Perhaps you are right, Zelal. You ask me why I bother about you. I've been asking myself the same question ever since the night you were shot. To help those in difficulty and so on, that's all true; but I think my main purpose is to write my own story, to find my own word, as it were.'

'Then why don't you look for your tale in your own land among your own people?'

Good question, he thought. Perhaps the girl doesn't realize the significance of what she has asked, but this is the question I must answer. 'My own land has dried up. My own people have changed. Perhaps I have changed – not them. I have become a stranger to them, to myself. I have lost my tale. Every storyteller wants to tell his own tale. But when the source runs dry, you build your hopes on new springs to quench your thirst. It's complicated. What I'm trying to say is this: don't dismiss my help, and don't be suspicious either. I'm doing this more for myself than for you.'

'If you are a storyteller, a bearer of the word, then tell me a tale of escape. Let it be a good story. Let it end well. Let lovers be reunited, brothers be reconciled, travellers arrive safely, babies not be shot and killed. As it is only a story, let no one be unjust, no one oppress or kill anyone.' This was how Zelal spoke, as if she were telling a story, reciting a poem. Her voice had mellowed; it sounded sad and tired. It was the voice of a child asking her mother to sing a lullaby or tell a bedtime story.

Ömer turned the girl's words over and over in his mind. How strange, the girl had said, 'bearer of the word'. That was what they used to say to Ömer; that was how he was known in literary circles. What was the source of this intuition that came from beyond her alienation, her remoteness, her poverty and reached her heart and mind?

Only he and Elif knew that 'the bearer of the word' had not delivered a word for a long time now, that he had lost those words. Elif had told him cruelly, 'When you entered the world of bestsellers, you broke away from feelings, from the sources that nurtured you.' Whereas she had said, 'When your readers changed, your writing also changed. You are busy playing to your audience. That is why you can't write what you want,' he was filled with the hope that Zelal would say something something more tender, more beautiful, more encouraging.

'I will try to write the tale you want,' he said quietly. 'It will have a happy ending, if I can write it. You know, you keep asking "Why?" Why I'm interested in you, why I'm trying to help you? Precisely for this reason: to find the word.'

'There was an old woman in the village, a storyteller who delivered the word. She not only told tales herself, she also brought forth the words of children. She used to tell us stories so that we could pass them on to other children. I was good at telling stories. She liked me. She used to say, "You will replace me one day." Then when I went to school I was not allowed to tell stories in my mother tongue, our own language. The teacher told stories in Turkish. I learnt fast and grew to speak Turkish well. However, I lost the language of stories. I could no longer tell stories – not in Turkish nor Kurdish. I lost the word. That is why I became so interested in numbers. Numbers have no language.'

'I, too, lost my tongue – although not quite like you. Language is not just words. "The word" is more than words. Whether it's Turkish, Kurdish, English, French or Arabic, you may know all the words and yet sometimes you're stuck, you can't express yourself. The "word" has become empty. Well said, Zelal; you may not have grasped the importance of what you said, but it is true!'

His spirits rose; he relaxed, mellowed. Perhaps there was no need to panic. They say it happens to every writer. Suddenly one day, you realize that you get writer's block. Something similar to temporary impotence . . . What was it that nourished me when I was happy to be writing and happy with what I wrote? I was writing our story; the story of people who wanted the whole world, who didn't limit themselves only to their own lives, who believed they could overcome, change and create a better world but who were defeated. I was writing about the poor, the workers, the slums, little people who didn't have to be important, who didn't have to be heroes. I was writing about hope, hope of changing the world, hope of salvation. This was because we were a generation whose faith fed on hope, whose values were founded on hope. 'You write well about us,' an old friend had said. He had added, 'But we were defeated so badly and have become so few that there aren't many people left who want to read these stories.'

I really did write well about us, but, as my friend said, we were few. Even we had grown tired of our grand narrative that the new world didn't want to hear, our lofty ideals that were already obsolete, our overwhelming desire to save the world. No, I never rejected my past, never denied it, as some people seemed to think. Yet I didn't get stuck there. I searched for a fresh approach that would be marketable. I wrote my transition novel, *The Opposite Side*, which broke sales records, and my publisher, in a state of happy amazement, struggled to keep up with demand for a reprint. I hadn't thought of it when I named it, but with that novel I passed to the opposite side. An explosion in the number of readers, in three weeks a rapid climb to the top of the bestseller list, staying for months at number one . . . *The Opposite Side* was a book in which I used all the clichés in which I had become so adept; in which I launched into bold experiments in form and structure with the audacity of professionalism; that if I had been a critic I would have called 'insipid and shallow'. I had spilt and scattered all that I had in my repertoire, inadvertently exhausted it. I had learnt the rules of the market, the taste, the demands of readers. Then, without thinking or calculating, similar novels followed one after the other. I increased the love interest and added some suspense, mystery and mysticism. My books sold well. The more humdrum my work became, the better I got at embellishing empty ideas with showy sentences. The more I distanced myself from important subjects and human situations that people didn't want to read about, the more my books sold. I used up my reserves, I exhausted my inner world: love, faith, hope, man . . . the internal richness that carries one from words to the true word . . . When my inner world was exhausted, the word became exhausted, too. Yet the word was all that I had. Now I'm completely empty.

'If you want to find your word, and you are searching for it in our footprints,' said Mahmut, 'go and look for it on the spot, *hocam*. You can't reach the right word from a distance. You have to hear the voice. You have to listen so that you can turn it into the word.'

When they left the room and were alone in the corridor Ömer gave Mahmut several phone numbers to call in case of emergency and other things to make their lives secure, including the address of a place they could stay while Zelal recovered – a villa on the outskirts of Seyran Vineyards, the bachelor pad of a friend who didn't use it much because he was now living abroad – and an ATM card for an account he had opened for them in his own name, just to be on the safe side. In return, he made one request: 'Wait for me. Don't make any major decisions before I get back. First let Zelal recover and get yourselves sorted out. Then you can think – we can think – with a clear head. Whatever I tell you or you tell me now is pointless. Wait. All right? I'll return before long.' He said this in the imploring tone of voice he used when he spoke to his son Deniz. He added to himself: I shall return when I find the word.

Mahmut nodded faintly as though in agreement and was silent. He didn't make any promises, but he didn't say no.

Thus Ömer started on his journey. The road had only been a vague intention, a longing when a few days ago he had told Elif, 'I'm going east.' With Mahmut's words, 'You must hear the voice to turn it into the word,' it became fate, inevitable, a fantastic adventure as he set out to find the word he had lost.

FOUR

Leaving Us With Our Snow, Our Poplars and Our Crows...

Now, as he walks along the streets of the substantial village that Mahmut, with his strong Kurdish accent, had called a town, he tries to put into words the ideas taxing his mind and his heart. He is searching for that 'everything' he called 'the word', which he had wasted and lost in another world in this small town surrounded by bare hills. The walls of the poor decrepit houses are still scarred with bullet-holes, flying poplar pollen attaches itself to one's hair and ears, and large crows perch in the poplar trees and dive down on the heads of passers-by, cawing loudly.

He senses that he has come here not to share the fate of those two young-sters tossed in a storm, certainly not for adventure, humanism, intellectual responsibility and all that stuff but for another purpose that he can't quite express. Is he here to run away from his arid earth, to journey towards a new life on soil where rivers and springs turn rebellious pastures green? Or is he here because he sees the reflection of his own fugitive son mirrored in the two fugitive youngsters? Is he here to look for the word? Or is he here to search for Deniz, the son he lost?

Zelal had said, 'If you don't hear the voice in your heart, you won't have any words left to say.' As your heart becomes calloused, and an arrogant, indifferent, selfish, heartless choir deafens your ears, you stop hearing the voice of the people. If the word does not reflect the voice of the people, their scream, it is doomed to remain empty and hollow, like the last things you wrote. Or you become silent and lose the ability to write at all. As is the case at this moment.

He asks himself why he is looking for the word here. How will the voice that rises from this ruined, destitute world be transformed into the word? He doesn't know. He must try to find it if he doesn't want to be condemned to silence. He will risk it. He will try.

There is only the name of the neighbourhood – Republic District, Number 17 – on the address that Mahmut has written on a piece of paper, not the name of the street. Perhaps he forgot to write it; perhaps there is no need for street names around here. The broad street, Flag Avenue, that cuts through the town, leads to a small square, Republic Square, in the centre of which there is a lead-coloured bust of Atatürk on a concrete plinth; barbed wire drawn taut around the statue and surrounding it limp, faded daisies, dead in patches . . . On a hot, dry midday in late June the square is quiet, almost deserted. The shops around the square are shut. The door and windows of the ramshackle single-storeyed building with the sign 'Internet Café' are wide open.

He walks in. Several young teenagers are seated in front of computers, playing games, cursing and quarrelling.

'Hi, guys!' he says. 'Is there a Republic District round these parts?'

'Yeah, this is it. It's the area around Obligation Square. Where are you looking for?'

'Number 17, but I don't know the street.'

He reads out Mahmut's father's name from the piece of paper in his hand.

'My elder brother would know him. He'll be here in a minute. Are you from the state? Who sent you?'

'I'm not from the state or anything like that. I'm a relative. I happened to be in the area, so I thought I would drop by.'

The boy looks at him suspiciously, mistrustfully. 'You are not one of us. What are you looking for? Why would you come here?'

'Why not? Isn't this our country – yours and mine?'

'It is my land and your colony.'

A bigger boy sitting at the computer says to his friend, 'Cut it out! Let's see what the gentleman wants. Let's wait for your brother. He'll be here soon.'

'The shops are closed, and the streets are deserted. Is it a holiday or something?'

'The shutters are down in protest. And it's Friday. Some have gone to the mosque for prayers, while others have made that an excuse so that it can't be said they closed their shutters in protest.'

'So why are the shutters down?'

'It's because there's so much persecution. There are so many deaths, bombs going off. They sent word from the mountain that the shutters must come down.'

'Then why didn't this place close?'

'This isn't a shop. This place is always open. This is where everyone learns what they should do.'

'Shut up, damn it!' the older boy intervenes. 'You'd better talk to our big brother, *abi*.' A young man walks in. 'Why, here he is. Now you can ask him what you want to know.'

The young man looks at the stranger mistrustfully, suspiciously, from under his brow.

'*Selam!*' says Ömer in greeting.

'*Aleykümselâm!*' says the young man. His voice is unfriendly, questioning.

'I was looking for someone.' Suddenly Ömer decides to tell the truth. 'I'm looking for someone to bring them greetings and good news from a relative. Republic District, Number 17. Hüseyin Bozlak.'

The youth peers at the stranger. He doesn't wear spectacles but stares at Ömer as if he were looking over a pair. 'What relative? Where did you see him? Where did you meet this relative?'

It's best to stick to the truth, just as it happened. 'I met his son in hospital.' It's true up to this point; but now a few lies become necessary, a rather different story. 'He was wounded. They brought him to hospital. That's where we met. He asked me to go to his parents and tell them he was all right.'

'Are you a doctor?'

'No, I'm a writer. I had gone to visit a doctor friend of mine.'

The young man continues to look at him suspiciously, distrustfully, strangely. He says, 'As far as we know his son is in the mountains.'

'I don't know where he is. But a young man I met at the hospital gave me this address. You seem suspicious of me, but you may have heard of me. My name appears in newspapers and on television from time to time. I mean, I'm telling you this not because it's significant, but perhaps you've heard of me.'

'What's your name?'

'Ömer Eren.'

The boy puts his thumb and forefinger to his temple as though wanting to draw strength from his fingers and is lost in thought. 'Yes, you were the one who spoke on our television. You said that Kurdish shouldn't be banned, the mother tongue must be taught, and things like that.'

Did I really say that? We say such things for the sake of political correctness and to make ourselves feel good. And then we forget. He cannot remember appearing on the broadcast that the boy calls 'our television'. However, they might have taken the interview from another channel and rebroadcast it. It is best not to spoil things, not to elaborate. The important thing is to win the young man's confidence.

'I don't know. I can't remember where I said that, but I have said it. That's because it's true.'

The young man's look of apprehension and mistrust disappears and his brow lifts. His face lights up. Now he resembles Mahmut, a laughing Mahmut, a happy Mahmut. 'You're telling me, *abi*! Why, of course! Ömer Eren. I should have recognized you!' It is clear that the youth does not know Ömer Eren. However, he remembers someone friendly defending his rights, his language on what he calls 'our television'. He wants to believe that the person facing him is that man.

'I'll take you to Hüseyin *Dayı*. One of his sons died on the mountains, and they didn't even give him the body. He constantly worries about his other son. What a good thing you came, that you've brought good news and that he's in good health.'

Ömer's heart feels like lead. What good news have I brought?

They go out on to the street. This time he looks more carefully around him. The shutters of the shops are closed. There is not a sign of life in the ones that have no shutters. Pieces of paper, plastic bags flying around Atatürk's bust on the plinth in the middle of the square, crows landing and taking off, the sense of abandonment, melancholy...

'Why do the boys call this Obligation Square?'

'There's nowhere else to go. That's why. Not another street, no cinema, no fairground... In the past tightrope walkers used to come, men on stilts, magicians and conjurors used to turn up. Once, even a mermaid came, my father told me. Since the war no one's been. Children, young people, the unemployed gather around this square. That's why it's Obligation Square. They spend time at the internet café when they have a few *kuruş*, or they hang around the statue.'

'How old are you?'

'I must be twenty-two. I did my military service in Uşak. I didn't take to the mountains. I enlisted. Everyone condemned us. They condemned my father and me. However, they didn't say anything out of fear. I enlisted, but if I had known then what I know now... I was beaten a lot. We people are good shots. Did you know that, *abi*? Look at my fingers.'

Three fingers on the boy's right hand are bent inwards, rigid.

'Was that from using arms?'

'No, it happened because I didn't want to use a weapon. There was this sergeant of ours; he saw that during target practice I hit the target spot on, not missing a shot and he got it into his head that I had learnt to shoot in the mountains, that a separatist bandit had taught me how to use a gun. I kept telling him that I had never been up the mountains, but he didn't believe me. One day he got really angry and kept going on at me saying, "Why don't you say it? Why don't you admit it?" I almost said that I'd been up the mountains and admitted to something that hadn't happened. However, I was frightened that they would throw me in prison, take me to court for belonging to the rebel organization. I stood my ground saying, "I've never been on the mountains. I've had nothing to do with the guerrillas." Then he thrust metal rods between my fingers and kept on hitting them. I fainted from the pain. My fingers have never been right since.'

'So you can't you use a gun any more.'

The boy gives an innocent, roguish laugh. 'I'm good with my left hand, *abi*. If you've a good eye and the will, you can hit a target with your left hand just as well. In the barracks at the shooting range they had a sign up saying, "Shoot, hit the target and be proud." By God, we can be proud of our shooting skills!'

Passing along the dusty streets in front of single-storeyed mudbrick houses, ugly, depressing apartment blocks of two to three storeys that have not been plastered and empty shops with broken windows, they arrive at a sizeable square of beaten earth with rubbish piled up in a corner.

'Look. Here it is,' he says, pointing to the house that has been painted with blue limewash in a corner of the square. He leads the way and taps on the half-open wooden door. 'Hüseyin *Dayı*, you've got a visitor!'

The swarthy, hairy man who comes to the door in a white vest and blue tracksuit bottoms is astonishingly like Mahmut. For some reason Ömer had imagined that he was going to meet someone old, decrepit and slightly bent and had prepared himself accordingly, yet the man looks about fifty, well built and robust.

'This man has brought news from your son. He's one of our writers – one of us.'

The boy's rash ingenuous trust unsettles Ömer. Only ten or so minutes earlier the boy had been mistrustful, suspicious and distant. To have half-heartedly defended the boy's right to learn his mother tongue was enough to win his friendship, his trust. Innocence still maintained amid so much blood . . .

'I hope there's nothing wrong. Come and sit down,' says the man somewhat anxiously. From inside he brings out two plastic chairs and places them on either side of the table covered with a floral plastic tablecloth. The lad who has shown the way sits on the door-sill. A little girl with black curly hair wearing a long printed cotton dress is running around.

'Our grandchild,' explains the man, 'a reminder of my eldest son. Mahmut is the youngest.'

His speech and voice remind him of Mahmut. What am I going to tell him? How am I going to tell him why I came? 'My name is Ömer. Ömer Eren. I met Mahmut by accident in Ankara. He's in good health. I was coming this way on business, and he said that if I happened to pass by I should call in on his parents – tell them not to worry about him. He told me a little about you leaving your village and your efforts to encourage him to study and get a good career.' He is aware that his words sound artificial and insincere. These words would not open any doors, reach people, reveal any truths or pull the word out of the depths in which it was lost.

The man, to buy time or to save himself time, calls to the little girl in Kurdish. As far as Ömer can make out, he asks for tea. She runs inside. A few minutes later she returns with a the bottom half of a plastic bottle with yellow, red and green artificial flowers in it. She places the vase, the sight of which pulls at Ömer's heartstrings, in the middle of the table covered with the plastic cloth. She says something in Kurdish. Her eyes are sparkling with joy, crystal clear, wide open and gleeful.

'She has brought you flowers,' says the man. 'She says she likes you very much. Ever since her father left she always does this when a strange man comes to the house. She gets really excited.'

They cease talking. The lad who showed the way breaks the silence. 'She doesn't know Turkish. None of us do until we start school when it gets beaten into us. Then we are angry with our mothers because they don't know Turkish. We are angry because they are not Turks. The teacher bans Kurdish, and we remain mute until we have learnt Turkish.'

A tall, very slim young woman brings tea on a copper tray. She has a band of gold coins on her forehead, and her black hair escaping from her white headscarf has fallen on her shoulders. She says something to the little girl who has knelt down at Ömer's knee. Perhaps she doesn't want her to annoy the guest. She leaves the tray on the table and goes inside trailing her long colourful, flowery skirt. It is hot. The breeze that blows intermittently causes the fresh leaves of the poplar trees to tremble and pollen to scatter in the air. Crows fly about in the sky, emitting a continual hideous cawing.

'Our tree is the poplar,' says the man. 'No other tree grows, and if it does we don't know how to cultivate it successfully. Our tree is the poplar. Our bird is the crow. No other bird comes to these parts. And we have snow in winter. It stays on the ground for seven or eight months. Then the roads are completely closed. We can't get out of the town even if someone is desperately ill.'

From where they are sitting Ömer looks at the bare grey hills visible on the horizon. Soft hills that are unlike the formidable majestic, rugged mountains that he saw on the road, that have a mysterious attraction and stretch in waves as far as the eye can see. 'How beautiful the hills are over there – but quite barren.'

'Those are our burnt mountains,' says the man in a voice resigned to fate and sadness which no longer harbours anger.

Damn it! Why didn't I think of it? How could I forget? Is this the fire that burns the place it falls on? We spoke a lot, and we wrote a great deal about the burning and destruction. But then we forgot. I forgot. That means that the fires that scorch the villages, forests and mountains could not get past our tongues and reach the depths of our hearts. What we said and wrote remained merely an idea, a political stand, and could not be transformed into conscience, emotion, pain and rebellion. Ömer Eren feels a strange uneasiness. He could feel his scalp prickling with sweat. Now the little girl returns with some sickly-looking daisies with crushed petals and puny stems. Holding out the drooping flowers to her beloved stranger, where words are insufficient, the child tries to speak with the language of her eyes in which all the hopes and longings of her childhood are concentrated.

Opposite burnt mountains; the artificial flowers on the table covered with a plastic cloth, the drooping daisies in the child's hand, the longing in her heart for the father she doesn't know, the square of beaten earth stretching away in front of the house – it's obviously the place where the youths play football – poplar trees here and there and cawing crows . . . Within him sadness that grows more oppressive the longer it stays and is internalized and which sits on his chest like a cannonball, and shame that brings tears to his eyes – why am I ashamed? – desperation and rebellion. He sits the little girl on his lap. 'What a pretty little girl you are! How do you say thank you in Kurdish?'

'*Spas dikim*,' answers Mahmut's father.

'*Spas dikim*,' repeats Ömer. He strokes the child's hair. She laughs. Murmuring a song she climbs off his lap and runs into the house.

The lad who showed the way seizes the opportunity and begins a repetitive passionless tirade. 'If only our intellectuals came here and saw for themselves, if the press came, if they got to know us and reported that we are not dishonourable terrorists and separatists. We are Kurds, human beings. We just want our language and our identity. We want to live like people in the west.'

He pauses for a moment, not sure of the effect of his words. He wants to say something more persuasive. 'This land, this country of ours, is not just death, mines and fighting. There are caves for tourists in these parts. There are ancient ruins ten thousand years old. How great it would be if people came – if tourists came to visit them.'

Mahmut's father is silent. Ömer is silent, too, and his eyes rest on the youth's broken fingers. The desperation for ten-thousand-year-old ruins and tourist attractions and the longing for so many things that don't exist, the boy's resignation and the pitifulness of his dreams upset him. The two men remain silent. The tea becomes an excuse for silence, a refuge.

After a while in a voice that has become heavy with the burden of these words, Hüseyin Bozlak says, 'I lost one son on the mountain, the father of that poor boy over there. And now you've brought news of the youngest one. You said that he's well. I trust he is. Do you know what it's like to lose a son, *beg*?' The strong eastern dialect and accent so perceptible at times when Mahmut was overcome by a wave of emotion and anger are echoed in the father's voice. 'God knows, I didn't want any of them to take to the mountains. I always wanted them to study. In our parts some people see the state as the enemy and send their children off to the mountains. I didn't want them to consider anyone, either Turks or Armenians or Arabs, as a foe. If you think of people as the enemy they will think of you as the enemy, too. I have always wanted my children to live decently with their families, to earn their living somewhere and be happy. Do you know what it means to lose a son? What cause is more sacred than life? Which war is more important than the well-being of one's children? I've lost one son. Should I lose a second now? Do you know what it means to lose a son?

'I know,' says Ömer. The words 'I know' are uttered involuntarily and without thinking. Perhaps it was just for this that he came here: to say, 'I know', to be able to share the pain with someone who feels it in his heart, to be free.

'I know. I had a son. He didn't die, but I lost him all the same. Children don't just go and get lost on mountains or in wars. Mine was overcome by the state of the world. He destroyed himself. Whereas I wanted him to fight, to conquer his own mountains. I wanted him to be better than me. I wanted him to champion my causes, to support my values. Rather than vegetating, I wanted him to fight for what he believed in, to have the courage to die if necessary.' He is aware of the callousness and lack of love in his words and falls silent. Once put into words and uttered, harmless, innocent thoughts clothe themselves in flesh and blood and become guilt. He panics. What have I said? Did I say I would prefer Deniz's dying? Like grief-stricken fathers at martyrs' funerals saying, 'I have another son, I will willingly sacrifice him for my country.' What is the difference between my words and that mental attitude, those statements that freeze people's blood?

'Our children are not our mirrors that they should reflect our values, Ömer *Begim*. No value, no victory can be measured with a child or substitute for the life of a son.

To Ömer there seems to be reproach, disdain and pity in the other's voice. He is ashamed of what he has said. He is astonished, too. Is this man really an ignorant and poor Kurdish villager? That is how we see him and how we think of him. We can't ascribe what he has said to him. This is because we think we have the monopoly on eloquent and profound remarks. Only I can say such words or write the phrase, 'Our children are not our mirrors that they should reflect our values.' Mahmut's father does not have the skill to use those sort of words, does he? Surely it should be me who asks 'Which cause is more sacred than life?' This is because we writers and intellectuals have been gifted with the word, so we assume we have the monopoly of profound thought.

'We cannot know which life is more precious, which life is more superior, who is more heroic. You haven't lost your son unless he is actually dead, Ömer *Begim*,' says Mahmut's father, as though reading Ömer's mind.

What did they talk about for hours, there in front of the door of the wretched single-storeyed, blue-washed house, under the sun that the shade of the poplars couldn't hide? Now, when he thinks about it, he is amazed that he was able to talk so openly and honestly about all those private and almost intimate subjects with this man that he had only just met. I hadn't talked about Deniz with anyone; not even with my wife had I been able to share the sorrow that dwelt in both our hearts. To those who asked, I said, 'He's well. He's chosen to live abroad, the rascal', and changed the subject. I had declared my son missing long ago, and I was afraid of sharing the pain. Elif used to say, 'Men don't share their suffering even with their closest friends, because suffering seems to them like defeat. They are reluctant to show their weaknesses even to those closest to them. Men have no confidants, because to suffer is to them a disability.' And now I'm sitting here and saying things to this man that I haven't been able to say even to my wife. This is because, like a mute, he will keep whatever is said to himself, because I am not afraid of being scorned by him, because I'm the master. I can't share my defeats with my equals, but I can share them with him without feeling wounded. Damn it! Am I such a scoundrel!

As the man speaks Ömer is amazed at how clearly, how well he expresses himself. His figures of speech are simple but apt. The metaphors he uses are striking, his sentences short and unequivocal. He remembers the father's eyes filling with tears as he talks about his sons; as he asks repeatedly about Mahmut his anxiety about the answer he will receive, the fearful look; the tremor in his voice as he says, 'When we stop saying "Every Turk is born a soldier and every Kurd a guerrilla" then there will be peace'; and the beseeching tone in his voice when he says, 'If you see Mahmut again, tell him, *begim*, that if he can he should go to a big city. Please help him if you can. He should find work and lead a decent life. Tell him it's his father's wish, his last request. No offence, Ömer *Begim*, don't take it to heart, don't think I'm giving advice but don't sacrifice your son. Don't abandon him because he chose life. Look how the world is going to pot, drenched in blood. We are not Abraham that we should sacrifice our children . . .' And then, when the time came for them to part, his holding Ömer's hand between his own and looking long into his face as Ömer boarded the minibus that started off from the corner of Republic Square. And the reproachful parting words that he would never be able to forget for the rest of his life. 'You just go off like this and leave us with our poplars, our crows and our snow.'

The loneliness left by the departure of the friendly stranger who had brought news of his son slips through the man's words and settles like a mist over the small town. There is still time before the snow, but the poplars and crows stay behind like a symbol of the distance, the loneliness and the alienation. Looking out of the minibus window at Hüseyin Bozlak, his right arm crossed over his chest in a last show of respect for his visitor, he seems to perceive why he has come there, what he is seeking and where his path is leading. He suddenly understands that his road will not end here. The voice that will revive the word is here – albeit just a whisper. I haven't yet heard the rousing choir. He has to go to the east of the east, towards the place where the voice is a scream that calls him with an irresistible power, like the voice of the sirens who seduced the sailors.

Ömer left behind him Mahmut's father, the little girl who embraced every man who came to the house in her hope for a father, the small town that manifested its sadness and hid its anger, and the crows, the poplars and the snow that disappeared from the ground with the spring, and continued his journey. This was an exciting journey to the east of the east, to the limits of his own feelings, to their hidden depths, towards the beginning and the future. He did not know where the journey would take him or where it would end, but he sensed deep inside him that when he had run the distance – that is, if he were able to – he would never be the same again.

A banner with the words 'One country, one flag, one language' flies over the sole entrance to the town surrounded by an invincible fortress built with fear and revolt, mountains, rocks and outposts, provocative fire and commandoes, and as they pass through it Mahmut's words come to his mind.

'I don't know whether I'm in a nightmare or a dream. In a fight a person's feet are on the ground. You shoot. You are shot. Yet there is nothing real about what I've been experiencing recently. Ever since I rolled down the slope, since I met Zelal, since Zelal was shot by that stray bullet, ever since we lost Hevi before he was born, since you came along to the rescue, nothing has had any reality. You know, *abi*, you said, "I'm a storyteller." Well, for days I've been asking myself: Is all of this a tale, a dream, a figment of the imagination? How will this story end? I'm frightened.'

As Ömer enters the town in the battered coach, weary from constantly being stopped and searched all along the road, he realizes that he, too, does not know how the tale will end. He has come to this town to find the chemist to whom Mahmut has entrusted Zelal and whom he was told to see. Instead of unsettling him, this thought gives him pleasure; his heart lifts. Where he is going is not even important. He is looking for someone in an unknown unfamiliar town, and even to remember her name he has to look at his notes. To entrust to her if necessary – which clearly it is – Zelal whom he does not know, under the directions of Mahmut whom he does not know, and perhaps unwittingly be a messenger for fate.

This is a town between valley and mountain where during even the longest days of the year the sun quickly surrenders to the peaks and disappears behind the steep mountains and where the coolness of dusk swiftly descends. He remembers a similar place between the rocky mountains in Macedonia, and another – was it in Tibet? The same early chill that suddenly comes down cleaving the suffocating heat; the same purplish light, the same flickering of colour and shadow. As he gets off the bus with his case in his hand he asks the driver for a hotel in which he might stay.

'There's not just one. There are several,' says the driver with pride. 'They are next to each other. We have places to stay because it's close to the border, on the way to the crossing. Go from here to the main road and keep walking straight. There is only one street anyway. You can't go wrong. You'll see the hotels just ahead. They say that Yıldız Hotel is good. Foreigners always stay there.'

Ömer feels the suspicious, thoughtful stare of the man on the back of his neck – or he thinks he does. Should he first look for the Hayat Chemist or should he check into the hotel? He walks with an undecided step along the road lined with poplar trees, amid the rustle of leaves and the cawing of crows.

There is the Yıldız Hotel in front of him, right at the entrance to the market, the kind of small-town hotel that one encounters everywhere. He goes in through the main door with its gilded metal bars. There are old armchairs covered with maroon leather, maroon curtains down to the floor and a strange smell, a mixture of kebabs, mildew and soot. At the entrance, on the left, is a wooden panelled corner with the sign 'Reception' written over it. On top of the counter are yellow and red artificial roses in a vulgar plastic vase . . . He leans his arm on the counter and waits for someone to turn up. After a while he presses the bell.

An elderly man comes out of a door at the back. 'May I help you?'

'Do you have a single room?'

'Yes, we do. How many nights will you be staying?'

That's a thought! How long will I be staying? 'It depends on my work. I shall probably be here a few nights.'

The man holds out a long registration form. 'You have to fill this in. They ask interminable questions. You have to answer them all. Your Turkish identity number is required, too. And you must leave your identity card. We'll send the information to command headquarters.'

'What has it got to do with command headquarters?'

'That's what they require for foreigners.'

'But I'm not a foreigner. I'm a Turkish national.'

'I didn't mean it like that. I meant to say, people from outside; anyone who isn't local. Here everyone is a foreigner.'

If only I had gone first to command headquarters, to the district governorship or whatever and introduced myself. I would have said I was working on a new book. They would have made things easy for me.

Just to be awkward he hands the man his driving licence instead of his identity card.

The man wearily gives the driving licence back. 'It's all the same to me, but command headquarters wants your identity card.'

He is angry with himself. What's the point of causing the man trouble? Beating the saddle instead of the donkey. He produces his identity card. As he fills in the registration form he asks, 'Is the Hayat Chemist near here?'

'Yes it is. Cross the road, and it's immediately on the left. If you look out of the door you'll see it, just at the start of the market. All foreigners ask for the Hayat Chemist when they come here.'

He senses relief, a friendly tone in the man's voice. 'Why is that?'

'Our Jiyan *Abla* knows how to speak to strangers, and she knows these parts well, too. She also speaks English if required. She is our only lady chemist. Everyone loves and respects her.'

He thinks that she must be one of those small-town interfering women who are too clever by half, who have studied a little and moved up the social ladder by opening a chemist's shop; and, to top it all, the daughter of a clan leader – whatever that means – and a Kurd to boot. All the Europeans trying to keep in with the Kurds, this mission or that commission, look her up first.

For a moment he thinks about exploring the town or going to the military garrison, the Governor's residence or anywhere instead of the chemist's shop. After all, he always finds someone who has heard of Ömer Eren. I'll tell them that I'm working on a new book and I've come to absorb the atmosphere in these parts. Nobody will be suspicious. What is more, it's true. I can't be considered an undesirable person. That was in the old days, twenty-five to thirty years ago. After all, we were revolutionaries then; communists. Now I'm the famous author Ömer Eren. 'The darling of the system and bestselling author, a writer who gives the correct dose of opposition, the correct dose of apostasy, the regime's fig leaf . . .' Who wrote this about me? Which son of a bitch? Damn it! Elif mustn't hear me swear. She used to say, 'You profess to defend women's rights and feminism, but your swear words degrade women.' Is she wrong? And when that bastard said 'the correct dose of opposition, the correct dose of apostasy', was he altogether wrong?

'Let's go, sir. I'll show you your room,' says the man. He picks up his case and leads the way. They go up stairs covered with a dirty and stained maroon carpet to the second floor. Room number 204. There are not 200 rooms in his hotel, he thinks. They always do this as though prestige increases with numbers.

The room is hot, suffocating even.

'There's air conditioning,' says the man.

There is air conditioning, but despite the man's heroic – and hopeless – efforts it does not work. He pulls back the net curtain and opens the window. It looks over a wood yard at the back. Flat-topped brick houses without roofs and plaster and with metal rods sticking out of the top are visible, buildings set next to each other like skulls; poplars here and there on which silent night birds perch, and behind, so near that if you stretched out your hand you think you could touch them, the mountains whose peaks are snowy even in June. Mahmut's father had said, 'You just go off and leave us with our poplars, our crows and our snow.' He remembers the acute sadness in the man's voice.

'Is it all right, sir?' asks the man from reception.

'Fine. As long as the sheets are clean, that is.'

'They are clean. You are only our fifth customer. They'll do for another five people!' He laughs mischievously, in a friendly manner, pleased with his joke. 'The sheets are changed regularly if not every day, sir. The cleaning ladies have to earn their keep. Don't worry.'

He turns down the covers and examines the sheet and the pillowcase as though wanting to confirm what he has said. The sheet is worn and there is a hole in the middle. 'Look – as white as snow. It's been worn with washing. Well, this isn't the Presidential Palace, is it?'

After the man has left leaving the key, Ömer opens his case and takes out his shaving things and his toothbrush. He hangs a few shirts and a spare pair of trousers in the cupboard in the corner. He goes to the bathroom and washes his hands and face and looks at his face in the mirror above the basin. He has some stubble. Never mind. Here there is no need to shave every day. His face looks a little tired. That is to be expected. How many hours has he been on the road? And with all the tension as well. He locks the door and goes downstairs. He is still undecided about whether to visit the chemist straight away. Instead of sitting in the hotel's stuffy lobby, to go out towards the market, to go into a restaurant for some local food and, if available, a small drink such as *rakı*, would do him good. He goes out on to the street. Young teenagers are sitting on the steps in front of the hotel and at the roadside, passing the time fooling around. There are also young children selling tissues, trinkets, eucalyptus sweets, toffees with rhymes on the papers and other knick-knacks from cardboard boxes hung around their necks with string. In a shop next to the hotel all kinds of souvenirs are sold, from local kilims to honey, from silverwork to regional dress. I must take a look later. Elif likes that sort of thing.

The road that leads to the market is livelier, more crowded than he had expected. He walks towards the Hayat Chemist thinking that it will already be shut.

The streetlights have not yet been lit, but the lights of the coffee houses and one or two shops have just come on. There is a red fluorescent light over the chemist's sign. It is illuminated inside. The metal shutters that evidently come down to the ground when the shop is shut are half open. On a sign stuck on the window it says, 'Tonight our chemist is on duty.' He gently pushes the glass door protected by metal bars. A long tinkling of a bell is heard announcing that the door has been opened.

The woman arranging some products on the shelves with her back to the entrance turns and looks at the door. 'Yes? What can I do for you?'

Ömer's first thought is how the voice and the face could be in such harmony and his second whether the woman's raven-black hair is dyed or natural. No, it can't be tinted. Under the yellowish light one or two silvery white hairs are visible at her temples.

In the following days he would relate to Jiyan the moment of that first meeting. 'I first saw your hair, only your hair. It was as though it had got entangled with your voice. I noticed your face much later.'

'Please give me something for a headache – something more effective than aspirin. And . . . I've had a long journey, so something relaxing as well, something to make me go to sleep for the night. Herbal if possible.'

While checking the shelves for suitable products the chemist asks, 'Is this your first time here?'

A few long curls escaping from her thick hair loosely gathered at the back of her head and held by a sizeable ivory-coloured slide fall on her shoulders. Ömer is surprised that the woman is so tall and so slim. As she reaches up to the medicine cupboards, he immediately sees silver bracelets with a black inlay that she wears on her graceful wrists and slim arms and also the huge, striking, strange rings on three fingers of her right hand. All these contrast with the simplicity of her clothes which consist of black trousers and a tight black combed-cotton blouse. They are like a natural extension of the woman's body, a part she cannot conceal.

He has not yet seen her eyes. He will see them when she brings the medicines down from the shelves and places them on the counter and when she looks and smiles at the weary stranger who really doesn't know what led him to these parts.

'I think these should help you. Our roads are indeed long and gruelling. Here the medicines I sell most to foreigners are mild tranquillizers and antidepressants. It is difficult to survive otherwise.'

Her eyes are a deep black, surrounded by long black lashes; huge in relation to her face. 'Her eyes are not just eyes, they are the land of eyes' . . . Which poet wrote those lines?

'Your eyes are a distant country. Your eyes are the mirror of your town, your country; so sad, so fearful, so mysterious, rebellious,' he was to say later, referring to the lines of the poet.

Now, as he prepares to take money from his wallet to pay for the pills, he asks himself whether or not the woman is beautiful. At the same time he attempts to gain time in order to say something else to her. No, she is not beautiful. One could not call the chemist beautiful. It's not exactly beauty. She leaves one with a different feeling; the feeling that the question is absurd – should not be asked. Different, unusual, striking . . . No, none of these adjectives describes her well. For someone who has seen her for the first time to ask these questions is a sign that she is unusual. Perhaps she is just a rather dark ordinary if presentable woman with jet-black hair, and my impression is merely the result of what I have been through the last few days; her extraordinariness just a delusion.

'I'm sorry, but are you Jiyan *Hanım*?'

'Yes, that's me. Why are you sorry? she says, smiling again.

He realizes that the woman is young, despite the small hollow under her left cheek at the corner of her mouth and the odd white hair. About thirty-five years old – perhaps not even that.

'I've come to visit this area and to see you.' He does not know why he has difficulty in saying this. Suddenly all that has happened since that frightful night at the coach station, and especially his being here now, seems strange and unreal. He falls silent, not knowing how to carry on the conversation, undecided whether to continue or not.

'If I could have your name,' says Jiyan. 'It's as though I know you from somewhere.'

'Ömer Eren. I'm a writer.'

Of course, of course, I know you. To tell the truth, I haven't read all your novels, but I did read your essays in which you discussed the east–west question. I thought it was about Turkey's east–west conflict when I bought the book. I was wrong, but, still, I found it informative. I've watched you on television a few times. Please forgive me. I should have recognized you at once. When you meet someone you don't expect to see you can't place them immediately.'

'To tell the truth, my being here amazes me just as much as it does you. It is a coincidence. Mahmut . . . He wanted me to see you. Does the name mean anything to you? Do you remember Mahmut?'

'I'm sorry I cannot recall him. In these parts there are many with the name Mahmut.'

'Mahmut is also from the east but not from here. Whether his real name is Mahmut I don't know either. That was what was written on his identity card, and he introduced himself as Mahmut. As far as I understand he was on the mountain for a time, at Kandil and perhaps in Bekaa and thereabouts. After that he came over to this side of the border. Then something happened. I believe he was wounded and left the mountain unit. I don't know exactly. I didn't ask for details.'

'When they talk about being on the mountain, you immediately think of Kandil, don't you? I don't think he was there. But anyway . . . It is not so easy to be parted from the mountains. If he surrendered and was recruited as an informer, that's different.'

'No, no, it's nothing like that. There was a very young woman with him. She was pregnant. They were running away together. The girl's brothers and family were after her. She had run away to escape the clan laws. They were together. Then the girl was hit by a stray bullet.' He realizes that he has been forming disjointed inarticulate sentences like an excited child's breathless narration of an incredible adventure, and he starts to laugh. 'Oh, forgive me. Trying to summarize things for you I've got everything mixed up. Basically, I met Mahmut and the girl by accident at the Ankara coach terminal. There was an incident, and the girl was hit by a stray bullet. In trying to assist them I found myself involved in their story. And now I'm here. Mahmut was looking for a safe place for Zelal. Zelal is the name of the girl. He said that you might be able to help and gave me directions to your pharmacy. Perhaps you do remember him. His father's name is Hüseyin Bozlak. I've been to see him, too, before I arrived here. He's a wise, dignified man, grieving . . .'

'I think I do remember Hüseyin Bozlak. We are distantly related through my husband's father. We once went to their village, which had been forcibly evacuated. The person you are talking about must be Hüseyin *Amca*'s youngest son Mahmut. I have never seen him. As I said, we are not very close, but I did know his elder brother who was killed. I had heard that Mahmut was studying at university. His father wanted his youngest son at least to study, to get a proper job and a career. What a pity!'

As he listens to the woman Ömer notices the strong emphasis on the syllables, the shortening of the vowels, the narrowing of the broad 'e's and the word 'husband' more than what she says about Mahmut. For some reason it had not occurred to him that the woman might be married.

'Tonight we are on duty. My assistant has taken a few days off. I have to stay here at least until around midnight. Please sit down. We can talk comfortably here,' says Jiyan indicating an old chair in the corner. 'Where are you staying?'

'At the Yıldız Hotel opposite.'

'It's safe and clean. Foreigners who come here mostly stay there. They're on good terms with the state and the garrison headquarters. They send the registrations of all the visiting foreigners directly to the centre, so there is no problem. I wouldn't be at all surprised if you don't get an invitation to drink *rakı* with the Commander before long. After all, someone as famous as you doesn't come to these parts very often.'

'I really don't think the Commander will know of me, but to tell the truth I'm not minded to refuse anyone's invitation to drink *rakı*. I'm tired, tense and in need of a drink!'

He feels he has behaved too familiarly, shockingly, and he is embarrassed. I have asked the woman to find me a drink. She's think I'm a typical author with alcohol problems whose hands begin to shake when deprived of his booze.

They hear snatches of conversation outside the door, strident voices, the clinking of metal . . . They fall quiet and look outside. The streets lamps have not yet come on, but the road outside is illuminated by the light from the chemist's shop. A few armed men with black snow masks and wearing camouflage stare into the shop, their hands and noses pressed against the window.

'It looks as though the invitation to drink *rakı* has arrived,' says Ömer, trying to contain his anxiety and excitement.

He recognizes them from newspaper photographs and the television screen. He remembers he wrote an article years ago on the subject when the Special Team was first formed as a part of emergency measures against terror. The editor-in-chief who, whenever Ömer sent an article, had always put it on the front page and sent an acknowledgement signed by the editor, had on this occasion requested that he tone down the article 'taking into account the delicacy of the situation and sensitivity of the relevant authorities'. Ömer had been enraged and had withdrawn his article saying, 'In that case, don't print it.'

The men are really intimidating in their masks. Ömer thinks that on a summer's day the function of them is most probably to terrorize. Perhaps they enjoy going around like that. They wear the masks not just to remain incognito but because the masks give them an air of menace; because they know that to wear them increases their power, their influence. After all, they are young men. That is how they add spice to their miserable lives in this intolerable place. They see themselves as the masters of terror and fear. They think that they can bring the whole town to its knees if they want to. They get a kick out of this.

Instead of turning his back and trying to hide his face, he looks straight at the window as though challenging his fear. A small part of this is his novelist's instinct to perceive the individuals behind the masks and their frightening weapons. These men in masks, armed from head to foot, appear more real, more frightening in the newspaper images and on the television screens than they do here. In the dark streets of this remote, dismal and strange town – where they should be at their most frightening, their most intimidating – to Ömer's eyes they lose power and substantiality. They remind him of extras trying to play their parts in a scene from a science-fiction film staged in a different galaxy in the distant future or else bad jesters, half-clothed in superman costumes and half in shrouds attempting to frighten children at a street carnival. In the photographs their faces seem more potent than in real life, because the originals are too scary to be real.

'Don't worry. This is the Special Team's welcoming posse for newcomers to the town. A routine visit. The message to say that nothing goes unnoticed.' Jiyan moves towards the door. The length of her neck and the slimness of her body are accentuated as she walks. She resembles a tense pedigree black cat – no, a black panther; it would be wrong to liken her to a domestic cat. She opens the door slowly. 'I'm on duty tonight. Did you need something?' There is not the slightest quaver in her voice, no trace of nervousness. 'I'm here until midnight, and after that if you need anything I shall be at home.' She closes the door slowly, without haste. The interior is filled with the cheerful tinkle of the bell entirely out of harmony with the atmosphere.

'They are frightened, too,' she says. 'Don't take any notice of their swagger. Here everyone is afraid. Tyranny makes people frightened, intimidates them, but fear also nurtures tyranny. The more we fear, the crueller we become, all of us. Until a few months ago we were more at ease; tension had lessened, a détente had begun, and we had started to hope. Imagine: even the streets lights were on at night. I realized how much I hate pitch-black streets and how much I miss wandering around lit streets once they started to turn on the lamps once more. Back then houses were not raided in the middle of the night as frequently as they used to be. The women were not prodded with bayonets and forced to lie on the floor with army boots on the nape of their necks, and their menfolk were not carted off to an unknown place. At least, this sort of thing didn't happen every day and every night. The number of unsolved murders decreased. How hopeful we were, how ready we were to forget everything . . .'

'Then?'

'I don't know whether you've noticed. It doesn't mean anything to you – you probably haven't even noticed – but, look, the streets are dark again. The street lights aren't being switched on. The snow-mask brigade has taken over once more. You probably cannot hear it, but our ears are very sensitive to certain sounds. We can hear the skirmishes, provocative fire, the mountain raids, the Cobras, the noise of the helicopters in the far distance. Mines explode, soldiers die, military operations are carried out, our children die. In other words, life has returned to the same damned rhythm. And, well, then there is this.'

They see that the men have silently moved off. The woman opens a corner cupboard with a wooden door. She takes out a bottle from a small fridge in which there are medicine bottles, boxes and equipment for dressing wounds.

'A drink will be much better for you than those tablets. There is only a little whisky. How would you like it?'

Released from the tension of a moment ago, Ömer puts his head in his hands and begins to laugh. 'It looks as though I won't have to accept the Commander's invitation after all!'

'Not this evening at least. I have faith in my whisky. It's the best con-traband. I suppose you realize that we are on one of the most important smuggling routes in the country.'

As he looks at Jiyan's face, he grasps what it is that spoils her unusual beauty, what hardens the expression on her face. It is the thickness and harsh curve of her eyebrows and their closeness to her eyes. It is a blemish that can easily be remedied.

'Perhaps you are hungry. I forgot to ask. Alcohol won't be good on an empty stomach. Let me order some kebabs from the shop across the road. I haven't had anything to eat since this morning. I would have invited you to eat trout at Soğukpınar, but we can no longer go there at night; it's forbid-den. It was, however, the only really pleasant secluded spot in the vicinity.

Is she constantly going to complain about local conditions? It does not matter whether these people are ignorant or educated, whether they come from villages or towns, they all talk of oppression, discrimination and privations. Not because they want you to pity them; it is because they expect something from you, to wear you down with their their victimization, to make you feel inadequate. Ömer simmers with rage. All that trouble he faced to protect their rights; being denounced as a traitor, tried under this or that article and other things beside, and none of it is appreciated. They neither trust nor thank you. In their eyes you remain a Turkish collabo-rator from the west. A good Turk or a bad Turk: at the end of the day you are a foreigner. This talk of victimization begins to destabilize one after a while; it alienates those who want to help . . .

'This is because such talk pricks people with a conscience who have not yet lost their sense of justice. You feel inadequate; you try to come to terms with yourself and you succumb to your conscience. And then, naturally, you get angry with us. You take refuge in your anger and find an excuse to cover up your lack of courage and your indifference,' Jiyan was to say later when he mentioned the issue to her.

As he sips the whisky that she has poured into dark cola glasses saying, 'Here you cannot openly drink alcohol,' he asks, 'Is your husband a chem-ist, too?' As soon as he has enquired he regrets it; he is embarrassed. You are appalling. You are wondering whether the woman is available, if she might be interested in you. You don't give a damn what her husband does for a living.

'My husband was a jurist. He was murdered five years ago.'

When she says 'my husband' he hears the passion in her voice, the pride as well as her firmness. He is shocked to hear the unspoken challenge: 'Stop right there. This is my private area. You don't have permission to enter.' The emphasis on the word 'husband' pre-empts 'he was murdered'.

'I didn't know,' he says in a low voice with genuine embarrassment. 'I'm sorry. I couldn't have known.'

'You couldn't have known. How could you! But now you do. Welcome to our town, Ömer *Bey*.'

To say cheers, Jiyan does not raise her glass that she has filled with water; instead she merely flicks it with her middle finger. This must be a part of the 'concealed drinking' ritual.

A strange woman, thinks Ömer; unlike anyone he knows. There is that phrase 'a very special woman'. This lady chemist is a very special woman – attractive but at the same time disturbing. Before taking a sip of whisky, he says 'Your health' without lifting his head and trying to avoid eye contact with her.

Towns have sounds. This has none. Especially at night this seems particularly quiet and characterless. During the day the market square is noisy and the area around the coach station is, too. Rows of shops line the market road, two arcades and a commercial building. The last, an office block housing lawyers' offices, a notary, a dentist and a doctor's surgery, is large and ugly. There are blocks of flats as well. Most of the upper floors are without plaster, unappealing, grey and grim-looking apartments. And between the many peeling, unsightly buildings a six-storey commercial building in glass with an internet café underneath rises from the ground as though it has fallen from outer space . . . It is a market similar to those in small Anatolian towns that no longer have any local colour or vibrancy – just a little more straggling, a little shabbier and poorer.

There is activity in the market: people going in and out of shops, people moving about in local dress with kaffiyehs and silk headscarves, idle men, women shopping and military vehicles rushing by. Ömer is amazed that people do not find armoured cars alien or take any notice of them or the new black jeeps that seem as out of place as the modern commercial building covered in coloured glass which stands in the middle of the market place, surrounded by horse-drawn carts and donkeys with panniers. Noise and humming; Kurdish, Arabic and a few Turkish songs, folk songs rising from the stalls of cassette-sellers, horns, children's screaming, swearing, doleful folk songs that emanate from building sites, the calls to prayer, the 'Tenth Year of the Republic March' echoing from the military garrison at the end of the market road, orations recorded on cassettes booming from loudspeakers, verses of the homeland–nation–flag theme and the 'One land, one language, one flag' slogan that rises from time to time, followed by 'I'll destroy the nest of the bird that ogles you . . .'

During the day the town is filled with a medley of sounds like every other town: however, it does not have its own distinctive sound. Its sound has been lost. It has been suppressed, drowned amid the noise and the hum. The sounds that can be heard belong to others. The town has withdrawn into itself and stifles its own sound. And especially when the light is trapped early by the mountains and night falls suddenly, one hears in the dark, hastily emptying streets only the barking of stray dogs, the footsteps of one or two people and from time to time the sound of guns and sirens that pierce not only the night or the town like a dagger but hearts, too. None of these are the town's own sound.

When he tried to explain this impression to Jiyan, she had said rebelliously, 'We have lost our voice. Our voices and words have been silenced. It was the thousand and one sounds of the mountain pastures, the plains, our weddings and the drums of our herdsmen, the laments of our women, the songs of our brides, the weapons of the hunters, the rebelliousness of our language, our joy, our sadness and, above all, our hope that lent colour to our voices. Our voices used to break loose from the plains, rise up to the mountain pastures and echo on the mountains. They used to mingle with the rivers, pass through the gorges, hit the rocky cliffs and return to the town – and become the sound of the town. Our voices are no longer heard. Our whispers do not break away from here and reach the mountains. They do not echo in the mountains and return to us more more powerfully. Now other sounds come from the mountains. One should say the sound of death, but death has no sound. It is for this reason that the town is silent – very noisy but silent.'

When he heard Jiyan express her feelings in these elaborate words that seemed to have been derived from an epic poem he had found it strange. He had found it unnatural. This woman speaks as though she is holding forth in Manukyan's theatre. In trying to impress she has the opposite effect. It seems to alienate. But then he got used to her mode of expression and became almost addicted.

When he told this to Jiyan and asked why she spoke in such pompous language she said, 'We either clam up or speak like this. perhaps it is the vestige of a tradition. Our mothers and grandmothers speak like this, too, as though they are reading an epic poem. But they speak in Kurdish. Then it sounds better, more natural. When I translate the thoughts that are in my head and my heart in Kurdish into Turkish, my ideas and my feelings become a little confused. This is why it seems odd, unnatural and pretentious to you. Do you know what *dengbejlik* is? Let us say it is our minstrel tradition, our oral literature. Perhaps I have been inspired by the *dengbej*. I don't do this intentionally or with premeditation. It comes out spontaneously. That's how it comes to my lips. In fact, the truth is as I tell it. I'm not embellishing it, believe me. I understand that it seems strange to you because you haven't learnt the language of our region with its emotional range. The style you use when writing I use when I'm speaking. In your last novel which you gave me you form the same sort of sentences as mine. The man says to the girl, 'Your eyes are not eyes. It's as though they are the whole world, a whole life.'

He had been embarrassed: because he could not produce a special word for Jiyan, because he had won the admiration of readers with trite phrases such as these; because he had become famous not for the enquiring, deep, challenging ideas of former days but for the novels he had written full of florid sentences and feelings lacking in originality – and most importantly because Jiyan had perceived the inadequacies he had tried to hide even from himself.

Ömer Eren is thinking about all this as he crosses the market and slowly ascends the slope that leads to the military garrison at the end of the road. He mulls it over, but his mind is confused, his thoughts disconnected. There is a fog in his head that he doesn't want to disperse, and he is in a state of drunkenness from which he is afraid of sobering up.

On his left lies a wide earthen area where in the past youths played football, funfairs were held at festival time and where, infrequently, third-rate folk singers gave concerts and where tent theatres and visiting acrobats performed. The place is now surrounded with barbed wire, and makeshift lookout posts have been erected on either side. He thinks that although the town has no sound it does have colour: yellow-grey, the colour of dust and smog; a colour, bereft of the joy, laughter and excitement of being completely open to the horizon, a mixture of grey earth, smoky-grey cliffs, milk-blue snow. Further along, on the right, are the grey concrete blocks that cover the town, the army quarters and garrison buildings that merge with the gloomy colour of the town. And at the end of the uphill road, steep rocky mountains suddenly rise up like an impenetrable fortress, a frontier without a crossing. Jiyan had said, 'This town is an open prison, but for women it is a closed prison.'

'Where are you in this prison, Jiyan?'

'I'm the officer on the gate. The collaborator, who, although sentenced for life, has been promoted to being a warden for good conduct. The officer with whom prisoners and the prison administration have to get on because they both need her help.'

Her statements embellished with metaphors and similes astonished Ömer. He had noticed that not only Jiyan but also the ordinary people that he had been able to talk to expressed their views articulately in their distinct eastern dialect with its harsh accent; some of them poetically, in an epic manner like Jiyan; some of them in speech that was frank, clear and to the point. But all said what had to be said as it should be said, reaching the heart of the matter . . . Perhaps because in the solitude of the mountains they thought a lot and said little.

He shows his identity card to the heavily armed soldiers on duty at the door of the garrison and tells them that the Commander is expecting him. He waits while they make a phone call.

A few minutes later a junior officer comes running and cordially shakes his hand. 'Ömer *Bey*, welcome. The Commander awaits you. Please come this way.'

As Jiyan had guessed, the Commander's invitation had not been long in coming. If not the following day, a few days after he had arrived in the town, an officer – perhaps it was the adjutant – coming to the hotel at night had informed him in a courteous manner that the Commander would be honoured to meet him and expected him in his office the following evening at 19.00 hours. He said that a car would be sent to the hotel to pick him up, but Ömer had politely refused the lift saying that he preferred to walk. For a while he had wanted to stroll towards the military zone and take a look around, but he had abandoned the idea so as not to draw attention to himself and create a problem. The Commander's invitation was a good opportunity to take a look round the military zone. He now had a response to the question 'Where do you think you're going, buddy?'

He had made trips with Jiyan or with the people to whom she had introduced him, entrusted him or, it would be truer to say, delivered him. They knew the area well. They could navigate this menacing land that kept its secrets from strangers. On these journeys that were officially 'surveys', for which they had to notify their route and get permission from command headquarters and the Governor, Ömer felt as though he had discovered a completely new continent. Yet I knew every inch of this land, or I thought I did. In our youth, in the years of our revolutionary ideas, we had argued not a little, were frequently divided as to whether we should lay siege to the cities from the countryside or whether we should go from the cities to the countryside and save the peasants, with the working class taking the lead. Were not the cotton pickers of Söke and Çukurova, the landless villagers of the east, the labourers, the tenant farmers groaning under the exploitation of aghas and masters waiting for us to come and save them? Is it we who have changed? Is it I, is it the people, the times, this place? Is it I who have changed, I who have become alienated from these parts, or is it they who have lost touch and gone, become estranged? I don't know these lands any more. I, too, am a stranger here.

On the main roads where the mine-sweeping teams – with their young men, beloved sons, their hearts beating at every step with the fear of death – sweep in single rows; at the crossroads where armoured vehicles wait; at the checkpoints that rule one's fate; while waiting for hours for no comprehensible reason at interminable roadworks; in the deserted countryside from which they had to turn back because of signs declaring 'Dangerous from this point' or 'No entry! Access forbidden'; in the deserted villages, the solitude of remote hamlets, his loneliness, foreignness and helplessness increased a little more.

Where am I? Which country is this? Years ago when I was going around Bosnia, then Afghanistan and a short time ago Iraq, writing features on the theme of war, I used to know where I was and didn't have to ask. There I was a proper foreigner. Perhaps that was why I wasn't overwhelmed by a feeling of foreignness. I wasn't embarrassed about being foreign. I wasn't responsible for what I saw. I wasn't an actor in the play. I was just an observer witnessing the suffering caused by calamity, the tragedy of man. However, here . . . where is this place? This lost country on the bottom and last leaf of a foldable Turkish road map. Where is this land crushed under its secrets, its suffering and the rebellion of its mountains?

The Commander of the Garrison is sitting in his office behind a solid desk between the Turkish flag and standard in front of the large photograph hanging on the wall of Supreme Commander Mustafa Kemal, walking thoughtfully at Kocatepe before the Great Offensive. He is not alone. He gets to his feet when Ömer enters the room. The two other people in the room, one wearing an officer's uniform and the other in civilian clothes, follow suit. Stepping in front of his desk to welcome Ömer, he introduces the others saying, 'The District Governor and the Commander of the Mountain Commando Troops.' He points to a black morocco-leather chair immediately in front of his desk.

'Please sit down, Mr Eren. It really is a great pleasure for us to see you here.'

Ömer notices that the man is choosing his words carefully. Is he sincere, or is this a standard speech? Have I been summoned to be intimidated or be warned off or because an officer, a man of pleasure fed up with the suffocating, tense atmosphere here, needs to unwind and talk to a writer who has come from the world he is missing. Not knowing what to say, he smiles and nods slightly.

'Here, among the mountains, we spend our days involved with mines, battles, death, attacks and military operations. And when we find someone like you we don't easily let them go before they have had a cup of tea with us.' He laughs brightly. 'Of course, you don't have to drink tea. We can offer something more tempting. You are our window to distant regions, Ömer *Bey*. So we want to show you that the people on duty here, who face death in these remote parts, can be different from what you suppose. Recently' – he mentions the name of a well-known Turkish reporter – 'came here. It was after the incident of this latest unsolved murder. He had made his decision some time earlier. I expect you have read his articles. You know, he doesn't look kindly on the army, soldiers. He doesn't mince his words. We took him around so that he could see the situation through our eyes, and we allowed him to contact local people. Believe me, in a few days we were friends. We began to trust each other. When he left, I won't say his mind had changed, but he had new questions in his head. Not everything is as black and white as the terrorist organization would like to maintain.'

Again Ömer cannot decide whether the man's words are a hidden threat, a hint or whether they are sincere. 'Commander, it is a great joy to hear from a soldier that not everything is black and white. You are right. It is a different matter to see and to study a complex political situation on the spot. One must not be prejudiced. However, some things are clear cut and should not be swept under the carpet. I know the journalist well. I might even call him a friend. He has always argued that there cannot be any reason or excuse for the principles of the constitutional state to be suspended.'

He realizes that his words are too bullish and tries to soften his remarks. 'But then I'm a novelist. The reason for my coming here is to do with the new book that I have started. I need to get to know the surroundings, the local people better. Perhaps my timing is a little out; my visit seems to have coincided with a period when trouble has broken out here once more. My journalistic streak is not overly developed. I write features from time to time on subjects that catch my interest. That's all.'

'You are modest, Ömer *Bey*. I read with pleasure your article in the paper written from Baghdad while waiting for the allied attack and also your previous Afghanistan notes. And I have watched you on television, too. I haven't been able to read your fiction. I must confess that we military men don't read novels very often. We don't have time.'

'I don't read fiction much either,' says the District Governor joining in the conversation. 'When I was at high school I read *Goldcrest* and later *Mehmet, My Hawk*. Recently I thought I would read a novel by one of our fashionable writers. I started it with good intent, but I couldn't get on with it and didn't get to the end. My wife reads a lot of fiction. She is one of your fans. She likes your books very much. I think she's read most of them. When I told her you were here she said, "I don't believe it!" She would love to meet you.'

'I should be happy to meet her. Please convey my respects to your wife. If she would accept, I should like to sign one of my books and send it to her.' He is pleased that he has been able to speak in such a courteous, polite and restrained manner. Here one has to get on well with the state.

'Are you going to be staying long, or will you be abandoning us soon?'

'I haven't made up my mind when I'll return. It is not enough to see a place superficially. Writing requires sensitivity, getting under the skin of the people, talking to them, looking into their eyes and understanding their characters through contact. I think I need a little time.'

'Never look too deeply into the eyes of people around here. And don't put too much trust in what they say. Leaving politics and politeness to one side and speaking openly, honestly as a soldier, they are all enemies of the state. Even the most peaceable, those who appear to be loyal to the state,' says the Commander of the Mountain Commandoes firmly.

As Ömer prepares to respond, the Garrison Commander changes the subject. 'We are glad our intellectuals come here. Of course, it is good for them to see the real side of terror, the realities of the country. It's also very important for the people here that they come; important to show that they are not forgotten, that those in the west are not ignoring them. The

Commander speaks harshly with good reason. He's very upset. Only two days ago he lost a petty officer and a private as well in a treacherous ambush; a very young soldier, just a boy, and Kurdish to boot. The petty officer was an excellent lad, a patriot who had come here voluntarily. He has left three children behind. Unfortunately, under these circumstances, it is not really possible always to be lenient. In fact, if the state could be more welcoming, if the civil government could bring food and work to this area – if it could dress its wounds – the people here are mostly trustworthy and good. You can find a handful of traitors anywhere. Unfortunately the conditions here make it easier to influence people.'

'I understand your difficulties,' says Ömer half-heartedly. 'This war, terror and bloodshed has wearied everyone. You know this much better than I. You are the ones confronted with these events. You are the ones risking your lives fighting. As far as I have been able to see in these last few days, the people here want peace and justice, their identity recognized, respect shown to them and they don't want to be considered dishonourable, traitors or to be badly treated. Perhaps you think this is the pipe dream of a writer, but despite all the bloodshed, these are people who have not lost their innocence. I say there is still hope.'

'Try not to fall under the influence of the people you have met since you arrived, my dear author. Those who decide to be militants of the terrorist organization under the guise of campaigning for human rights and those who behave divisively cannot be true guides.' Once again it is the Commander of the Mountain Troops who issues the warning.

Ömer can tell he is starting to lose patience with the man's entrenched attitudes and his hectoring talk. For heaven's sake, stay calm, he tells himself. There is no need to get on the wrong side of these people. After all, they are the rulers of this region. And, what is more, we writers do go on about empathy; one has to understand these individuals, too. They are surrounded by death, war, fear and hostility. In addition the man's petty officer and his soldier have just been killed. Who can guarantee that others won't die tomorrow? Just as he is about to ask who they mean when talking about 'behaving divisively', he notices the District Governor giving him a kind but warning glance. He seemed to want to look after and protect his guest from the stern officer's fury.

'I'll heed your warning,' he says curtly.

The Garrison Commander breaks the tense silence. 'I won't offer you tea, Ömer *Bey*. I dare say our author wouldn't say no to something stronger.

This gives us an excuse to have a drink, too. Isn't that right, my dear Governor? Tonight we'll let the Commander off. He has already offered his apologies beforehand and asked to be excused. The last two days have been a great strain for him. Our condolences, Commander. We'll see you tomorrow. This way please, Ömer *Bey*. The chef at our modest club is not bad at all. He cooks local dishes very well, too.'

Despite Ömer's fears, the evening passes pleasantly. The Garrison Commander and the District Governor are moderate, charming people. They are the kind of people who think: if only all this had not happened, if only we did not have to fight here. The conversation is warm, friendly and frank. The local dishes are excellent, and the *rakı* is not bad at all.

They watch each other carefully and drink only a little; indeed the District Governor has diabetes and does not drink spirits. For a time they discuss healthy eating, diabetes and blood pressure. As they weigh each other up and feel more at ease, as they stop being commanders, governors and writers and become simply men, the conversation relaxes and flows. They talk about about clans, codes of honour, leaders and sheikhs, communities, the circumstances of the rich, the plight of the ordinary, law-abiding citizens, smuggling, terror, soldiers' hardships, forbidden areas, fear, anger, ambition, hope and even a little politics.

At some point, when the conversation comes around to the situation of the women in the region, the Governor says, 'Jiyan *Hanım*, the chemist, is very active when it comes to women's rights as she is in every field, *maşallah*.' Did you know her before, or did you get to know her when you arrived?'

'No, I didn't know her. Where would I have met her? The first evening I was here my head was aching. I'd had a nightmare journey. You know the road. The two-hour journey lasted almost six hours. I dropped by the pharmacy to buy some painkillers. That's how we met. She seems an intelligent and interesting woman.'

'She is, and she also belongs to one of the region's powerful clans. A large clan that has relations both with the state and with the separatist terror organization. One branch consists of wardens; the other branch aids and abets the terrorist organization. You must look into this clan issue, Ömer *Bey*. It's a completely different world. What is happening there throws all the old values to one side. I was not around during the incident. I was appointed subsequently, but as far as I can understand the murder of the chemist's husband was linked to the clan. He was an important person in this region. A writer; well thought of.'

'The chemist said that her husband was the victim of an unsolved murder. She didn't go into the matter, and I didn't think it fitting to probe. Besides, it's not my sphere of interest.'

'Around here, when someone close to the terrorist organization or somebody whose opinions carry weight is murdered, it is immediately ascribed to the state. The separatist organization spreads such propaganda straight away,' says the Commander. 'To tell the truth, on the whole, we keep quiet in order to intimidate, so even if we are not involved we don't openly disclaim responsibility. After all, if you do you will then have officially addressed the terrorist organization. The military would never do that. The incident to which our Governor refers is an interesting case. No one admitted to the murder, but neither did anyone deny it. There were rumours that it happened with the wife's knowledge. However, in my opinion all that was fabrication. Here the waters are murkier than you think, Ömer *Bey*.'

'If the chemist were not under the protection of the clan, she would not be able to act so freely. Human rights, women's rights and so on – please don't get me wrong, Ömer *Bey* – at the end of it, these, are grist to the separatists' mill. If the lady did not have the protection and support of both sides she wouldn't be able to get involved in her political work in such a reckless way. It's not my place to advise you, but accept this as a friendly warning. For our intellectuals this region has an attractive, alluring side. And if they get too carried away by its charm, they will be like the sailors bewitched by the sirens' voices who wreck their boats on the rocks.'

Smug about showing off his knowledge of classical mythology, the Governor leans back in his chair and smirks from under his moustache. He doesn't notice that the Commander has a long face and has turned his head the other way.

Ömer thinks it expedient to pretend not to have heard the Governor's warning. He decides to change the subject. He turns to the Commander and asks if he can suggest where else and who else he should see. He wonders whether the Commander could facilitate visits if he had time. Would the military be able to give him special permission to visit certain places? If they saw fit, would he be able to watch preparations for a military operation – at least the preparation at the barracks?

He says this purely to gain trust, to make conversation. There is nowhere he especially wants to see, no one he wants to meet, to talk to, and, above all, there is no operation in which he wants to take part. He is not actually writing a novel; he is incapable of writing. In fact, there is no reason for him to stay any longer apart from the irresistible call of the sirens and the sound of the mountains.

As he returns to his hotel along the dark deserted roads in the Commander's car, for a moment he considers visiting Cihan – no, not Cihan; Jiyan . Why do I always mix these names up? Either to say goodbye or to succumb to the desire that he has been suppressing for days, to wreck his vessel on the sirens' rocks, to remain on this bewitched, sinister, forsaken island never to return to the mainland.

As they approach the hotel his phone rings. The ringtone is the sound of a cockerel . . . The soldier driving the car is at first surprised and then cannot help laughing. After all, the Commander's guest is a civilian. There is no harm in relaxing a bit.

The cockerel sound belonged to Elif, the miaowing of a cat to Deniz – that is, in the past, before they lost him. He had set his phone to make other ringtones, too. For example, his publisher, the old revolutionary who had become rich at his expense, was set as the Internationale. This was a pleasant joke between his close friends. When Elif asked, 'Why am I associated with a cockerel?' he would answer, 'Because you are my wife who always wakes me up and keeps me on the alert through life.' It really was like that. Before Deniz had run away from their world he was their beloved kitten, their dear son. When he phoned, the miaowing of a kitten heralded news of their son. Now, not just physically thousands of kilometres away but emotionally thousands of kilometres from the cockerel, the cat and the Internationale, he thinks how alien they all seem, with a slight sense of bewilderment and a strange feeling of freedom . . .

Ömer doesn't answer the phone. The cockerel crows for a long time, this time without waking anyone up, and then becomes silent. It is either a cock that crows very early or one that is too late. He says to the driver who is still grinning, 'It tells the time, even if it's midnight.' He gets out at the door of the hotel and goes straight to his room.

I had come here to look for the word I had lost. The lonely, wounded, fugitive young people had said, 'Go and look for the word in its place. To find the word you need first to hear the voice. You have to hear the voice to put it into words.' I believed them and came. Was I just in pursuit of the word I had lost? I don't know.

He guessed he was looking for that indefinable thing that had, at one time, filled him and then got lost leaving in its place a cold dark emptiness. Without realizing it, in the daily comfortable bed of life he had been consumed by a selfish insensitivity. But why here? Why in this distant, foreign land and not there – where he had lost it?

When Zelal had asked the same question in her own language, he had answered that his source had dried up. But to think that the springs in these parts gush more freely and are purer and cooler, isn't that some sort of intellectual romanticism? Isn't this also an eastern myth that we have created?

Jiyan had said, 'If you are trying to capture the spirit of our people, go to a mourning house. I'll introduce you to a friend, a lawyer. He was like a pupil to my husband. He's from round here. He is one of those who, instead of staying at university and making a career for himself, opening an office in Istanbul and becoming a rich and famous lawyer, preferred to remain here and become a country lawyer. He will take you to a mourning house.'

He knew about community centres, but he had not heard of mourning houses. 'Is it the home of the young lad they shot as a terrorist a few days ago?'

'It's not just his, but it's everyone's home. It's a place a bit like a local community centre. After someone has died, people gather there, relatives of the deceased accept condolences, there is lamenting, poems are recited, and songs are sung for the dead.'

She gives a cynical wry smile. 'It is a social, public place, like a mosque or an Alevi assembly house. There beats the heart of the town's deep sorrows.'

'Is it always open?'

'It's always open because people are always dying. A lot of people die here. Death is our most important social activity.'

As she introduces him to her lawyer friend who is going to take Ömer to the mourning house Jiyan says, 'Surely I don't have to introduce you to Ömer *Bey*. If I remember correctly you said that you had read *The Other Side*.'

'Of course I know Ömer Eren.'

He shakes Ömer's hand in a friendly manner. 'Don't take any notice of Jiyan. Sometimes she's pessimistic like this. She makes everything more tragic than it really is. It must have been her suggestion that we should visit a mourning house. Of course we'll go, but we have happy, hopeful, lively places, too: our cultural centre, the women's cooperative, the women's shelter, our recreational areas. We know about living, not just dying. We know about dancing and music, too. In one night there are dozens of henna parties. In a day there are dozens of weddings, especially in the summer.'

'There must be, I'm sure. I wish there were a wedding. I would love to attend. I wanted to meet the family of the child who was mistakenly shot as a terrorist two days ago and ask if I could help in any way. That is why Jiyan *Hanım* directed me to the mourning house. I'm putting you to a lot of trouble.'

'It's no trouble. I don't have any hearings or anything else on today. In fact, I must talk to the murdered boy's family. They'll be there. I'll see them at the same time.'

As they talk and walk along a neglected dusty street with plastic bags and newspaper flying around and rubbish piled up at the side of the road, the lawyer says, 'The worst thing is the feeling of loneliness inside us. Loneliness and mistrust . . . That's why it's important that people like you come here. It decreases our sense of isolation. But of course it raises our expectations and hopes. We think that those who take the trouble to come this far will will appreciate our situation and, from what they have learnt, will stand in solidarity with us and help us resolve our problems. It doesn't work like that. Then, as you have observed, the mistrust and the sense of isolation deepen. Please don't get me wrong. We know you are helpless, too. Time is needed, patience is needed, but people's time and patience are running out.'

'That boy who was shot as a terrorist . . . Did you say he was twelve years old? Why him?'

'Even you have doubts when asking that question? Mistrust has settled in our hearts. We cannot overcome it with ease. The boy really was innocent; whatever innocence means in these parts . . . Of course he could have been a courier for the organization. He could have been taking messages to and from the mountain. He could have been stashing weapons or something. Sometimes even children get involved in the fighting. This place is not the world of innocent angels; no one has wings on his back. It's war. War destroys innocence. However, this boy, believe me, was just a child. I think the real target was his father. Perhaps it was a mistaken target, perhaps intimidation.'

'I hope the truth will emerge. If you look at the newspapers the incident has had quite an impact on public opinion. They say that committees are being organized to come and do on-the-spot inspections.'

'This is what I wanted to tell you, Ömer *Bey*. They will come here in droves and with the best intentions, with feelings of righteousness against injustice. They will share the family's grief, our grief. As you will, too, in a little while. They will promise themselves and us not to let the matter rest. Then they will return to their homes. They will do their very best and they will see that their very best is not much – as always. More important work will crop up or they won't have the power to do anything, and they will be without a solution. Things will be put off and then forgotten. In the meantime children will continue to die, to be killed. Your children, our children, the world's children.' There is no weariness, reproach or dejection in the man's voice. It is as though he's making a cool professional analysis.

'I came here not to be like them,' says Ömer. He realizes that he says these words not to the lawyer but to himself and that he has been thinking aloud. 'It is not enough to understand. One needs to be the other person in body and soul. Suffering cannot be shared. One has to endure the suffering. For some time I've been thinking that solidarity is self-deception. And now I don't know what to do.'

He remembers his conversation with Mahmut's father. The spindly daisies brought by the little girl who missed her father, and Hüseyin Bozlak's query 'Do you know what it means to lose a son, Ömer *Begim*?' He recalls what they talked about, pouring his heart out, saying things that he would not tell anyone else. There is something about these people that encourages honesty. Something that makes one talk without worrying about betraying oneself. Perhaps it is because it is the only way that one can reach their hearts. The lawyer had mentioned mistrust. Perhaps it is to dispel mistrust.

The mourning house is a largish room within a coffee house in a poor neighbourhood on the outskirts of the town. Chairs have been arranged around the walls. The relatives of those in mourning sit on chairs directly opposite the door that has been left open because of the heat. The young woman in the middle must be the mother. A corner of a long white scarf hanging from her head trails on the ground. Here the colour of mourning and death is not black, thinks Ömer. Their mourning is so deep, such a part of them, that there is no need to express it with symbols. The colours of life and the colours of death are one and the same here. There are other women near the mother; elderly women. They are repeating a prayer-like chant in low voices, mainly just moving their lips. The mother does not cry; she does not participate in the prayer. With her eyes fixed on her old plastic slippers, her hands clasped under her stomach, she remains motionless. The father is seated by himself, a little to one side, a few chairs away from the women, and he is looking at those who come and go.

As they enter, the lawyer silently greets the people inside. Together he and Ömer go over to the father.

'Ömer *Bey* is one of our writers. He has come from Ankara to share our grief. He would like to offer you his condolences,' he says in Turkish and then repeats what he has said in Kurdish.

The father stands up. 'Welcome, *begim*. My son has been shot. *Zarok kuştin!*'

Zarok kuştin! Zarok kuştin! Zarok kuştin!

The scream that rent the night in the Ankara coach station: Mahmut's voice, Mahmut's words. *We zarok kuşt! Ev zarok kuştin!*

It's as though a circle drawn with a compass has met the point where it began. Ömer is seized with the feeling of being imprisoned in the middle of the circle he has drawn himself. Without knowing what he should do he pats the young father's shoulder. He feels that every word he utters will be empty, insincere and soulless. I have no part, no blame in the murder of this boy, in these people's grief. Then why is there this feeling of shame, of guilt? Was it not the same feeling that dragged me here in the footsteps of Zelal's and Mahmut's suffering? His heart and mind are illuminated by a light that filters through from the walls of the mourning house, the suffering of these people. Was not Deniz's defeat, his running away, leaving everything behind, abandoning everything, a result of this feeling of guilt, this shame, too?

He feels he must say something, even if it is a useless remark. 'This time they will be punished. This time they won't get away with it.'

'No one will be punished. They won't even be tried. Neither a lawyer nor anyone else will have enough might to oppose these tyrants,' says the grief-stricken father. 'You've come all this way, *begim*. Thanks. The lawyer said you are a writer. You have a pen. They say the pen is mightier than the sword. We also believe in the power of the word, the pen. We want peace, for death to end. But now my only son has been shot. Write as much as you like – you can't bring him back. Round here the sword is more powerful than the pen. Don't let anyone ever tell me about the power of the pen or the word.' He falls silent.

Everyone is silent. One of the women brings tea on a plastic tray with gilt decoration. An enlarged passport photograph of the dead boy in a black uniform with a white collar has been hung on the wall. It must have been taken when he started school, for registration purposes. The sadness in his eyes touches Ömer's heart. It is as though the boy is watching his own death, his own mourning. Yellow, red and green flowers have been arranged in a water bottle on the small table that has been placed in the middle of the room with chairs arranged on three sides; flowers identical to those on the table with the plastic cloth where he and Mahmut's father had drunk tea.

Since Ömer and the lawyer entered the mourning house the women have stopped praying and lamenting. The room is silent. It is as though the silence is about to become a sound and turn into words.

When they are outside again the lawyer says, 'Don't take the father's words to heart. He would not have talked like that if he hadn't thought of you as a friend, if he hadn't expected help. He opened up his heart to you. It's difficult to explain, but he trusted you. He needs you, people like you, me, all of us. In fact, we need all of you. When I think about it, it seems that our anger, our reproach, stems from this need.

'Is this why you are here?'

At first the lawyer does not understand the question.

'What I meant to ask is whether you stayed here because you knew you were needed? Jiyan *Hanım* said that if you had wanted you could have been a lawyer in Istanbul or Ankara or somewhere else; you could have stayed at university and become an academic. But you chose to stay here.'

'You could say that. This is my country, my homeland. They say that something is more valuable when it is in its place. Whether we take to the mountains or whether we stay in the town – right or wrong – in our own way we believe that we owe it to this land, this people of whom we are a part, and we try to repay this debt.

'What has this land given you other than suffering? This town where mourning houses are considered normal . . .'

'It is not this land, nor the people that create suffering. Suffering was imposed on us by the pressure of history, by the cruelty of those in power. We, the children of this land, feel the shame of this suffering inside us. The *Hoca* used to say that if you lose the shame you feel for the suffering of the world and the people then you lose the essence of man. We learnt many things from the *Hoca* – I mean Jiyan *Hanım*'s husband whom we lost.'

Ömer's thoughts that, a little while ago in the mourning house, were a formless quest begin to settle and take shape. I used to feel the shame for others' suffering inside me. I used to feel responsible for the exploitation of workers, people's poverty, their oppression, their wars, their murders and their dead children, for all the suffering of the world, and I would attempt – we would attempt – to atone for the sins of mankind. When this sense of responsibility diminished, when I became absorbed in my own concerns, I lost the word and myself.

'And what about Jiyan *Hanım*? Is she, like you . . . ?'

'Jiyan can't leave this area either. If she goes, a mighty tree under whose shadow everyone shelters will have been toppled. If people like her go, the conscience and hope of the town will collapse. The blind rage of the mountains will have complete control. I'm not using going in the sense of moving or leaving here, Ömer *Bey*. People can stay and still be gone.'

People can stay and still be gone. Perhaps I was one of those like that who stayed but was gone. A woman chemist; a country lawyer; the *Hoca*; others like them . . . Those who stay, those who fight. The last strongholds of conscience . . .

Not able to overcome his curiosity, Ömer asks, 'Jiyan *Hanım*'s husband, the *Hoca* . . . Who was he?'

'He was one of our philosophers, one of our writers who came from this region. He was originally a jurist, but he had worked on our history, our language. He was respected both in the region and throughout the Kurdish world. After 1980 the *Hoca* lived for many years in exile in Sweden. Jiyan's elder brother was in Stockholm. They met there when she went to visit her brother. There was more than a twenty-year age gap between them, but they loved each other very much. Theirs was a passion fit for a fairytale, a love that knew no bounds. At the beginning of the 1990s when a pardon was granted for some of the political exiles the *Hoca* returned home. They married and lived here.'

'What about his death?'

'Didn't Jiyan tell you?'

'I could only talk to Jiyan *Hanım* briefly on the subject. I didn't want to intrude into her private life, and she plainly didn't want this either. However, I did hear something about it.'

'I'm sure you have heard something. Here one hears a lot of things – everything but the truth. One shouldn't believe too much in what one hears, Ömer *Bey*. If you are in the middle of a war each side has its own version of events, its own truths. That applies particularly to unsolved murders. I know. I have dozens of unresolved cases on my hands.' It's obvious that he does not want say more.

Ömer feels a strange jealousy and frustration. The doors that look as though they've been partly opened are again closed to the stranger. This man knows everything about Jiyan. I don't know anything. 'Wasn't it difficult for Jiyan *Hanım* to stay here after her husband was killed?'

'It was, without doubt. But, then, she had no other choice. Before she met the *Hoca* she had thought about leaving, even going abroad. At first one felt that she wasn't local, that she wouldn't fit in. But after she got to know the *Hoca* everything changed. For Jiyan this land, these people – I mean our own people – and the love she felt for her husband became inseparable. It was as though Jiyan had stopped being Jiyan and become the sum of them all. She won't leave this area. She can no longer leave. If she left she would not be Jiyan any more.'

Ömer feels a strange unease within him that he does not comprehend. He thinks how well the lawyer has described Jiyan in so few words. He said, 'If she left, she would not be Jiyan any more.' This was what I have been unable to put into words, that I sensed but could not express clearly. Jiyan was not merely a woman. For that matter she was not just Jiyan. She was the sum of all that the lawyer said. And it was this that made her special, beautiful and remarkable.

To change the subject he asks, 'Are the families of martyred soldiers – martyrs' funerals – brought to the mourning house, too?' He realizes that his question is stupid and falls silent. 'I'm afraid I've been talking nonsense,' he says like a student asking his teacher an inappropriate question.

'If this happened, there would be no need for mourning houses. Neither guerrilla nor soldier would be martyred. But you haven't been talking nonsense, Ömer *Bey*. This was Jiyan's latest dream. She was striving to get a quiet, modest ceremony organized for dead soldiers at the mourning house; for all to gather together in the same place, if not in joy then at least in mourning, and to mourn for those who died for their country and those who had been captured dead, whether they were Turk, Kurd or whatever.'

'Why do you talk in the past tense? Has she relinquished the idea? Has she given it up?'

'Let us say she hasn't been successful as yet. Jiyan doesn't give up. What is more, for her this is something like the *Hoca*'s last request. In this region of ours the hardest thing is not fighting, dying and killing. What is really hard is being able to cry together for our dead, to feel it inside all of us. Both sides resist it. It doesn't suit the interests of those who strengthen their power using the dead, those who use the dead as weapons. And just think of two fighting armies embracing each other's soldiers! What commander could stand that?'

By the time they reached the market Ömer felt in so great a need to mull everything over and put his emotions and thoughts in order that he abandoned the idea of getting in touch with Jiyan just then. He decided to phone to find out whether the Governor's invitation on behalf of his wife, a great reader, still stood. Yes, they were expecting his visit. They would be very happy to see him and to have dinner with him.

There was still time until the evening. He went into the internet café to check his emails.

FIVE

In the Footsteps of the
Unknown Deserter from Life

After midnight she awoke to the howling of the wind and sound of the waves. She was in the room with the large bed and high wooden ceiling overlooking the sea on the upper floor of the Gasthaus: the room in which she, Ömer and Deniz had stayed as a family twenty years before.

'The weather is extremely changeable here. Sometimes the sea is as calm as a millpond and stays like that for days, then a storm will break out. You can hear it really loudly in the rooms above. It rumbles and roars. You won't be able to sleep,' Deniz had warned. But, still, she wanted to stay in the room. Was it nostalgia or masochism?

The wooden shutter had slipped its latch and kept on banging. She gets up and opens the window to shut it. The storm and the raging waves seem to fill the room. She hastily closes the shutter and pulls down the window. In the darkness outside the night is frightening and wild. It reminds her of the rocky island with the bad witch's castle in illustrated children's books or the setting of a horror film. However sheltered and protected this place is, at the end of the day this is Norway, the North Sea. If Ömer were here he would say, 'We are just a smoke away from the Pole.' A cold emptiness descends on her, a feeling of foreignness, a sense of not belonging, of being alone . . . She realizes that she misses her husband and that she wants him with her. Couples should not be so much apart, should not separate their lives so much if their hearts have not already been completely severed from each other, if they haven't become totally estranged. Worlds that aren't shared fall apart in the end.

'You to the west and me to the east. We are gradually drifting apart,' Ömer had said. Elif feels a pang of sorrow. We must come together again, reunite our hearts. Hearts unite when they walk the same path. We must find a path that we can walk together. Outside is the storm; a roar, penetrating the shutters and windows and filling the room. Sounds like those of animals being slaughtered, perhaps the screams of giant seagulls, perhaps the whistle of the wind that slithers through the rocks like a snake.

She takes out a packet of cigarettes from her cluttered bag that she had thrown on to a corner of the table and lights a cigarette. She is not really dependent on nicotine but is one of those who smokes from time to time, for pleasure or from stress. She needs a cigarette at this moment as well as a strong drink – the sort the northerners call schnapps.

They had slept in this room, in this bed. It was the end of December. It was Christmas Eve, and it was freezing. The tiled stove hastily lit with embers brought from the fireplace made no impression. They had tucked their little son between them so that he did not get cold. He had slept soundly all night long. Husband and wife had joined hands over their son's head. Locking their feet together, they had tried to cuddle one another and get warm. It was a cold but calm night. They were happy. But tonight . . .

Contrary to what she had feared, her meeting with Ulla's grandmother and grandfather had not gone badly at all. Of course, there was the language difficulty, but Bjørn made everything easy. Even if he did not believe that his father had a mother, and that this mother was facing him now, the child liked the foreign woman. On the table was cold and raw fish, dried fish, salted fish, sweet and sour sauces to be eaten with fish and a tasty dish of boiled potatoes mixed with fried onions. They had offered her a strong drink they had made themselves. The memory of Ulla was not overwhelming at the table, as she had feared. If it had not been for the photograph mounted in a frame of pine twigs over the fireplace whose heavy metal doors stood half open, one might have thought she had never lived here. The Ulla in the photograph looked much younger than the girl she had seen when she arrived with Deniz in Istanbul – and died there. In the picture she must have been fifteen or sixteen years old. She was looking into the distance with her sad smile and lacklustre eyes that had upset Elif then, too. So that they did not notice that she had been looking at the photograph, she put on a smile and focused her gaze on the grandfather sitting directly opposite her. She felt that if Ulla's name were mentioned Pandora's Box would open and all the unspoken blame, suffering and regret would come pouring out. Or it would be suppressed, and the suffering, blame and regret would be buried and spring up from the soil of their hearts as rancour, anger and enmity.

During the meal the little boy was so over-excited he could hardly contain himself. He kept getting out of his chair and coming over to Elif, trying to hold her hand and closely examining her face. Pointing to Bjørn, Deniz said, 'He likes you.' Then he translated what he had just said into Norwegian for the benefit of the grandparents. In her son's manner, in his face and voice, she had sensed a strange shyness, an effort to ingratiate himself with these poor folk, and she felt upset.

The meal passed with stories of how they had come to the island years ago; Deniz's insistence that he must see the Devil's Castle, the elderly German that they had met introducing himself as 'the unknown deserter' and how that night they had not come across a single soul apart from the woman with the baskets on her arm and how they had begun to think that the island was bewitched. Deniz tried his best to translate the conversation so everyone could understand.

'We northerners tend to believe in sea spirits, mountain fairies, wood elves and in fairytales and legends,' Ulla's grandfather said, 'perhaps because of the mists, storms, the twilight that lasts for months and then the long dark nights, the foaming seas and the dark forests.'

'But now all this is over. Modern life has changed everything,' the grandmother that the boy called *Mormor* argued. 'Now television brings the world to our homes. Even tiny children no longer believe in elves and fairies. They pretend to believe – just for fun. In the east, presumably fairytales and myths are still popular. Everyone knows *The Thousand and One Nights*, don't they?'

'The situation is not so different in our country,' Elif replied. 'The world has become small now. As you say, technology has broken the spell. And there is this fact, too: Turkey is not really the east. We feel closer to Europe. Geographically we are, in fact.'

God knows, these Norwegian villagers probably think that in Turkey all women live in harems and men wear fezes and smoke hookahs. That is why they look down their noses at Deniz. He should be told that he must not be put upon.

'It's a bad world,' the grandfather bemoaned. It was obvious that her descriptions of modern Turkey had not interested him. 'Evil has beset the world. We are trying to protect our island from wickedness. We don't know how much longer we can do so, but nothing bad has happened here for years. Sometimes neighbours fight, then, at church, they make it up. Sometimes a boat has an accident and we lose people. We are sad, especially for those who die young, but we put our trust in God and look after those they leave behind. However, on the island people are not bad to each other. Children are safe here.'

It seemed to Elif that 'Ulla' had just been mentioned. She sensed that Deniz was not translating everything. Perhaps the grandfather had said something about Ulla being killed in Turkey and to avoid a tense atmosphere Deniz had not translated those words. Then they had spoken about the preparations for the fish festival to be held the following day.

Deniz said, 'Tomorrow there's the herring festival, Mother. They are discussing the preparations for it. Tomorrow the island will be full of people. Visitors will arrive by boat. They will stop by the Gasthaus to have something to eat and drink. They may stay overnight as well. Bestemor and Bestefar, I mean Grandmother and Grandfather, are talking about what still needs to be done. I don't need to translate this for you. I don't think you'll find it very interesting anyway. It's one of the simple activities of the fishing village.'

She sensed in her son's voice a feeling of inferiority towards her, of inadequacy, and the pang of sadness deepened. But still it couldn't be said that dinner and the evening had passed badly. So in that case who had dug this deep dark well in the middle of her breast? Why did she feel as though a wild cat had been scratching her breast with its claws, making it bleed?

Outside the storm rages, and its roar penetrates the windows. She is seized with a sense of panic that the waves might reach the house and that they could come through the windows and fill the room. She remembers that the strong drink tasting of iodine they had offered her after dinner is in the large room in which they ate their meal. I must have a sip. I don't know what good it will do, but I need a drink and a cigarette! She leaves the bedroom light on and the door open and goes down the dimly lit stairs. The door of the dining-room that also functions as a kitchen is open, and a light is burning inside. Damn it! What will she say? I'll say I was thirsty and came down for some water. I can't say I want a drink like an alcoholic, can I?

Luckily the grandparents are not around. Deniz is sitting at the end of the long solid wood table. He is busy fastening fish heaped in front of him, of various shapes and sizes cut out of colourful bright mica or a similar material, on to a fishing net.

'I woke up to the sound of the storm and . . .'

'I told you. When a storm blows up one has to plug one's ears to be able to stay in the room you're in. That's why I sleep downstairs in the room at the back now.'

Elif looks searchingly around. She looks for the bottle of alcohol on the table, on the kitchen worktop and on the carved wooden sideboard. 'Give me some of that drink we had or whatever – something strong. Not beer.' She sits down directly opposite her son at the other end of the long table.

'What's the matter, Mother? You aren't that keen on alcohol.'

'I need it tonight.' She pauses, mellows and says, 'It's because of the storm. If I wake up at this hour I can't get to sleep again. A glass of spirits will do me good.'

'It's difficult to find alcohol in Norway, and it's expensive, too, as you know. However, because this house is considered a tourist lodge, even though it doesn't have many customers, alcohol is always available. Would you like some of what we had at the table or something like akevitt?'

'Not what we had earlier. The other stuff should be better.'

He fills his mother's glass. 'I don't drink strong drink much. Alcohol-free beer goes down better.'

'What is this you're doing? Preparations for tomorrow?'

'I don't know if the storm will have died down by tomorrow morning, but at the fish festival they have a tradition of decorating the square at the quay. These have to be finished in time.'

'And this is left to you?' She is unable to hide the condescension in her voice and falls silent.

'Not just me. Others do it as well. Ulla and I used to do it together. She used to love all sorts of handicrafts and was good at it. You know that I'm not very good at handiwork. In any case, I can't produce enough. Masses of decorations are needed. I get satisfaction from doing this sort of thing, Mother. Your son enjoys occupying himself with simple tasks like this.'

'I didn't say anything. Don't get all prickly. This is your choice. I can't pretend it would be mine. If stringing fish made from glossy paper, plastic or whatever this stuff is on to nets for a fish festival on this godforsaken island at the edge of the world makes you happy ...'

'I don't know if it is my happiness you're concerned about, Mother. But, yes, making these colourful fish, decorating the nets for a silly fish festival makes me happy. Mending the fishing nets on the ocean-going boats, cooking for the people on the vessels and giving them drinks, carrying the fishing baskets and crates of prawns make me happy. I'm sorry that I'm happy doing this. What would you suggest?' He speaks softly, trying not to raise his voice. At the same time he continues threading the netting through the eyes and tails of the colourful fish and clumsily ties knots with his long, slim fingers. The long, slim fingers on this fat, clumsy body are like a reminder of the graceful youth of the past.

Elif gets caught in the whirlpool of the complex feelings she feels for her son and is silent. He was always clumsy. He was hard-working, well-meaning but always inept, particularly where handiwork or sport was concerned. She remembers his efforts to ingratiate himself with the other children so that he could join in their ball game. She feels a little depressed. And here he's trying to ingratiate himself with these stupid Nordic villagers by working for them and preparing decorations for a stupid festival. Suddenly she begins to weep softly and quietly. Tears trickle down her cheeks.

'Mother!' he says. 'Mother Cat . . . please don't cry. Look, your kitten is playing with fish. Cats like fish.' He wants to embrace his mother, to hug her, but he cannot do so. Why is it so hard to overcome the distance, the lack of communication, between them?

Helplessness settles on the table, a heavy silence. Only the roar of the storm and the waves can be heard and the ticking of the cuckoo clock on the wall.

'I would suggest you leave this place and return to real life. That you get away from this false refuge and return to us, to the world, however cruel, however savage it may be.'

'Are you really sure you want that, Mother? Are the famous author Ömer Eren and Professor Elif Eren, nominee for Woman Scientist of the Year, prepared to support their son who is disabled when it comes to life?'

Elif senses the reproach in the boy's voice. Her tears cease to flow. She can't breathe. The question becomes an iron ball and smashes into her breast. Is she ready to support her son? Her unsuccessful, awkward, defeated son, this unkempt, slovenly, dull, fat man?

'I don't know, but I'm ready to pay the price. If you make up your mind and have the courage, both your father and I can try to begin a new life with you. The thing you call happiness is in fact nothing more than a state of lethargy, putting life on hold. And all this talk of "famous author" and "famous professor" is a part of your self-defence mechanism. I cannot remember ever humiliating you or putting on airs.'

She gets more and more angry; the angrier she gets the more the pain diminishes and her fury increases. At the end of the day people always find an excuse for everything they do. Being put down by one's mother and father is a good excuse much favoured by smart-aleck psychologists, too.

'Perhaps you did not do any of those things, but while I was with you I had the feeling that you always expected more from me and I could not live up to your expectations. Here no one expects anything from me. I don't fight with myself. I'm not ashamed of being what I am. I don't feel anguish because I am what I am. You have to accept me for myself. In your mind, what should your son be? To which peak should he aspire? Well, I don't know the answer to that. It seems to me that it's wherever you can get to, wherever you are. Look, Mother, listen to me for once. Accept that I, too, have some ideas of my own. Listen . . . The storm outside doesn't pretend to be anything other than it is. The sea is the same; fish, cats, seagulls, these cliffs, in other words nature itself, doesn't try to be anything other than it is. There is harmony, great harmony. People jeopardize this harmony with their ambitions and destroy it. Putting harmony under pressure results in brutality, war, blood and violence. I want to be a vibration of harmony, not involved in violence and savagery.'

'We didn't expect a Nobel Prize from you or for you to be famous or that you would be the head of a business enterprise or that you would end up – I don't know – powerful or rich. Of course it's good to be opposed to violence and brutality. But you could have opposed such things not by passive submission, not by running away, but by striving to eliminate the suffering of mankind and working for justice and peace. That's how you could have lived. You could have been a part of a food programme for starving children in Africa or Médecins Sans Frontières or a green movement or an organization opposing war. You could have had an aim, a cause to fight for. You choose to run away, to hide. You choose to be like that old German, to get buried here on this island – to be the unknown deserter from life. Don't expect us to applaud, to support this, to be happy about it. You are a pain in my heart – in our hearts – a pain too deep for you to comprehend.'

'So I have managed to be something: I have become a deep pain. I'm sorry, Mother. But ever since Ulla's death, since I disappointed you, since I tried to retreat in dreams and untruths, I, too, have known suffering. Suffering seems to ease in a fishing boat battling the waves in the dark. It can't be felt when I'm fixing these paper fish to the nets or when I'm handing out beer to visitors. When I'm playing with Bjørn and watching him grow day by day it disappears altogether. Suffering stops if you accept it, if you absorb it. Resisting increases suffering. I'm not going to try to resist it because I don't have the strength. Don't feel sad for me. Just consider me your lost son if that's easier for you. I'm telling you this so that you can feel better. I'm fine, Mother. I'm very, very, very well.'

'I'm very, very, very well.' This expression he had insisted on since childhood; emphasizing it when he was at his worst, when he had hit rock bottom, accentuating and underlining the words as though he wanted make himself believe them first. Perhaps he really is fine, thinks Elif. And perhaps he is right. Do I – do we – have the monopoly on what is right? Can't he have his own sense of purpose? Her eye lands again on her son's clumsily tied knots. Preparing decorations for a fish festival may very well have meaning, bring happiness, make life more enjoyable. Very well, if we are to ask the question plainly, ridding it of any embellishments: So what am I doing? What am I doing other than shutting myself in a laboratory and examining the brains of the little animals I've killed and dreaming about the prizes I'm going to win?

Elif wants to believe her son when he says, 'I'm very, very, very, well', to be free of guilt, to feel at ease. She wants to be rid of the mental strain and to relax, to be able to ignore her anxieties and feel at ease.

'Give me another drink and I'll help you. At this time of night I don't think I'll be able to sleep.'

She pulls an armful of fish in front of her. Mother and son work together for the first time in years, leaning over the fishing net spread out on the table. Immersed in their thoughts, they silently attach the colourful fish on to the nets.

When Elif awoke the following day she was amazed to see that the storm that had raged all night had abated. The North Sea was like a millpond, as though the last night's storm had never occurred. It was almost nine o'clock. Had she overslept? She had gone to bed very late, almost morning. She wasn't used to strong drink. She had drunk a great deal and had passed out as soon as she lay down. As she collapsed in bed, having been instructed to do so by Deniz before her head fell on the table, she remembered that her son was still beavering away downstairs on those unimportant decorations.

'You go to bed, Mother. There are only a few fish left to do anyway. I'll finish them and then get to bed myself.'

Her son's bearded face looked fatigued. It was the look in his eyes that seemed really tired; a resigned, humble, defeated look. At the end of the night's long conversation – perhaps the most intimate, longest and friend-liest conversation that mother and son had had in their lives – Deniz had asked, 'What do you think is the recipe for happiness, Mother? Examining changes in the brains of mice? Smiling and signing novels for readers in queues, like my father at book-signing days? Fighting and dying or killing for a cause? Perhaps all of them. Well, I'm happy here. Don't be upset. Your son is fine.'

But the look in his eyes did not reflect happiness; it reflected defeat, submission, capitulation. My son has found happiness in defeat, because he has not the strength to look for it anywhere else. He has been defeated without fighting at all.

Last night, perhaps under the influence of the drink, perhaps out of desperation, she recalled that she had found peace for an instant by accepting Deniz as he was and that she had asked herself: What is right? What is good? What is happiness? What is the meaning, the value of people's lives? But now, with the beginning of the new day, all the overwhelming values with their unconditional and acute truths that had been shaken in the night once more proclaimed their sovereignty.

She got up and washed her face in the basin in the corner of the room. She liked what she saw in the mirror. Ever since I was young the more tired, the more depressed I get, the better I look. 'You should feel sorry for yourself, darling. With that face you can't possibly make others feel sorry for you!' Ömer used to say, hugging his wife and stroking her hair. When he said this her worries would evaporate and troubles became meaningless. When did we lose the therapeutic power of our love? When did the river that watered our feelings dry up? Was it when we realized that we had lost our son? Or was it much earlier when you were in pursuit of the magic of the word, when you were climbing the slippery slope and grew away from us? Or was it when I lost myself among the fascinating images transferred from the microscope to the screen and forgot to come home from the laboratory? Was getting yourself caught up in your writing, your books and your admirers and drifting away and my getting lost in the kaleidoscope rings of my childhood dreams not a reason but a result?

A slight stroke of a pencil on her eye and her eyebrow, a touch of lipstick, a hint of foundation to soften the deepening lines on her forehead and at the corners of her lips were rituals she performed daily, as natural as brushing her teeth. As she puts on her expensive designer jeans – not one of the usual well-known brands – that fit her perfectly, that skim her body without being too tight, she smiles with the pleasure that she feels at still being slim, lively and active at over fifty. What was that? Fifty. She repeats the compliment that she is used to hearing: 'Fifty years old? I don't believe it! You don't look more than forty.' Deniz has become overweight. He has become clumsy, with a body that is harmful to the eye and to his health, reflecting the phrases that she retains in her memory from his childhood: 'He doesn't know his lessons, and he's fatter than the other boys.' When she realizes that she is ashamed of her son's body she dislikes herself. I'm slim, graceful and well groomed, and I'm Professor Elif Eren. But what use is all this? What does it mean, for example, to Ömer?

She knows that her husband cheats on her periodically. She gets stuck on the word 'cheat'. It is an ugly word, an inane, vulgar expression. It doesn't reflect the truth. Ömer does not talk about these kinds of casual relationships, but he does not hide them either. All this belongs to a different part of his life; to a part that has nothing to do with me, that does not take anything away from me or diminish me . . . This has nothing to do with the body, desire, sex: it is a male instinct, a need constantly to prove himself; an obsession with being wanted, being considered important, being flattered and with making conquests. I'm the real one. I'm the woman to whom he returns every time. No, this is not true. He never parts, never goes away from me that he should return.

The bond, that instead of being worn out with casual relationships has stood the years and been made strong and firm, although no longer a passionate love, a blind love, seems to Elif like a safe haven. To be Ömer Eren's wife, his woman . . .

'How does it feel to be Ömer Eren's partner?' the young arts reporter had asked when she came to interview the famous author and his wife in their home for a national broadcast. Elif had been the the perfect interviewee. She hadn't put a foot wrong and, to make a feminist point, she had responded, 'It is also possible to ask the question in this way: "How does it feel to be the husband of Professor Elif Eren, known for her work internationally on the subject of genetic transfer of forgetting and recollection?"' The young reporter had been stunned and wrongfooted by this and had continued the interview in an amateurish and hesitant manner. However, the last question that the girl had posed before leaving was now troubling Elif in mind and heart.

The hapless girl had insisted on speaking to Deniz who was at home at the time. Oblivious to the young boy's fretfulness and unwillingness to participate in the broadcast, she insisted on asking just one question: 'What is it like to be Ömer Eren and Elif Eren's son?'

'It's dreadful,' Deniz had replied in a rough voice. 'I don't recommend it. No one regards you as "you". They simply see you as this or that person's child. And you feel you have to perform impossible feats so that you can be yourself.'

Elif remembers the young reporter's astonished expression. At least, she had had the decency not to include this last question when editing the interview.

Is being our son like that? Is it preferable to live on a remote island in the north at the other end of the world, on the island of the unknown deserter from life? Which conversation, which interview, which photograph reflects the truth about a person? Which one can explain why I'm here, the suffocating feeling inside me, the sadness? Why should I feel so disturbed? I, someone who, the day before, presented one of the most significant papers at an international symposium and received masses of praise – perhaps not least for being, unusually, a Turkish woman presenting such interesting findings. Someone who is beginning to make a name in the international community and getting close to achieving the Woman Scientist of the Year prize. What is this feeling of cold dark emptiness inside me, of not having succeeded? Why do I feel alone, helpless this morning? Is it because of the boy? Is it because I'm missing Ömer? Or is it both?

I need you. I need your voice. I need to hear your voice. When I return I mustn't let you go again. Even if you want to go, I must cling and hold on to you. I've always hated the thought of being a clingy woman, and I've tried not to be. But now I must cling to you. We must never go again, you to the east and me to the west. The east and the west are big enough to take both of us together. On the telephone you said, 'Me to the east and you to the west . . . We are gradually drifting apart.' At the beginning of our journey we were so intimate, so close, that however much we separated it always seemed to me that our road, our roots, our bodies were one.

Perhaps it was for this reason that she hadn't made an issue of her husband's affairs, her escapes where she used her own academic studies as an excuse, their separations, their distance. It was as though their being together was a necessity rather than a state. Ömer was not a separate entity. He was an extension of her mind, her heart and her body. The fact that his being there felt so natural may have been down to her self-confidence, or perhaps – quite to the contrary – from her fear of losing him. Perhaps it was because secretly she did not notice the erosion of the years or have the strength to stop it.

I am gradually getting old. Reaching fifty would never have crossed the tip of my mind. I've come to it. I'm pushing it. I've even passed it. I love you. I need you more than ever before. I'm with our son, our wounded son, our son who wounded us. Last night we spoke until dawn. We had never before spoken for so long. He was fastening fish of coloured aluminium foil on to old fishing nets to decorate the fairground for today's fish festival. He said that it made him happy. He asked me why a life full of peace, a conciliatory, decent pastime was bad in the midst of the violence that surrounds us in this world of blood and fire. I could not find an answer. I'm tired, darling. I need your wisdom, your voice and your words.

To rid herself of the depression that is hanging over her, the feeling of suffocation that rises in her breast and sticks in her throat and a feeling of deadlock, she understands that she has to separate the issues out and solve them one by one. First of all you systemize them: you take the questions one by one and eliminate them. You start with the ones you can solve, you establish the links, and you progress step by step towards a solution. The Cartesian method that makes the job simpler and prevents one getting lost in the maze; rationalizing and systematizing . . . But in life it isn't like that. You cannot always isolate problems and solve them. Rationalism does not seem very analytical in this world where quantum theory and the metaphysical interpretations of chaos theory raise a storm even in positive sciences where positivism is almost obsolete.

What is it twisting my insides? Is it my son who has deserted life, who has been trapped on this lonely island? Is it the distance that I feel has grown and deepens day by day between Ömer and myself however hard I try not to accept it and however much I try to deceive myself? Is it the fear of losing him? Or despite my paper being met with praise and applause at the last symposium and the offers I received from important universities for visiting professorships, could it be my inadequacies and limitations that only I am aware of? If I were to tell this to someone else they would think it was false modesty; they would think that I want even more applause, more recognition. Yet I know how far I can go, where I stand and that I am no genius. If I were to tell Ömer, he would say, 'Perfectionism is your incurable illness, my girl. If you were in my shoes, you would not like anything you wrote and you would not produce even a single novel.' Ömer, like most men who are considered successful, is self-satisfied and does not work meticulously. If what he writes sells well, is well liked, that is enough! Am I doing him an injustice? Why hasn't he been able to write recently? He obviously has his own problems. There is something that he worries about, that stops him writing. How little we share things, how little we speak now. Everyone has loaded up their heavy bundle and is dragging their donkey along their own path: me to the east and you to the west . . .

Outside the weather is clear. It's going to be a fine day. What a strange climate. You can't trust the weather even at the beginning of July. If the night's storm had continued, if it had rained the fish festival would not have been any fun. All that hard work would have been for nothing. She catches herself: as if I care about the fish festival on this bloody godforsaken island! What she does care about are the decorations going to waste that her son has prepared all night long, clumsily but with enthusiasm, patience and care, and little Bjørn who has been looking forward to the festival being disappointed . . .

She goes down to the kitchen to get a cup of coffee. She cannot pull herself together in the morning without drinking a large cup of strong coffee, a pleasure or an addiction that Ömer never shared with her. He has tea for breakfast or a good soup.

Breakfast had been prepared on the long wooden table in the middle. Yellow unsalted local cheese, another type of cheese resembling *lor*, wild strawberry jam, practically raw salted fish in separate small dishes, black bread beside the toaster with board and knife and coffee in a thermos. There was no one around. She recalls the solitude of that December evening years ago when, by some strange chance, they had first set foot on this island which she has begun to think is bewitched.

She was not in the habit of having breakfast as soon as she got up in the morning. Leaving the fine china cup to one side, she filled a large mug that was hanging on a hook on the wall with coffee. The smell of it was good; it was full of memories. With her coffee in her hand she went out of the wide wooden door at the side of the house that faced the sea. She breathed in the smell of salt and seaweed. Well, this is different from what we are used to, but this is another type of beauty. A dull, slightly misty sky, milk-blue, grey, sometimes navy water, and a light that is yellow at sunrise and verges on purple rather than pomegranate red at sunset. Serene, solitary nature that smoulders and does not blaze, that does not evoke violence, passion and ambition, whose colours do not flare up or compete with each other. In this land there is nothing harsh other than the storm that has long since died down, the waves that have settled down and retreated, and the granite rocks. It is impressive and beautiful, but if I were to stay longer than three days I would suffocate here. We are Aegean, Mediterranean people. We miss the hurly-burly, the burning sun, the dazzling light. We cannot stand solitude, a lack of people.

As she goes out of the door of the Gasthaus on the seaside and walks towards the sea, she spots him. When she faces the sea he is sitting with his back to a rock on the cliff to the left of the house. He has his head between his hands, his face turned to a point below. He seems to be talking to someone there; someone he can see but Elif cannot.

She shivers. A hot wet snake breaks away from the nape of her neck and sinks into the bottom of her spine. In the vast loneliness of the desert, perched on a broken-down wall or a rock of marble, the Little Prince is speaking to the snake under the rock; one of those terrifying poisonous cobras that can send a person to his star in one bite.

He tells him it's the right day but not the exact place and that he shouldn't be afraid, as he won't feel any pain, even if he looks a bit like he's dead. He won't really die ... He tells the snake to try to understand that his planet is far away and his body is too heavy for him to carry it so far ... It will be fine, as he shall watch the stars and they will give him water ... He stops, because he is crying, and he sinks to the ground in fear. He continues, 'You know ... the flower I told you about ... I'm responsible for her' ... He stands up, takes a step, and a flash of yellow strikes silently close to his ankle ...

Deniz's favourite book, *The Little Prince*, the last chapter that the child never tired of listening to and had repeatedly made her read, the scene where the Little Prince makes the snake he meets in the desert bite him so that he can return to his own world ... The boy would open his eyes wide every time and listen with bated breath as though he was listening to it for the first time, and sometimes he would cry.

She panics. It is as though the snake is lying coiled up just under the rock, the place that Deniz is staring at. 'It's the right day but not the exact place ... My planet is far away, and I cannot carry this heavy body that far ...'

Elif rushes towards the cliffs. There is a fence between the Gasthaus garden and the cliffs. She does not know how to get over the fence and reach the cliffs. Presumably you have to go around from the back somewhere. She panics. I have to get there before the snake keeps its promise, I have to prevent it biting! The Little Prince had said his body was very heavy and he couldn't carry it. Deniz's body is also very heavy. He cannot carry it. Not only his body but also the sadness in his heart weighs him down. He cannot carry it. The snake must be stopped. He must not feel the need for the snake's help: he must stay a little longer on the planet earth. The fox must not abandon his friend so quickly: you know the fox that had told the Little Prince to tame him, and, when the day came for them to part, said that he would cry, but when looking at the wheat fields he would remember the Little Prince's wheat-coloured hair. And then what will the pilot whose plane had crashed in the desert do without the Little Prince? No, he mustn't be abandoned.

She hears her own voice, like a muffled cry: 'Deniz! Deniz! Deniz!' . . . Her voice reverberates on the rocks.

'What is it, Mother? What's happened?'

Now it is Deniz's turn to panic.

Elif slumps to her knees on the other side of the fence before she can cross to the rocks. She does not even notice that Deniz has rushed down the cliff, grabbed Bjørn, who has been playing below the cliff, in his arms, got the boy over the fence and then jumped over himself and reached her side in agitation.

'What is it, Mother? What's happened?'

She buries her head in her arms and begins to cry shaking with sobs. Deniz does not know what to do and kneels down beside his mother. With clumsy pats and timid touches he tries to calm her.

Bjørn asks in amazement and rather anxiously in Norwegian, 'What is the matter with *Farmor*?'

'There's nothing wrong. It'll pass in a moment. Now off you run to the quayside and see if everything's ready, if the nets have been put up. If anyone asks, say, "Daddy will be along soon."' He smacks the boy on the bottom. The child runs off.

'What the matter, Mother Cat? What's wrong?'

'I don't know,' she says between sobs. 'I don't know: when I saw you on the cliff I suddenly got really frightened. You were talking to someone, something. It seemed as though you were talking to a snake. I was terrified.'

'Oh, Mother . . . What snake! Bjørn was standing below the cliff and was insisting that we went to the fairground, and I was saying that we would wait for Granny to wake up and then go. I was waiting for you. That's all.'

'I'm sorry,' she says. 'I'm sorry, my nerves are in shreds. I've started to hallucinate. Last night was a difficult night for me. As a matter of fact, everything has been very hard for years. Well, off you go. Don't leave the boy alone. Never leave your son alone. I know the way. When I've pulled myself together I'll follow you.'

He helps his mother get to her feet. He hugs her; just as he hugged her when he was very, very small, with the same submission, the same amiability.

'There are no snakes here, Mother. Don't be afraid. Go inside and wash your face and freshen up your makeup. My mother should look beautiful to the islanders. I'm not late, and, besides, I've no more work to do there. It's much too early for serving beer. I'll wait for you, and we'll go to the quay together.'

This time Ömer answered his phone. At last he had managed to reach a civilized place where mobile phones had a signal! She had grown fed up with hearing the message 'The number you have called is unavailable. Please try later', and she had been hurt that he had not replied in spite of seeing her number on the screen. He had said on the phone that he was going east. Where is the east? Van is east and so is Tunceli and Hakkari, Iraq, Syria and Afghanistan . . . The east is everywhere. Even Europe is the east when looking at it from here, from the North Sea. The stress of following the symposium that had passed with interesting presentations, the excitement of putting the finishing touches to her paper on 'Ethical Issues of Gene Technology' – she thought that the paper would make her a strong candidate for the Woman Scientist of the Year prize that she had her sights on for years – and the question 'Should she or should she not go to see Deniz?' that was gnawing away at her mind and her heart had prevented her from thinking too much about Ömer. In the bustle of the last few days he had sent a text message saying, 'There is not always a good reception here. Don't worry. I'm fine. I shall be here for a while.' Well, that was a sound and valid excuse for both of them: there's no reception. What can I do?

Now she was standing in a relatively calm corner where the row of houses began, a little way from the festivities, and looking at the square by the quay that had been decorated with fish, starfish seahorses and large mermaids made from colourful foil, pieces of material and thick cardboard, dangling from nets. She had taken refuge in the corner of a house in order to shelter from the noise of the festival where a wide range of fish was displayed on long tables covered with white wax cloths, where biscuits, cakes and coloured sweets were sold and where preparations were being made for serving beer, and with her mobile in her hand she was waiting to hear Ömer's voice.

'I was going to phone you, dear. I phoned several times before, but I couldn't reach you. Where are you, or have you returned to Istanbul?'

'These phones are to blame. I expect mine didn't have a signal either. What with you in the middle of the mountains and me on the Devil's Island, what can we do?' Her words are sarcastic, but her voice is not bitter or despondent. One could even say it is cheerful with a subtle vibrancy. 'Guess where I am!'

'You're on the island, Deniz's island.'

'How did you know that?'

'Didn't you just say I was in the mountains and you were on the Devil's Island?' He pauses for a moment and in a voice different from his previously teasing, childish voice he says, 'Thanks for going. I didn't feel ready yet, and I put the burden on you. I didn't support you either.' His voice sounds subdued with a faint tone of embarrassment and apology.

When we talk about our son we always seem to be scared, shy and apologizing to each other. Why? Is it because we each feel guiltier than the other, or because we each think that the other's inadequacy is greater? Or is it because of our weakness, our helplessness?

Trying to sound cheerful she says, 'Now, forget all that. There is a fish festival today, a herring festival or something here on the island. We are at the square by the quay. Do you remember the quay? They've decorated everywhere with fishing nets and multicoloured fish. Your grandson's dashing around. He's having a wonderful time.'

'My grandson! I have a grandson, do I?'

It is then that Elif realizes what she has said. 'Yes, you have a grandson, and he is really sweet. Little Bjørn who waits for Princess Ulla, who, when he realized that we didn't speak the same language, showed his affection by rubbing against me like a cat.'

'How is Deniz?'

'Deniz . . . Deniz is well. Everyone's fine.'

They both think at the same time of that heart-wrenching film that they love: *Everyone's Fine* . . . When the elderly Sicilian father who has gone to see his children living far away returns home, he replies to those who ask how the children are and also says to his wife in her grave, 'Everyone's fine.' The summary of the desperate grief of their children's lives wrapped in dreams and lies; their children who have perished and been crushed in a distant city; the daughter who is a prostitute, the elder son who has committed suicide and the young son who has gone to prison for drug dealing. Everyone is fine.

She continues, 'We'll talk about it when I come. I'll tell you about Deniz and Bjørn. I've missed you, I suddenly had this feeling, and I couldn't resist it, so I just had to phone you straight away.'

'Why on earth were you resisting it?'

'Your not getting in touch, your clinging to the excuse that there was no reception. Get out now from among those mountains and caves and get to a place where your phone has a signal. There is a meeting in Switzerland in a few days. I'm going to take part in it and then return. Come home, too.' She is astonished at what she has said. She had made the call to put her own mind at rest rather than Ömer's as well as to be seen to have made the effort in asking after her husband – or that is what she thought. When one was incapable even of understanding one's own feelings how could one tell others that one could understand them?

'I'll be there when you get back, dear. We'll talk. Give my greetings to Deniz . . . Well, say whatever's appropriate – whatever will make him feel better . . .'

Elif ends the call. The little boy comes running over to her, and, pulling her by the arm, he says something that she doesn't understand. His eyes are flashing. He's excited, joyful, full of life. She walks towards the quay following the child. He points to the fishing boats that have been decorated for the festival and that are drawing up to the quay. Women and men, old and young, people in regional dress from the surrounding islands and from the mainland get off the boats singing cheerful songs to the accompaniment of a strange instrument, something between a fiddle and a mandolin. The square by the quay comes to life. It is as though this far-away island that has exceeded the limits of serenity, silence and peace and threatened to be bleak has had a fit of jollity and excitement that it finds somewhat alien.

Holding her hand, Bjørn drags his grandmother to the middle of the square by the quay. The square is surrounded by stalls of fish, food, decorations, fishing tackle and drink and with the fishing nets she and Deniz decorated during the night. The area in the middle of the square that has been set aside for the young people to dance, the fishermen and the musicians to show off their skills and for races and competitions to be performed is still empty. Bjørn stands right in the middle of the square without letting go of Elif's hand. No one notices them at first. and then slowly they begin to take an interest. Bjørn shouts, 'Look, look at us! Attention please!' Elif, even though she does not fully understand, senses the gist of what the boy is saying. Then the boy shouts, as though he will burst his lungs, as though he is letting out his final scream, 'This is my father's mother! Look, *farmor, farmor, pappamor*! I love her!'

She hears the scream and – how strange, as though it is in her own language – she understands. She feels that she is suspended in the air at a point of infinity. The last conscious moment before death must be a moment like this. This is a film, no, a scene from a musical: in the middle of the décor of a fairground erected in the square by the quay that is licked by a beguiling sea clothed with a semblance of innocence and calm is a tiny very blond child challenging the whole world and clinging to the hand of a slim middle-aged woman whose face is well cared for but who looks fatigued in jeans and a white T-shirt. A scream piercing the ears of those surrounding the square and winding round their hearts, passing the quay, the sea and the square and reaching the castle perched on the cliffs and from there mingling with the ocean's waves; the scream of a child weary of waiting for Princess Ulla. 'This is my father's mother! Grandmother! I love her.'

She tries to observe the scene with the eye of an outsider. She sees herself for a moment as a witch to be burnt later in the village square or, like Mary, waiting for the angel to fly her to heaven with the child. Both are different images of the same feeling, the same phenomenon. How strange! She leans down and takes the child in her arms. I used to take Deniz in my arms like this and hug him him tight. She feels the boy's heart fluttering like a little bird. Opposite, behind the beer stand, Deniz is watching them, smiling. I hope to goodness he doesn't try to come over. Then the picture would be gooey, intolerable. Deniz does not come. He stays where he is behind the stand. As she walks slowly towards her son with the child in her arms cheerful voices rise from the crowd. She does not understand the words but senses they are some kind of greeting, a welcome. Then, a different sound is heard from the corner where a group of youths in strange attire and with motorbikes have congregated – cars cannot enter the island but they don't say anything about motor cycles –'The foreigner's mother! The foreigner's mother!' She understands what they are saying and that they are not friendly. With the child in her arms she turns to the direction of the noise and regards the small group dressed in leather, tattooed, some of them skinheads, up and down with marked contempt and disgust on her face. Just as she is about to swear in English she catches sight of Deniz. She notices the anxiety and panic on her son's face and walks quickly over to the other side of the square to join him.

'Until now nothing like this has happened on this island. In any case, these bastards aren't from here. They must have come from the other side,' says Deniz as though in apology.

'They are the same everywhere. Whether Turk or Norwegian, German, English or Greek . . . The primitive prejudice and their grudges are always the same. Everyone is a foreigner in this world! Everyone is an enemy to one another.'

'They are frightened, Mother. Always the same fear. People are at a loose end. They are afraid of their future in this savage world. The more they fear, the more aggressive they become. Don't worry. Don't take any notice. Norway is the last country where skinheads and fascists will prosper. This place will not shelter such people.'

He strokes the blond head of his son who draws close to them. 'You don't say my father's mother; you say Grandmother. Not *pappamor farmor*.'

'But she's a foreigner. You're a foreigner, too. The older boys on motorbikes said "the foreigner's mother". Didn't you hear them?'

'We have talked about this before. Everyone is a foreigner to each other. On our island the youths on the motorbikes are also foreign, because they are not from here. If we go to a different country we are considered foreign because we are not from there. To be foreign doesn't mean being bad. Am I bad, in your opinion?'

The boy jumps up at his father's neck. 'You are the very, very, very best *pappa*. When Princess Ulla comes she'll marry you, and the three of us will be very happy.'

Elif can only understand the words, Princess Ulla, daddy and foreigner. The deep love between father and son simultaneously warms her heart and makes it ache. Perhaps this was what Deniz needed, this unconditional love, this trusting surrender, to be there for a tiny person, to bear responsibility for him.

They linger in front of stalls selling junk food – which really appeals to the child – along with fish, biscuits and other things to eat as well as toys. She buys Bjørn a huge remote-controlled pirate ship and a large red car that works on a powerful battery system. The car has been put out not because there is much hope of a buyer on this quiet, small island but to make the display more impressive. The boy cannot believe that the car is his.

'But you said that this car was just for decoration, Daddy. You said that no one would buy it. Granny bought it for me. Look! Or is Granny a magician?'

'She's not a magician but perhaps a bit mad.'

At the risk of upsetting the child's frenzied joy Deniz tries half-heartedly to protest. 'There was no need for this, Mother. You never bought me such expensive toys. You were always against such ostentatious consumerism. Haven't you gone a bit over the top?'

It dawns on Elif that she has paid all this money for the toy car not merely to please the child but to leave the Nordic peasants' mouths gaping, to gain respect for her son in the eyes of the local people. So you despise us as foreigners, do you? Particularly because we are easterners, Turks, you ignorant fishermen! Well, the expensive toys that you haven't been able to sell for years we buy without even bargaining – just like that!

She feels that she has been caught red-handed. I'm obnoxious. I'm like those Arab sheikhs who think that the more money they fritter while shopping in London and Paris, the more respect they will gain.

The boy has already got behind the wheel of the red car. He is racing round the middle of the square in the magic car that his fairy grandmother from far away has brought him on her magic carpet from a distant fairytale country. Elif puts the pickled herring with onion and lemon that Deniz has handed her into her mouth, screwing up her face, and tries to swallow it in one go. Deniz is getting ready his beer and akevitt stall made of wide planks of wood thrown over beer barrels. In due course he will hand over the stall to someone else and board one of the boats that have been made ready to take part in the 'Biggest Fish' contest and head out to sea. On this distant forgotten Nordic island the summer or fish festival is in full swing. What am I doing here at this festival? Why did Ulla die? Why is Deniz here? Every island, every community, needs foreigners. Is it to prove their own local identity, to strengthen their tribal self-confidence? And what about Bjørn, the boy taking his irrepressible joy for a ride in his red car? Where is his real home? Is it the fairytale country that he has created in his broad imagination? That vast country to which Princess Ulla will one day surely return, where he and his father will defeat the Devil and settle down in the crystal palace that is waiting for them . . .

She looks at the people filling the square, the fishing nets draped from all sides of the small yellow hut next to the quay, the fish-shaped colourful balloons, fishing vessels especially decorated for the day, the grey-blue sea, the blue sky with little white clouds scudding by and the ruins of the castle on top of the cliffs behind, the Devil's Castle. Here I have neither my husband, nor my friends, my relatives, my students or my own people. I don't even have my mice or my test animals. My son is distant, a stranger. The little boy doesn't understand our language and I don't his . . . She feels completely alone, and if she were not embarrassed she would cry like a lost child.

Deniz comes over to her. With genuine enthusiasm he tells her about the Big Fish contest that is about to commence. 'The Big Fish race isn't in fact a real contest. It's just a festival tradition and one of its highlights. Nets are thrown or lines are cast into the sea. Sometimes an old boot is caught or a piece of driftwood. After the jury have got tanked up on booze, they announce whoever they want to be the winner. You never know, your son might be the winner – and then you will swell with pride, Mother!'

He realizes that his joke has upset Elif as soon as the words have left his lips, and he panics. He knows that every word he says, every effort to made to correct his gaffe, will make the situation worse. There is a crushed, desperate, apologetic look in his eyes.

Ever since his childhood she has never been able to resist this look. When he was just six months old she had seen the shadow of it in her baby's eyes. Why should a baby look so sad even though he didn't have any aches and pains or worries? Did he feel something lacking in his little heart? she wondered. Was it something I failed to do?

Again that look. That look that has become even deeper, hidden too deep to fathom. She glances away from her son. 'Go on then. Don't be late. Go and join your friends! Which boat are you going out with?'

'That one in the middle; the one painted blue and white.'

'A nice boat. It looks big, too.'

'You never know, we might catch the biggest fish. I have spoken to my friends, and this time we are going to take it seriously and catch a real fish. Bjørn really wants our boat to win. We'll celebrate together this evening.'

This time she sees the hope of victory in her son's eyes. Elif knows this look, too. The downy velvet light of his optimism, his wish to believe that bad things will not occur. Deniz has another look: the look of pride he felt in success. His eyes would become slightly moist and flash brightly. She had noticed this look for the first time at a ski resort they visited when he was seven or eight, when he came second in skiing, at which he was in fact no good, and a medal of shiny chocolate foil was hung round his neck; and another time, when he received his diploma the day he graduated in third place, although no one expected it, from that elite school famed for its strictness . . . The child who wanted the success expected of him but who shrank from the price to be paid.

When he came home like a defeated soldier, leaving his education, his school, everything behind, she had asked her son, 'If you had wanted you could have done it. There was nothing to stop you succeeding. You had everything you needed. Why didn't you do it?'

'So I didn't have all I needed to succeed. Sometimes that everything that I think I have is not enough.'

'What was lacking, Deniz?'

'I have thought about this from time to time. Perhaps I didn't have a strong enough drive. I mean, a case of so what if I study? So what if I succeed? Father is successful and you are, too. You seem to be, and you are considered so. Well, what is the result, Mother? What does success do for you? More important, what has your success cost you? How many little lives have you ended? How many creatures have you killed? What and who did my father sacrifice? What did he give of himself to become Ömer Eren, the bestselling author?'

'Don't be silly. Success ensures respect in society, ensures recognition. Apart from all that, it ensures that a person is content. It bolsters a person's self-confidence and happiness.'

'That's because your society has been conditioned to worship success and victory. People trample over one another for victory, for success. They step on one another and try to advance. They even kill each other. I don't want that sort of success. You can say our son was not successful. It's just one of those things – and that's that. I want a simple life. I want to be just an ordinary normal person.'

'Stop rambling! You make excuses for the things that you cannot do and philosophize about failure. However, to philosophize a person has to have experience and a valid concept of the world,' she had said cruelly. Now, when she recalls this conversation, she is upset and amazed that she could have been so obtuse, so horrible. She hopes that he cannot remember the discussion, that he has forgotten it long ago. But, damn it, he does remember.

'Once you spoke to me of success. When we started speaking about catching the big fish, about being first and so on, for some reason I remembered that conversation of ours. You said that I had wanted success but that I hadn't made enough of an effort. So much water has run under the bridge since then. Years have passed. But you were right. Do you know that? At the time I hadn't been able to tell you what was lacking, and I said a lot of stupid things. Now I know.' He stops talking. He waits for his mother to respond.

'What was it, dear?'

'I think I had no confidence. Is that right? Is it self-confidence? How terrible! I'm forgetting my Turkish.'

'Yes, you could say self-confidence.'

'I think I didn't have enough self-confidence. Look, now I'm saying, "I think". I always used to look at your faces – especially at your face – when I said something, wondering whether I had said it right, whether you would approve. Ever since childhood I have not been able to believe in myself. I didn't want to show it, but the world around me used to frighten me. I sensed I wouldn't be able to cope with it. Then I saw that the world really was frightening and savage. War, violence, blood and death . . . It was not for me at all. I would never have the stomach for the fight that even you weren't able to overcome.'

He laughs briefly, unnaturally, to lighten the mood and to disperse the regrets that are beyond retrieval. 'When your son returns with the most enormous fish then you will see what success is!'

No, there is neither resentment, nor mockery, nor revenge for the wounds opened by his mother's bitter words of years ago. It is spontaneous. He just wants to catch a large fish. If he catches a big fish and comes first, he really will get great pleasure. He and Bjørn will be happy. Hadn't he asked late the previous long night, 'What is happiness, Mother?'

A flood of love wells within her, and she blinks back her tears. She hugs her son like a cheerful villagewoman sending her man off to the sea for the great hunt.

'Well then, the best of luck. What do they say when fishermen go out to sea. Have a good catch?'

'Yes, I think so, but here they say, "*Skitt fiske!*"'

'Well, off you go. In that case, *Skitt fiske!*'

She gazes after him. She watches him walking slowly towards the quay, lurching from side to side and boarding the fishing boat; greeting those at the quayside with the air of a sea captain who is about to cross the ocean. She stands there surrounded by this foreign sea, in this foreign clime, with a turbulent breast and a scream stifled in her throat unable to share in the festival for which she feels no joy and which has no meaning for her.

The boy, waiting for his mother, Princess Ulla, who, in the fairytale world that his father has created, has managed to escape from the Devil's Castle, is drawing circles with his car in a corner of the square, letting out squeals of joy. If only I knew Bjørn's language; if only we had a common language. If I knew the island's language perhaps I would be able to understand the secret of the peace that Deniz finds here. Ömer had written, 'Language is like a key; it opens the secrets of a foreign country, of a person you don't know, of a heart.' Perhaps he is looking for the key word, too, in the places he visits.

It occurs to her that she must leave. I must go before Deniz returns. I must go before seeing him step on to the quay carrying the biggest fish like a triumphant commander, with the ridiculous welcoming ceremony and his counting all this absurdity as happiness, before witnessing yet again his defeat – our defeat.

Trying not to attract attention, she walks quietly with pensive steps in front of the green, pink and yellow wooden houses towards the Gasthaus. She does not notice that two of the skinheads on motor cycles who have congregated in front of the drinks stall, knocking back bottles of beer not always available in these parts, have separated from the group and followed her.

The door is not locked. It was not locked either all those years ago they arrived on a dark winter's day when evening fell early. Do these people feel so secure? So far away from evil . . . Suddenly she gets angry, annoyed. When one half of the world is a bloodbath, when bombs are raining down on people, when violence, death and tyranny are erupting, this indifference, this devil-may-care selfishness, this stupid local festival seems insane! Don't they live in this world? They've retreated to this blasted Devil's Island; catch fish, swallow it raw, down beer and come forward and dance in time to the music. Keep your doors unlocked and open, brag that nothing bad will happen here, lord it over the real world, the world in which there is evil!

No one is in the house. The bearded grandfather with a pipe who seems to have sprung from a Van Gogh portrait of a sailor is at the fairground. The grandmother must have gone out, too. That is good. I will not have to try to explain my sudden departure to anyone. And in what language would I try to explain? I'll leave a note for Deniz and I'll write that I'll come again and so on. He'll be happy anyway for the tense atmosphere to lift and for life to return to its natural course.

She goes upstairs to the room she stayed in that night and collects her bag and her jacket. As she glances around the room for the last time, in case she has forgotten something, she becomes angry again. This stupid island, that stupid girl that went and died, these peasants ignorant of the world, my stupid son burying himself alive in this grave having pushed away the opportunities presented to him with the back of his hand ... However much I appear to understand him so as not to upset him, I really don't understand him at all. I just repeat all this stuff and nonsense, without believing any of it, those clichéd philosophies for living derived from television culture; 'as long as you're happy', 'if you're happy that's fine', and so on *ad nauseam*. But it's not enough. It's really not enough! The happiness of swine should not be adequate for human beings.

A little while ago, while she was talking to Deniz at the square by the quay, she was calm, understanding, as she watched little Bjørn's joy that warmed her heart and made her eyes mist. Now she is becoming more and more furious. Like a safety valve, her anger prevents her from becoming emotional, bowing to the inevitable. Why am I angry with them because they don't lock their doors, because they feel secure, because they are not frightened and because really little things make them happy? Don't we all long for a world when locks are unnecessary and doors can be left open? Damn it! Why should tranquillity be such a bad thing? Must people invariably live on tenterhooks, be constantly stressed because of unfinished work, with the burden of duties unaccomplished? Her mind is now totally confused. She sinks on to the bed unhappy with herself and her negative thoughts and her unwarranted anger that acts as a safety valve for pain.

We were here, on this bed. Ömer, little Deniz and I were trying to get warm by huddling up to one another in the damp December chill. In the middle of winter one would have expected the weather to have been even colder. However, we knew that the shores of the North Sea were more temperate than the interior, at least seven or eight degrees warmer. I had cuddled Deniz and was trying to warm his tiny feet. He used to like sleeping in our bed; however, generally, so as not to break the family rules – largely to make sure he didn't become a spoilt brat – he wasn't allowed to. That night when he heard that we were going to sleep together, he was delighted. He had jumped up and down on the bed; this bed ...

This bed, this house ... Places, houses, rooms and beds remain. You can visit a place, an area again, you can return. Objects remain. You find objects where you left them. The place is still in its original position. Objects withstand time. What about time ... What about the me of twenty years ago? Us ...?

Just as I have returned to this room I should like to return to that time.

To that December night of so many years ago. To that night when Ömer and I could not reach each other because Deniz lay between us, when we passionately tried to touch each other, when we made love with our legs and our toes, when we got warm with the heat of desire that enveloped our bodies and when we felt warm inside with the love we felt for our tiny beautiful son lying between us. Not to begin again but to be able to experience and appreciate times of happiness more slowly, to be better equipped to understand the value of beauty, to be able to grasp that all this is not at all commonplace – that it has been bestowed. To be able to stop for a moment and ask: What am I doing? – while irresponsibly and dissolutely wasting the future day by day and year by year. To be able to prevent the monster of tedium shredding and engulfing our love, our son, the things we shared, our common values.

Elif, sitting on the bed of twenty years ago with her aching head between her hands, is attempting to fit twenty years into a few seconds. She is trying to catch the fireball that Deniz has perhaps unintentionally thrown into the ring. 'What is the meaning of success? At what cost? Sacrificing what? How many little lives has your success cost?'

Then she had been furious with Deniz. She had thought he had been taking the pain of his failure, his weakness, his defeat, out on me, on her and Ömer. Now she turns the question over and over in her mind. What is the meaning of all the things I've done? She realizes that she has never asked such a question. What need was there to ask, the meaning was in my work itself.

Was it really like that?

Mice would utter a feeble little 'eek' before dying; people not used to it do not even hear it. Then you cut them open, look at the microscope screen, take notes, form equations and write formulas. The little bodies remain there before they are disinfected and thrown into a special rubbish bin. The human equivalent of 'eek' is more distinct in the scenes of war and violence to be viewed daily on television screens. People 'eek' more loudly. Which important meaning did I grasp, which value did I create, in cutting up these tiny animals? How have the lives of these small mammals contributed to making the world a better, more habitable, tolerable place? She knows all the classic answers. In her paper that received much applause and praise at the symposium the day before she arrived on the island she had asked these questions herself and she had answered them herself. Now she thinks that the questions and answers were clichés and that she had answered none of the questions and, furthermore, that she had not really asked them. My aim was to present a high-flown text and secure my place in scientific circles, to rise step by step to an elevated position in the hierarchy and to honours. Even if no one else knows this, I do.

Ömer would ask, 'Why are you so hard on yourself? When you are so uncompromising about yourself, then you become intolerant of those around you. All right, we appreciate that you are disciplined, hard-working and clever. But others can be different to you in ability and attitude. What entertaining rogues, what jolly tramps exist around us. They scorn the world, and they pass like a pleasant shadow from this world. The effect of stroking a velvety-soft cat is all that remains of them after their deaths.'

'Don't speak to me in that florid literary style you create to impress your readers, Ömer Eren. The traces of the wretchedness they suffered while they lived will certainly remain – not the stroking of a cat or anything else,' she had said with her strong relentless logic. But, still, in a corner of her heart a contented cat had passed by purring, spreading softness within her. Without revealing it to her husband she had thought: You swine, this must be what they call the power of words. The stroking of a velvety-soft cat . . . What an appropriate metaphor!

On this island, in this room, on this bed I have missed you. I have missed you like I haven't missed you for years. My mind, my feelings are in utter turmoil. Our son has got me all confused. I must return home soon. I can put off taking the classes that they offered me for a term. If I don't take them at all, what will happen? What will I miss? I must return and say that I want to be like the stroke of a velvety-soft cat. In fact, I must tell him on the phone. I must say, 'Be at home when I return', without being afraid of being a pestering or clingy wife.

She gets up and freshens her makeup, she rearranges her hair, cut in an artful and dishevelled way according to the latest fashion, raking it with her fingers to provide more volume. The flesh that gently bulges over the waist of her narrow trousers vexes her. I must start dieting; fat beginning to collect around the waist is not a good sign at my age. She stashes the few belongings lying around, such as makeup and hairbrush, into her capacious handbag.

She goes down the stairs with the wooden banisters feeling lighter with every step. On the ground floor she pauses for a moment at the door of Deniz's room, then she turns the handle and goes inside. It is dim and cool: the room of the elderly poet who had introduced himself twenty years earlier as 'the unknown deserter'.

The room has not changed at all. Deniz has taken the place of the old man. On the desk in the corner sits the framed picture of Deniz and Ulla with baby Bjørn in their arms. She thinks that Ulla's face is more beautiful than she remembers – or that anyway she looks good in this photograph. Deniz and Ulla are smiling but in the expression of both is a sadness that has become a part of their faces as though there from birth. On the desk there are two notebooks. One is old and worn with a leather cover; the other is a new book with the pages open. First she opens the ancient notebook. She recognizes the Fraktur italic script of Germans educated before the war. They must be the old man's poems, the verses of that strange man who styled himself 'the unknown deserter'. She picks up the other book. There are a few lines on the open page:

> I am a sea, a fugitive from the ocean
> Saved from the bloody seas
> Running away from the sacred lies, all of them
> In the calm harbours of my own lies
> Content with licking the shores
> I am a sea of nothingness . . .

The last line has been scored out. Beneath are two lines in Norwegian. Deniz must have tried to translate the verse from Turkish or else tried to write something else in Norwegian. She opens the first page of the notebook: *Deniz's Journal*. There is a date; the days following Ulla's terrible death, when he blocked his ears to our implored advice that he remain in Turkey, rather than return to Norway, and after which he never returned to our world . . . She flicks through the pages of the notebook: German, Norwegian, Turkish; notes, odd lines and verse. Most of the writing is in Turkish, although one of the longest entries is in Norwegian.

Language is a person's homeland, they say. So which is my country? Day by day I'm losing my mother tongue. That surely means my language couldn't have been my country. Where am I from? Can one be a citizen of the world? To be a citizen of the world one has to understand the language of the world. I can't understand the language of this world. I can't speak it. I'm frightened of it. Can one be a citizen of nowhere?

She closes the notebook. She places it on top of the old fugitive poet's book. With a curiosity she cannot control – fully aware that what she is doing is wrong – she tugs at the handle of a single drawer in the middle of the desk. The drawer is not locked and is in a mess – just like Deniz's childhood desk drawer. Blank paper, coloured pencils that perhaps at one time belonged to Ulla and a whole lot of useless little bits and pieces . . . A folded white envelope attracts her attention. On it is written in Turkish and Norwegian, 'For Bjørn when he grows up'. The envelope has not been stuck down and there is a compact disc inside. She never tampered with Deniz's private or personal possessions until now. She used to think that even with a child one should respect a person's privacy, that one had no right to intrude on it. But now she wonders what is on the disc. What does Deniz want Bjørn to know, to see when he is grown up? She has an idea that if she finds out she will be able to understand her son better and reach out to him.

Deniz's small computer – his camera and this computer were like an extension of his hand and arm in the old days, too – are on the table in the other corner of the room. With her heart in her mouth, afraid of her own heartbeats, she turns on the computer and pushes in the disc. The device, an old model, seems slow, and she becomes impatient. Finally a window opens on the screen. It is a disc of photographs; just four photographs. The first frame is an image of the wounded father in Iraq with a sack thrust over his head who is embracing his son; one of those photographs about which Deniz had said, 'I did not want to be party to murder by taking a photograph of suffering and spending the money earned from it. I deleted them all.' Elif looks at it again and again. Enlarging the picture, she stares at it as though wanting to engrave all the details of the helpless man and the child enfolded in his arms in her mind, in her heart. She scrutinizes the black sack thrust over the man's head, his torn plastic sandals, the child's bare feet, his small face dazed, as a result of sun, fever or shock, his lips slightly parted and parched with thirst. She sees the fear surrounding the bleeding desperate father behind the barbed wire, the fear of not being able to protect his child, his submission to fate. She sees all too clearly the suffering that Deniz has been trying to express in words to her and from which he is escaping. That year, a similar photograph, the same subject but perhaps taken from a different angle, was chosen as the photo of the year, she recalls.

When he asked about her achievements, was it revulsion at her routinely killing laboratory animals and receiving prizes for doing so that Deniz had wanted to discuss? Was her son right? She might be better off if she ejects the disc and closes the computer down at that point, but instead she clicks on the second picture. The father and child are lying dead on the dusty yellow sand of the desert. The sack over the man's head has been slightly pulled away and blood is flowing from his neck. The child has fallen on top of his father, as though he is asleep, his parched lips are still parted, his tiny feet bare . . . This photograph was not published anywhere. Deniz had told us a bit about the first picture to explain why he had run away, but he had not mentioned this one, had not been able to talk about it. It is now too late to turn off the computer. She clicks on the third photo file. In the foreground Ulla is smiling vivaciously with her wheat-coloured hair flowing round her neck and face, clasping the toy camel to her bosom, wearing the sequined belt Elif remembers and her pale-blue frumpish dress. Sultanahmet Mosque, in all its glory, can be seen in the background, and there are red tulips immediately behind her. And the last image: it is as though it has been taken the wrong way, upside down. In the background once again are the dome and minarets of Sultanahmet, while red tulips seem scattered, indistinct, lines amid grey and white smoke, pieces of paper, a toy camel and . . . and human body parts! Pieces of Ulla fly around in the air.

She remains frozen in front of the screen. Obviously the digital camera had taken the last picture with the shutter being depressed accidentally. At the moment of the explosion, before rushing over and before he lost consciousness, Deniz must have somehow hung on to the device. He must have spotted the last picture that the camera had taken some time later. An image of violence, terror and suffering; the intolerable burden . . . He has carried this burden for years! He has not shared it with anyone – not allowed us to help him. He internalized it and buried it within him. He threw it all into his bottomless black pit.

She closes the computer down. She replaces the disc in its envelope and puts it back in the drawer. Deniz will tell his son when he grows up and reaches an age when he can understand why Princess Ulla will never come back, and only then will he share with his son the reason he could not stand the world's suffering – the burden, the very heavy burden, that he felt unable to share with us.

She realizes that she will not even be able to tell her husband what she has seen. Whatever I say, it won't be enough. I do not think that we will be able to endure this together. When suffering is this painful it won't diminish the more it is talked about. When shared, if anything it will increase. I do not have the strength to deal with this. Deniz is happy with his little boy, and Bjørn is a darling. They have established a way of life to suit themselves.

When you see them you can believe that there is not just one recipe for happiness.

She realizes that from now on everything that she experiences will be in relation to these photographic images. In the background of her film of life there will always be those four rectangles. Just as they have been in Deniz's life . . .

On the desk are various pens. She does not touch them but takes out her own purple fountain pen from her bag. She writes a few lines on a blank piece of paper in front of her.

My dear, don't be angry that I didn't wait for you to return with the biggest fish. I'm sure you caught it and that Bjørn was delighted. At the moment my heart, my mind and whatever I have are all confused. I don't have the strength to stay any longer in this place that in your childhood you nicknamed the Devil's Island. I hope that you will rest for a while in this sanctuary away from the oceans and bloody seas and lick your wounds better – because you are my cat son and you know that cats heal their wounds by licking them – and live happily with your little boy. I think that this time I have managed to understand you, if only a little. Perhaps it's too late, but it is better than not at all. You're probably right. There is no single route to happiness, no single definition of a fulfilled life. I love you whatever you are and wherever you are. Kiss Bjørn for me. Tell him that fairy *Farmor* has climbed on to her magic carpet and returned to her land of mice. Very many mews and even miaows . . .

She closes the door of the room and then the front door of the house and goes out. Not locking doors is a good thing; not having to do so offers a strange sense of security. The security of those who have never experienced crime, those who have nothing to worry about or fear, those not under threat and those who have no concept of evil. Still, if I knew where the key was I would lock it just the same. My son and my little grandson live here. I'm responsible for them; just as the Little Prince is responsible for the poor rose that has only four thorns to protect itself. Deniz and Bjørn don't have any thorns.

She has emerged from the Gasthaus's door facing the sea. The dog yelps. She looks one last time at the cliffs. The image of Deniz sitting at the top talking to an unseen person below – no, the Little Prince speaking to the snake – appears before her eyes. The Pilot says 'What are you thinking about? You frighten me, my little man' to the Little Prince, who asks for help from the snake under the rock so that he can leave the world and return to his own planet.

At these big fish competitions, at the festival beer stand, on one of the thousands of tiny islands that don't even have a place on world maps, under a mask of happiness you are so lonely, so sad that you make me frightened, my little man.

There is no one around, she cannot make out why the German shepherd dog tied up in front of his kennel is barking so persistently. She guesses that he barks at strangers. Am I that stranger?

She walks with rapid steps toward the square by the quay where the jollity of the festivities is evident, by now lubricated freely by the whisky, akevitt and beer produced by traditional methods. I must reach the opposite shore before Deniz returns from fishing. I just hope there is a boat ready and that I don't have to wait long.

SIX

Can a Person Reach Other People?

On both sides of the road are shanties, poplar trees with cotton-wool-like seeds, plum trees that have shed their flowers and are beginning to bear fruit and pear saplings in blossom. As Mahmut climbs swiftly to the top of the uneven earth road he mulls over the situation. In his hand he has the address that the writer has given him and on a small piece of paper the plan that he has drawn; in his pocket is the key to the house in which he is to stay . . . No, things don't go this much according to plan; they don't run this smoothly, as if there are angels waiting by the road asking, 'What more can we do for you?' Is this all because of Zelal's pure heart? How did the writer come to be so providentially at the coach station? How did he get there? Who sent him? People like him do not travel on overnight buses. They go by plane. How did he happen to appear at our side just when Zelal was shot by that treacherous bullet that killed our child? Let us assume that he is a kind man and simply felt sorry for us. He would have given us a few *kuruş* and gone away. Or he would have taken her to hospital and vanished. A famous man; a great writer. Why should he put himself out for us?

Because he wondered what sort of person Ömer Eren was he visited a bookshop and asked for his novels. The slimmest was fifteen new lira. He had left the shop without buying anything. The author had given them money, and he had even opened an account at the bank, but, still, one must be careful. Who knows what tomorrow will bring?

The shanties lining both sides of the uphill road are surrounded by trees, hedges and tiny gardens. It is a good place, even though filthy water flows on either side of the earthen stony path, children play in the dirty water and mangy dogs rooting through the mounds of rubbish fawn around one with their tails between their legs, too lazy to bark. It is more pleasant than any of the places Mahmut knows or has lived in and is far better than the big city where he went to study.

The heaviness in his heart and the lump in his chest ease a little. The child has gone, but at least Zelal is alive. Thank God. We are still young; we can still have children. The writer had said something to that effect as a sort of consolation to him. He had said, 'New Hopes will be born.' It is true: *Hêviyên nû derdikevin pêş, ji cane te, ji xwîna te lawikêk tê dine.* And next time it would be a boy of my own flesh and blood. Perhaps the wheels of fate have started to run true now. Perhaps God has said, 'These servants of mine have suffered much. They've been sorely tested and deserve goodness and beauty from now on.'

He feels the pain that he thought would never diminish gradually wane. A pregnant woman passes by. Wearing rose-patterned baggy trousers, a headscarf edged with embroidery and carrying a bucket in each hand, she is heading for the fountain a little further down that he has just passed to collect water. So that's how it is here, too. And, what is more, this is the outskirts of the capital – barely outskirts, as we are actually in the city. Women fetch water like they do in our region – even when heavily pregnant. His thoughts turn again to the unborn baby. It was such an all-embracing love that Zelal and the child had become one. I loved them both as one person. The more I loved Zelal, the more the child seemed mine. Now . . . now the child is no more. It is as though Zelal is incomplete, is half. As though something has vanished between them, its place left empty. He cannot understand or explain. A moment ago he had felt a little less anxious, but now he feels depressed once more.

We were going to go towards the sea, to those boundless waters. Zelal yearned for the sea; for the sea that she had not seen, that she did not know, the sea that was a dream. A person's longing for a dream is greater than anything. The unknown is magical. That is why. Mahmut knows Lake Van. When he was studying at university he and his friends had been there a few times. What a beautiful stretch of water that lake was; how vast, how blue. 'But Lake Van is nothing! What they call the sea is a hundred Lake Vans, a hundred thousand Lake Vans,' Zelal had said, as though she had seen the sea. We were going to reach it. The child was going to be a child of the sea, not the mountains. 'The sea softens people; the mountains harden them,' one of the lecturers at the university had said. My father had expressed a similar sentiment. He used to say that mountains make people hard. Perhaps it is true. People are like plants; they grow hardier the more they are put under strain. The flowers at the foot of the mountains, along the riverbanks, in the valleys, have a more intense scent, while the grass is softer and its leaves more slender. Plants become tougher, thornier and more stunted the higher one climbs, but they also become more hardy.

The address he holds in his hand is where the shanties stop and the little houses with gardens begin. There are only ten or twelve houses. Some have not been completed yet; the rough construction work has been undertaken and they have been left half-finished. This must be a cooperative or something. To judge from the electricity poles, pipes and cables, they have electricity and other facilities. A tarmac road goes down the other side of the slope. People with cars do not need to climb up between the shanties. Admittedly it is a long road, a road that no one uses apart from the owners of the villas who have cars. So a road has been created just for these people!

He immediately sees the two-storey white house that the writer had described, with roses and flowers in the garden: number 7. Ömer *Abi* had said that the house belonged to a friend of his who lived abroad, that he stayed there occasionally but that no one was using it at the moment.

He had said, 'Use the lower floor, and you can take care of the house and garden. For goodness' sake, don't let me down. Look after the place well. Don't let anything get broken or ruined. In any case, there is not much in the way of furniture – no valuables or anything. But, still, be careful. If anyone around asks who you are and what you are doing there, say that you are acting as caretaker and give them the owner's telephone number or mine. Mind you don't talk too much.'

What especially warmed Mahmut's heart was the writer trusting him. He had not asked himself: Who are this couple? Are they honest? What are they going to use the house for? Neither had he wondered whether they would get him into trouble. He's obviously a good man, a man of the world.

Mahmut opens the gate, which is entwined with rambling roses, with difficulty, and he enters the garden. It is pretty, but the ground is dry. At the first opportunity he must water the garden and give the path and steps to the house a thorough cleaning. And when Zelal is better and comes here she will turn the garden into a paradise. There are two locks on the front door. Which key belongs to which hole? He has to fiddle with the door for a while. There! It's open.

The house is clean and light inside. As the writer had said, there is not much furniture. The rooms are almost empty, just the bare essentials: a sofa, two armchairs, an old round table with four chairs; in the inner room a large double bed and a wardrobe; and in the kitchen a fridge, stove, pots and pans, plates and cutlery. They are probably wealthy owners, but there are no carpets, no kilims or embroidered throws. These people have strange taste. And clearly no one has lived here for any length of time.

Once more he is astonished that everything is going so well. Only a week, ten days ago they were in deep distress. The state, the organization even the code of honour were hounding them. They were fugitives, homeless, penniless and without identity . . . Now look. He stretches out on the sofa. It is well sprung, soft and comfortable. If this is the house the owner lives in occasionally, uses just from time to time – perhaps its purpose is for bringing back women or other shady business – then God knows what his real home must be like! Things he learnt from a female comrade when she was giving them ideological training on the mountain spring to his mind. As she was explaining the concept of exploitation in her class on the principles of Marxism-Leninism, she had said, 'We cannot even begin to imagine the money the wealthy spend on their houses, food, drink and clothes, their luxuries. All this is only possible because the bourgeoisie exploit the working classes and the poor. And then the exploiters and the exploited get together and exploit us all. The workers and those who are exploited wage a class war against the bourgeoisie – the exploiters – and take power by revolution. And, as for us, because we are all exploited and crushed, our rich, our poor, our aghas, our peasants, all of us together wage a national war of liberation against the ruling nation that crushes us.'

Yes, that is true! The houses of the sheikhs, the masters in our region, even their tables cannot compete with the ones here. He suddenly feels hungry and thirsty. What a good thing I had the presence of mind to get a portion of *döner* and bread. He goes to the kitchen and opens the fridge. There is just water, a few bottles of some kind of alcohol that he does not recognize, a few eggs and a pack of margarine. But the fridge had been left on; no one worries about electricity bills or wasting energy.

The cold water does him good. Am I out of condition? Of course not! Climbing that slope in the heat of Ankara's early summer would affect even a guerrilla. A guerrilla, eh? A fugitive guerrilla, a traitorous guerrilla, a guerrilla who deserves execution, a *caş*! I hope to God they think I died as a martyr. If they saw me rolling down the hill they would have thought there was no hope for me. Perhaps they didn't even see me; everyone was preoccupied with their own troubles. No, the *hevals* would not do that. If they had noticed that I was wounded they would have done everything in their power to help me. They would not leave a comrade there like that; they would not leave him to die. We've been through a lot together. Our belief, our hope, our enthusiasm, death, fear, rage, pain and disappointments . . . Lying on our backs under the starry skies and taking drags from a shared cigarette, our traditional songs, our little secrets . . . When he thinks about the people on the mountains his heart aches. Bad things used to happen, too. For sure, there were also rotten guys, but what about the others, my close friends? I left them there and ran away.

'I ran away,' he says in a loud voice. Who will hear it here? 'I ran away, see? I ran away . . .' He has to assimilate this, his mind, his heart and, above all, his conscience has to get used to this fact.

I ran away because I was scared. If I hadn't run away I would have been disciplined. This time it would be no joke. It would not be like the first time.

At the camp, during the second month of training, he had been sent for discipline for two weeks. In the disciplinary cave there were almost twenty men; he recalls the smell of sweat, foul breath and dirt, having to request permission to relieve oneself three times a day and receiving two meals of bread and water. What had I done? What was my crime? He had wondered about it then, and he thinks about it now. They had wanted him to undergo a public self-criticism in front of the whole camp. He had not regarded it as demanding. A militant who had committed a crime should face what he had done and be prepared to make a frank confession in front of his comrades. He should expose his misconduct, should purge himself. That much was agreed. But I wasn't guilty. I didn't feel guilty. I hadn't done anything to warrant self-criticism. I had just secretly taken a few cigarettes, a piece of mirror and greetings to one of the troops in discipline – someone from our neighbourhood who was very young. Apart from those on duty, contact was forbidden with the men being disciplined. However, I knew the boy was afraid and that he needed support – not punishment. Perhaps the traditional methods of discipline would have continued, but Mahmut was in luck. Just then, for some unknown reason, tension had erupted in the command of the region's mountain cadre and, according to rumour, it had turned to infighting. The revised training advice that came down from the top, in which it was emphasized that discipline and democracy were inseparable, that the broadest democratic debate should not conflict with inflexible punishment, had changed the atmosphere in the camp, and disciplining had been brought to an end.

If he faced punishment again he might not be so fortunate. This time there was no tangible accusation. But, still, he felt he was continually under surveillance.

It was when the operations and fighting had intensified. They had brought a young girl to the camp, wounded and covered with blood; they had dumped her on the ground. She was moaning and still bleeding from her wounds. She needed immediate attention. He had been amazed that no one took any notice of her or asked where the medics were, and when he learnt they were in the commander's cave had run to fetch them. He had tried to explain the situation as speedily as possible and asked them to come immediately to look at the girl or at least allow him to tend to her. After all, he had studied at medical school. He had not even noticed that the medics were busy attending to the commander who had stomach cramps. While waiting for the medical team to assist, he had held the hand of the girl who was pleading in fear of death and moaning in pain, and he tried to give her hope. But by the time they arrived she was dead. He had just looked at their faces and gone off without a word.

When he was summoned to the commander's cave he had not felt nervous. The man had asked just two questions: whether he had met the girl before and why he hadn't spoken to the medics after she died. The commander had said, 'Those who cannot stand the sight of blood, those who cannot stomach our female comrades being martyred for the sake of the cause, cannot walk this gruelling path. If she was left on the ground like that, there is a reason for it. We had information that she was an agent. Everyone must do their duty, comrade. Recent reports about you are not encouraging. They say you are incapable of teamwork. We are going through difficult times. Watch your step!' The meaning of the man's words was clear: if we were not in the middle of fighting, if we did not need men to bear arms, you would be locked up.

Was it really like that, or was I getting paranoid? Hadn't we witnessed many comrades being taken for disciplining or even being executed? Were all those who ran away traitors? You cannot call what happened to me running away. I was shot – by whose bullet? If only I knew! I was shot, and I rolled down the slope. I didn't run away. Don't lie to yourself. You didn't roll – you rolled yourself down the slope. And what's more, your wound wasn't serious. '*Xayin*, traitor!'

What is the point of brooding about this now, just as things are beginning to improve? He tries to cheer up. I'm not the first to run away. Hundreds of them came down from the mountain and gave themselves up. What happened to me was different, that's all.

He had not wished to surrender in the conventional way. First you go to the north and seek asylum with Barzani's forces. Then, accompanied by them, at the border you give yourself up to the authorities of the Turkish Republic or TC. Or else you drop into the first military post that you reach. *Aleykümselam*! Then it is time for prison and confession. Well, that just would not do. I'm not a *caş*. A *caş* is one of the living dead. Better to die than to be a *caş*!

When he dwells on the word *caş* he realizes that he is thinking in Turkish and is astonished. In the village, at school and on the mountain and when he was with Zelal he used to think in Kurdish. Since the night Zelal was shot and lost her child he often thinks in Turkish. Isn't that also a form of treachery? Isn't that losing your language, your identity? 'What is more important than independence and armed conflict is to form and strengthen our national identity, to gain our self-confidence as individuals, to build up our identity through our self-confidence,' so said the *heval*, called 'the Doctor', who had joined the movement from the west. He was a good man, courageous and with profound wisdom. And he also said – this had lodged in Mahmut's mind – 'Identities must not overpower each other. If you are a Turk you must not think of Kurds as the enemy, and if you are a Kurd you must not think of Turks as enemies. Nationalism is an evil virus. You must not let it enslave your soul. You can fight for your national identity and if necessary for independence but not by violating the rights of others to their identity. Let us not forget; the worst tyranny comes from the downtrodden.' This was typical of the Doctor. Some listened to him attentively, and others would drift away from his inner circle less impressed or even hostile. One day he quietly and unobtrusively disappeared; no explanation was given. It was said that he had been sent to Europe, that he had been promoted. And there were those who said that he spoke too much. He broadcast the dilemmas in his mind.

What the Doctor had left Mahmut was a sense of the importance of self-confidence and of being reconciled to one's identity. While he was at school they had been made to read poems for National Sovereignty and Children's Day as well as Republic Day: 'I am a Turk. My religion and my race are great'; or every morning before lessons began, 'I am a Turk, I am just and I am hard-working . . . May my existence be a gift to the existence of Turkey.'

He used to think: why don't I read the poem as 'I am a Kurd. My religion and my race are great'? Why don't we say, 'I am a Kurd, I am just and I am hard-working.' Cannot a Kurd's religion and race be great? Cannot a Kurd be just and hard-working? In history lessons, in civics, in Turkish lessons, they used to learn about important Turks, Turkish customs and Turkish victories. But are there no important Kurds? Have the Kurds never won victories? Why does Atatürk entrust the country to the Turkish youth? Does he not trust the Kurdish youth? They used to debate such matters among themselves. Their childish minds and childish hearts could not comprehend what was at stake.

At school their teacher used to say, 'We are all Turks. There is no such thing as a Kurd. It's a fabrication of the separatist traitors.' Then one day they shot him as he was returning from holiday to the village. Actually he was a good man; he had never so much as lifted a finger to a pupil in punishment. He tried desperately to teach the children Turkish, about Atatürk and how to read and write. The pupils had been sorry when he was killed. But if we are all Turks, what is this language we speak among ourselves? Why do they scream, 'Dishonourable, separatist Kurds! Armenian spawn!' when they come to raid our villages? If everyone is a Turk, what is it you want?

These questions arose in their minds but were not expressed in words. At school Mahmut had happened to pose a question one day. 'In our village people spoke Kurdish. No one spoke Turkish until they moved to the town. Wouldn't you call someone who spoke Kurdish a Kurd, sir?' He received an answer from the sharp edge of a ruler landing on his head. They had investigated whether there were members of the Kurdistan Workers' Party or PKK in his family. In those days his brother had not yet taken to the mountains. He learnt that Kurdishness was shameful, was a lie, that some traitors convinced the mountain Turks that they were Kurds, that everyone living in this country was Turkish and that to claim otherwise was a betrayal of the homeland and the flag. The main thing he learnt was that he should not ask questions on the subject. It would be better for him to forget Kurdishness, a sorry fate, a punishment that God had given to his wayward servants.

In his childhood and adolescence, especially after their village was burnt and they had moved to the town, his mother's threat 'I'm going to come to school and speak to your teacher!' was what Mahmut feared most. This was because his mother did not know Turkish. She used to go around in clothes typical of Kurdish women. He knew he would be humiliated if she came to school dressed like that. He would be ashamed of his mother, then ashamed of himself for being ashamed of her. What was all that about being reconciled with your identity and self-confidence, Comrade Doctor?

How can we be reconciled to this identity that we carry as a curse and shame? When our identity is so battered and derided, how can we have self-confidence? If, for example, the owner of this house arrives and asks where I'm from, what answer do I give, especially if he were to ask directly if I'm a Kurd? It never used to occur to people very often to enquire, but now they ask quite openly: Are you Kurdish? Are you Alevi? What would I do if someone came and asked me outright? He makes a decision: if anyone enquires he will stand and answer, 'I'm Kurdish.'

I ran away, but all those people are not fighting in vain; all those people have not died for nothing. It would not be manly to betray them. Again he feels a pang of sadness: I ran away from the front. Was it because I was afraid? No, that wasn't it. Fear is not unconquerable. You steel yourself, and you overcome it. And sometimes you are so tired of life that death is preferable.

No, it was not from fear. Nor death, pain or the arduous conditions in the resistance . . . If you have faith in the leadership, trust in the comrades and belief in the cause then all this is of no importance! It was neither the hard life in the camps, nor the fighting, nor fear that led to all those people, young and old, being branded 'traitors', '*caş*', 'turncoats'. You see it was that question; that treacherous question that gnawed at the enthusiasm of the first days and first months: the question, 'Why am I here? I'm here, and what has changed?' Woe betide that it should start to trouble the heart and mind! Then it grows inwards and turns into a malignant growth; and, whether one is on the mountain or is a prisoner, it eats a person up.

In the small town we call our village, our hamlet or '*bajar*', which consists of a main street (either Republic Street or Homeland Street), a square (either Atatürk Square or Republic Square), two rows of squalid shops and an imposing office block, we have people as rich as Croesus, grand state buildings and, a little further away, the military garrison. We, who live there without hope, without a future, downtrodden, poor and bereft, go up the mountain to fight to be regarded as human beings – as somebodies – and to have hope and dignity in our identity. The fires burning on the mountains (not shepherds' fires but the fires of rebellion), the songs echoing in the valleys (not songs of love but calls to war), the cries rising from the villages (not laments of mourning but the yells of daily life) are all sacred signs promising a paradise on earth. We run like moths flying towards the light, to take a stand in this fight and escape from being nobodies and 'spineless bastards'. We listen to the sounds of the mountains; we obey their call.

It's a little like when you walk along a road and hold out a match to some-one who asks for a light; well, that is how we offer ourselves up – simply and without ceremony. We do this to reconcile ourselves with our identity, to gain self-confidence, to enter the ranks of men and, primarily, to be heroes in our own eyes. Then one day we see that every step we take to strengthen our identity, to gain self-confidence, all the values that until then have been exalted in theory – to ask, to question, to think freely – have suddenly become a crime. Then the Devil whispers the question that would make a saint swear, 'Why am I here? What am I fighting for?' Some people ask no questions. They just carry on like that until the end . . . The end? What is there at the end?

It was not death he was running from. Even though he could not bring himself to think it or to say it, a voice inside him whispered, 'You did not betray. You are not a traitor, you are a human being.' The real escape – perhaps betrayal – began not when he was rolling himself down the slope; it began in Zelal's arms. They had dreamt of far-away seas together. Embracing each other, they had imagined the unknown blueness, the balmy air, the little two-roomed house and Hevi playing in the sand, swim-ming in the waves and growing up like the children there, as one of them. Like Adam and Eve, the world consisted of just Mahmut and Zelal. They had no need of temptation by the snake or the forbidden fruit to be cast out of that paradise of a refuge in which they had shut themselves and nurtured hope in their hearts and bodies. It fitted the whole universe into the hollow of a cave and the lee of a grove impervious to light and was as eternal. What they had experienced was the forbidden fruit itself, the original sin. It was the first step towards betraying the mountains.

Now, having been cast out of the mountains, having betrayed the cause, exiled from love and passion and feeling all alone – and without hope of making the happiness that life had offered with the unborn child and of recreating themselves together with the child – Mahmut is sitting forlornly in a strange house in the unfamiliar distant district of a city that he has never been to before. In one hand, half a loaf stuffed with *döner*, in the other a bottle of water, a lead weight in his heart and fog in his mind. We are not used to comfort. These negative thoughts, this pessimism, is because comfort grates. Everything will come right when Zelal is better and we are together once more. The fog will lift. We have lost the child – but not to worry! We are still young. We have a whole life in front of us; our Hevi, our shared hope, Zelal's and my son will be born.

The writer had said, 'Don't wander around too much. Be careful. You know that better than I. It's obvious that you're in trouble. Wait for my return to decide what you are going to do. Zelal should first get out of hospital and recuperate. I'll join you, and then we'll think of a permanent solution. And mind you don't forget; you are responsible not only for yourself but for Zelal, too. It's your mutual decision that will determine your fate – not yours alone. At the moment you are safe in the house. If you are careful, no one will be able to locate you. If anything happens, call me straight away on my phone.'

He really was safe in that house – safer than ever before. No one would come and set fire to the place. No one would drive him out. The house would not be raked by heavy machine-guns during night raids, the walls would not be full of bullet-holes. For the first time he had access to money in his pocket – even if not in his own name. The writer was smart; he knew about these things. If anyone was following us he could potentially track us down from a bank account. But here Mehmut had a secure bank card whose pin number he knew and which he could use if he needed to. He even had a mobile phone provided by the writer.

The man who had supplied all this – was he a human or a guardian angel? – had embarked on a journey to the burnt mountains, houses riddled with bullet-holes, derelict villages, charred landscapes and mourning houses. Mahmut could not understand it. Did comfort disturb him, too? Was he a little nuts? He could not make out the answer to these questions.

When he put it to him and tried to find out, Ömer had said, 'It's hard to explain, but perhaps you can grasp my situation. Did not you and Zelal say to me, "If you are looking for the word, then go and look for it in its place"? In fact, I'm heading to your homeland for the same reason that you went up the mountain. I've been in a state of confusion for a very long time. I have to pull myself together. I have to come to terms with everything, with everyone, with myself.'

'Why our region, *abi*? I'm not saying don't go – don't misunderstand me. But it's our homeland, our land. We would give our lives for it. But what's someone like you going to find there? Poverty, hopelessness, burnt-out and wrecked villages, mined and deadly roads, hamlets where the traditional songs may no longer be heard, countryside that has lost its herdsmen and its flocks . . . And the area is dangerous. Operations have started up again – landmines and all. After the war, what is left in our homeland for people like you?'

'Perhaps there is still something. If there is still a slim hope, a light, perhaps it has remained there. In our youth we used to believe that we would save the world. Of course we didn't succeed. We were defeated. Most of us gave up the struggle, surrendered and toed the line. But there was always something lacking within us. That's what I'm in pursuit of.'

'In other words you're going to look for what is lacking in you in our homeland. *Inşallah*, you'll find it, *abi*.'

'There is a saying – I don't know whether you've heard it – "The morning light comes from the east." There is something stirring, alive in the east, a sign of life emerging from death, a hope of change. But perhaps it just seems so to me; perhaps it's intellectual romanticism, the illusion of a writer. However, an inner voice tells me that I shall achieve something there, that even if I don't find what I lost I shall understand better why I lost it. It has something to do with my son. Perhaps following in your footsteps to the east will help me to understand, find and regain him.'

Mahmut had not quite grasped what the writer was talking about, but he had sensed the integrity in his heart. He kept remembering his saying 'perhaps' and understood that there were some things the writer could not unravel either. For the most part he had been curious about the writer's son. If a man saw his woman blown to smithereens before his eyes what would happen, how would he live, how does he manage not to become a killer? If I had found the person who shot Zelal I would have killed him. You die on the mountains, in war, and you kill; however, you don't kill each other out of revenge. There has to be a cause for which people die and will kill; an abstract thing, born of ideas. Neither soldier nor guerrilla knows the other. If there weren't a war and they could meet in the village coffee houses they would be friends. There are many guerrillas whose mates, cousins and neighbours are soldiers. There are even those whose brothers are soldiers. There, in the midst of gunfire, you are a heartless weapon of destruction, anonymous and without feeling, just like a stray bullet, a mortar or a mine . If you start to think about this, you won't be able to fight as you did before. God forbid that you should begin to have doubts! Once you have doubts, you are finished as a fighter. First you question why you are fighting, and then it gradually starts to seem meaningless; in time you will forget why you are fighting, lose focus and become confused. Finally you will end up being regarded as a murderer or a traitor, a traitor to that side or this – whereas you had set off on this road to be a hero.

Perhaps the writer's son had originally wanted to be a hero, but apparently he had failed and run away. Who knows why? If you see your woman killed in front of your eyes, you either kill or run. But the son never saw who killed the mother of his child. Dirty work, treachery. One plants a bomb or one lays a mine; now they are all remote-controlled. Then whom it strikes is the luck of the draw. He thinks about the mines he has laid and shudders. When you lay mines or plant bombs in rubbish bins and buses, when you are operating in a city, you don't know who it will strike: treacherous hand, treacherous bomb, treacherous heart. But still you do it. Someone has to do the dirty work for the noble cause of the people, to comply with the leaders' orders, for victory. You have to accept from the start that the 'one' will be you. This, too, is a kind of heroism; self-sacrifice. The whole issue is about having no doubt that this dirty work contributes to the final victory; not asking what sort of victory is won by killing or maiming innocent people, wasting innocent lives. Not questioning the leadership or the organization even for a moment. If you question, if you doubt, you cannot function. Everything is organized for you not to think, not to hesitate. Isn't it like that in the army, too? Let us say you are a soldier, a Turkish soldier. Can you afford to challenge the legitimacy of an operation on which you are engaged? God only knows what would happen to you if you were to question your superiors! You cannot fight asking questions. Even at home, as a child, if you ask too many questions grown-ups say, 'You mustn't delve or dwell on that. You mustn't think too deeply, or you'll lose your mind.' It's the same in war.

He is thinking about all this as he goes down the slope between the shanties decorated with spindly poplar trees, colourful geraniums and fuchsias flowering in tin flowerpots. From the yellow rambling rose trying to climb a wall of one of the jerry-built houses he stealthily picks a few buds to take to Zelal. There are no roses at home, but they are the flowers of love, the flowers of fairytales. She likes wild flowers: snowdrops, the harbingers of spring, bluebells, yellow daisies and purple wild tulips. Now, like the townspeople, I'm taking her roses. What more can she want!

As he approaches the main road he looks carefully around. Among the long-coated headscarved women waiting for the bus, girls in jeans, poorly dressed men with sweaty armpits and creased jackets with sagging pockets at the bus stand opposite he notices two rather tall men in dark suits, with dark complexions, standing very straight. Taking cover behind the electricity posts, he observes the men. They are some way off. He cannot make out their faces, but it is clear they are not from round here. Mainly people from the Black Sea and from Sivas live in the shanties on the hills that over-look the capital from a distance; the people in the district on the one side of the hill are from Sivas and Çorum and the people in the district on the other side are from Kastamonu, Cide and Inebolu.

These two men are from our region. A person knows his fellow country-men from their mien, their gait and their appearance; he knows them from the way they swing their arms and the way they walk, from their nervous scanning of the surroundings and their tense stance like that of animals on the prowl. I am not suspicious of others but of my own people. I am wary of them because they look as though they are from the east. How terrible is that! Well, what about me? Am I not nervous like them, ready to flee like a trapped animal? If they saw me they would recognize me, too – immedi-ately realize that I am a Kurd.

The two tall swarthy men stand there combing the surroundings with their eyes. A bus and two minibuses stop briefly and the stand becomes relatively empty, but still they wait. Perhaps their minibus or bus has not yet arrived. Perhaps they are from Sivas; the Alevis there look like us. I am being overcautious. He remembers the words he heard during the training on the mountain. One of the comrades from the capital who had been to university and had come to train them had said, 'Being paranoid does not mean that you are not being followed.' Perhaps I am right to be wary. He considers all eventualities: they could be from the state, from the organi-zation or they could be from Zelal's family. When he thinks about the last possibility a chill runs down his spine, despite Ankara's late June heat. He breaks into a cold sweat. So as not to attract attention he retreats slowly back up the slope and turns into the first street he reaches. He has the same bad feeling in his chest as he did when he went off to fight on the mountain. A feeling as though millions of voracious insects are chomping at his heart, as though a cold bubble of air comes from his chest and grows and bursts inside him. When the fighting begins you no longer feel afraid and you don't think any more. You programme yourself to kill so as not to be killed. While you fight you are as brave as can be. And even now, if the men drew their guns and came at me, fear would vanish. Waiting is the worst. As you wait, you think, and the more you think the more you fear. He remembers that he is unarmed. He has not had a weapon since he and Zelal came down from the mountain. He does not want to carry one any longer. Recalling the arms on the mountain, he smiles to himself. How absurd it would be to wander around the city with such weapons! He looks at the rosebuds that he still clasps in his hand. The thorns have pricked his palm and have made it bleed a little. As he walks slowly between the shanties he feels that roses are safer than weapons, that they protect people better. No one would suspect somebody wandering around with a bunch of roses. Such a person would be less likely to get shot. His fear and panic evaporate as he walks, but, still, he decides to go down to the main road from the south side of the hill and catch a minibus from the bus stand immediately before the one he had just approached. I mustn't get into trouble because I'm trying to take a short cut.

The minibus is so full that he can hardly get on. He holds his arm in the air trying to protect the roses. They must not be crushed; nor must they wilt before he arrives at the hospital. Someone in the crowd accidentally jabs his bad arm, which aches horribly. To avoid arousing suspicion and being interrogated he has not received professional medical treatment for his injury. He had not even mentioned it to the writer. If he had, Ömer would have had a trustworthy doctor friend look at it. However, he does not want to get the man into more trouble. His wound is healing by the day. Zelal had laughed when she was dressing it one day and said, 'You were shot from behind while running away. The bullet just grazed you, so don't make a fuss.' How smart she is. Some men find it hard to deal with clever women. He knows it can be hard, but it does not bother him. He loves everything about Zelal, including her mental agility .

His arm keeps aching. I hope to God the wound does not open up again. He clenches his teeth and keeps quiet and focuses on keeping the roses safe. The minibus is crammed so full that passengers are hanging on right at the door. The vehicle does not even stop at the bus stand where the two tall men are waiting. What a good thing I did not wait at that stop! Anyway the minibuses on this route are infrequent. If I had waited there I would not have been able to get on at all. Every cloud has a silver lining. Ignoring the pain in his arm or the jeopardy to the roses, he cranes towards the minibus window and tries to see the stand. He glimpses one of the men still waiting there, leaning against the post of the bus-stand. Perhaps I am mistaken. I'm nervous and overexcited. It's because I'm frightened. Fear makes a person imagine things.

He has known fear ever since his youth, and he knows that it exaggerates the object of fear like a magnifying mirror, distorts it and makes it worse. From the depths of his memory a saying or proverb comes to mind: 'A rabbit does not run away because it is frightened. It is frightened because it runs away.'

We wanted to run away from fear, to conquer fear; we thought we could quickly cross to the other side of fear like crossing the border. Now the more we run, the greater our fear . . . He is overcome with despair. You think that things have sorted themselves out, that your luck has changed, that it's smiling on you, and suddenly you see the frightening dark night again. Not even your love, though it is as mighty as the mountains and vast as the sky, will suffice to reach the daylight. However firmly you embrace the ones you love, you cannot keep them, you cannot protect them – neither Zelal nor Hevi. What we experienced beside the spring in that secret corner of the grove that did not allow even light to penetrate was a dream, a fantasy, a story, or another life that we visited through God's wisdom. Real life is full of hazard.

He feels totally exhausted. His head is spinning, and if he was not in a public place he would slump to the ground. He thinks it would not even be possible to slump in the overcrowded minibus. He would just stand there suspended. It was not *déjà vu*. He had already experienced this feeling of anxiety a long time ago in his childhood when, stuffed like tinned sardines in the trailer of a tractor, he went to work with others down on the plain. It was anxiety about the days to come rather than claustrophobia that had caused his sense of panic. Is life something like this? Is a better life, another world, not possible?

He had asked this question for the first time as a small child, as he rested his cheek against the chest of the black-nosed puppy he had clutched when their village was evacuated and they had to migrate to foreign parts, to foreign regions, to places unknown. Behind them the village had been set on fire. The onions in the garden ready for harvesting, the mandrakes and the spindly pear saplings, cats, dogs and chickens were burning fiercely. Those who could had taken a few of their large animals, cows and goats, with them – not to raise but to slaughter and sell when required. Such a lament rang in his ears that it was as though a sob had broken forth from the village and mountain and had echoed on the peaks and reached the migrating caravan. Was life something like that? If it was like that, what was the point of it? The question had gone round in circles in his childish head and was answered in the language of a child. If it is like that, then better that it isn't; if it is like that, then better not to live. Years later when he had become a young man and was looking for the answer to the question 'But how?' he had realized it was not that simple.

'Study and get a career. I've set aside everything I can to ensure your future. I'm going to send you to university. You are going to study. You will become a doctor. If not, you can become a teacher. I couldn't do it for your elder brothers. I could not save them from the mountains, but you will be saved,' his father used to say.

'You cannot be saved on your own. You cannot be saved by selling your people. You will be saved with your people,' his elder brother used to say. When they went to pick cotton or nuts in the summer the bigger boys from the towns used to lower their voices and say, 'The workers, the proletariat, will be saved by revolution, by socialism.' In the camps in the mountains, the comrades who trained them used to talk about the salvation of the Kurdish people and explain that it would not be individual salvation, just as his brother had said. However, the answer as to how the Kurdish people would be saved was less clear. It would change from time to time.

Only the Doctor said anything really original. 'The key to salvation is within the people themselves. If you really know why you are here, what you are fighting for and if you believe in yourself and the job you are doing, you will be close to salvation. The salvation of a person and the people comes from their attaining an identity and their proud and confident sense of belonging.' His statement was clearly significant, but it was less straightforward than Marxist dogma. For this reason some were suspicious of him. If someone said something tricky to grasp – not the standard revolutionary maxims committed to memory by most of the mountain leaders – one should approach that person warily.

When they arrived with all their belongings – pots and pans, beds and quilts wrapped up in bundles in the kilims handwoven by the women – that they had carried on their backs and dragged all that way, with their poverty and homelessness, and their fears, desperation and rebellion, to the banks of the streams of the other city where the capital city's sewage flowed, the question had already been answered. A prison sentence awaited; like a seal of fate, an irrevocable, irreversible, iron-clad sentence.

A discordant polyphonic choir composed of poverty, deprivation, abuse and humiliation had provided the answer. What Mahmut wanted was to be considered a human being, not a doormat; just Mahmut, the person Mahmut, the man Mahmut – not a contemptible separatist. It was that simple, straightforward and innocent . . . Afterwards it became compulsory. It was the mountains. The mountains that would not let you be Mahmut but called you as a conscript to the liberation army, a hero, a guerrilla, a *havel* Mahmut. The mountains that promised to take those wriggling along the ground like worms, hanging around the shanties and rubbish heaps of the cities, without food, work or hope, and carry them to the peaks, to a world in which they could live without fear or shame . . . The mountains that sucked the blood of so many and spat out the dregs, that, at the risk of your life, brainwashed you into believing that there was no other life and never would be. The mountains from which he ran away . . .

Now here in the minibus, the wilted and now crushed yellow roses in his hand, squashed between people packed tightly like sheep being taken to the market for slaughter, miserably thinking that he has been unable to find the right answer to the question, he is afraid that he will yet again fail the lesson of life.

He is confused, troubled and exhausted. If he could sing a folk song it would cheer him up, but this is impossible on the bus. He feels suffocated, stifled. Gathering up all his remaining strength he calls out that he wants to get off – without paying heed to where he is and without worrying as to whether anyone is following him. His voice is like a cry for help. The driver brakes suddenly, and the passengers lurch forward and fall on top of one another. As Mahmut hurls himself out the door he does not even notice the man who gets out behind him.

While Zelal waits for visiting hours and for Mahmut to appear at the door she closes her eyes and pretends to sleep so that she does not have to speak to the elderly patient next to her. A few days have gone by since the woman had been operated on and put into the empty bed in the room. The first day she had barely regained consciousness; the next day she had started to come round, and since then, apart from when she slept, she had not stopped moaning and groaning. 'How can I wait until a single room is free? How can I lie here among peasants – Kurds to boot?' she wailed. She cursed the hospital management and the insurance company, asking every nurse when she would be able to move to a deluxe single room. 'Do you know who I am?' she demanded and would cry when no one paid attention to her.

The more the woman went on about 'peasants' and 'Kurds' the more Zelal's patience was tried, and in a thick eastern accent she had raged, 'Why are you going on about having to share a room with Kurds and peasants? I'm the only one here! Or are you seeing double, you old witch?'

The elderly woman was not to be intimidated. 'What are people like you doing in this place? This is a private hospital – not for the likes of you!

Before long you will be driving us out of our own land, our own hospitals. You Kurdish separatists! I guess it's not your fault. It's the fault of those who have put you here!'

Zelal had not backed down. 'Now look. Don't go on like this, or the real PKK will be along – and then you'll be for it!'

When Mahmut came in to visit with the battered yellow roses in his hand – he had learnt from Ömer about bringing patients flowers and thought the sight of them would make Zelal feel better – the expression on the face of the woman in the next bed was a sight to behold. It was a mixture of fear, contempt and despair . . . Meanwhile Zelal had cheered up. She thought to herself: It serves you right! Be terrified, you horrid old witch! She winked at Mahmut who was nervous anyway when he saw a stranger lying in the bed that formerly had been empty. Zelal had said loudly in her best Turkish, 'This lady does not like Kurds very much.'

Mahmut held out one of the rosebuds to the old woman saying, 'Why is that then? Kurds, Turks, Arabs – aren't we all human beings?' He added politely, 'Get well soon!'

The woman did not actually decline the rose but put it beside her pillow without a word of thanks and turned her back on the couple. Zelal knew that she was listening to them, trying not to miss a single word.

Mahmut described the house Ömer Eren had arranged for them at length. He spoke Turkish when necessary so that the woman did not get suspicious. Chiefly he talked about the house's garden to please Zelal, mentioning especially the roses, pansies and the expanse of grass. He was cautious. He did not utter the writer's name; he referred to him as *abi*. And he did not give away the location of the house. It did not matter how much the woman heard. She would not be able to work out whether the little palace was to the west or the east.

Zelal asked in Kurdish rather sadly, rather indifferently, '*Ya paşê?* And after that?'

'After that? After that will be fine.' If it worked out they could stay on as caretakers in that house, at least until they had managed to recuperate a little, until the writer returned and a place could be arranged near the sea.

As Zelal listened to what he was saying with closed eyes and a faint smile on her pretty face he thought that they were sharing the same dream and was happy. Since those days when they stayed in the cave on the mountain, his wound washed by the healing waters of the fountain and dressed with the heat of Zelal's kisses – how many days, how many weeks had passed, perhaps even a month, he didn't know – it was their sharing the dream of salvation and happiness that kept them alive, strong and hopeful. Until the stray bullet came and killed the hope in Zelal's womb, their dreams were full of life as though they could come true at any minute. Now perhaps once again . . . once again . . . The light entering the window struck Zelal's face, which had grown slightly thinner and appeared drained, and her corn-coloured hair spread out on the pillow. The rays on her face promised new hope.

Mahmut gets carried away and as he becomes emotional he reverts back to Kurdish. '*Edî çarenûsa me ji me re dikeni, tu saxbe bes e.* Fortune is smiling on us now, Zelal, you'll see. Just get better!'

Zelal remains silent, her eyes closed.

'You just get better. We are young. We'll work. And we'll reach the sea. The writer promised me; he said that on his return he would take us to the sea. He is hurting, too. His son went off and left him. He hadn't grown into a responsible man. We are, in some way, a substitute for his boy, he told me. He's in our homeland now. You know, you told him, "Go and look for the word in its place." Well, off he went!'

'The writer is a good man, but he doesn't know anything about us. Even if he travels every inch of our country he still won't understand us. He will get upset, and he'll worry about our situation. Now that he's met us he will never be the same again. However, he won't know us. Don't get angry if I say that his word won't be enough to get us to the sea. And even if we reach the sea, the day we arrive we will begin to miss the mountains. At the moment we are dwelling on our dreams because we are confused. When I get better and get out of here and we start working as caretakers in the stranger's house, then our hearts will be divided between here and there. The mountains will lure us – even if there is death at the end.'

Why is the girl so pessimistic, so bitter? Supposing she had died right there, supposing the writer had not come to their rescue in time . . . Why can't she be pleased? Why can't she be thankful? My beloved trusts neither man nor fate. It's as though she doesn't even trust me. Has she been so intimidated, so badly treated?

Just as he is about to respond they hear the woman lying in the next bed. 'What language is that you are speaking?' Her voice is not kind, not curious either, but menacing.

'You know bloody well, so why do you ask? It's Kurdish. That's how we speak. That's our language! If you don't like it, ask them to move you to another room!' snaps Zelal.

Mahmut grows nervous. He admires her recklessness and obstinacy but is afraid that they will get into trouble.

'God forgive us, we have got to the stage where we can't protect our own language. You've overrun our cities, taken them from us, and we can no longer walk safely in our streets. There is no peace – not even in hospital,' says the woman angrily but somewhat subdued.

Mahmut jumps in quickly before giving Zelal a chance to reply. 'We are not doing you any harm, *teyze*. This is our language. Where we live they speak Kurdish and in some places Zaza. We can talk to each other more easily in our own language. It is the language of our mothers. Our mothers don't know any other tongue. It's not their fault. Everyone speaks better, more sweetly in their mother tongue. If the words we speak are about love and goodness, what does it matter if they are spoken in this language or that?'

The woman turns her back on them again and is quiet. Mahmut is filled with unease.

'That's what I mean,' says Zelal in Kurdish. 'What am I doing stuck next to people who insult the language I speak, the language I heard when I was born? With whose words I was loved, with whose lullabies I was lulled and with whose oaths I was beaten.'

How poetically she expresses herself, thinks Mahmut. This woman is something else . . . And, what is more, what she says is true. His heart warms, his youthful body warms and he desires his woman. He thinks how much he loves Zelal and trembles with the fear of losing her. I must not leave her here next to this malevolent old woman. Zelal is a wild rose, a wild but very beautiful rose. Her thorns cannot protect her. If she is plucked, she will be crushed and she will fade. Just as he is thinking he is the legendary Rüstemê Zal, happily riding the horse of hope at full gallop, his heart is overcome with despair. I am the only support she can rely on, that she can trust. How far can I protect my rose? And who will protect me? If only the writer had not left us before Zelal was discharged from hospital. If only I had told him not to go. I don't know whether he would have listened. He was obviously in a hurry to leave. It was clear that his heart was troubled, constricted. Whether it is to do with him or the world or whatever is any-body's guess, but he is undoubtedly troubled.

The other patient's visitors arrive carrying plastic bags. They are a pleasant-faced, kindly couple. They wish Zelal a speedy recovery as they pass by. The old woman says something in a low voice to them. She is evidently complaining about her neighbour in the next bed. Mahmut says in Turkish in a loud voice so that the visitors can hear, 'I've spoken to your doctor, and they will discharge you within a few days' – although they both know that Zelal should stay for at least another week or ten days.

With her sharp wit Zelal grasps the situation and joins in the game. The frown on her face gives way to the wicked, roguish expression of a child. 'We seem to be disturbing *teyze*. Let's hope I'll be discharged as soon as possible so that she will be comfortable. Besides, we keep on talking in our own language with its harsh tone,' she says in Turkish loudly.

The young male visitor interjects, evidently trying to apologize for his mother. 'Oh, my dear, don't mention it. Why should you think you are disturbing her? Why should you think you speaking in a harsh tone of voice? Everyone's language is beautiful. Our mother is rather old, and her illness has unsettled her.'

'You can see that the son knows what she's like!' murmurs Zelal to Mahmut in Kurdish.

'It doesn't matter,' says Mahmut in Turkish. '*Teyze* is right, too. It's difficult to share a room with a stranger. *Inşallah*, we'll all feel better soon.' Then he has a idea. 'Something totally unexpected happened to us. We were waiting in the coach station for our bus to go home and kiss our parents' hands. A stray bullet, some hooligan's bullet, hit Zelal, and we lost the baby in her womb – our baby.' He is no longer himself and gets carried away by the tragic tale that he tells to move the bad-tempered woman and the young couple. For a moment he forgets it is his own story.

'Good grief,' says the woman visitor. 'What sort of country has this place become! You never know what will happen when you are walking in the street. I hope you get better soon. At least you're alive, thank goodness. You're still young. You'll have healthy children, *inşallah*.'

'Thank you, *kardeşim*,' says Zelal. Now she's not acting. She is thanking the girl sincerely; this is evident from her tone.

Mahmut's eyes fill with tears. Kurd, Turk, easterner or westerner; how good it is when people reach out to one another, sharing their grief and their smiles! Sometimes one word, a single word, is enough. The word 'brother', a greeting from the heart, sometimes a look, a touch, holding a hand and jumping a stream, rubbing a bleeding finger on a spider's web, putting a hand on a forehead is enough; you become friends with the person you previously thought of as an enemy. So what is it? What is it that we cannot share in this transitory world?

'Thanks,' he says, addressing the other patient and her visitors. 'I hope you get better soon, too. If people love one another, if they don't despise each other, if they think of each other as brothers and sisters everything will improve. One day this country will improve, too. Guns will be silent. Stray bullets will not hit babies in their mothers' wombs.'

Mahmut mulls over what he's just said. He wants to believe this himself. Will there be such a day? Will it come? Will the day come when babies in the womb, mothers big with child, young girls, youths, Turks, Kurds won't be killed, won't destroy one another, when no one will be captured dead, be martyrs, when all can live without fear? This day will come, the instructor in the camp used to say. Not the female instructor but the older one known as the Doctor.

The female instructor used to explain things parrot fashion, as though reading from a book. She wanted her students to recite by rote, too, and would not allow questions. She used to itemize, like checking off a list, how mankind had arrived at the present day: how they had passed from primitive society to feudal society and from there to capitalist society and how things were moving towards communism. Somewhat bizarrely, while her students were being taught in an almost totally incomprehensible fashion about the transition to communism through working-class revolution, the syllabus seemed to change without warning, and the era of Eastern Bloc communism was swiftly glossed over. Those who enquired were told peremptorily that they were going to skip that subject for now, that the urgent question was the liberation of the Kurdish people and that they were going to learn about the people's revolution.

The Doctor was different. He did not teach by rote. He conducted his lessons as though holding a conversation. A different world would be established one day. We will not see it, but our children will; if not them, then our grandchildren will. It would be a just, enlightened world where people would not oppress or tyrannize one another and where everyone would have food and work, where everyone would live their life without harming others, freely according to their own choice, their own will. Nature, animals and people will live in harmony. Humanity has been dreaming of this world for thousands of years. If there had not been the hope of such a world people would not have struggled for thousands of years. People only fight if there is the hope of a better world, a better life. If we lose this hope we cannot fight. If we lose our faith we surrender . . . He would say wonderful things like this. He would talk about life and hope, not about war, death and the organization. His students used to love listening to him, asking questions and receiving considered responses. Then he disappeared. He was too large for the mountains.

Mahmut shrugs off his memories and dreams and returns to the ward. 'As long as there is no enmity in our hearts, as long as we don't despise people,' he concludes.

The bad-tempered woman scowls with the disappointment of not having found support from her son and his wife. The visitors shake their heads in agreement, as though to indicate it is to be hoped that things will get better. A nurse pokes her head round the door and reminds them that visiting hours are over. The son and daughter-in-law say goodbye to the patient and prepare to leave. As they pass in front of Zelal's bed they wish her a speedy recovery from the bottom of their hearts. They ask whether she needs anything. No, thanks all the same – she does not need anything, thank God.

Today Mahmut does not feel like leaving Zelal there on her own. Crazy ideas pass through his mind. If I were to put her in a taxi and take her away, she would be able to walk as far as the door on my arm. She's a tough girl; she wouldn't even let out a peep. Hadn't the doctors said she should take a few steps every day, walk around a bit? Would they look for her if we were leave now before they considered her ready to be discharged? Would they follow us? As if there are not enough people pursuing us! All we need are doctors as well! He thinks about the men waiting at the bus stand. He shudders. All right, I was suspicious for no reason, but my nerves are in shreds. I am wary of my own shadow. That's certainly the case, but what if . . . ? Without mulling it over, without thinking things out, he walks over to the woman in the other bed almost instinctively.

'I'm entrusting Zelal to you, *teyze*,' he says. 'Please don't take it personally if she's sometimes rude or insolent. A lot of things have happened to her. It's because she is shy, because she is afraid, that she puts out her prickles. She feels a stranger here, and when I go she is completely alone. Please look out for her. She's just a young girl. She does not know this place – she does not know the city. Please help her. You have children of your own. There is love in your heart. Please take care of her for me.'

The woman had leant back against her pillows and was silent and unresponsive as though she had not heard what he said. It seems to Mahmut that she imperceptibly moved her head and said 'All right'. He is not entirely sure, but he wants it to be so to ease his heavy heart.

Just as he is going out of the door he turns back. 'I read somewhere that someone has written, " People can reach other people." What good are our hands and arms if we don't reach out to help one another?' His voice is mild but not meek and much wiser than one would expect from his appearance. He stands at the head of Zelal's bed and with a clumsy, shy movement strokes the girl's hair that resembles a sheaf of wheat spread out on the pillow. 'I'll come again tomorrow at the same time, and then perhaps, if the doctor allows, I'll get you discharged early.'

The hospital corridor is crowded. It is leaving time for all the visitors. He gives a quick glance in both directions; everything seems normal. Before going out through the main door he lingers for a while at the end of the corridor. There is no one suspicious in evidence nor anything out of the ordinary. But, still, we must leave as soon as possible, I must take Zelal away from here right away. We have almost forgotten to be cautious. We have forgotten what a dangerous situation we are in. The people on the mountain used to say that the city air makes one relax. That's true; we have let our guard down. I've relaxed. It is as though we thought we were normal citizens.

He goes out of the hospital and with rapid, determined steps mingles with the city's crowds.

After Mahmut had left, Zelal felt worn out. They were giving her a great deal of oral and intravenous medication. The young nurse had said that the surgical wound site would hurt for some time so she should take medicine for the pain. Zelal liked this girl. Her highly sensitive antennae with which she continually combed her surroundings had picked up on the vibrations emitted by the young nurse; they had reached the touchstone of her heart, and she understood from the radiance that spread inside that only good would come from her. Among the many doctors and nurses who entered the room this was the one she warmed to most: Nurse Eylem, with the pretty face and strange name; Nurse Eylem who visited the room without fail whenever she was on night duty, who personally gave her her medicine, who spoke softly, who did not ask questions but who could read her looks.

Like a cat trusting its whiskers, Zelal trusted her antennae to sort out friend from foe. She was never wrong. Her teacher was a good man, the headmaster bad, her father was good, her uncles bad, her father's second wife was good and the midwife was bad. Mahmut was good, very good. Before he went up the mountain her Mesut *Abi* had been good, too. she had loved him very much. However, when he returned from the mountain and came to the village he had changed. He had become bad; he had become somebody else. And those foul-faced dark men with cruel looks who had accompanied him . . . She had been afraid of them, had run away. When her father had thrown himself to the ground, beating his breast and crying like a woman because, he said, 'My son is a collaborator', she had not understood what was so bad about it. But when her Mesut *Abi* had returned to the village with those two youths, laughing unpleasantly and showing off his gun with a swagger, and had told her to run and tell their mother about his arrival, she had sensed evil with all her five senses. She had run away from them and had could no longer bear to see, smell or touch her Mesut *Abi*, whom she had previously loved so much. She had thought that her father had been right to beat his breast. People change, the good become bad – and perhaps the bad become good . . .

Zelal had complete faith in her instincts. Nurse Eylem was good, a friend. When she talked to a person she looked them straight in the eye. One did as she said, took the medicine on time. She had said she was on duty that night. If she were on duty it meant she would drop by. When she was there, there was no need to worry or to be frightened.

She pushed the pillows that Mahmut had piled up behind her to make her comfortable to the top of the bed and lay down. She savoured the drowsiness that spread through the warm droplets of water that drained from her forehead and trickled into her eyes. Drowsiness gradually became sleep and sleep turned to dreams.

They were running down a very green steep slope. They were running, but Zelal had no legs. She was a cloud, water, vapour from the waist down. Who was the person beside her? Was it Mahmut? It was, and it was not. She was carrying a baby in her arms. The baby's face was Mahmut's face. Mahmut did not have a face. His face was in pieces; it had merged with green grass. They were running in a cold sweat. She did not know why or from whom. It was dark behind them. There was a storm, a deluge. A smoking burnt forest appeared in front of them, pitch-black stumps, branches and ashes. Mahmut's faceless body threw the baby from her arms, embraced Zelal and threw her down; she felt the gentle warmth of the ashes on her body. She suddenly saw that she was stark naked and bleeding. Men had surrounded her, and none of them had a face either. Then the baby wrapped in rags stood up. It had a huge head, and Zelal saw her Mesut *Abi's* face: it was not the good, kind face of her brother before he went to the mountain but the evil, frightening face he had when he returned to the village with the two young men. Mahmut got off her and disappeared into thin air. She wanted to get up and go after him, but she could not. She began to scream at the top of her voice in fear, but no sound came. The more she screamed, the more her voice was stifled. It was stifled screaming. The more she screamed the more she turned to stone, and the stone came and blocked her throat. She heard sounds, shrieks. Then . . .

She awoke to her own voice. First she thought it was from the pain, the ache she felt in her womb. She noticed the dumbfounded face of the woman lying in the bed next to her and her staring eyes. Intuitively, by some strange force, she turned her head to the door. In the half-open door opening on to the hospital corridor she saw just a face, a disembodied face like a continuation of the frightful dream that she had seen: the face of her Mesut *Abi* . . . Like a rabbit mesmerized by the eyes of a snake, she remained frozen, motionless and silent watching the door.

Then the face vanished. The door was quietly pulled shut. Was it Nurse Eylem who had closed the door? It seemed to be her. Zelal held her breath, then she took a deep gulp of air and tried to calm down. She was drenched in sweat. Her body felt very cold in the heat of the early summer evening. She felt embarrassed, especially when she thought that the old witch would have seen that she was afraid, heard her crying out in her sleep and perhaps talking – and what if I spoke Turkish rather than Kurdish! She closed her eyes so that she did not see the woman's face, but when she shut her eyes her head spun as though the ground and the sky were merging. Spinning round she fell into such a dark well that she let out another shriek. When she recovered, once more she saw the patient's anxious face. Suddenly she realized how much she needed this woman to be there at this moment. She was surprised. Mahmut had said something as he went out of the room: he had said that a person can reach out to another person. Was it this feeling that he wanted to communicate? If that was so, why should people be afraid of people?

'You had a bad dream. Don't be afraid.' For the first time the woman's voice was soft and kind. In tone it resembled her mother's voice. Like the voice of my mother as she took me in her arms and comforted me when I was afraid of the jackals howling at night and cried '*Dayê, dakilê.*' My mother who had given her sons to the mountains, my mother who doted on me, my mother who could not protect her child when they took out my death warrant and dangled the rope in the hayloft, my mother who had gone out and hidden, crossing houses and roofs to God knows where so as not to see my death. My mother whose smell and warmth I longed for.

'I disturbed you. Forgive me,' said Zelal, turning towards her room-mate. 'It's true, I had a bad dream. I screamed my head off, but no sound came out.'

'You screamed. You did scream. You made a noise. You uttered muffled shrieks. You awoke to the sound of your own voice.'

Worried that she had given them away she asked in a sweat, 'Why on earth did I shout, *ana*? What did I say?'

'I don't know your language, do I? I didn't understand. You were shouting someone's name, was it agha or *abi*? You were obviously afraid. You were terrified. What happened? What did your *abi* do to you?'

'I don't know . . . In my dream I saw someone who resembled my *abi*. I saw a baby who had Mahmut's face. I saw burnt forests.'

'It's over now. It was just a dream. There is still some water in the glass beside you, take a sip and calm yourself.'

Zelal took courage from the woman's voice that had become quite mellow and friendly and asked in a whisper. 'Did you see him, *teyze*? You know, that man who was peering through the door just a moment ago?'

'You know we keep the door slightly ajar because the room is hot, so people passing along the corridor peep inside. Somebody did look in, but perhaps they were looking for someone. What's wrong with that?'

'No, it wasn't like that. It was a young man with a dark face. He was there just as I woke up.'

'Your nerves really are in shreds, my dear! You've been frightened by something. I didn't see anyone. This is supposed to be a hospital, but it's more like a thoroughfare. Everyone barges in. You see, that's how these second-class private hospitals are. If it were a public hospital, especially a military hospital, they wouldn't let any old person in. But, still, we'll tell the nurses when they come. They can place your bed in front of the window, and I'll move over near the door, so don't be afraid.'

Zelal suddenly began to weep, silently, quietly, burying her head in the pillow to stifle her sobs. Not from fear or weakness but out of the gratitude she felt for the woman's unexpected concern and kindness.

'Let's call the nurse, and she can give you some pills to calm you down. It's evident your pain goes deep, that bad things have happened to you. Illness makes one edgy. Look, I've been unfair to you, and I behaved unkindly. But you snapped at me, too. Anyway, don't be upset any more. Soon we'll both get better and be out of here. You're young. You'll recover more quickly than

I. You had a nightmare: the baby in your dream, the burnt forests, the figure of a man . . . Clearly losing your baby has greatly distressed you. You're still young and your man is, too. You'll have very healthy children – sons and daughters who will be good citizens. Don't be upset.'

If Zelal could have got out of bed and walked unaided she would have gone over to the woman's bed and put her arms round her neck. Not only that but buried her face in her bosom and cried to her heart's content. I miss my mother, my mother who even gets on well with my father's second wife and consents to sharing her man. My mother who gave her sons to the mountains and her daughter to strangers. My mother who is possibly much younger than this woman but looks old enough to be the woman's mother, all the same.

There was such a fire right between her firm breasts scorching her heart, such a longing to return home, such a longing for her mother that it was more than words could explain. Neither the writer nor the *dengbej* could describe it. How could a person put into words the pain that they had never felt? And when pain is this strong it does not translate into words. So pain is indescribable.

'God should not make his servants suffer so much pain, if indeed he is God.'

'You mustn't say that. One cannot question His wisdom. A person must not lose faith.'

The door opened. An orderly who eventually had heard the call buzzer asked what they wanted.

'She's had a nightmare, and she is very tense. It would be good if you could give her a tranquillizer,' said the elderly patient. Then she added, 'I don't want to sleep beside the window. Please change our beds round.'

The orderly looked at Zelal as if to say, what do you think?

Zelal said, 'Whatever *teyze* wants.' When the orderly went off to ask for help to move the bed, she asked in a whisper, 'Why did you want to change places, *teyze*?'

'I realized that you were afraid, that there was someone you were running from. I don't know whether it's your brother or someone else, but your fear will increase if you stay in the bed by the door. You won't let either of us sleep. That's why I asked them.'

'Perhaps I saw a ghost; perhaps he was real. He put his head round the door and was looking inside. Did you really not see him – or did you see him and won't tell me?'

'So many heads peer inside, but I really didn't see anyone who attracted my attention. Even if I did see him I didn't notice. Perhaps it was that swarthy male orderly. Come on. Don't dwell on it any more. If someone comes they'll see me first and go away.'

Zelal was silent and withdrew into herself. Does a person mellow when they feel a person's pain in their heart, or do they love only when they feel love in their heart? If I had not screamed with fear in my dream, if I hadn't wept, she would not have reached out to me. She would have thought of me as an enemy because I was a villager, a Kurd. But when she understood how afraid and upset I was, she mellowed. She is upset, too. Perhaps some people do not feel another's pain and therefore bear enmity, and because they don't feel it they kill? Has God not granted them love? When they raped me like wild animals, making me scream with fear and pain, did they block their ears, or did it give them more of a kick? Did it add to their enjoyment? The one who fell upon me last; he was different. There was love and pity in him. There are good people, and there are bad. Sometimes the good ones fall prey to evil, and being frightened of evil makes them worse. The Devil was banished from heaven but is very powerful. It is the Devil who is powerful in this world, not angels.

She counted the days; she counted the months. How many days was it since the seed had sunk into her? How many months would my murdered baby have been? The girl who knew about numbers calculated exactly. She was lost in warm thoughts for her unborn child. 'He's my child, my son, born from war. But he will bear peace. Peace will become hope, and his name will be Hevi,' Mahmut had said while stroking her stomach.

That was all very well, but how will peace be born of war? How will the forests that had been set on fire become green again? How will the destroyed villages and hamlets be repopulated? How will wounds be dressed? How will the blood be cleansed? A warmth and tenderness has pervaded me because this woman has treated me well, but my suspicion and resentment has not passed. I feel less fearful and lonely but still foreign and out of place.

The food trolley arrived. The trays were left on the small tables beside them. She had no appetite for soup or pilaf or yogurt.

'Try to eat a little something. You have to be strong to get better,' Zelal's elderly roommate said.

'I don't feel like eating. It's as though a lump has got stuck in my throat,' she said. She swallowed a few spoonfuls of yogurt not to upset the woman.

'Where are you from?' the woman asked.

'We're from far away. From the east, from one of the villages of Van,' she lied with her instinct for preservation.

'My husband was a military man. We travelled around that area a lot. It used to be called eastern service. Erzurum, Ardahan, Doğubeyazıt, I know them all. I don't know Van. My husband was a gendarme. In those days there was the Moscow threat. They guarded the Russian border. And they also went after bandits. The bandits would go up the mountains with our men in hot pursuit. The bandits in those days were not like today's ones. They were like innocent babes compared with the present ones. At the moment trouble is further south. The separatist terror is striking the south-east. It is in your area, in Van, too, isn't it?'

Zelal swallowed a few times. 'Yes . . . It is in our area, but we don't know about it. We left our own village and migrated to a hamlet. When I was in the village I was very small. The guerrillas would raid the village and demand food, shelter and weapons if there were any; if not they wanted young men, and then the soldiers would come and collect the men and take them away saying, "Why are you harbouring guerrillas?" They would enter the houses and drag us out. First one would strike and then the other. We were in a terrible situation. Then we left the village. We heard later that the village supported the militia. We moved down to our uncles' hamlet far away.'

'If people didn't protect them, the separatist terrorist organization would not take hold. That's what my dead husband used to say. The PKK did not exist at the time, but, as I said, there were bandits. My husband used to say, "The people protect the bandits. They hide them." The people there have been hostile to the state for as long as I can remember. Now they have become real enemies. There are so many inciting them – that's why. Yet when I was in the east, especially in Erzurum, I had such good neighbours . . . I was young at the time, like you, inexperienced and timid. My husband, as I said, was a gendarme. He would go off into the country in pursuit of bandits. In those days there weren't quarters or anything. We lodged in a house in the town. I couldn't stay alone, I got frightened. The neighbours' wives used to come and stay the night. They would help me with everything. In those days the Kurds were not like that – they were not hostile. The most loyal batmen were Kurds. They would die for you. They were so trustworthy, so loyal. But now . . .'

Zelal was tempted to say, 'Now their eyes have been opened. Everyone has trampled on us because we have been such loyal servants. A dog that is beaten a lot will become ferocious', but she refrained. She just said, 'Now there is a lot of tyranny. This one tyrannizes, and that one tyrannizes. And so everybody goes up the mountains.'

'A beating from a teacher or the state does no harm. You have to be biddable to a certain extent. If you rise up then you will be beaten down. If they were not drawn to the agitators it would not be like this. If you turn your gun on a soldier then of course you'll get what you deserve. The Turkish army won't abandon this land to one or two looters.'

This time Zelal could not contain herself. 'Now look here, *teyze*! You talk well, but if your village were being raided three times a day, your brother and your father were struck with the butts of guns and dragged along, if you were beaten for speaking Kurdish, if the gendarmes raided and took your flocks and animals, if you were stopped constantly, if when you fell sick on the road you died before you reached a town, then there comes a day when you see that tyranny and beating does harm and you revolt. When we met, to begin with, you looked down on me. You saw me as an enemy. But you seem to be a kind woman, a mother. You have love to give to others. And, thanks, you're protecting me now. So I thought I should tell you how I feel. Please don't get angry or upset. But you should know that no one wants their loved ones to die, their children, their husband, their father or their brother. You talk about the homeland; the homeland is the homeland of both those who die and those who kill. But it isn't like that. Our village was our homeland. We were frightened, driven out, and we ran away. They shot the child in my womb, as you heard. I – we – don't have anywhere to go. We will live a dog's life in strangers' houses at strangers' doors. The Kurds are loyal, aren't they? You said that. We can be loyal servants.'

Breathless, she fell silent. I've been running off at the mouth. I'll make the woman angry again. She regretted what she had said. If I said you're right, what you say is justified, it wouldn't be any skin off my nose! But I'm like this. I've been like this ever since my childhood. *Seri hişk*: headstrong they used to call me at home. Only my teacher used to say, she is not headstrong, she's clever, proud. The teacher was a good man, a special man.

She was afraid that just as she had got close to her, begun to like her, she had made the sick woman angry. 'Don't be angry, *teyze*,' she said. 'You are older and more experienced. You know about such things. Let it be as you say.'

The excitement of talking was added to the sedative effect of the medicine, and just before nightfall, as the lights on the far hills were lighting up one by one in the dusk, she took refuge in sleep. Sleep swathed her wounded body and her wounded heart. She began to run after the goats in the green meadows. She gathered violet, purple wild tulips and yellow daisies among the rocks. She reached the spring before the animals and filled her cupped hands with water. The water was cold, and she drank eagerly. The sky was a deep blue in the land of dreams, the earth a green kilim sprinkled with sparkling iridescent flowers. The peaceful happiness of her dream was like a warm quilt and enfolded Zelal like Mahmut's body, Mahmut's arms. She slept.

SEVEN

Jiyan Means Life, Commander!

Whether in fiction, or in real life, it was inevitable that they made love. That they came together and loved not just with promises, not just with eyes, words and silences but with glowing hearts and bodies was no momentary madness, no fleeting fancy but their inevitable fate.

The evening they met at the chemist's shop – and was it not a sign that it was the Hayat Chemist which was open that night? – as they talked about this and that, the region, Mahmut, they realized it when they parted and their eyes met at the moment of farewell. They had got the message, had not pretended not to understand, had not resisted; they had acquiesced. The following days during which they lived as though nothing had happened, no spark had been ignited, were no more than a delay, a fearful expectancy that did not suit their independent personalities. Now, as they lay side by side, they were ashamed not of their love-making, their union, but of having waited until now, of putting it off, of their moral scruples. They had deceived no others, just their own passion, their own bodies and their destinies.

Freed of hairslides, elasticated bands and the other fetters of a virtuous widow, Jiyan's raven-black hair that spread out in ripples and curls like a raging river was the only barrier between their perspiring bodies, the only covering for their nakedness. It seemed to Ömer that everything, every incident and every development following that extraordinary night at the coach terminal, had occurred with mysterious and unerring teleology for them to find each other. The strange woman in the Ankara coach station: the one who had lost her child while fleeing across a central European river . . . The woman who was shot there: Zelal who had lost her baby to a stray bullet . . . Mahmut who had fled from the mountains; neither coward, penitent nor confessor, a naked person who had cast off his guerrilla uniform, his militia clothing, somebody who yearned for the open sea he had never seen . . . Elif, his wife, whom he always kept in the depths of his heart even when he was with another woman, who was going west after her lost son . . . Everything, all of this, seemed to be leading up to his meeting with Jiyan.

Now at a moment without yesterday or tomorrow, making love sometimes roughly, sometimes gently, and lying side by side damp, sweaty, naked, satisfied and tired on the mattress spread out on a rainbow-coloured nomadic kilim that covers the floor of the room, they experience the serene happiness of a cat that has stretched itself out in the sun.

One can also reach Jiyan's house by a wooden staircase from the depot behind the chemist's shop, through a door hidden by a cupboard with shelves. The main door to the building is in the back street. Looking at the building from the outside, it is difficult to imagine that the interior can be so large and luxurious. Jiyan's flat is nothing like the houses typical of the town's notables. Having prepared himself for ornate, tasteless heavy brocade armchairs, gilded suites of furniture, carved sideboards stuffed with crystal and silverware and elaborate lace cloths, Ömer is surprised to be greeted by the restful aesthetics of simplicity and emptiness. In the huge sitting-room there are only a few pieces of furniture: in one corner a plain white sofa and armchairs; in the middle, a large, long dining-table with a cream-coloured cloth decorated with white pearls and simple white embroidery; against the wall, a solid wooden sideboard with hand-carved tulips in the corners; in the opposite corner, huge cushions with colourful flowers hand embroidered on white and scattered all around the cushions, newspapers and magazines . . . This must be Jiyan's corner.

One wall of the room where they now lie side by side, naked and content, is taken up by a wooden cupboard of many doors resembling the closets of old mansions. In the middle of the cupboard is a recessed section designed as a dressing-table. There is a mirror behind two wooden panels that open out on either side and are decorated with pretty flower pictures. Immediately below it is the wide shelf that Jiyan uses as a dressing-table, with rings, pots of creams, makeup, combs and brushes and in front a small stool. And then there is this large comfortable mattress spread with snow-white linen sheets on the floor.

When he first arrived and she was showing him around her home, Jiyan had said, 'For me, mattresses and cushions on the floor are essential items. I brought the kilims, the embroidered cushions and so on from the mansion in the village, I mean, from home and also the doors of the cupboard in the bedroom. Did you notice the panels of the mirror? In my father's village was a young man. He used to draw and paint pictures on paper, cardboard, wood, whatever he could lay his hands on. If he couldn't find anything else he would make figures with small stones on the dry earth. I bought him lots and lots of paint, oils and watercolours in many colours, and coloured pencils. It was he who painted the flowers on the panels of the mirror. They are lovely aren't they?'

She stopped talking and ruefully attempted a smile. 'I miss the village, the mansion with forty rooms . . . Of course, it didn't have forty rooms, but that's how it was known. In my great grandfather's time it was described as quite palatial. That's why it's still known in the area as "the mansion". The family also call it that. I miss the people, my animals and the countryside. I was able to live in the village only for a very short time. Sometimes I wonder whether it was all a beautiful dream. You know there are some dreams that you can't get enough of, and as soon as you wake up you close your eyes again wanting them to continue. Were those days a dream like that?'

When he asked why she did not go to the village very often and what had happened to the mansion, she had said with the same sad, soft voice, 'The village was evacuated. It was because of a disagreement within the clan. My father had already left the village anyway. The family had moved here, to the town. But we used to go back in the summers. There are mountain pastures, it's cool: the air and the water – everything is good. Then when war broke out my family refused to join the militia. Don't imagine that it was because they were on the side of the rebels on the mountain. Being part of the militia is considered collaboration. That really would not be in keeping with clan law. Besides, contrary to what one would expect, it would be dangerous. When they refused to join the militia, pressure from the state increased. The rebels on the mountain thought they had found an easy prey and began harassing them. In other words, there was no peace any more, and everyone migrated. After that the military evacuated the village. My father also had houses in the town, but they loved the village and the mountain pastures. They were their – how should one say it? – their kingdoms. In our parts, whether you are a clan leader, a khan or an agha you are lost in the town, your sultanate lies in the countryside.'

'What happened to the boy who did pictures, who painted the panels of this mirror? Tell me something cheerful. Tell me that he studied art, he became an artist, that he holds exhibitions!'

'Became an artist? . . . The things we suffer here are too painful to make light of. Fairytales are not real. People do not attain their desires and live happily ever after. It was better in the past, before the war. There were people from this region, the villages, who got somewhere, but now . . .'

He saw that the young woman's eyes had become misty and that her lips were trembling slightly, and he regretted his thoughtless words.

'The boy who painted pictures is dead. One cannot become an artist here. Depending on one's background and nature, one becomes a guerrilla, a terrorist, a traitor, a separatist, a collaborator, a martyr or an informer. Or you are captured dead. You are going to be angry with me again, and you are going to say don't politicize instances of oppression or injustice, and don't fight for your right to justice. Well, how do we fight for our rights? We have only our dead, our suffering and our privation.'

What impressed Ömer was the extreme sensitivity, the defiant fragility, the heat of a volcano about to erupt that was concealed beneath Jiyan's hard shell, her serene poise. When she became excited, emotional – and the smallest incident, a word used randomly or a memory were enough for her to get excited and emotional – a shadow would pass across her eyes, the left corner of her mouth would twitch slightly and lift, and her long, slim fingers adorned with silver rings of multi-coloured jewels would begin to tremble imperceptibly. What had she been through, what had she witnessed, what had she left behind? He did not know. Was she really so mysterious? Or was she just a charming, pretty woman, and was Ömer writing the scenario with his writer's imagination and his own troubled mind? Her harsh, clipped eastern accent that to someone else might seem unattractive, her speeches that resembled theatrical tirades and which bordered on affectation, her enigmatic silences were all a part of her. When local women who came to the chemist's shop to buy medicine, to have their blood pressure taken or to ask for advice, and men in local dress resembling that of the peshmergas, young girls with or without headscarves began to speak to the chemist or Jiyan *Abla* in their own language, he realized how much a part of the community she was, and he was astonished. When Jiyan passed them in the street, the men raised their right hands to their chests and greeted her with an exaggerated respect peculiar to the region. Sometimes the women asking for a cure for their troubles or an ointment for their wounds would hug and kiss her, sometimes take her hand in theirs and lovingly hold it fast. No, Jiyan was not merely the product of his poetical fancy, the heroine of a novel that he had created influenced by the strange mental state into which he had descended. She was the fruit and the essence of this wild impenetrable land whose soul and mystery was impervious to invasion. A unique and cherished fruit, a beautiful and splendid essence.

When she invited him to come and see her house, her naturalness, her recklessness and her self-confidence had amazed Ömer. A young, pretty – and respected – widow in a provincial town in the east of the east, who did not shrink from inviting a strange man to her house. So confident in herself, so comfortable. The confidence and comfort deriving from a conviction of her invulnerability.

Jiyan's home . . . The large sitting-room that gave one the feeling of walking in a white cloud, cream-white curtains, white armchairs and the white carpet that covered the floor from wall to wall – for this reason one had to leave one's shoes outside on entering – her study with its bookcases with glass doors and elegant desk, and now this room where they had lain beside each other naked, satisfied and happy; her bedroom.

They were standing in her bedroom in front of the panelled mirror on which fairytale birds and the many-coloured flowers of the mountain pastures were intertwined. Jiyan was standing behind Ömer's right shoulder. Her face, surrounded and shadowed by her black mane of hair that had fallen on to her shoulders, was reflected in the mirror. Ömer turned his head slightly back to the right and his lips found her lips straight away as though it were not the first time but the thousandth time, as though she were his wife of many years whose body's every point and curve he knew by heart. As a soft but burning fire spread through his throat from his tongue and from there to his breast and towards his stomach he had thought of two things: Jiyan was the same height and she did not avoid his lips. Was it from indifference or from desire; at that moment he could not decide.

The long black hair spread out on the pillow of the woman wrapped in white embroidered linen sheets beside him now seems at that moment to Ömer, even more feminine, more sensual, more inviting than her naked body. A meddlesome sliver of light filtering through the folds of the tightly drawn curtains strikes her hair and roams through her curls. Without her hair her face would not be so attractive, thinks Ömer. The total change when she lets down her hair, her transformation into the likeness of a legendary goddess stems from this. The spell of this woman is in her hair. It's as though the magic would be gone if she cut it. He thrusts his hand through her black mane. He winds her curls around his fingers. He wants to say to her, 'My woman.' There is a term of endearment associated with every woman, and he associates the expression 'my woman' with her. If he had a good voice, if he could sing, he would sing that folk song he loved in her ear so that only she could hear:

> There is myrtle in front of your house
> Oh, water doesn't flow upstream, my woman . . .
> Take the dagger, my woman, strike and let me die
> Oh, let me be a slave at your door, my woman . . .'

Yet Jiyan is not his woman; he senses this. She has been the woman of only one person and she has always remained so. She is no one's woman any more. She is mistress of her own body. She is a jet-black lynx that uses its body as it pleases, taking pleasure but not offering itself, not allowing the male to have the feeling of possession but not trying to possess. The moment you think you have tamed it, it reverts to wildness. He remembers the tone in the young woman's voice as she said 'my husband'. Had those men wanted to say that she was connected with her husband's murder? It was evident that they had never heard the passion, the longing with which she said 'my husband'; evidently they did not know her. In any case, even if they had known her they would not be able to understand her. The lawyer had said it was a 'great love'. What was it that nurtured their love, made it grow and made it survive even after death? Jiyan's loyalty to the husband she lost was intertwined with this land, the sufferings, the hopes of this land and its war. For this reason even if the object of love is absent it retains its power. As for me, I'm the stranger. The good stranger but from outside. Her relationship with me depends on the boundaries of her body and her desire and with me will vanish off the face of the earth.

Jiyan lies quietly beside him without touching him. She is tightly wrapped in the sheet, and her naked flesh does not touch his. Women cuddle up to a man after making love, especially the first time. As for men, they prefer the freedom of a satisfied body and enjoy being alone, withdrawing into themselves. Jiyan is like that now. I am the one who feels the need to touch her, embrace her and be tenderly caressed. A strange reversal of roles!

Jiyan gets up from the bed and goes to the adjoining bathroom dragging the white sheet she has wrapped herself in behind her. Ömer hastily gets dressed while she is in the bathroom. He wants to freeze and keep what they experienced as it is in his body, in his memory and in the centre of his feelings. Those moments should remain there. They should not flow into the present; otherwise the spell will be broken. He opens wide the decorated panels of the mirror and looks at his face. They say that satisfying love-making makes a woman more beautiful. It's done me good, too. I don't look at all old. He feels content in himself. The negative feelings inside him have vanished. If he weren't embarrassed he could even whistle and sing songs.

Evening falls. It is evident from the light filtering into the room and gradually turning to a reddish-yellow that fades by the minute. The hum from the market gradually dies down. A distant call to prayer is heard. It mingles with the military's more resonant orders for the flag ceremony and the marches. The cassette-seller opposite puts the *Come to the Mountains, to the Mountains* cassette in Kurdish that he plays every evening at this time in the cassette player and turns it up full volume. Ömer had thought that this town had no sound; now he begins to realize how the town lost its sound. Here the sounds are each other's enemies, drowning each other and trying to silence one another. When the town's own sound is silent, then only the noise of conflicting foreign sounds or nothingness remains.

When she came out of the bathroom and stood by my side, her raven hair was wet. It spread out in waves and curls on her forehead, face and shoulders. I feel the excitement of a teenager who has been united with the one he loves for the first time. There is not a sign of the annoyance, the lethargy or the regret felt after having slept with somebody on a whim or under the influence of alcohol – or sometimes with the laziness of not be able to say no, perhaps not to hurt the other person or their pride.

I watched Jiyan in front of the mirror trying to gather up her hair and attempting to wipe away any trace of love-making from her face and body. I did not know whether I should admire her ease and her naturalness, be amazed at it or be upset that what we had experienced should be for her such an everyday event. The water had washed from her all the traces, all the feelings of our love-making.

Was it nothing more than a sexual experience that an ardent young woman had had with a stranger who would pass briefly through her life, unimportant because it was fleeting, harmless and because he was a stranger?

When we spoke during the following days, you were to say, 'We mustn't forget how attractive Ömer Eren's fame is. After all, all women like strong, famous and powerful men. You must admit that you took courage from your preconceived notions of the Orientalist to approach me. Weren't women in the east females waiting ardently for their men, like courtesans?

That east is not far away, even if it is only our east . . .' Then you saw that I had become disgruntled and tried to correct yourself by saying, 'But, still, what we experienced was a spring that appeared before me when I was in the desert without water. Thank you for wanting me and choosing me.'

You stubbornly insisted on using the formal 'you'. When I asked why, you explained, 'Perhaps it is a habit, a method of self-preservation.' I learnt to say the familiar 'you' in Kurdish. I tried to understand, to hear to whom you said it. The old, the young, the worker, the tradesman, the mayor, the party leader, your own people were all 'thou'; we, the others were all the formal 'you'. The unacknowledged foreignness, the distance and lack of language that lies between the formal 'you' and me and that does not exist in the familiar 'you' and me came between us even when we were making love. When I said to you that it was not me but you, not us but your people that had created this, it seemed to me that the tone in which you said, 'you' became even harsher. I spoke of the couples I knew: Kurdish-Turkish, Laz-Circassian, Turkish-Armenian couples. In trivial, trite expressions I repeated the phrases that you knew by heart: differences in language, religion and race should not separate people, should not make people enemies, as though you did not know that. You said in a tone that was half mocking and half joking, 'Now you sound like the fundamental principle of the constitution.' Then you added, 'But you know better than I that things don't go according to the book.' You were right, and I kept quiet. I spoke to you about another language: a new language that did not factionalize, did not separate the differences, that was purged of politics, power and conflict. You asked, 'How can I create a new language without finding my own language first, without being myself?' I did not have an answer. I was silent. I was angry with you because you made everything so complicated, I took out my frustration in love-making. Realizing that I would not be able to possess you, I tried to enslave your body. And I managed to do this to a certain extent: I whipped up your desire, I used your sexuality, I got you addicted to my body. The more I thought about it, the more I understood that this was a form of rape, and I was ashamed of myself. But I loved you. I loved you as I did my wife. I loved you deeply. She was a part of me, and I wanted you to be a part of me, too. I thought that we could meet in the language of love. I – we – did not succeed. Were our languages too different to unite in love, in passion?

Jiyan says, 'It's late. Please go now.' She is stroking Ömer's cheek. They are standing side by side in front of the mirror. They are like a picture in which the attractiveness of the young woman overshadows the man who has passed middle age. They resemble the keepsake photographs taken in front of a scenic backdrop of engaged couples who have come down to the town or new recruits who have come home for the weekend. Behind them there is the feeling of emptiness of the white wall, not a view of Istanbul or fairytale birds and flowers of paradise. Jiyan murmurs a folk song in her beautiful, deep voice: 'Let them print our photos side by side . . .' He remembers the song. Wasn't it the story of two lovers who had been involved in some crime and had been caught by gendarmes?

Swiftly he shuts the panels of the mirror and embraces her. 'What will happen if I don't go?'

'Nothing, of course, but there is a society meeting this evening. And I'm the speaker.'

' And which separatist organization is it this time, my darling?'

'This time it's a harmless organization: a woman's organization, closely linked to the state. Even the Governor's wife supports its work. That's why our women keep their distance, but they will come this evening because I'm the speaker.'

'What's the topic?'

'The health of mother and child. The midwife at the polyclinic is the main speaker. I'm going to be there as support; an extra speaker so that our women will come, too. In fact the problem for our women is birth control. Young people don't want many children, especially after giving birth to a boy. However, they are frightened of birth control methods such as the coil. They don't trust them. When people talk about preventing the Kurdish population increasing and birth control, they are frightened that they will be sterilized.'

'You're kidding!'

'No, I'm not. When people's trust has been shaken so badly, when they've felt so trapped, downtrodden and desperate, they are wary about others' intentions. Fear makes a person suspicious. I understand our women. In fact none of them wants a lot of children. They don't have any ambitions to increase the Kurdish population either. These are the issues of politicians, men scrambling for power. However, should they become infertile, especially if they do not have a son, then a second wife immediately comes along. And no one wants a second wife.'

'That's a difficult situation. It's not for me. But how come the state trusts you?'

'It doesn't trust me, but it needs me. It uses me to make contact with the local people. We each walk our own path with little steps, covering for each other. The Governor's wife and the Commander's wife, the teacher, nurses and midwives need me if they don't want just to talk to one another at the meeting. And, as for me, I need to convey a message to my people. As you see, we manage to rub along together.'

He feels the weariness, the feeling of being trapped, in her voice.

'Forget about advising women about birth control, my woman, and give me – us – a child. A Kurdish-Turkish child to replace my lost son, a child of the common language of love, of hope and the future.'

'Why did you say your lost son?' Now she sounds not just weary but sad.

Ömer realizes what he has said. He becomes confused. He feels like a skein of betrayal. It's as though he really has lost his son – just now in saying these words. Yet I came here to some extent to look for him. While I was speaking to Mahmut's father I had thought I might be reunited with my son if I took the path that the wise man had paved for me in my heart. I humiliated Elif, not by making love to Jiyan but with these words. It's as though I erased my son from within me. What was traitor in Jiyan's language? *Xayin! Du rû! Caş!* When I said 'my lost son' and wanted a son in his place, then I really did lose Deniz. I killed him. I killed Elif, too.

Was he to lose his way completely in this foreign land where he had come to look for his very nature, his inner being, his values and the word he had lost, to be cleansed and purified? The Governor who had tried to show off his knowledge of mythology had mentioned the sailors who had been enchanted by the voices of the sirens.

I must save myself from being dashed to pieces on the rocks. I'm a complete mess. I'm disorientated and alone.

He does not answer Jiyan. He gently touches her forehead with his lips.

I have never loved like this. Like loving the earth, the sky, the sea, like loving the mountains and loving myself. So naturally, inevitably, indisputably . . . No, this was not a sentence from the book he could not write. It was no fiction. It was exactly what he had experienced. The overflowing enthusiasm of an eighteen-year-old youth wildly and madly in love: a bird constantly fluttering in his breast, his throat, his head and at the tips of his fingers. A love without beginning or end, time or space. As they made love it was as though their bodies melted, as though they evaporated, a sensation from head to toe. As they stand silently side by side they are a folk song for two voices; as they speak they are the word that reverberates on the rocks. Then comes the meaninglessness, the emptiness into which he falls when he is apart from Jiyan, when he is without her. The question that is never asked when he is with Jiyan, that has no equivalent in any language and that resounds in his brain and heart in every language and sound when he is by himself, alone: why am I here? What am I after? Where am I going?

Ömer is surprised at himself. He wants to apologize to all the women he has known and loved, especially to Elif – to his wife to whom he thought he was inseparably bound. No, not because he loves someone else – Jiyan is not someone else – but because he has grasped that what he offered them as passion, as love and desire was a lie with which he tricked himself, not them. In any case, what were all those women who had come and gone in his life other than the satisfaction of his male ego that was so utterly inflated by his fame and success? But Elif was different. She was the strong safe lap of youthful years when we ran flat out in pursuit of a revolution we had no doubts about, our shared ideas, the plane tree I rested my back against, the mother of my son. For a long time there has been no passion but essentiality, necessity. He feels depressed by these thoughts, but he no longer feels guilt. Elif would understand this; she would understand that this feeling is not directed at her, does not take anything away from her, does not belittle her. She would understand that the nameless, indescribable, irresistible attraction that I feel for Jiyan has clinched its own place, its own meaning and bound her more strongly to me.

Would she really understand? No, no man or woman would understand, and even if they did they wouldn't acknowledge it. I'm making all this up to comfort myself, to live for today. I want it to be like this. I'm resisting reality. Jiyan never asked about my wife. It's of no importance to her. In fact, I'm not very important to her either. She is not jealous because she doesn't feel as though she is sharing love and passion with another woman. She lives in the moment; she keeps it alive. Then she returns to her own world that she never reveals and whose narrow door and tiny window she doesn't leave ajar which is hidden behind her thick black eyebrows. Just like this town. Strangers cannot fathom Jiyan or get through to the realities of that world, its secrets and its fears.

He knows that he should escape from her magnetic field immediately and from this frightening, magical, strange town before being carried away and sinking completely, before leaping over the threshold of no return. If he were to take his small case and board the first coach, jump on the first plane to take off from the nearest airport to his own land, his own world, if he were to return to himself . . . If he were to return to his wife, to his son who still gave him hope of returning to life, to his readers queuing at his book-signing days, to his arrogant intellectual circle so pleased with themselves and full of their public image, to the comfort brought by alcohol, the lethargy of emptiness, the meaninglessness of life . . . Before it is too late, before all his bridges both inside and out are entirely burnt?

He knows very well that he will not return, that these questions are an attempt to purge his conscience. He knows it, but he is trying to deceive himself. He finds fault not with Jiyan but with Mahmut and Zelal, the mountains, the region and the town for leading him astray, for enticing him. Sometimes he thinks: put Jiyan in the middle of Istanbul and she would at most be a fairly pretty countrywoman. And if she began to speak she would be a *bacı* from the other country. But in these lands, under this sky, in the shadow of these snowy peaks, with the secrets that envelop her like mist, with the invisible halo that she carries like a crown, and with the power of the mountains and the traditions that have filtered down through the centuries, she becomes Jiyan. She becomes life. Ömer likes this new life whose door he has pushed ajar. With Jiyan he is reborn from being burnt out. It is as though he is going back many years, to youth, to hope, and perhaps to the word he lost. As he tries to penetrate the depths of the town, to reach its soul, to hear its scream, Jiyan and the town intermingle; they overlap. The secret that entwines them both, that renders them unattainable does not manifest itself to the stranger, be he lover or friend. The moment he thinks he has lifted the curtain, town and woman withdraw into themselves. They take on the identity of an ordinary town, an ordinary woman. The stranger remains outside the shell that he feels he will not be able to pierce. Or it seems like that to the stranger.

Yet in appearance both Jiyan and the town are so welcoming, so inviting, so friendly that Ömer sometimes has doubts about himself. Or am I making all this up? Is it all about me, a man in his fifties going through a mid-life crisis, Jiyan, a small-town widow, and the town, a poor underdeveloped eastern town? Am I making up a love story, a legend of the east to overcome burn-out, the boring routine of life, to be able to write again?

He wanders around the streets, strokes the stray dogs, greets the tradesmen and spends time in the coffee house. The owner now knows that he drinks his coffee without sugar and that he likes a glass of water with it.

He is delighted that 'our author' has come. Even those who have not even heard of his name until now, who haven't seen one of his books, call him 'our author'. People talk about him. Pupils come and ask for his autograph. Because they are not able to find his books they have his autograph in their school notebooks or the girls have it in their diaries. They part from him giggling with delight. Although it is not his custom he has a shave at the barber's just for a chat. He visits the town hall and talks to the mayor. He goes to the Culture and Solidarity Association and then, to be even-handed, he goes to the District Governorship and drinks tea with the Governor and listens to his complaints. When the Commander asks, he does not decline his invitation to have a drink and a chat. When evening comes and darkness falls and the sinister armed special force in camouflage and snow masks begin their daily display of terror in the streets that open on to the market square, he realizes that he is not intimidated as he was on the first day and that he has got used to it. They are all a part of the town and its secret: the key to the puzzle. It is only the town's cats that he has not yet got to know. Cats are in the streets, in the shops, on the walls, in front of the doors, everywhere. When you approach them they disappear; they vanish into thin air, become invisible. Or are the cats the carriers of the secret? he thinks sometimes, laughing at himself. This idea would please Elif. She is a cat person. She always used to say that without knowing each individual cat and its nature you don't really know a place; you haven't made it your home. I haven't been able to get to know the cats. I haven't yet become part of this place. The cats do not disclose the town's and Jiyan's secrets. They hide them in the quivering of their whiskers.

Even though it appeared that everyone including the Commander, the hotel-keeper, the Governor, the cassette-seller, the organization and the military had believed the rumour that he had come here to write a book, he knows that in fact no one really believes it and that everyone has a different story about him. For them I am also a mystery. And what about Jiyan? Does she know, does she understand why I am here and why I didn't leave within a few days?

She never asked why I was here. In any case Jiyan did not really ask any questions. Once, when he had not been able to cope with things and had asked himself out loud, 'Why am I here?', she had said, 'To seek and to cleanse your heart.'

'What am I seeking?'

'What is missing . . . What you had and then lost.'

What I had and lost: my youth, my enthusiasm, my dreams of self-sacrifice and revolution, my vision of a better future – well, we were going to save the whole world, all mankind, weren't we? – my son who became a stranger and slipped from my heart and . . . and the word.

'Why do I want to cleanse my heart? What is the dirt in my heart?'

'Not dirt. Let us say rust. You have got carried away by the spell of your readers, your books and your reputation. Your signature has become your cocoon. It has wrapped you up soft and warm. It has distanced you from human suffering. I was curious. I thumbed through your books again; before you became famous you wrote about poverty, hunger, the underdog, the victim, the worker, men crushed yet resisting, and then I saw that you had stopped writing about these things. As you became more famous as the writer of 'the psychological depths of love, of people, the postmodern novelist of alienation, east–west conflicts' your books began to sell more. But you had broken away from your roots. You had become estranged. And then . . .'

He had secretly been annoyed, angry, but on the other hand his admiration for this fearless woman grew.

'But I don't just write novels, I often discuss the subjects you mentioned in articles I write for newspapers and so on. Literature is a different kettle of fish. I'm in no position to turn out ideology in a novel. My readers would not appreciate that, and if no one reads my books I won't be able to convey the more universal messages about humanity and conscience that interest me.'

He realized that he had gone on the defensive and was ashamed; he became defiant. 'Aren't you being unfair, Jiyan? I never shirked from defending the truth when necessary.'

'When necessary, yes. But when you begin to weigh up when the time is right to deal with a subject and when it is not, then you have digressed from the subject. You have put it at arm's length and alienated yourself from it. You have now become the judge. Can one judge between hunger and satiation, death and life, love and hate? And you know you said "to defend the truth". Defending the truth is looking on from the outside. One has to live the truth, not defend it.'

'Is that the rust you mentioned?'

'Forgive me. I'm afraid the word exceeded its intention. I always speak rather plainly, just as I feel. The more I love, the more openly, sometimes harshly I'm inclined to speak. I love you. That's why I'm saying that your heart does not support you. It wants to have the rust wiped away and shine. That's why you are here, and you are in the right place, Ömer Eren. The fountains of the west have dried up. It is no longer possible to be purified there. Here we still have fast-flowing water. Water that is cool and healing, even though the blood of brothers mingles with it from time to time. And if only we can cleanse it of the blood . . . Knowingly or unknowingly, you came to wash in this spring.'

'It's true I was looking for a healing spring, cool water that would quench the aridness and dessication within me, my withering, my thirst and that would wash and purify my heart. Perhaps you are right. I did come here to look for water, but now I'm not sure if the spring is here. This climate is too harsh, and, what is more, as you have said, the waters have mingled with blood.'

'They say that flowing water does not retain dirt.' She realized that their conversation had become too serious, and she said, 'Since we have been talking about springs, I would like to invite you to ours to eat trout. They have closed the mountain pastures but one can still go to Soğukpınar during the day. Some enterprising citizen has put out a couple of tables and created a trout pool near the water. Our people like that kind of thing. They are enthusiastic about tourist amenities, even though they don't always show it. At this hour there is no one around. Anyway folk are wary of going into the countryside, of going too far from the the towns. We'll take my stepsister and my brother-in-law, too, if you don't mind. A widow shouldn't be seen alone with a man, isn't that right? Even if that man is "our author"!'

Two details preyed on his mind, her insisting on saying my stepsister and not my sister and the slightly mocking tone of voice as she said 'our author'.

Throughout the journey the step-sister and her husband had talked incessantly about the beauty of Soğukpınar: 'A little corner of paradise, a natural wonder; oh, if only this war would end and peace and quiet return! Our homeland is paradise, Ömer *Bey*. If we could show you every part of it, believe me, you would write a novel about this place. If only tourism were allowed to develop people would be able to breathe a little easier. We have no factories and no real pastures or fields left. War has put paid to livestock farming. Smuggling, the mafia and terrorism are rife. Don't expect honesty from starving people. A starving person has neither hope nor honesty. What will a starving person do? He'll either go up the mountain, become a village guard or start smuggling.'

Jiyan was silent, thoughtful. She was sad. It was as though she regretted suggesting this trip. She looked exhausted, as if she had been without sleep for days. Later she was to say resentfully, her eyes full of tears, 'I realized that even if you didn't show it or admit it to yourself, you would look down on us; you would feel sorry for us because we cannot share our paradise, and that would estrange us even more.'

In fact, it was a lovely day. The sky was as blue as could be, the little white clouds did not obscure the sun. The brother-in-law's black jeep – Ömer had not found out how the brother-in-law earned his money – left the main road and turned on to a stony, dusty country road. From his first day Ömer had been amazed at the abundance of luxury jeeps, some armoured, some with dark-tinted windows, perhaps bullet-proof, amid the poverty, the neglect and ruins of the town. When she saw that Ömer was surprised, Jiyan explained that the vehicles represented security and prestige and were symbols of power.

'Even in the big cities it would be difficult to find as many of the latest jeeps with massive amounts of horsepower or the luxury cars you come across here in the street. You wouldn't believe that you were in one of Turkey's poorest and most underdeveloped regions,' the Commander had said during a conversation on the subject.

Now, as they travel in such a jeep along a road covered with bushes and scrub, the brother-in-law says, 'Ten years ago this was all woods and forest.'

Ömer asks in an unguarded moment, 'Then what happened?'

There is silence. Damn it, why don't I keep my mouth shut! 'Oh, I understand. I keep forgetting. I'm sorry.'

'You don't forget,' says Jiyan who has been sitting silently in the back during the whole journey. 'You don't have to apologize either. No, you don't forget. To forget you have to know. You never even registered it so that you could forget. There are things that a person cannot feel deeply unless they've experienced them. At the end of the day, the images on television screens are just pictures, unreal. Even if they are our whole life, for you they are bad things that happen in distant places.'

Later, when they were alone, she would say, 'Please forgive me. I can't stand this thing between us, this line that divides us. I can't accept it. I get angry.'

Jiyan's words subdues the mood in the car. There ensues a silence that seems longer than it is.

'A girl has been born,' says the step-sister.

'We say, the Devil passed,' says Ömer. The jeep turns off the earth road and progresses slowly along a dry river bed. When armed men – whether soldiers or civilians, Ömer cannot make out – block their path, no one except Ömer gets excited. Here everyone is used to everything. The extraordinary has become ordinary. What need is there for a state of emergency? Every state is always an emergency anyway.

'Don't worry. It's a routine check,' says the brother-in-law. Their work is difficult, too. Everyone's priority is their lives. They know us, but should they see a car that they don't recognize, believe me, their hearts will be thumping, too. All men are the same. Everyone has just one life. Everyone is afraid. We are all afraid.'

'They treat us well,' says Jiyan. 'We will sort things out with a reciprocal greeting. We are considered the region's gentry. We even have dealings in common with the state and with the military. Conversely if some poor person were to pass by on a donkey then there would be no deference or respect.'

The jeep stops and the heavily armed men approach.

'We are taking our guest to Soğukpınar,' says the brother-in-law. 'He's one of our writers, and he's come to get to know our region. He's a friend of the commander.' Then he says something in Kurdish.

The men glance briefly at their identity cards. 'All right. Pass. You don't have anyone with you with a foreign passport, do you?'

'Which of us would be a foreigner? This gentleman is one of our best-known authors. Perhaps you've heard of him: Ömer Eren. He has come to acquaint himself with the region, to write. We are looking after him.'

The man does not seem impressed. 'We don't know what these writers write. It's all right for the Commander. If something goes cock-eyed, or anything happens to him, we'll be held responsible, not the Commander. There is a lot of action again in the area these days, so you must get back before nightfall.'

The arrogant and abrupt manner of the man, who appears to be the head of the patrol squad, his all-powerful demeanour, offends Ömer. The brother-in-law's almost grovelling humouring of him and Jiyan's silence upsets him further. Here even going to a spring on a hot day comes at a price . . .

Soğukpınar: a few poplars, a few willows and a little further on clear water gushing from the rocks. And a hut with thick plastic over the holes that pass for its window and door. In front of it, by the water, are three tables covered with wax cloths with dilapidated wooden chairs arranged around them.

The dark, wizened man who emerges from the hut at the sound of the engine comes running with a dirty cloth in his hand in the hope that his unexpected guests may be good customers. Welcoming them in Kurdish, he makes a show of wiping the chairs and the table surfaces with the cloth.

'Well, this is Soğukpınar,' says Jiyan. 'The surroundings used to be much more beautiful – or at least it seemed like that to us. In spring when the snow melts it's really lovely, when the snowdrops begin to show their heads.'

She has the timid melancholy of a child who is worried that the beautiful picture she has drawn will not be admired or of a poor little girl who suddenly realizes that the frilly dress she has donned to impress the others around her is in fact old, cheap and pathetic. She knows that Ömer will compare it with country restaurants near water he has known and belittle it, thinking: Was this the picnic place you praised to the skies? She knows that even if he does not say so he will think it and lie, saying, 'It's beautiful.' Indignant and depressed, she knows that Soğukpınar is a sorry place of three poplars and a willow and that the standards of the best and the most beautiful of this land have changed, that in the eyes of the country's giants it has shrunk to the size of the land of the dwarfs. Later on she would tell Ömer this, in an attempt to explain herself.

She leans down to the clear water that flows in front of the table where they are sitting. From the edge of the water, she picks a daffodil with glossy yellow petals, the constant adornment of the riverbank. As she tries to pin it to her hair, her slide springs open and her hair tumbles down towards the water like a thick black mane. At that moment such desire swells within Ömer that he can hardly prevent himself from embracing her, reaching out for her lips and holding her tightly to his breast. As Jiyan straightens up and comes to the table with the gracefulness of a black cat or a lynx, he understands from the moistness in her eyes and the flush spreading around her prominent cheekbones that she shares this desire. He thinks that her hair is the conductor. When her hair is freed from its restraints, we fall into its net. Their eyes meet, their eyes make love, commit adultery.

Ömer sends a sign of his passion, his love and his respect in a single phrase to the woman that he cannot embrace and kiss right there, whose net of hair he cannot get entangled in. A sentence that he murmurs from the heart to himself, that has not been coated with sugar, dipped in the sauce of mock respect, that does not give solace: 'When I can see this place, this land with your eyes and embrace it with your heart then I will have found what I am looking for. When I feel in my heart that Soğukpınar is not just a few poplars and a few willows.'

Instead of the thoughts that he could not express, he says in a loud voice, 'I shall learn to love these parts.'

Jiyan comes over to him and sits on the broken wooden chair. She tries to match the yellow flower in her hand with the flowers on the wax cloth. 'The fact that you are even making the effort is important, Ömer Eren. There has been many a person who has understood us in mind and has extolled us with speeches, many a politician, intellectual and writer such as you. We must not be unfair to any of them. However, because they have not understood with their hearts, because their hearts and language have not reached our hearts, they have always remained outsiders. Perhaps we have done them an injustice. We have not been able to open up our hearts enough to them either. Isn't it like that with love, too? It is easy for the strong one, the one who dominates, to love and trust. Those who are meek and more submissive find it hard to love, hard to trust.'

Trout fried in butter, a salad with plenty of onion and an appetizer with yogurt and garlic resembling *mantı* with bulgur arrive at the table. The man rushing around with a napkin in his hand, trying to please the customers, says something in Kurdish.

'The bread is not fresh. They had not kneaded dough because they were not expecting anyone today. His wife is making fresh *kete* inside,' Jiyan translates.

'The trout from these waters is unique,' boasts the step-sister.

'If you were to ask us, we have nothing that is unique,' says Jiyan mockingly.

Ömer recalls that wherever he goes and is treated to trout he hears the same sentiments. Wherever trout is the only fish available, the locals boast about how amazing it is. Is it that the less one has to boast about the more valuable it becomes? His feels a faint stab in his heart. I, too, should like to believe that my trout was unique, I should like to believe that what I have is unique, he thinks with a pang of sorrow.

'Well, now it's time for a drink of *rakı*,' says the brother-in-law with glee. He calls out to the man, 'Bring us *rakı*, Not that state *rakı* or whatever. Some of ours if there is any.'

The colour of the *rakı* that was brought in a water bottle is slightly yellow.

'It is a sort of bootleg *rakı*. I advise you not to add water to it, Ömer *Bey*. First try it like this.'

Ömer takes a forkful of trout. The fish really is delicious, and it has much whiter flesh than the trout he has eaten in the past. He takes a sip of the *rakı*. It glides down his throat leaving a slight burning sensation. He admits to himself that he was expecting a much stronger, spirituous, unpleasant taste. We tend to think that the other person's fish and drink do not measure up to ours. Even if we pretend to have liked them, our praise is just for politeness, a show of cordiality.

He seems to sense the source of Jiyan's hidden anger, her distance and her open rebellion which she cannot rid herself of even when they are at their closest.

The fish, the *rakı* and the water filled from the spring all taste divine. Real butter has been spread on the hot *kete*. The chattering poplar leaves turn their never-ending talk into song and the little bee-eaters defy the crows. Jiyan's wild hair flies around; it ripples as she talks, as she shakes her head. Ömer Eren understands that without realizing Soğukpınar's beauty, without tasting the healing power hidden in its water, without being in love with Jiyan, it cannot be said that he knows the area and likes it, and if it is said it won't go beyond words that remain on the edge of his lips. I can stay here for the rest of my life, at the water's edge listening to the rustling music of the poplars and stroking Jiyan's hair. When the snow melts and the snowdrops shoot up through the green grass, while looking for cool-ness in the summer heat, in autumn when the leaves of the poplars assume the colours of sadness and fly around, and when the snow settles and the wolves come down, I can stay in the hut by the fire I have lit. A whole life is not a very long time for a man who has reached his mid-fifties. I will stay here; not as the other or the one who alienates and not as a stranger, just as me, just Ömer Eren . . .

That day, when he returned to the hotel towards evening, pretty drunk, pretty tired but with a heart that for a long time had not felt so light, he stroked the ginger cat that was dozing in the old morocco leather armchair near the reception desk. 'What's its name?' he asked the youth responsible for room service who was wandering around. 'Virik,' said the boy shrug-ging his shoulders and grinning.

'And what does Virik mean?'

'How should I know, *abi*? It's just a cat's name.'

As the boy chased the cat away with his long-handled mop, he remembered something and added, 'They came from the military. The Commander sent a note. They could not reach you on your phone. It's on the counter under the customer records book.' He came over to Ömer, bent his head slightly and whispered in his ear. 'These days there are a lot of people asking about you, *abi*, both civilians and military men.'

'What do you tell them when they ask?'

'I say, he's writing a book in his room.'

'Even if I'm not in my room?'

'Well ... how will they know? If they go up and have a look, I'll say, so he went out without my noticing.'

'Why do you say that then?'

The boy shrugged his shoulders, 'You're Jiyan *Abla*'s friend, that's why. Here they get suspicious of foreigners. I wouldn't want anything to happen to you.'

Ömer opened the envelope. This time the note from the military was not an invitation for a chat; it was an official summons to the Commander's office around noon the following day. The Commander had not allowed other units to do the interview or questioning because of Ömer Eren's reputation and because of the good relationship they had formed between them. Apparently he preferred to resolve the problem himself. Ömer thought, I've stayed long enough to attract attention – although it hadn't been three weeks since he had arrived. He stuffed the envelope into his pocket and went up to his room.

The bedroom was hot and stuffy. He opened the window wide and drew back the net curtains. He threw his dusty shoes on the floor and lay down on the bed just as he was.

When he awoke it was past midnight. His head was thumping, his tongue was furred, his throat dry. He felt terrible. That homemade *rakı* had really knocked him out, he thought. Yet how good everything was at the edge of the water. How easily the sips of *rakı* had glided down his throat. He emptied the rest of the water in the bottom of the plastic bottle on the little table in front of the window into a glass and began to look for the painkillers he had bought from Jiyan's shop the first night he arrived in town. He rummaged through his trouser pockets, the side pockets of his bags and the empty drawers in which he was sure he had not put anything. After that first night he had not needed painkillers. He thought that perhaps he had left the box at the shop on the counter after he had taken the pills with the water Jiyan had provided. He washed his face at the basin. He needed some ice-cold water, but the tap water was almost warm. He decided to go downstairs and ask the boy on night duty for cold water and to send him to one of the two chemists in the market or town – whichever was open – to buy some analgesics for his headache.

The boy on night duty had rested his head on the counter and was snoring lightly. Ömer did not have the heart to wake him up. He thought he heard a noise from the kitchen. He went towards it in the hope of finding someone to ask for water and whom he could send to the chemist's. The cat Virik streaked out of the kitchen and hid under one of the armchairs in the lobby. Ömer pressed the light switch beside the door. A feeble yellow light illuminated the room which looked more like a place for making coffee than a working kitchen. As he turned to the corner where the fridge was, he noticed that the window opening on to the side street was open. They must have left it open to air but, still, what careless behaviour! A shadow passed in front of the window. He shuddered and was angry with himself for doing so; he was angry with this sinister town and the clouds that had descended over it.

'I want to live without the fear of masked men raiding my house in the middle of the night and wandering around inside, taking me away to some unknown place; without the fear of being hit by a bullet in the neck on a street corner; without experiencing the fear of losing my loved ones or turning against them. This is all I long for, all we long for,' Jiyan had said. 'And I want to wander as free as a bird on summer nights along streets lit by street lamps, where people sit in front of their doors, where they sit and talk in front of their shops, without fear weighing on my heart,' she had said. He understood.

He took a bottle of cold water from the fridge. Although it was not his job he shut the window. As he closed it he did not stick his head out of the window but took shelter behind the wall. This time instead of being angry with himself he laughed. This is what I call adapting to the environment; if someone who was not from this area were to see me they would make fun of my behaviour. He went out of the kitchen leaving the light on. The boy at reception was still fast asleep. The cat was waiting in front of the hotel's glass door, watching for the door to open. When it saw Ömer it rubbed itself against his legs and miaowed. 'Do you want to go outside? Come on, Virik.' He liked addressing the cat by its name. Virik stopped being any old cat and became a cat he knew, that knew him; it was as though it smoothed out his feeling of foreignness.

As he was trying to open the door to let Virik out, the youth at reception awoke and leapt up befuddled with sleep. Ömer glanced at him and saw the gun that had suddenly appeared on the counter. He pushed Virik who had begun to miaow away with his foot.

'Don't worry. You were asleep, and I didn't want to wake you up. I came down to get some cold water, and the cat wanted to go outside.'

'Let him go out, *abi*. Wait, I'm here now. I'll open the door.'

As the boy was opening the door and pushing the cat outside, he stood for a moment as though riveted to the spot and then hastily closed the door. He said something in Kurdish. Ömer did not understand what he said but gathered from his tone that he was swearing.

'Has something happened?'

'No, *abi*. You go up to your room. They've surrounded the market again. They're over by the chemist's.'

Ömer rushed towards the door.

'Don't open it, *abi*. Go up to your room. This is our business.'

'What do you mean, our business, buddy? Don't I count as a man here? Isn't this my country? If there's a nasty situation developing here, then it's as much my business as yours.'

The young man stood in front of the door without moving a muscle. In his harsh eastern accent, emphasizing his words one by one, he obstinately reiterated, 'I'm responsible for your safety.'

Buddy, you were asleep just a moment ago. If I had gone out, you wouldn't have known, thought Ömer.

'You are right, *abi*. It's your country, too. But you don't know this area, what it's like. We fight, and you are the judge. If the judge gets beaten up there will be even more blood and tyranny. Just stand back and leave things to me.'

'I can't stand back. Your Jiyan *Abla*'s chemist's shop is over there. My friend is there . . .'

'Our Jiyan *Abla* knows how to handle them. She has survived till now. She knows death, blood and tyranny. Nothing will happen to her. No one would dare touch her. Anyway the men are not coming just to see her. It's a general raid on the market, and in passing they've stopped by the chemist's shop.'

'But, still, let me go and look. If they see me they will steer clear.'

'Here no one will steer clear of you. If they take you in, they will question you like there's no law or constitution – or even God. Here no one has a

God, not in the mountains nor on the plains. Men you drank with, talked to, yesterday will suddenly disappear. There will be no one behind you to offer support.'

'Are we just going to stand here with our hands tied? If I call the Commander . . .'

'It won't do any good. Anyway the Commander knows. Sometimes it's beyond the Commander. Who's really in charge here is anyone's guess!'

Ömer sank into the armchair next to the door. He realized that his headache and the throbbing in his temples had passed. This must be what they call the hair of the dog that bit you. Years ago, when they arrested him and took him to the police station – was it when they went out flyposting or was it during a protest to support a workers' boycott? – he recalled them saying, 'Even if the Son of God came, he would not be able to save you from this place, so spill the beans! Tell us about the organization.' Such things get forgotten . . . Years pass, our lives change, no one cares any more, we pass over to the other side and we forget. Tyranny and terror recede from our surroundings because we have become compliant, respected members of the system, the cogs of the cutting machine. As the boy said, at best we are the judges. Here rights, justice, even God have long since fallen victim to unsolved crimes.

'Well, ring the chemist's shop.'

'That won't do, *abi*. In any case they will have connected the phone to their own line. To telephone from here is not on.'

My mobile phone! Why didn't I think of that before? Luckily it's in my hip pocket. He dialled Jiyan's number and waited, his heart constricting. 'The number you have called is unavailable at present. Please try later.' He looked at his message inbox. Two new messages: the first was from Elif. Without reading it he quickly skipped to the second one. It was from Jiyan. 'Don't worry. It's a routine check. I'll call later.'

He sank a little deeper into the armchair or, rather, he shrank. Out of the corner of his eye he watched the youth on night duty take the gun on the reception desk and place it under the counter.

'While you were asleep I went into the kitchen and the window was wide open,' he said to put the boy on the spot.

'It can't be. I closed everywhere up myself,' replied the boy. He took out the gun he had hidden under the counter. As he walked towards the kitchen he turned to Ömer and with the smile of a naughty child he said, 'You're angry so you're teasing me, aren't you, *abi*? Was the window really open?'

'Yes, I was angry, but the window really was wide open. I closed it.'

He saw the shadow of fear passing over the boy's face, and he felt sorry.

'If the latch wasn't closed properly perhaps the cat opened the window. After all, it was in the kitchen, and it shot out when I opened the door.'

'But, still, I should look. They might throw something in or something…'

'What sort of thing?'

'Four or five years ago they threw a couple of Molotov cocktails – bombs and stuff. I wasn't here then, and after that nothing like that happened, thank God. But nowadays things are stirring up again, so you never know. They could throw something different, such as smuggled goods, I mean, white stuff. Then they mount a raid and extort money.'

'Who does?'

'All of them. How do you think people get by here? Is there regular work? Where are the factories? The military and the government don't even shop from local tradesmen. Even their jars of honey are surreptitiously imported from some way away. The people are destitute, and they try to get by through their own means.' Lowering his voice he whispers, 'Smuggling, especially drug smuggling, serves everyone in these parts. Jiyan *Abla* doesn't get mixed up in that sort of thing. That's why they keep raiding the market and the chemist's shop to conduct searches. They don't find anything and off they go.'

Ömer remained quiet and contented himself with watching the boy carefully searching the kitchen through the open door.

'There does not seem to be anything here,' said the boy. He stood in front of the door and looked outside. 'They are not coming this way. They are going into the market. Don't call Jiyan *Abla* straight away though. Leave things to settle down a bit. Your calling would not be good for her either. Here things resolve themselves, and, if not, nothing can be done about it.'

Two steps away Jiyan is in trouble, perhaps in danger. And I can't do anything. I can't help. My hands are tied. This rascal of a hotel boy gives me advice, tells me what I should and shouldn't do. I'm of no use to anyone. I cannot help either of the two women I love.

He slumped into the torn leather armchair. He began to fiddle with his phone. There were new messages in the inbox. Why can't I just switch the thing off? Why don't I take the SIM card out and be free of it altogether? Frustrated by his indecision, displeased with himself and also a little worried, he reads Elif's message: 'I can't reach you. I'm with the boy. Call me.' He looked at the date of the message. It must have come while they were at

Soğukpınar. Suddenly he felt shattered, all done in: weak, feeble, hesitant and homeless. Not even in limbo – at a complete loose end.

I've slowly rolled into this chasm, destroying myself, forsaking myself. Writing with an eye on customer satisfaction, calculating the number of editions, measuring the length of the queue of admiring readers – mostly women – that stretch in front of me on signing days . . . And then that difficult question: What was I really? What did I have to destroy? Elif had written in her message that she was with the boy. The boy . . . my son who ran away from violence, life's cruelty, the savage world of grown-ups; whom I abandoned because he longed for an insignificant, happy life and I considered him lacking in courage and drive. My wounded son who ran away and sought refuge on a distant island. What noble cause was I espousing when I accused him of being worthless? Was I courageous when I flung his failures, his incompetence in his face?

He felt as though he were in a bad film with a stupid script that had no proper beginning or end but which one could not help watching. The décor, time, place and actors were all strange, and unreal. What if he got up and left? He didn't have to watch it, did he? But the doors of the cinema were shut. The youngster who showed people to their seats was of no help to the inconsiderate latecomers. He looked at the mobile's inbox again. He reread Elif's message. He felt he could not call her at this hour. She would be sleeping now. He would have to wake her up. He thought he might feel relieved, be purified if he heard his wife's voice. He wrote a short message: 'I received your message too late. I'll call you early tomorrow, dear.'

He felt like crying his heart out. The youth on night duty was still standing in front of the door. The sun must have risen from behind the mountains to the east. A glow had appeared in that direction.

'Day is breaking.'

'Not yet,' said the child hoarsely. 'There's been an assault, The glow you see is our mountains burning.'

It would be good if he could go up to his room and sleep a little. He was in no state to collect his thoughts and think sensibly. When had the Commander wanted me to come? At twelve, if possible, he said. It's a long time until noon. What's more, the request was quite deferential in tone. There is no sense in rushing off at the crack of dawn.

'I'll go upstairs and try to sleep. If I don't stir, wake me at ten.'

'I'll leave a message for the colleague on day duty, *abi*. Do as you please. I'm here. If anything happens I'll let you know.'

What can happen? he thought to himself. The Kurd enjoys scaring me and making me anxious.

He slowly climbed the stairs, entertaining himself by counting the stains in the maroon stair carpet, the luxury fixture of provincial hotels. Exactly thirty-two large stains. What do people fixate on when they are tense and knackered! The corridor was dark and stuffy. His headache was developing again. As he turned the door handle he remembered that he had not locked the door when he went out. He paused for a moment as he opened it, then he became ashamed of his panic and angry with himself. You're not on top of your game, Ömer Eren! You're behaving as if you've always been safe, as though you never rushed into danger before. It's as if you've entirely forgotten the soldiers with Sten guns kicking the door down and barging into the house at dawn, the screams you heard as you waited your turn to be tortured in the cells where they took you blindfolded, the years of your youth when you were on the run to avoid giving yourself up. No, I haven't forgotten. I haven't become so estranged from my past. But it is different here. It feels foreign here. In those days I knew where the threat and the danger were coming from, what I was up against, what I was fighting. Here I don't know. I cannot comprehend. People fear the unknown.

He had left the light on, and the room was bright. He realized from the coolness of dawn that filled the room that the window was open, and he shivered. As he walked over to the window to shut it his eye caught on the envelope from the Command Headquarters that he had left on the small table. On top of the envelope there was a second piece of paper torn from a chequered notepad. He was sure that this piece of paper did not belong to him and that it had not been there before. He had always hated chequered notebooks. He never used them. Perhaps it was because they reminded him of maths lessons, the nightmare of his childhood. He held the paper to the light and read the two lines on it: 'Don't interfere in our business. Stay away from the chemist. Go home.'

Where is my country, my home? Whose business is it? Who are you? Who am I? Who is the chemist? When was this paper put here? Who put it there?

He thought that he would hear similar advice from the Commander a few hours later. Jiyan had said, 'People who do not take sides are put aside. I am trying not to be on the side of the people holding weapons and I'm also trying not to be put aside. I'm just attempting to be on the side of human-ity and life. It's very difficult, if it weren't for the power of the clan and my being a woman I wouldn't succeed.'

Who wants me to stay away from the chemist? Why am I upsetting them? At the end of the day, I'm a writer looking for a subject for my book in this area. Neither the organization nor the state would bother with me. That leaves the clan – and the possibility of some child's game. Even that rascal downstairs might have done it to frighten and taunt me.

He began to learn that in this land no question had a single, clear, indis-putable answer. The shadow of the mountains, the flames of the fires, the colour of blood and the power of violence wiped out all truths, rendered the answers doubtful and obscured them. Here everything seemed differ-ent to what it was, was different to what it seemed. Even Jiyan's face, her identity. But perhaps, on the contrary, everything was open, as clear as day, simple. And there was no secret, no secret side, and we were writing – I was writing – this complicated scenario as an outside observer embellished by my overactive imagination.

He lay down on the bed. He was amazed at the solitude, the calm inside him. His fear had subsided. I'm not anxious. How strange – and how good! It was a feeling of having overcome that which had been imposed upon him. Was it from helplessness? Perhaps I am gradually adjusting to the region. His eyelids, brain and heart grew heavy. He fell asleep. If they had not called him from reception and woken him up at ten he could have slept until the evening.

As he was shaving and getting dressed in a leisurely manner, his mind was not on what the Commander was going to say; it was on Jiyan: her hair that was demure in the street and unruly in bed, her changeable face whose real exression he had not managed to catch, her anger, mutiny, pride and submission, her mystery, her secrecy. Jiyan who could not be possessed even at the moment of union, who did not surrender even when moaning with pleasure, always belonging to another world, to another lover.

When he entered the market he purposely walked on the pavement opposite the Hayat Chemist. As he came level with the shop he restrained his desire to enter and glanced over casually from across the road. Jiyan was not there. The young female assistant was arranging the shelves. He walked slowly across the middle of the market road as though he were challenging the unknown enemy. Two stray dogs lazing in front of the butcher's shop feebly wagged their tails without getting up. The barber, who was sitting on the wicker stool he had put in front of his shop and sipping his very strong tea, gave a friendly greeting. He slowed his steps as he passed in front of the internet café. When one of the youths chatting away in front of the door saw Ömer he left the others and came across. With a strong eastern accent he respectfully asked him for a book. There was no bookshop in the town, and they would be delighted if the writer could send some books. Then he added, 'Write about us, *abi*. Our voices don't reach your parts. Our language isn't sufficient. As you are a writer, be our voice.' Ömer promised to send some books, but he could not promise to be their voice.

As he passed in front of the photographer's shop two girls emerging in local dress ran off giggling. His eye spotted the honey pots on the shelves of the honey-seller who sold every imaginable kind of foodstuff, from cereals to potatoes and onions. He craved honey; he longed for it. I must buy some on my return. He fell in with the ginger-and-white piebald dog that followed him whenever he went through the market and reached the end of the market road. A military jeep passed him by lifting the dust from the earth road. The dog gave up following him and turned back with its tail between its legs as though he had been spooked by something. The dusty, deserted road sloped gently up towards the military zone. At the side of the road, yellow daisies had opened despite the dust. He picked one. As he passed the first checkpoint he only had to say his name. They knew him by now, so they did not ask for his identity card, but he produced it as well as the invitation from the Commander for the guards on the main gate. There was a short telephone call with 'yes, sirs' and 'no, sirs' and then 'The Commander is expecting you.' He remembered the day he had first passed this gate. It was as though there used to be a kinder, friendlier atmosphere. Come on, I'm imagining it. It's always the same formalities!

The Commander was alone. He was composed and respectful as always. He stood up from his chair and stretched out his hand from behind his desk and bade him sit down. Ömer remembered that the first day they had met the Commander had got up from behind the desk, come over to him, shown him to a place and then sat down in his own chair again; not like a superior but like a host welcoming guests of consequence.

Contrary to what he expected, there were not the awkward, silent moments, and the formal enquiries after his health did not drag on. The coffees without sugar were ordered straight away. What needed to be said was said, as the Commander put it, 'in plain, soldier language', without prevaricating and hiding behind polite, meaningless sentences. It had been quite some time since Ömer Eren had arrived. He had been given sufficient time and opportunity to scrutinize the area, its problems and the people *in situ*. The Commander said, 'You can be sure that we have given no other civilian such extensive freedom of movement. You are one of our most prominent writers, and I have no doubts about your patriotism. We wanted you to see things with your own eyes, to evaluate things in your own mind.' Of course it was their duty to provide the country's eminent intellectuals with such opportunities, and the army and state were extremely grateful to him for taking the trouble to travel so far to see things for himself. However, as reflected in the media, tensions were increasing in the region. The 'cease-fire' was, as always, just a tactical diversion. There was reliable intelligence that the separatist terrorist organization was about to attack, and at times like these – the Commander felt the need to lower his voice as he was saying this – it was impossible to separate the good from the bad, and it was not certain how and from where provocation would manifest itself. From the sake of the writer's safety, it would be better for everyone if he were to leave the region as soon as possible.

For a moment Ömer thought of mentioning the note left in his room and saying, 'There are others beside you who want me to go.' Then he remembered his words 'It's impossible to separate the good from the bad' and remained silent.

'Is that an order, Commander?'

'Let us say a request and a friendly warning, if you like.'

'I understand.'

'Now, relying on your tolerance and confidence, as a friend I'm going to tell you something in all honesty. Something that I should not tell you, something you should not hear from me.'

Ömer felt like saying, 'If you like, don't tell me.' Whether it was because he was afraid of what he would hear or whether he had doubts about the veracity of what he was to hear, he did not know.

He just said, 'Please go on, sir.'

'I don't want you to misunderstand, to construe this as our interfering in your private life. Besides, we might be wrong. But, still, I wanted to warn you about the lady chemist. We get far more intelligence leaked to us than we can deal with. We get overwhelmed by what we know and learn.' He stopped talking. It was as though he were waiting for permission to carry on.

For a moment Ömer thought about not giving his consent, thanking him and getting up. Then he was overcome by his curiosity and his emotions. 'I would not wish you to be overwhelmed by what you know.'

'Jiyan *Hanım* is a very unusual woman. She is a mystery to everyone, even to our intelligence units. Her secrets are hidden in the depths of this land. I'm telling you, swearing on my honour, that we have no evidence to prove for whom she is working and who her inside and outside connections are. It's as though some invisible force is protecting her. Clan relationships, especially since the war has escalated in the region, have become so complicated, so thoroughly confused, that even we cannot work them out. I can't even claim that we completely understand the militia clans who cooperate with us. The shield provided by the clan that protects the lady chemist is important, of course, but it does not explain everything. What is more, the clans are gradually disbanding. They are dabbling in politics and are to an extent losing their former power and unity. You know they always talk about the 'deep state'; well, in these parts, there are systems even deeper than the deep state, and it is not known who is pulling the strings.'

He stopped talking again. He looked down trying to avoid meeting Ömer's eyes. It was evident that he was deliberating what to say. Then he lifted his head as though he had come to a decision and spoke looking straight into the other man's eyes. 'There is no one who remembers the woman's birth and her childhood. It is as though she suddenly appeared when she was sixteen or seventeen. And after that she studied abroad. She calls all of her father's wives "Mother". The woman who appears to be her mother on her birth certificate, let us say her real mother, is dead. We know nothing about her.'

'Couldn't she have been adopted? Or could she have come into the family through the exchange of brides – you know, what they call *berdel*? They say that in this region there are people who do not know how many children they have or remember their names.'

As soon as he had had spoken he was sorry; he was ashamed of himself. I said, 'this region', displaying all my white Turkishness. These strange lands that we believe harbour every disease known to man! I used the Commander's language. I betrayed Jiyan. I got caught up in the story, and I began to contribute to it. Instead I should have shut the man up immediately.

'If that were the case, it would be known. Here such relationships cannot be hidden. It's out in the open. It's just the right subject for you, Ömer *Bey*. These are the kinds of things that happen in novels, don't they? They never seem very plausible when one reads them.'

'Thank you for your suggestion, but there is something I still find difficult to believe. Let us say this scenario is true. What does it matter to the state whose daughter she is? I mean, what is the objection in the political sense? Or what has it got to do with me?'

'Let us say danger rather than objection. I have a hunch that the lady's husband was murdered because he learnt some of the truth. And his wife did not prevent his execution. She could not. At least she kept quiet.'

The Commander using the term 'lady' when he talked about Jiyan annoyed Ömer almost more that what he actually said. It was the macho culture's language of bogus respect that used the word lady in contempt, like an insult.

'Now I'm really confused. Where does this information fit in the Jiyan *Hanım* legend?'

'It seems I should speak more openly. I'm not saying that the chemist had her husband killed. There are those who believe that that's what happened, but there can be no condemnation without evidence and proof. I say that she could not prevent her husband's murder and, most importantly, that although she knew the murderers she did not denounce them. She did not denounce them because . . .'

'I can tell you that she still loves her murdered husband. She is still attached to him.'

'That's true. As far as I have heard the man was an important Kurdish sympathizer. He wrote books and so on. He did his doctorate in France. He lived for many years in Europe, in Sweden, I think. They say that he had a great influence in the chemist's development. There was a difference of more than twenty years between them. It is true that she was attached to her husband. However, it fails to explain everything. I haven't delved very deeply into the subject. According to the reports I have read, her husband was a Kurdish nationalist. However, he was against violence. I'm a soldier, Ömer *Bey*. I'm involved in the war and the security side of things. I keep my political judgements to myself. However, I can tell you this much: in this area such a person is the target of every hawk from every section.'

Ömer did not want to hear any more, and the Commander did not want to tell him any more. The conversation had ended and both of them understood this.

'I hope you are not angry and that you have not been hurt. What I told you was to warn you, to protect you,' the Commander said in a friendly tone. 'And perhaps in a way you are right. You know I told you that we get intelligence leaks. Sometimes they want to mislead even us. I mean, disin-formation spreads this far. I have moments of doubt, too, about who knows the truth or, more to the point, who plans and dishes out what is presented to us as the truth. I'm a soldier. I cannot always gauge who is right and what is just. Soldiery and war do not allow this type of analysis, Ömer *Bey*. This conversation did not take place between a commander and a writer; it was just between two friends, I rely on your understanding in this matter.'

'I understand. Thanks. Don't worry. Of course what we have discussed will remain between us. If you ask me, this is all very complicated. We reputable novelists don't like such complicated stories. We consider this the stuff of crime writers or of mediocre writers who seek to embellish their work with intrigues and conspiracy theories. Perhaps the truth, I mean the truth about Jiyan *Hanım*, is much more ordinary than all these conjectures, these conspiracy theories. But thank you again, both for informing me and for trusting me. What you have told me won't go any further. Don't worry. You are right, even if the truth is in the hands of certain people, we are all being manipulated.'

The two men, about the same age, shook hands in a friendly manner. It was a warm, simple parting without ceremony but one that neither of them would forget. A current of feeling reaching from person to person, man to man, flowed between them.

When Ömer had passed through the garrison's barbed-wire gate with its sentry boxes and watchtowers and reached the road, he paused for a minute at the top of the slope and looked at the dusty, grey, barren town bleakly lying in the valley below. The dilapidated houses mainly with flat roofs, virtually identical government buildings placed without the least nod to aesthetic considerations, schools, some lead domes sparkling under the sun, a few minarets and the market road which from this viewpoint looked thoroughly seedy, neglected and rundown. And the poplar trees . . . The poplar trees in rows with crows perched on their branches. Then he turned his eyes to the mountains. The mountains that rose on all sides to spite the town's dismal wretchedness, their peaks quite white with summer snow, their slopes fresh spring green and with cataracts gushing from the precipices. He remembered Mahmut's words, 'We look at the mountains, *abi*, and we listen to them. It has been like this for generations. The town is captivity, the mountains are freedom . . . Or that is what we think.'

He feels upset when he thinks about Mahmut. What will they do? What will happen to them? Has his helping them been of any use? By embracing

Mahmut and Zelal how much can we solve? How can people be saved one by one? How can they keep their heads above water? In my youth I believed in individual salvation. We used to say that malaria would not end with killing the mosquitoes one by one, without draining the swamps. Did I say being saved? Well, who will save me? Who will save us?

He took off down the slope with rapid steps, a great number of unanswered questions hanging over his head and about his feet. Thinking about Jiyan with a solid lump in his breast, impatient to be reunited with her, and trying not to think about Elif, he walked back to the town.

EIGHT

The Subtle Pain of Killing a Mouse

A faint stab clawing at the middle of her breast. The echo in her heart of the thin muffled 'eek' uttered by the laboratory animal as it dies. One gets used to it. After a while you begin to think of your victim as a rubber toy. A little mouse, a guinea pig or sometimes a cat; a life entrusted to you hanging on your orders and your mood. You are God. The little creature in your hand does not even understand from where and from whom death comes. It resists with all its strength, reacting with fear as life does towards death, existence towards non-existence. All its strength is this slight, feeble 'eek'. The sound of a person is a little louder than a mouse, a test animal. Sometimes it is a scream. Even if the sound is a scream it cannot rebel against extermination. It cannot conquer death. Can't it rebel? Can't it conquer it?

As Elif, in her hotel room in Copenhagen, makes the final corrections to the paper she is going to present at the congress in Göteborg two days later, she ponders the sentence, 'Even if the sound is a scream it cannot rebel against annihilation, it cannot defeat death.' There is something in this statement that is troubling. To reduce life and death to this single dimension is a precept too simple and superficial. If all the dozens of guinea pigs and hundreds of test animals were all to scream with one voice, if they were to rebel against their executioners *en masse*, they would be able, for a time at least, to hinder their annihilation. They could succeed in living for a while longer. To live for a while longer . . . For what? For what purpose? What would be the use of extending the life of a little mouse for a few hours? What is the sense of a mouse's life? Well, what is the use of extending a person's life for a few hours, a few days or even a few years? What is the meaning of a person's life apart from the fact that it is a person asking the question and not a mouse?

Well, that is a question thinks Elif. That famous question that Hamlet posed with the skull in his hand: 'To be or not to be', where we come full circle. The moment you ask what the point of a mouse's life is, then to kill it for a higher purpose gains legitimacy. And so it is quite possible to leap quite easily from the question 'What is the point of a mouse's life?' to 'What is the point of a person's life?' The transition from killing a mouse to killing a human can theoretically be less difficult than one thinks. If death is the annihilation of a living creature then the difference is of quantity not quality. You can sacrifice the lives of people one by one for the sake of a noble cause thought to be for the benefit of all mankind. You can kill half of mankind in order to save the world. You will risk dying and killing for your country, your homeland and your nation. For the sake of beliefs and ideology you can sacrifice the lives of people. You can sacrifice a great many lives, animals or people in order to find the cure for a deadly disease. Which noble purpose, which noble cause justifies death and killing, exterminating life? Can good intention, the right purpose, legitimate violence? Then, what is the standard for good and right? Who defines the standard? Whose morals? The thousand-year-old questions of philosophy and ethics ...

I am not a social scientist and I'm not a psychologist either, she thinks. But still, in most of the scientific congresses she attends, especially those that are predominantly about ethics in science, she inevitably finds herself caught up in a debate about the position of man versus the violence fed by the technological revolution of the age.

All types of violence, all their aspects, are in need of investigation; from the violence considered innocent of the child who tortures a mangy dog, ties tins to cats' tails and who treads on flowerbeds and grass, to the violence of the researcher who kills guinea pigs for science; from the violence of a man who beats the dog he loves, his child and his wife, to the violence of the death sentence legitimized, legalized by politics and war; and from the planned organized violence that has enveloped the whole world to daily violence. No one has any doubts on this matter. Everyone is united. And then what? When people cannot produce solutions to eliminate it what is the good of exposing violence, explaining it? Was it not Marx who said, 'Philosophers have only interpreted the world, the point is to change it'? Our generation was nurtured by Marxism, and even if we didn't study it in depth we knew these quotations by heart. For a moment she considers ending the paper she is to present by quoting Marx. For example, a sentence such as 'We content ourselves with explaining the unethical, shocking developments that gene technology can give rise to and the violence that it can create, but it is necessary to produce solutions to resolve this.' She stops at this point. Quotations from Marx no longer go down very well in scientific circles. They may even cause loss of prestige. So how am I going to end this paper? Suddenly she feels inadequate. She can't think of anything other than the rebellious collective eeking of mice as a possible solution. A naïve joke to add pleasantry to the debate – that's all.

Whenever her son comes to her mind, she thinks of Deniz with a keen, clinging sadness. Was it not a form of violence when we looked for what we held to be right in him, condemned him to surpass us, to be success-ful, to be strong? When talking about violence we only think about wars, exploding bombs, mines, people killed randomly, women and children. Yet don't we all continually feed the source of violence? I, killing my test animals, another interfering with embryos, someone else trying to find the formula for the most powerful weapon of mass destruction, those who philosophize on violence, those who use the power of government, we all constantly produce violence. Deniz found the solution in running away. He even considered taking photographs of violence, suffering and the help-lessness of people as complicity, and he rejected it. We called him a deserter, a deserter of life! Perhaps the truly consistent, strong, moral person was our son whom we tried to erase from our hearts saying that he was weak, unsuccessful and a fugitive. Our son, who ran away from the sufferings of this world and from violence, from us, and took refuge on a foreign island, in his beloved who died, his little son and his hopelessness.

Elif had hoped that Deniz would call her on his return from the Big Fish competition when he did not find her on the island, or at least leave a message on her phone. Perhaps he was hurt because I had not waited. Perhaps he hadn't had the energy to call. We live in such different worlds. In a sense distance repairs our relationship. If we had been together for another three to four days we might have upset each other. We could have altogether lost the fragile bond that we thought we had found. But still she would have liked her son to call. Sometimes quarrelling is better than silence. There is even an affinity, a dialogue, in continual bickering.

Outside it is rainy and a little cool. What sort of a start to July is this? Elif likes the sun and sparkling blue water. The characteristic of Cancer. She had read in a women's magazine that included the signs of the zodiac and such things that Cancer always yearns for water. She feels depressed. If only I had stayed on the island or returned immediately to Istanbul rather than take part in this rather mediocre second congress. The symposium in Copenhagen really was important. All the famous names of the scientific circle were there. And I achieved the result I wanted. There was no need for me to participate in the Göteborg congress. Was it worth it to meet two or three more scholars, to make my presence known to a few more colleagues? Why do I always want more? Why do I put myself under more stress? This is a form of self-inflicted violence.

She closes her laptop. That's enough. I can't make it any better! Most of the papers of those self-important men and women are much ado about nothing. It's as though they are on holiday. They come unprepared and, apart from one or two brilliant contributors, most of them present unoriginal research and stereotypical views within their specialist areas. We put them on a pedestal because of our inferiority complex towards the west. And they with their western arrogance – 'Let's see what this Turkish woman has to say!'– listen to me out of curiosity. They mostly pay more attention to my uncovered head, my smart western clothes and my good English than to the science I have to present – although increasingly my papers are receiving prominence and getting noticed.

What really gets on her nerves at these international congresses is when a paper she presents which she evaluates as 'not bad' is praised to the skies. 'Your paper was wonderful, Mrs Eren. To tell the truth, we didn't realize that science in Turkey was so advanced.' Or 'You probably made these experiments, undertook this research at a research institute in America, didn't you?' Or 'I should like to congratulate you. You are an example of how a person can transcend their surroundings.' It is the same when she has to speak in her bad German. They say, 'Ah, how good your German is!' In other words, monkeys can dance, too! . . . Applause, applause, applause . . . At these meetings where you've been subjected to positive discrimination, you have received praise you did not deserve and where you have been the centre of attention, you perceive the attempts of the western scientists not to alienate – even to encourage – the others from countries less well known for producing world-class scientists. They treat scientists with dark skins and those from Asia like this, too. Their intentions are undoubtedly good, but the exaggerated praise and positive discrimination crushes the other person even more.

Perhaps I'm being unfair. Mine is the oversensitivity of a person from an underdeveloped country. None the less, at such gatherings we from the east and, to a lesser extent, the people from the Mediterranean tend to group together. We feel closer to each other. Anyway this circuit is coming to an end for now. A few days from now I'll be in Istanbul.

When she is abroad, Elif likes staying in good hotels but today the hotel room really depresses her. There is something that she cannot figure out, something that makes her uneasy, a bad feeling that keeps irritating her, a feeling of something lacking. Supposing she went out in the street despite the drizzle, walked a little, sat in a café and ordered herself a glass of wine. That's what they used to do when they lived here. Ömer liked the rainy, misty weather of the north. 'This weather suits the area. Sea, sun and heat go with our parts,' he used to say, and then he would add, 'The weather of the north doesn't suit Cancerians, but Aquarians don't complain about it.'

Suddenly she remembers: Today is my birthday . . . I wouldn't have remembered if there hadn't been the association with the signs of the Zodiac. Ömer forgets many things but never my birthday. She opens her inbox. There are three new messages. With her heart in her mouth she presses the keys of the telephone. Please let Ömer have sent a message, even a tiny one! The messages are not from Ömer. They are insignificant texts. There is not a peep from either Ömer or Deniz. With one tiny hope she looks at missed calls. There are none. How impatient I am! The day is not yet over, there is a whole night in front of me. Birthdays last until the twenty-fourth hour.

She looks out of the hotel window. Outside the summer rain is raining steadily. Today I'm fifty-two. I'm in Copenhagen. I'm a professor of bio-chemistry. I've been nominated for the European Women Scientist of the Year award. Even if it is not a Nobel, it is a prize not to be scorned. I'm looking out of the window of a hotel in Copenhagen. It's raining. It is misty and dark. The streetlights are on, although it's hours before evening. Everything is in order, but I'm depressed. It's raining. I'm married, and I have a son. I'm the wife of novelist Ömer Eren. My son's name is Deniz. He lives on a small island in Norway. It's raining. Raindrops are trickling down the windows. I have a grandson, little Bjørn. I have no daughter-in-law, she died in Istanbul. With the red tulips in front of her and behind her the splendid dome and graceful minarets of Sultanahmet. Her blood spattered on to the tulips and spread over the tarmac, her limbs flew into the air. It's raining here, soft fresh rain. Ömer and I have been married for twenty-seven years. I've never deceived my husband. It never occurred to me and I didn't feel the need. Recently we have been apart a lot. It's natural; our work, our spheres of activity, our professional circles are different. However, no one can say that we don't love each other, that we have become detached from each other, no! It's the beginning of July, and it's raining. That's northern weather for you! No one has remembered my birthday. I'm alone, and it's drizzling down on Copenhagen.

First she sends a short message to Ömer. 'Today's my birthday. Love.' Instead of a message, I could have tried phoning him. But no, she had promised herself that she would not call him unless he called her. She would keep her promise. Then she remembers that she has made a note somewhere of the phone number of the biophysicist who showed a real interest in her paper at the symposium in Copenhagen. 'We are researching similar topics. We could share our knowledge and our experiments,' the man had said. I think he was an Englishman working at the biochemistry or the gene technology institute here. He had given her his phone number and had asked her to call him if she found time. He was between forty and forty-five, a pleasant, intelligent-looking man.

She finds the man's number in the phone's 'contacts' section. So I did make a note of it! She dials the number. For a moment she is afraid that he won't answer the phone. She knows that if she cannot reach the man now she will not call him again. He answers the phone almost immediately.

'I'm Professor Elif Eren from Turkey. I'm in Copenhagen tonight. We could meet if you still think that sharing our knowledge and experiments might be of benefit.'

'In my opinion, it would be more than beneficial. It's crucial! When and where shall I pick you up?'

Elif gives him the address of the hotel. 'I'll be ready an hour later.'

She switches off the telephone completely. If anyone should call they can leave a note. I'm damned if I'm going to wait by the phone all night long for Ömer or Deniz to call! Rather than spending the night on my own feeling sorry for myself I'll talk to someone who understands the work I do. And I'll celebrate my birthday with a glass of wine – no, not just wine, champagne!

She decides to put herself first, to spoil herself. People give you only as much as you ask from them. Especially men. In hindsight I've been unfair to myself in being self-sufficient and strong, in not making more demands on anyone, even on my husband, than they gave. There is no one to nurse you if you don't cry. There are people who know how to get attention. I have not been able to be like them. Yes, not just wine; first champagne and, what is more, the best-quality champagne. I'll spare no expense, and tomorrow morning I'll buy myself a birthday present of the bag and blouse I spotted in the boutique of that famous fashion designer.

She takes the tight black trousers that she knows make her look slimmer than she is and the lilac silk blouse out of the cupboard and throws them on the bed. They will go well with my purple silk and linen jacket. I must be smart and well groomed on my birthday. This will be the first birthday for years that I have spent without Ömer, without having flowers from him. Long ago, when we were two penniless students, he used to bring carnations and roses that he had picked from gardens on my birthday; in the first years of their marriage a beautifully arranged bunch of flowers from the florist and with it a book or a cassette that she had been wanting for some time; and in more recent years expensive, exquisite orchids and tropical plants ordered by telephone from the florist accompanied by a valuable piece of jewellery, perhaps an unusual ring designed by a famous contemporary jeweller. As our relationship crumbled amid the gnawing teeth of time, the monetary value of the flowers and other gifts rose. I wonder if I could write the formula for the inverse proportion between love and the value of gifts.

She goes into the shower with a wry, bitter smile on her face. Standing for a while under hot water will do her good.

She carefully blow-dries her hair and puts on her usual light make-up. A woman must be well groomed and beautiful on the night of her birthday! Especially if she is going out with a man . . . The term 'going out with a man', not the idea, seems funny to her. She likes her reflection in the mirror. Lilac, purple and mauve have been her favourite colours ever since she was young. Ömer does not pay much attention, but he knows my colours. The lilac silk blouse was a present he brought from China.

She puts her jacket over her arm and walks to the stairs. It's not worth taking the lift for two floors. Elif does not like elevators. Electricity might be cut off when you are inside, or there might be a fault and then you would get stuck in the thing. Even the thought of it gives her palpitations.

Her English colleague is seated in the lobby that is furnished with simple elegant Scandinavian furniture of teak, thumbing through the newspapers while he waits.

Instead of hello he says, 'You look very smart. It's impossible to park around here at this hour. I left the car in a car park some way away. I won't make you walk that far. Let's call a taxi so that your clothes are not spoilt by the rain.'

He asks the young woman at reception to call a taxi. They wait by the hotel's glass revolving door. The rain continues to fall gently. The man is well dressed, neither too carefully, nor carelessly. Just as he should be. He holds a large umbrella in his hand. They had learnt at primary school that the British always carried umbrellas.

The man notices that Elif is looking at his umbrella and laughs. 'You think I'm a typical Englishman, don't you? It rains every day in England, so everyone carries an umbrella. Half the Englishmen are homosexual, and half the Englishwomen are frigid. They never miss five o'clock tea. They all drink Scotch and spend much time in the pubs. They have no sense of humour and so on . . . Let me tell you immediately that most of these stereotypes don't apply to me.'

Just as she is about to ask which do apply to him Elif changes her mind. 'Yes. You know there are stereotypes like that for every country. For some reason we like to put the whole of mankind into boxes, into moulds.'

'It makes things easier, that's why. Just like our lab experiments. If we were to think about the individuality of each guinea pig, it would be impossible to us to finish the test.'

The taxi pulls up directly in front of the hotel door. They have only to take a few steps but even so the man opens his umbrella and holds it over Elif's head. Without waiting for the taxi driver he helps her to get into the car.

'So the adage that all Englishmen are gentlemen is not wrong,' says Elif by way of thanks.

The driver waits for them to give him the address.

'What sort of restaurant would you like to go to?' asks her English colleague. 'I know the city well, and I'm fond of eating and drinking. Well, there you have another deviation from the norm. You know they say that the slimmest book in the world is *The English Cuisine*.'

'It's my birthday today. You are my guest. I don't want any argument on the subject. I leave the choice of venue to you. It would be nice to have dinner at a good restaurant with a champagne menu. Somewhere where we can talk; quiet but decent.'

The Englishman gives an address to the driver and the taxi moves off.

'I know of a very good French restaurant: Le Coq Rouge. Incidentally, half the French restaurants outside France are called the Red Cockerel. But it's still very early. It's not even dark. Let me take you to a Scandinavian bar first. From there we'll reserve a place at the restaurant.'

What a good thing I thought of my English colleague, thinks Elif. I could not have stood being in that hotel room tonight. He's really nice, has a good sense of humour, is natural and courteous. And we have subjects in common to talk and argue about. There is no reason for it not to be a good evening.

But what is this feeling of guilt, this uneasiness? She seems to hear the ring of a phone from the depths. She puts her hand to her bag, and then she remembers that she left her mobile in the hotel room. First I turned it off so that no one called, but then I turned it back on. Why? No, I didn't forget it, I left it behind on purpose, knowingly, so that I didn't have to bother with anyone. Be honest with yourself, Elif! You took precautions against the possibility of Ömer phoning you. Every moment you would be waiting for him to call, and the evening would have been spoilt. But still, if only I hadn't left the phone at the hotel. Now it would be rude to say that I'd forgotten my mobile, so let's turn back. Let others ring. Let those who phone learn to call and not get me every time.

When they get out of the taxi in front of the bar they realize it has stopped raining. There is a faint smell of the sea in the air. The sky is a milky grey and the clouds are gradually dispersing. Elif looks at her watch. It's just past seven thirty. It must be about nine thirty in Turkey. Her date opens the door of the bar with unexaggerated, natural courtesy and waits for Elif to pass through first. Then lightly touching her back he directs her to an empty table in the corner. As she settles herself in the chair that he has pulled out, she decides to be free of the vicious circle of anxiety and doubt and make the most of the evening. Let's see what happens. Don't get tense. Don't bottle up your feelings. Enjoy the evening as the fancy takes you. If you get bored, go back to the hotel. If you enjoy yourself, then carry on. Drink and eat as much as you like. After all, you won't get fat in one night. Listen to your heart and not your mind – if only for one night. If you like the man, prolong the evening, but, if you start finding him tedious, then leave saying you're tired. Make life simple. Don't tense up. Relax.

'What would you like to drink? They have good beer here.' Her companion's question brings her out of her reverie.

'I'll start with wine, so as not to mix drinks too much. A dry red wine please – sometimes when you ask for wine they bring a sweet one.'

The waiter takes the order.

Her English colleague broaches the subject of work immediately. 'In your paper you made reference only to your most recent experiments. Your subject was the ethical dimensions of gene technology and its limits of acceptability. For that reason you did not enlarge on your research. I think the work I am doing is very similar. That is why I wanted to speak to you.'

A typical Englishman, she thinks to herself. This man really does want to talk about science. Gracious me! And what was I expecting?

Ömer received Elif's message as he was waiting for news of Jiyan at the chemists. He did not get perturbed because he already was. He only remembered that it was 13 July. At that moment he did not even think of answering. What could he write? What could he say to Elif?

They were following him. They were after him. There were problems. He had to leave as soon as possible. He did not give a damn about any of this. He had left the Commander and gone straight to the chemist's shop to see Jiyan, to touch Jiyan, to speak to Jiyan and to be quiet with Jiyan. Not to become involved with her world and solve her secrets but to be buried in secrets and be part of them. She was a beauty whose attractiveness did not draw its power so much from what it showed but from what it concealed. Her impish intelligence, her forceful femininity and surprising self-confidence seemed to whisper, 'There are things that I keep a secret. You won't be able to reach them, and the more you fail to discover them, the more you will be committed to me. Just like this land, these rivers and mountains.'

Ömer sensed that the poetry of the yellow-grey earth, the barren hills and the craggy cliffs did not lie in what they revealed but in what they concealed. Now he really did understand the meaning of St Exupéry's words, that what made the desert beautiful is that somewhere it hid a well. These lands, these mountains, these people are beautiful because of the voice echoing inside them. It is not what she offers or shows but her secrets that make Jiyan beautiful.

Jiyan was not at the pharmacy. Her helper, the sullen girl, had said, 'Jiyan *Abla* is going to come late. Perhaps she won't come at all today', making it clear that she did not want to say more.

'How late? After the shop is closed?'

'I don't know. She just said, "Don't wait for me." That's all.'

'I have to find her. Her telephone is switched off. She's not at home, and she's not here.'

'She's gone somewhere. She has a lot of work to do.'

'Did you see her this morning? Was she all right? There was a search or something last night. There's nothing the matter, is there?'

'They're always raiding the chemist's shop. Well, whatever they're looking for, they don't find it – and off they go. We are used to it. Jiyan *Abla*'s fine. Don't worry. She'll come when she's ready. Can't a person have things to do? Can't they go places? She's not going to tell us everything, is she?'

The bitch, he thought to himself. She's just making fun of me. She'll come when she's ready! The girl is right, up to a point. Of course people have work to do. She has to go somewhere. She has patients to see. She has friends. I'm making an unnecessary stupid fuss. But after the events of last night she would not go off without a word. She would have phoned or sent news or at least left a note. Doesn't she know I would be worried? Then he remembered the lawyer with whom he had gone to the mourning house. Thank God I took his number. Perhaps he knows. The lawyer was not in his office. His young trainee assistant said that he was out of town on a case.

Again Ömer turned to the girl. 'Now look here. Did she leave me a message? I've got business with Jiyan *Hanım*. I've brought her some very important news. I must see her straight away. Who can tell me where she is? Her family, her friends, those who know her – where do they live?'

'Don't get worked up over nothing, sir. Don't worry. She'll come. Go and ask the military if you like. Ask the District Governor. Perhaps your lot will know. They are the ones who are following her. How should I know?'

Ömer wondered what lay behind the girl's brusqueness. She had said 'your lot'. In other words, the Commander, the District Governor, me – all of us are in the same boat. 'The TC state' as they say here. For her I'm a stranger from the west. It's as though she is trying to protect Jiyan from this me. Why are they so mistrustful, so distant? We say that a person can reach people, but sometimes one can't. One does not know how to; one cannot find the way.

He tried to touch the girl's weak spot, her attachment to Jiyan.

'My news is very important. If you know something, tell me. After all, if something bad happens to Jiyan *Abla*, you will be responsible!'

A shadow passed over the girl's face. Or so it seemed to him. Her lips went taut. She fixed her eyes on the counter and spoke without looking at his face. 'Why don't you leave us alone? You come here like this, infidels, Turks . . . And then you abandon us and we get into trouble. Whenever a stranger comes there are incidents afterwards and military operations. We are just trying to live here. We are used to it. We fend for ourselves. Don't come and stir things up. If you are Jiyan *Abla*'s friend, well, it's better if you leave her alone.'

A crowd of customers arrived at the shop. It was obvious they were from the village. A very young woman in local dress was trying to soothe her small baby who kept on crying. There was an older woman with her, perhaps her mother-in-law, her mother or her stepmother, with a headdress that resembled a kalpak, decorated with gold coins. Ömer was surprised at the loveliness of the woman's greenish eyes, the way in which she flung her skirt around as she talked, her free movements and the imperious tone in her voice. She must be one of these local agha women, he thought. The man with them held out papers, presumably a prescription, to the chemist's assistant. Ömer's eyes lit on the black Mercedes waiting outside. Well, here was yet another scene to shatter our south-eastern stereotype! From the few words of Kurdish that he had begun to get used to hearing he gathered that they were asking about Jiyan and that they were sending her their greetings. Perhaps it was the leading family of another clan. If I ask the girl, though, she would clam up again.

When the customers had gone and they were alone again, to put pressure on the assistant he said, 'I'm not going anywhere. I'm staying here until Jiyan *Hanım* comes.'

'Stay. At seven I'll be closing the shop. You can wait as long as you like. You can stay until morning if you wish.' She did not speak again. She concentrated on a new set of customers who had just walked in.

As he was trying to call Jiyan for perhaps the twentieth time Ömer remembered Elif's message. If it had been some other time he would be sorry that he had forgotten his wife's birthday and try to make amends for his forgetfulness. But now he was in no state to think about all this. He was focused on finding Jiyan – or at least getting news of her.

'I'll go, but I'll be back before seven. If you speak to Jiyan *Abla* in the meantime, please ask her to call me. My phone will be on.'

Perhaps the assistant really did not know where Jiyan was. The chemist did not have to tell the poor girl all her plans! She had said, 'I'll be late.' What need was there for more? Hesitantly he walked to the hotel. It was possible that she had left news for him there. How was she to know that I would sit stupidly at the shop and wait?

He was not wrong. The elderly hotel clerk in reception pointed to someone dozing in an armchair in the dimmest corner of the lobby. 'He has brought news from the chemist. He has been waiting for ages.' Then he called out to the sleeping man in Kurdish. '*Yazar hatin!* The writer's here!'

The man who got up from the chair and walked towards Ömer was dressed smartly. Not very young. Well built and handsome. His complexion and expression were western even if the lines on his face were not. In his walk and in his face there was something alien to these parts. He was wearing a fresh white shirt with the sleeves rolled up to the elbow over dark widely cut trousers. The gun at his waist in the large pocket of his trousers was immediately evident. It was as though he wanted not to hide it but to show it.

'I've come to take you to Jiyan *Hanım*. Jiyan *Hanım* said, "If he has time, if he wants to come."'

Ömer hesitates for a moment. Who is this man? What is he? He does not look like a driver, a bodyguard or a servant. Why doesn't she phone? Why send this man instead? How does one trust a stranger in this sinister land?

He turns to the hotel clerk, with whom he has now begun to be friends, with a questioning glance, as though appealing for assistance.

'He's a relative of our Jiyan *Abla*, a man you can trust,' says the clerk. 'She's sent for you. You should go.'

'Isn't Jiyan *Hanım* in town? I've been calling her all day on the phone, and I haven't been able to reach her.'

'She's in the country. There's no reception there.' He points to the invisible mountains. 'Near the mountains . . .'

The adventure is about to begin, thinks Ömer. This scene could have been the opening sequence for a film about the Kurds. The handsome, mysterious man with a weapon in his belt has come to take the lovesick writer to an unknown destination in the middle of the mountains. Will the writer go? Will he have the courage? The Governor had mentioned the voice of the sirens the day we met. Did I not come here to hear that voice? Am I not after a voice that will whisper the word I lost?

He would go. The story that began with the scream in the coach station in the capital would write itself step by step. It would come to an end. This time he would not be the godlike writer who decided the fate of his heroes and heroines and who played with them like a cat with a mouse. He was not going to write the story; the story would write him.

'At least wait five minutes and give me time to change this shirt.'

The man brings his right hand to his chest right on top of his heart with a gracious 'Yes, sir.' Yet another scene from a film, thinks Ömer as he walks towards the stairs. The man's gesture was not natural to him: it was as though he had had to learn it. Why can't I perceive my experience here as real life? Why does everything turn into a scenario, a film, a surreal adventure or poetry in my head? But it is all a part of everyday life here . . . Does the reality of other lands, other folk, other people always seem to us like a frightening or a seductive fairytale?

When he comes downstairs, the hotel clerk says, 'He's waiting for you outside, *beg*. He's a relative of Jiyan *Hanım*. Please go, sir. If Jiyan *Hanım* has summoned you, you should go. Besides, it's really beautiful in our mountains in this season.'

As he goes out of the hotel door he thinks about the way the man said, 'our mountains'. Mahmut also used to say our mountains, as did Jiyan, Mahmut's father and the others, too. It is as though the mountains are their most valuable, most prized possession. The refuge of hope, protecting spirits . . . Is that why those mountains are set on fire, to annihilate hope? Or is it the opposite: to revitalize hope? But how does this man know where to go? How much people here know, and how little they give away!

A black jeep stands before the door. The type of vehicle that challenged the widespread perception of poverty and deprivation in the region. As soon as the man sees Ömer in front of the hotel he springs with agility from the driving seat and opens the front passenger door. 'Do be seated. You'll be more comfortable here. We have over an hour's journey. That is, if the road isn't closed.'

Ömer doesn't ask where they are going. They are going to Jiyan. I am going to look for her in her own land, in the land of her own reality and legend, far from this town that has lost its sound, withdrawn into itself and is lying in wait. He remembers the message that Elif left on his phone. Today is my wife's birthday, and I have forgotten it for the first time in years. I must call her immediately. A little later when we leave the plain and dive into the depths of the valleys and gorges there will be no reception at all. He is going to speak to his wife without planning in advance what he is going to say, without making excuses, just as it springs to mind. Elif is the true me, my diary, she is a part of me: Jiyan is my legend, my fairy story, the mirage in the desert of lost words.

He dials Elif's number. He lets it ring for a long time. If the phone were switched off there would be a notification to indicate this. She's either left it somewhere or she's not answering. He looks at his watch. It must be six o'clock there. Perhaps she has gone out to dinner, perhaps the congress has lasted a long time. Those boring, scientific meetings where no one listens to the speakers, and when it comes to debate everyone competes to show off their knowledge. He rejects the idea of sending a text message. It is not something that he can write in a few words. There is nothing to say at this moment. At this moment he is going along a road that follows the bends of a gurgling river, passing the fortified checkpoints of the military, towards the mountains whose snowy peaks are streaked red by the setting sun.

'The surrounding mountains reach over 3,000 metres. The mountain that rises in front of us is almost 3,500 metres. No one has ever seen it without snow. Local folk say that if the snows of Mortepe melt the end of the world is nigh. They believe that the mountain protects them and that it has supernatural powers.'

Ömer is surprised at the man's polished speech, his ability to explain his views so well and articulately. It's as though his excellent Turkish has been learnt in adulthood. The difference in intonation calls to mind the accent of western foreigners rather than that of the east. The old man at the hotel had said that he was a relative of Jiyan *Abla*. A relative, a bodyguard or . . . Or what?

'The snow on Mortepe has started to melt,' says the man. 'The glaciers won't melt that easily, but global warming has come to our land.' Then he notices Ömer's welling curiosity and adds: 'I know you, Ömer *Bey*, but I haven't introduced myself yet. I did not want to do so in front of the hotel employee. Here words can easily be misinterpreted. There is no need for everyone to know everything about a person's business either. Sometimes information brings danger in its wake. My name is Diyar. I'm a relative of Jiyan *Hanım*. Or, rather, I'm the son of her murdered husband.'

'I had no idea,' mumbles Ömer. 'She told me that her husband had been killed – that was all.'

'I know. She does not like to talk about it. She loved my father very much, and my father loved her, too. Their marriage lasted a short time. Only five years. It was the worst phase of this ongoing dirty war.'

He stops talking. He breaks off the story at the most exciting place, like a professional storyteller. Suddenly Ömer has the feeling that Diyar knows about his relationship with Jiyan, that he is trying to pass on a message and that Jiyan wishes him to do so. But he does not want to be the first to speak. He pretends to be engrossed in the redness of the setting sun reflected on the water, the rocks and the mountains.

'Magical sights, aren't they? Whenever I see the setting sun reflected on the mountains I feel that I'm in a fairytale world. This view must be one of the reasons for my returning to this land and not leaving it.'

'Aren't you from here?'

'I don't exactly know where a person's homeland is. Is it the place where they are born, in which they grow up or the place they return to? I don't know.'

'Which is the place you've returned to?'

'I suppose it's here. The east of the east . . .'

'Where did you get that expression from? I'm sorry, it's a phrase that I use. I mean, it's not mine, though, and I don't know where I borrowed it from.'

'My father used to say it. In one of his books he mentions this region as "the most east of the east".'

'Your father's books . . .'

'Yes, he wrote quite a few. On the Kurdish language, Kurdish history, Kurdish literature. You must have heard of him.' He mentions a name that Ömer remembers from his youth. 'Didn't Jiyan tell you my father's name either?'

'No. We rarely had such conversations. We have spoken mainly about the region and its people. I wanted to write something about the area.'

'Every sympathetic westerner wants to write about the region and our problems. I was born in Diyarbakır, but I grew up in Sweden. I'm one of the children of the Kurdish Diaspora following 1980. In Sweden people who consider themselves intellectual are curious about our region, the Kurds and Kurdistan. Some just from sympathy, from their devotion to human rights, to pay blood money for the prosperity of the west; some to manipulate the balance in the region. But all of them look through their own glasses and write what they see distorted in this way. And they give us advice. Not just the Swedes, of course, I mean all westerners. Please don't be offended, I wasn't referring to you. However, to be able to write about this area you have to understand the spirit of the place, to feel it inside. I have been here for four or five years now. My roots are in this land, but even I cannot say that I have been entirely able to comprehend it as yet.'

'Forgive me, I'm asking you because you broached the subject. Your father and Jiyan Hanım . . . Was it in Sweden? I mean, I haven't quite got the hang of it . . . it seemed a little complicated. Was your mother Swedish?'

'It's not complicated. In fact it is simpler than the plots of your novels. My mother is from Diyarbakır. My father is from further east, from around here. I, too, was born in Diyarbakır. Then when the soldiers came in 1980 Diyarbakır and the whole of the east became hell. My parents had to escape and went to Sweden as political refugees. At the time I was six or seven, I can remember our arrival by plane. It was the first time I had boarded one.'

'And, after that, your father and Jiyan, I mean how did he meet her?'

'It was a love story. At the time I was a young lad of nineteen or twenty. Jiyan had come to visit her elder brother in Sweden. We used to visit them as a family. My father met Jiyan by chance at their home. He was over fifty then. And as for Jiyan – I don't know whether I have to explain – she was young and quite enchanting. Don't get me wrong. My father was not particularly interested in women. He was still married to my mother, and in Sweden there are plenty of beautiful women. All the same, my father had eyes only for his work and research. But Jiyan, especially at that age, was more than just beautiful. Now I understand it better. In those days I was an adolescent preoccupied with northern blondes. My father said, "It's as though the essence of my country, its heart, mystery and rebellion have come together in this woman. Jiyan is not just a beautiful woman but a country; the country from which I was thrown out, that I left, the country I long for." It seemed to me too romantic or even rather maudlin at the time. I was angry, too, because he left my mother. Now I understand what he meant.'

He is silent for a moment. 'Perhaps I shouldn't be telling you all this seeing that Jiyan has not told you herself.'

They leave the deep valley and turn on to an earthen track. The last shafts of light from the setting sun strike the steep cliffs. Like opposing mirrors the granite rocks reflect the light back and forth.

'We're almost there,' says the young man. 'There is a checkpoint a kilometre further on. If we can reach it before the sun sets, we can pass. Otherwise they close the road. They haven't quite evacuated everywhere here. Officially it hasn't been named as such yet, but after the last period of tension, the explosions and operations it has long since been a forbidden zone.'

The days are long, twilight has not yet fallen. They reach the point before sunset. It is a long wait. Papers, identity cards. ' Open the boot!' 'Where have you come from?' 'Where are you going?' . . . Questions asked in harsh, commanding, scornful voices. Ömer has now learnt to keep quiet in such situations, to hand over his identity card and wait in a corner. Like the skilful actors in a play that has been well rehearsed, the people here know the questions, the answers, the gestures, where to be silent and where to speak.

The leading office at the checkpoint – he must be a junior officer or a military police officer – gives the command in a deep voice with the air of a general. 'Pass! Next time you are this late I won't let you through. Go on, get going!' They make slow progress along the deteriorating road, full of pot-holes and stones, in the four-by-four that Ömer later realizes is armoured. They spot a clump of trees that seems to jump out at them from among the rocks as they take a bend.

'We're here!'

When Elif returned to the hotel she was pretty drunk. It was a night that began with champagne and ended with champagne. And, to top it all, the superb French wines that were drunk in between. By northern standards Le Coq Rouge was an excellent French restaurant. Her date really knew about food and drink. Was that all? His command of his scientific field was not to be sneezed at either. They spent half the night talking about their research, the latest findings in genetics and, of course, the resulting ethical questions. What she liked about the man was his talking with her as an equal – not patronizing her.

As she took off first her trousers and then the lilac blouse, her eye caught on the full-length mirror on the door of the wardrobe. She took off her tights designed to make her look slimmer than she really was, that squeezed in her stomach and her bottom and the specially cut bra that showed off her breasts to their best advantage. She examined her body objectively. Not bad at all for a 52-year-old! 'My youthful wife,' Ömer used to say as they made love. His words, his caresses, his closeness gave her far deeper pleasure during sexual union than the physical enjoyment. He used to say, 'You make love with your brain.' She never worked out whether this was a com-pliment or whether he was teasing her. She used to imagine Ömer knowing women who made love with their bodies, their whole beings, perhaps aban-doning themselves to their basic instincts like animals, and comparing them with her, and then she would be upset.

She thought how long it was since they had made love. Was it a month, two months? It wasn't more than that. Ömer had returned from a book-signing day at a major international book fair. In the past he would return the same day by plane when he had been to those sorts of events. However much they urged him he would never extend his stay, resorting to the excuse, 'I have to work, my publisher is waiting for me to finish my book.' That time he had stayed there almost a week, the length of the fair. This was because when he came back there was nothing to do. Elif knew that he had writer's block, that he could no longer write. She felt that it was for this reason he had gone east, that the source for his work had dried up and that he was looking for new inspiration.

'This time you stayed too long,' she had reproached him.

'You are right, dear. I did stay a long time. I've missed you.'

They had made love. Just like the old days, right there on the couch, covering themselves with the twilight. Calm, safe, sound, unexciting love-making without waste, without surprise, where they both knew each other's likes, all their sensitive points, the curves of their bodies.

As she looked at her body in the mirror, she had a feeling of longing that she had not experienced for a long time. She felt as though she had been left suspended in the middle of making love, as though she had been cut short just as she was about to have an orgasm. The bitter taste of adultery that had come to nothing and a feeling of humiliation coupled with shame. The emptiness of an intended but failed attempt at murder . . .

Why did I meet up with that English colleague? Was I really interested in talking science? And what about getting dolled up to the nines . . . Wasn't everything, from the bra to the silk jersey blouse, chosen to show off your femininity, to get him excited? At one stage you even considered at the last minute wearing a thin cotton top without a bra at all – so that your nipples would be visible. So why didn't you? Was it to play the mysterious woman from the east? You are Turkish. A man should find something in you that he can't find in western women; a little reserve, a touch of coyness or coquetry. Aren't all these pathetic ploys contrived to arouse a man, to ensure that the fish swallows the bait?

Why had she behaved like this? Before she leaves the mirror, she addresses her motives. With the habit she has acquired from her scientific studies she treats herself not as a subject but an object, as she does when examining the behaviour of a guinea pig. No, the reason was not the urge of the flesh, an irresistible sexual impulse, a desire that could not be curbed. If it were that, it could be seen as natural, understandable, healthy or even reasonable. It could be counted as a manifesto for woman's sexual liberalization. In fact, it was none of these. It was because I wanted to punish Ömer, because I rebelled against our drifting apart, because he had allowed it, because I felt he thought of me as a fixture. He hadn't even remembered my birthday. He hadn't even phoned me. That is why I called the Englishman. It could have been someone else. The only available opportunity in this city was the scientist – the easiest to reach and likely to be the most harmless and free of complications. Adultery as revenge. The familiar theme of bad melodramas.

If she had fallen madly in love with someone, if she had run to this other person sacrificing everything, burning her boats and leaving all behind, she would not have lost her self-respect. Love forgives much; at that point conscience takes off its hat to infidelity. My case is similar to that of a poor girl who has fallen pregnant, is deserted by the man she loves and who becomes a prostitute out of revenge.

She becomes embarrassed by her nudity in the mirror. She doesn't want to see herself. It's as though she has been raped, soiled, covered in the sticky fluids of the male. She tumbles into the shower. She has to be cleansed, purified. But what about my heart? How can I ease that? She adjusts the water to cold. She is frozen. She shivers, but it feels good and she relaxes. As the cold water beats down on her shoulders, her breast and her face, her self-confidence returns. She begins to laugh. What had the Englishman said towards the end of the evening?

'Mrs Eren, remember I told you to ignore the internationally perceived stereotype of the Englishman – about half the males being homosexual, taking five o'clock tea when not in the pub, being gentlemanly but emotionally cold and knowing nothing about food, constantly carrying brollies and so on . . . Just occasionally there is a modicum of truth in these preconceived notions about nationality. For example, I count myself as among the 50 per cent of Englishmen who prefer men. Otherwise there's no way I would have let you get away!'

He had grasped that I was after him. He had realized that the conversation about science and research between fellow workers was just a cover, and he had politely turned me down. Perhaps what he said was true, or perhaps it was just an excuse, but he did save me from being unfaithful to my husband. Otherwise I would have been lying like a mummy in the arms of an Englishman with a bitter taste in my mouth and regret in my heart.

As she dries herself with the hotel's soft snow-white towels she asks herself where the border for infidelity lies. Is it when you sleep with someone, when you seriously contemplate it, when you really want to but do not act on it or merely when you express your desire? As with the question where does violence start? Is it when you kill a laboratory mouse, physically intimidate your sister or when you become a suicide bomber and destroy people in the name of your beliefs?

Before she gets into bed she takes a sleep-inducing tranquillizer, a Chinese herbal remedy that is non-addictive. As she turns down the bed-spread, her phone falls on the floor. Of course . . . I left it on the bed. How could I forget? She is about to turn it off and place it on the side table when she presses the 'missed-calls' key.

There are two missed calls: one from Turkey, a number that she doesn't recognize which does not come up on the screen either. The other is Ömer's number. So he did ring! He has rung! Hooray! And he let the phone ring for a long time. Perhaps a few times. No one answered. Was he worried? Had he tried to guess where I was and what I was doing? Will he call again? Over there it is two in the morning. Very late. Never mind. If he's asleep then he can wake up. Today's an important day. She presses the 'reply' key. 'The person you have called is unavailable.' He must be out of range again, or he has turned off his phone. I'll call again tomorrow. Ömer will phone, too. A feeling of shame mixed with regret spreads over her. I owe my fidelity to the sexual preferences of the English colleague. How fragile everything is! How it all hangs on a thread.

Then she looks at her incoming messages. The most recent one is from her recent date. He must have sent it as soon as he emerged from the taxi that brought them back to the hotel. 'What I said about my sexual prefer-ence was true. You are a very special woman. I should like to have been able to fall in love with you.' She smiles. So the cliché that Englishmen are courteous was also true . . .

The other message is from Deniz. See, he has remembered my birthday as well. I am too negative, and I'm rather spoilt, I'm afraid. But, no, this is not a birthday greeting. 'They've set fire to the Gasthaus. Please phone me immediately on this number, Mother.'

What does he mean, they've set fire to the Gasthaus? For a moment she cannot make it out. Then a photograph emerges in fragments from the depths of her memory and the pieces pile up, one on top of the other. Sounds and colours complete the picture. It transforms into an image of the group of young skinheads with motorbikes in a corner of the square by the quay where the fish festival was celebrated on Deniz's island. When I went back to the Gasthaus to get my things and go the door was open as always. The dog yapped behind me. I thought that someone was there, but there was no one in evidence. I was surprised that the dog kept barking. Bjørn? Where was Bjørn at the time? No, no he wasn't at the Gasthaus. He did not come with me. He was with his grandfather and grandmother at the fairground. He was driving round and round the square in the car that I had given him as a present.

She tries to dial the number that Deniz has provided. Her fingers are trembling. He doesn't have a mobile. The number must belong to a friend of his. Isn't it very late? It doesn't matter!

The telephone is answered immediately. 'Mother!' says Deniz. This is the taking-refuge-in-his-mother voice when he was ill or in trouble in his childhood. Tears trickle silently down her cheeks. She is crying not for the Gasthaus being burnt and the distressing news that she is about to hear but for the way her son says 'Mother' in that helpless childish voice.

'What's happened, Kitten? Is it true?'

'The Gasthaus burnt that day, the day you left. They set fire to it. We saw the flames as we were returning from the Big Fish competition. They saw you leaving the island, the captain had already told me. You know there were those neo-Nazis on motorbikes. They suspect them.'

'The boy . . . how is the boy? Bjørn? How are the grandmother and grandfather? How are you?'

'Now everyone is a little better. Only Kurt, you know, our dog, he was tied up – he could not escape. They set fire to the place while the others were at the festivities. Even though Bjørn doesn't quite understand, he's still very sad. He says that the Devil has punished us because we took Princess Ulla away from him. He is convinced that you were Princess Ulla in disguise.'

'How are you, Son? How are you, Kitten?'

What a long time it's been since I said 'Kitten' to him. It feels as though he's snuggled up to me again, just like the old days. It's as though I've found my lost son.

'I'm very, very, very well, Mother Cat . . .'

Elif begins to sob. I know your 'very, very, very well'. Your helplessness, your loneliness and your fears . . . My fugitive son who has taken refuge on a foreign island. My dear son has been struck yet again in the place in which he took shelter.

'We must meet straight away, Deniz – right now or at the latest tomorrow morning. I'll come to Oslo on the next flight or to Bergen. I'll rent a car, and I'll be there very soon. Or would you prefer to come here? You and Bjørn? Immediately! You must come immediately!'

She sobs. She doesn't feel the need to hide her emotions from her son.

'Don't cry, Mother Cat. Please don't cry. It wouldn't be right for you to come. The people here might feel uneasy. If we set out tomorrow morning early we'll be in Copenhagen by the evening.' A silence . . . 'Do you remember the unknown deserter, Mother? He had a poem: "You have nowhere to go but yourself. The violence of the age will find you everywhere."'

'I remember it.' She gives Deniz the address of the hotel. 'I'll be here the whole time. I'll be waiting for you.'

She calls Ömer. Again and again. 'The person you are calling is unavailable.'

The person you are calling is unavailable. The person she is calling is right now among rocky mountains in a green haven. All phones, the past and the future are out of range of the fate of the world and his own.

The place the young man who brought him here pointed at and said, 'Here we are!' must be Jiyan's refuge. The family home that she talked about with longing, that she called a mansion and then become ashamed of the arrogance of the word, trying to change it by saying, 'That's what they call the fairly large houses of the governors and aghas in our parts.'

She had told him that the villages had been evacuated, had complained of no longer being able to visit them. Perhaps I am the one who remembers wrongly, perhaps she might have said, 'I don't feel like going to that house since they evacuated the village.'

As he gets out of the jeep Ömer takes a quick glance at his surroundings. Higher up, towards the slope, are dilapidated mudbrick houses, deserted ghost huts. All of them have merged with the mustard-coloured slope; have become one with the yellow earth and the grey rocks. At the point where the road they drove along ends stands Jiyan's family home amid trees and greenery, as though protecting the deserted village; like a door to the village or a secret gateway.

Large dogs appear around them, growling and showing their teeth. Ömer stays where he is without moving. They had taught him to do this in his childhood. When you see a fierce dog you must stand still. Two villagers, or guards, appear with sticks in their hands and weapons in their belts from behind the garden fence woven with brambles and thorns. They drive the curs away.

'Here we trust our dogs more than our guards,' says Diyar. 'They don't have any vested interest. A stranger is a stranger as far as dogs are concerned, but with people one never knows. Jiyan trusts our men implicitly. If she hadn't trusted them so much my father might still have been alive.'

What does the stepson mean? He remembers the Commander's words: 'I'm not saying that the chemist had her husband killed. There are those who believe that that's what happened, but there can be no condemnation without evidence and proof. I say that she could not prevent her husband's murder and, most importantly, that although she knew the murderers she did not denounce them.'

Just as he is about to ask Diyar what he meant by his remark he sees Jiyan leaning against one of the supporting posts of a veranda that runs the length of the front of the two-storied mansion of stone and wood. Instead of descending the few steps and walking towards them, she waits for them to approach without moving. Perhaps this is the custom. The head woman or *hanımağa*, whatever, does not walk towards her guests; visitors approach her as a mark of respect. Even though, in the town, she ignores the customs, here on her own ground, in her own kingdom, in her evacuated, deserted paternal home, she follows the traditions.

'I had begun to worry,' she says holding out her hand and giving his a friendly shake.

'We'll speak about who has been worried about whom another time. After the events of last night surely you could have sent news?'

She holds his hand and squeezes it in her palm. 'I'll explain. I needed to get away from the town for a few days and stay here on my own.'

She is wearing clothes similar to those worn by local women. A long green skirt, a wide-cut pomegranate-red thin tunic jacket of shiny silk, open in front, with a narrow bright-yellow blouse under it. Those colours again: red, green and yellow!

'Is this some sort of rebel zone? I see that you have hoisted the flag.'

She smiles with the sad smile that defines the dimple at the right of her lip. How I've missed this smile, this dimple, this hair and this face. No, this isn't the longing of a few days; it is the panic at the thought of not seeing her again.

'In spring, as the yellow daisies and red poppies open in the green grass we don't have any need of cloth flags,' she says as they enter the house from the veranda.

Ömer looks around to see Diyar. The man is not there. He has silently disappeared. It's as though he has gone to earth. One of the fierce-looking dogs that was growling before wags its tail in a friendly way and follows them. It is obvious that it has sensed that its mistress is not in danger and has relaxed. Ömer sinks on to the cushions on the floor of the hall. If he didn't stop himself, he could bury his head in Jiyan's lap and go to sleep. He is exhausted. Jiyan is not sitting beside him; she is some way off. She puts her legs together under her ample green skirt. His eye catches on the silver anklet on her right ankle. He wants to stroke her slim graceful ankle – not with desire but as one touches the statue of a goddess with the expectation of being exalted.

'Well, this is my sanctuary,' says Jiyan, 'This is the house I told you about.'

Ömer is silent.

'They turn a blind eye to my using this place from time to time. Of course, it's a privilege. In fact by law they cannot prevent me. But this place is in the region that is in a state of emergency, and laws and such don't apply. Why should they stop me anyway? It is easier to keep me, and those who come and go, under control here. Behind us are steep cliffs. No one can climb them other than rebels, mountain commandos and goats. In front of us is the road you came along. The entire place is under military surveillance.'

Ömer is silent.

'The surroundings are arid, but our village is like an oasis. Or, rather, it was before it was evacuated. A little further on we have a spring. The water flows this way and then goes underground. They say it joins the big river.'

Ömer is still silent.

'Are you angry because I didn't call you? It wouldn't have been right for me to call you. I know you had a talk with the Commander. I can guess what he told you. The stories that they make up about me, the suspicions . . . He also told you that your time was up, you have to go. There are others, too, who want you to leave. In these parts everyone is afraid of a stranger. Even though we are enemies we know one another, but strangers are regarded as dangerous. People who are fighting each other tooth and nail unite against strangers. And, of course, I'm their possession! They don't want to share their property or have it taken.' Again she smiles sadly.

There is something strange about Jiyan today. Different from usual. It's as though her energy, her anger, her rebellion, her inner fire have been extinguished. A Jiyan who is not defiant but one who has surrendered. A Jiyan who has buried her secrets, if there really are any, and forgotten them. Perhaps this is all in my imagination. I am writing a story again in my own way. I created a Jiyan, and now I'm looking for an end to her story.

'Who is Diyar?' Ömer demands. 'Who is this stepson? How long has this stepson been around? Your husband's death, all of it . . . You never told me about any of it! You remained silent looking through your eyelashes and putting on an air of mystery.' He realizes that he is shouting and that his voice resounds from wall to wall. He understands that he is jealous of this woman, of her dead husband, of Diyar, the lawyer, her damned alleged secrets, this house, this strange land, the local women who hug and kiss her when they see her, these people who speak the same language and even the Commander. They are a closed sphere, an egg, within which they fight and merge. I cannot break the shell of that egg and enter. I just hold the egg in my hand and look at it. That's all I can do!

'Clearly the Commander's tales have had an effect.' This time she doesn't smile sadly but tauntingly. Her dimple deepens, and her face can barely be made out in the twilight.

'It's got nothing to do with the Commander. What has affected me is what I see and what I cannot see, what I feel and do not feel. I reach out and think I have touched something, and then I find that it was only air.'

Fatigue and weariness sweep over him. I came here to look for my lost word. I came to escape alienation, to understand with my heart where reason falls short. Now Jiyan is shutting me out. Everything and everyone unite against the stranger.

'I wanted to explain to you. I wanted to say that there is no secret, that everything is so simple that it would disappoint you. That is why I wanted us to talk. It's quiet here. Here I feel at ease. It seemed to me that this was a place where I could explain certain things more easily. And besides, it is a haven that even a phone cannot reach. That is why I asked you to come here. I wanted you to see this house, this garden that we love as a family. And perhaps – as you are a writer, a novelist – I thought that this house, these surroundings would make an impression on you. The reason I did not come to the shop today is simple. I was extremely tired because I had been up until morning the previous night. I thought to myself that I could sleep here undisturbed, without anything untoward happening, I could rest and be by myself. Diyar is a chatterbox, I'm sure he has told you a lot of things. He is in fact a Swedish Kurd – or perhaps it would more accurate to say a Kurdish Swede. He is one of those who try to become natives of this place. Why he wants to be a native is a different issue. We can speak about it, if you like. I call it 'new Orientalism'. In fact my husband, or rather Diyar's father, used to say that. Let me tell you straight away that there is no connection between Diyar and me other than the fact that he is the son of my dead husband and some social activities that we are jointly trying to carry out here. I am sorry that I have disappointed you, Ömer Eren, but I cannot contribute to your vision of the "mysterious east".'

Ömer feels that his anger has passed, that he is more comfortable and relaxed. He is also embarrassed. This fuss of mine, these remarks about 'foreignness' and 'alienation' were all because I was jealous of her, afraid of losing her. It is as simple as that.

The fading light of the closing day filters through the veranda door. Darkness will fall a little later. Jiyan will light a lamp. A pale still light would suit the place. He gets up from the corner where he is sitting and comes over to her. He unties the bands of her hair. It is as though a raven-black flood is teeming down over cliffs. He gently strokes the anklet on her ankle. He lets his fingers wander not over her skin but the little round bells of her silver bracelet. He does not desire the woman now who has been the object of his lust and passion ever since they first met at the chemist's shop – 'Can I help you, did you want something?' It is as though he has lost his sexuality or has overcome it.

'You don't have to explain,' he says in a gentle, tired voice that is foreign to him. 'Don't explain anything. Leave it as it is. Let's write the tale as we wish.'

Jiyan pulls her naked foot with the anklet under her full skirt. 'There are no secrets,' she says. 'You create the secrets. The vision of the "mysterious east"; the fictionalized portrayal of woman that ranges from images of the harem, concubine and courtesan to Kurdish woman and me. The secrets are in your heads. They are in the heads of the Commander, intelligence, the District Governor and even in yours, Ömer Eren. Even in yours.'

It strikes Ömer that Jiyan is using the familiar you for the first time. It's as though the 'you' does not express familiarity but anger. Even though he is upset, he does not answer. He remains silent.

'There is no hidden agenda, secret or a word that hasn't been said. I know what the Commander told you. How often I've thought about going and talking to him person to person, to say exactly what I have told you now. Not because I had hopes of anything or wanted to protect myself but so that he should know and understand, for something to stir in his heart. Perhaps he would understand. I still believe in people, in promises. He would understand, but he would not be able to do anything. I'm sorry for the Commander, but, contrary to what he thinks and the assumptions and fabrications of his informers, there is nothing secret about my mother or my father. If there were, that would be my business, but there is not. It is merely that my mother died when I was very young. And she was from the Syrian branch of the clan. You know I look more like an Arab than a Kurd;

that is why. As for my father: Turkish intellectuals think they know what happened here in the 1980s, but they have no idea. How can they? My father was imprisoned in Diyarbakır prison for a short time. Politics were not for him. From today's point of view, you could even say that he supported the state. But they still picked him up. From there he sent news. "Here there is every imaginable form of cruelty and torture. Who knows what they will do outside! Don't stay." The family was frightened. They moved from this region. Until my father was freed and he returned I wasn't seen outside on our land. Later I was always at boarding-school, and I went to university in Ankara.'

As Jiyan explains, Ömer watches her language change to the local dialect – from her rather high-flown formal Turkish to her harsh eastern accent, favouring the present tense instead of the past perfect continuous. She is about to speak her own language, Kurdish, without realizing it.

'Let me tell you what you really want to know. When I met my husband I was twenty-three years old. I had gone to see my elder brother who had settled in Sweden. I first saw my husband at my brother's house. He was very much in love with me. He was almost my father's age. And I loved him greatly, beyond measure. It shouldn't have happened, but it did. It was a love story that the *dengbej* had not told. We told this story by living it.'

Don't tell me any more. Let's be quiet together. Let's go outside and listen to the silence of the deserted village in the remaining twilight.

He thinks he has said this but he knows he has not uttered a word.

'He taught me that my living here wasn't enough to make me a native. He taught me my history, my language and my identity and to look through the eyes of this place. He taught me to love this area and to be at peace with my identity. He taught me not to be hostile to other identities while being reconciled to my own, not to be cruel by taking refuge in our oppression. He taught me hope. He taught me to express feelings and thoughts that I sensed but could not formulate into words, that I recognized but could not express. He said, "We are going to try what is difficult. We will choose to be on the side of humanity and life and not on the side of persecution and tyranny." He said, "Being persecuted does not give you the right to be cruel." I loved him so much.'

Another of the age-old most deep-rooted themes of the literature of love, thinks Ömer: love that cannot be regained or is lost through death . . . You can deal with everyone or everything but not with a dead person. Death rivets, intensifies and increases the feelings that should erode with time or at least become normal. You have to put up with the residue of the dead.

'We used to stay in this house. He used to stay here all the time. He used to work here. I used to go back and forth to the town. He was not afraid. He used to say that he was of no harm to anyone, that no one would do anything to him. His room is inside. His books, his things are all as he left them. His last articles were on peace. He used to say, "We have always approached peace through politics. From now on we must approach it through conscience." He was preparing a major book on the subject, a kind of manifesto. It was the fifth year of our marriage. He was here alone. There were two men with him from our clan whom I trusted implicitly. Well, like servants, like bodyguards . . . I was in the town, at the chemist's shop. I was on duty that night. I received the news the next morning that he had been murdered.'

She stops speaking. She gets up and lights one of the gas lamps standing on the small table just next to the half-open door. 'I like these,' she says. 'We could use methane gas lamps or propane mantle lamps, but I like these.'

The lamp smokes, and a smell of kerosene evocative of former days pervades the room. She adjusts the wick. A pale, mournful light falls on her face.

'In the past, in my father's time, there was a generator, and we had electricity. When the village was evacuated it vanished, too, along with other things.'

Finally he has the courage to ask the question. 'How did he die? You spoke of an unsolved murder. Why are they involving you in this business?'

'He was shot in this house. The pistol that my father had given me as a present to protect myself if necessary had disappeared. In any case, I had never used the weapon. And the two men I trusted had run away. In my opinion, they were abducted. They picked up the track of one of them a few years later in an area some way off. Another unsolved murder . . . Not even the trail of the other was ever found. This is why the clan is implicated. My husband was shot from behind, in the neck with a bullet that came from my missing gun. There was no evidence. Everyone knew that I was on duty that night at the shop. The people thronged around the courthouse door to testify. However, it suited some people's purpose to create suspicion. Ammunition for blackmail. "If you go too far, we'll ruin you!"'

'But didn't you look into the truth of the matter?'

'We did try. It got lost in the murk. What he wrote last would not suit the purpose of any of those bearing arms. His proposals for a peaceful solution were no good to those who fed on war. What is more, his opinions carried weight, and he was respected in the region. He had begun to have influence on the cadre. He dreamt of a society where peace did not exist just as a concept in articles and speeches.'

'Would it be possible for me to read what he wrote?'

'Although his Turkish was very good, he wrote in Kurdish in order for our language to develop, be more widely acknowledged and become emancipated. If there were time I would translate them for you.'

'What do you mean if there were time? I have time. I'm not going anywhere, even if everyone – from the Commander to a bunch of anonymous djinns – tells me, "You've outstayed your welcome!" I'm not leaving you, and I'm not going anywhere.'

'I wouldn't be so sure. People sometimes have to go, despite themselves. They have to leave.'

'What do you mean, my beloved? What's going on here? What are you trying to tell me?'

'You were looking here for the mystery behind the obvious, for the voice behind what was heard. You had convinced yourself that you would find what you had lost here. You said so. But, look, in reality neither the land nor I have any special secrets, hidden voices or concealed words. Everything is clear. The ways of the normal south-east, the ways of the normal Kurdish woman are like the "normal native of my land" . . . That when stripped of the mystery that you've imbued us with become ordinary and have no attractions left.'

'I'm not after your secrets or anything like that. It is you whom I love – not your secrets. I'll stay here with you. Who can stop me? You can translate your husband's writings for me, and we will work on them together in Turkish. I told you that I had come to find the word I had lost. Perhaps the key to the word I'm looking for is in his writings.'

Jiyan gets up. The enchanting jangling of her anklet can faintly be heard. She takes the gas lamp that she had left on the table and stands before one of the doors opening on to the hall.

'Come,' she says. 'I want you to see this room.'

In the pale light of the gas lamp he sees a wall full of books, then a couch covered with a kilim and a desk with drawers full of papers and notebooks.

'This was his study. I could not bring myself to change anything after his death. In any case, what's the point?' She opens one of the drawers of the desk and selects a notebook there. 'Here are his last writings, the ones I mentioned.'

Ömer thumbs through the thick bound notebook with pages handwritten in Kurdish. 'Now I'll need to learn the language.'

Jiyan takes the book and randomly opens a page. She reads it, translating it into Turkish:

'People create legends. This is because we need legends and epics to uplift us. By wrapping ourselves up in legends we can escape life's cruelty and deprivation. We can commune with our legends, overcome being crushed and become heroes. All societies need heroes, not to be crushed or humiliated, in order to resist. The epics of our *dengbej* unite with the stories of mountain bandits; Dersim meets Cudi. In our territory the mountains are the symbol of mutiny. The epic of the mountains is passed on from generation to generation. And every new generation rewrites this saga.'

Skipping a little, she continues to read:

'But if legends and epics are turned into opium for the people and the cadre, then revolt will be tyranny. If heroism becomes a shield for tyranny, if violence is considered its twin, then legends and epics become stained with blood. Now the whole question is to return to the innocence and humanity of the legends of our foundation and liberation.'

'That's how it continues. I don't know whether it means anything to you.'

'I think I understand. It's like a non-rejectionist, non-external message of peace.'

'Recently he had concentrated all his strength, all his work on a peace programme focusing on the Kurds' right to live without fear or violence and the happiness of our people. Of course, it was extremely difficult. What we had experienced rendered such Gandi-like notions fanciful, reconciliatory and almost impossible. Now, after all these years as our people continue to kill and be killed, people are starting to appreciate that he was right.'

'Do people really understand? Can the language of violence be answered in another language? Do you believe this?'

'I believe it. We believe it. Here we have succeeded in creating a vital line that is fed from the mind and heart of my husband. I, Diyar, our lawyer friend and others here who you know and don't know have taken a chance on peace.'

'Taken a chance on peace?'

'Yes, taken a chance on peace! He was thinking of collecting these articles under the heading, *Taking a Chance on Peace*. You in the west and we here talk a lot about peace. There are peace talks, peace societies, peace initiatives . . . Everyone has their own version of peace, and everyone understands peace as the surrender of the adversary. This is because we only understand peace in a military–political dimension. We forget that of humanity and conscience.'

'That's because the dimension of humanity and conscience is an abstract concept'

'You are mistaken. What can be more concrete than human beings and conscience? But to be able to take a chance on peace, a price has to be paid. No one is prepared to pay the real price. Sometimes the price can be as severe as death; sometimes it is considered surrender. For those who fight, the state of war turns into a way of life, a habit difficult to break. It seems to people the only way. Take this notebook. In it you will find some of the ideas we have talked about. You can keep it. I had a photocopy made for translation. When you have learnt Kurdish you can translate it yourself – or you can get someone else to translate it.'

As she pick up the other notebooks and put them in the drawer a tiny mouse suddenly pops out from under their feet. Ömer prepares to kill it.

'Wait, wait! Don't hit it,' she says in a low voice. 'Let it go. Hear what it says right at the beginning of this book: "Violence can begin with shooting a gazelle. After that you cannot draw the line. And as the deer dies, only the bewildered sadness in its eyes remains."'

NINE

Concerning Mahmut, Zelal and Fate

While Zelal was burning with a longing for the sea that she had never seen, Mahmut was dreaming of the metropolis, the refuge for all fugitives and all those who were wanted by the authorities. For Zelal the sea was synonymous with escape, salvation and freedom; and for Mahmut it was the the cities and towns that clasped those who sought refuge to their bosom. If a stray bullet had not pierced their dreams that night and killed Hevi they would have already reached the town by the sea.

He has left the hospital, and as he is walking preoccupied, pensive and a little anxious, he recalls that dreadful night. He cannot decide whether everything that happened was God's curse, the Devil's trap or if the Almighty Protector who spares and forgives had felt sorry for their purity of heart and bestowed a favour on them.

He had done something crazy. It wouldn't have mattered if he had been on his own, but he and Zelal had done something really mad.

The madness was in not fleeing from the mountain earlier. There were people among the mountain troops, especially new recruits, who deserted from time to time. During the first days of his arrival he had witnessed the execution of a very young guerrilla who had been caught trying to escape during combat – just like I did – when they had been cornered on a slope. He had thought that if they were not treated so harshly there would be no men left to fight. It is not sufficient to talk about steel-hard discipline. You have to implement it for it to work as a deterrent. But he couldn't stomach the execution, the boy's eyes full of fear, his crying for his mother as he begged for his life to be spared; the cold-bloodedness and especially the high-handedness of those who issued the execution order and the inhumanity of those who carried it out – all this had grieved him. In those days I was a new recruit, I was inexperienced, had faith and was a part of the mythology, an anonymous hero of the liberation army. Today I, too, am a deserter.

Attitudes against deserters changed from time to time. Sometimes they would be stricter, sometimes more lenient. And sometimes a blind eye would be turned. However, there were specific rules about escaping. Previously one surrendered to Barzani's forces and they would deliver the deserter to the border. Nowadays one either defects to a village protected by the militia or surrenders directly to the nearest police station. There are also those who flee and vanish without trace. They say that Istanbul and Izmir are full of such people. If you have not been sentenced, if the state is not after you, if there is no record of you, if no one has squealed and mentioned your name, the safest thing is to give yourself up directly. Should luck go your way, you will save your life, you will stand trial and be given a short sentence. And if you become an informant everything will stay on track.

He thinks to himself: Everything will stay on track, but you will be off track. If you are an informer you will squeal on the *hevals*. You will tell where they are, you will tell of their plans and get them destroyed if needs be. You cannot merely give misinformation or lie. Is the state stupid? Would it have itself ridiculed? Of course not. First of all they test informants to see if they are the type to betray their comrades, their own people. You can go through all this, too, but still your new masters won't trust you. Someone who betrays once will do it many times. Informants are those whose hearts are tarnished with fear, who have sold their comrades to save their own skins. Wouldn't someone who sells their comrades also sell the masters they have clung to if they were in a tight spot? The state knows this better than anyone.

Mahmut walks among the crowds with an uneasy heart and mind. I couldn't have done it. I couldn't have surrendered. Thank God I didn't. I chose the most impossible, the most difficult way, but I did not become a traitor. I deserted from the organization, the mountains and the state – from everything. And everything's compounded by Zelal's flight from the code of honour. What a fix we're in! The craziest thing of all was to attempt to flee with my unhealed wounds with Zelal who was pregnant with Hevi. What happened that night was not God's curse but fate's blessing. If the stray bullet had not found Zelal's womb, then how would the writer have noticed us? If we hadn't run into him there, we would have been in even greater trouble. They say that every cloud has a silver lining. Well, perhaps it's true.

His dear mother used that expression. When they were still in the village before it had been evacuated and burnt, while there were still animals and flocks of sheep and goats, she used to say when wolves used to seize the lambs, 'If that bad wolf had confronted you, if something had happened to my children' . . . and comfort herself. When his eldest brother took to the mountain she had said, 'Let's hope for the best. Supposing they had come and shot him or I had found my dear boy's body riddled with bullets like Zara's Seydo.' When the village had been evacuated and they had seen the fire in the distance as they fled, she had cried, had lamented for her village as though for a loved one. But even then she had said, 'Every cloud has a silver lining. Supposing it had burnt with us in it', and his father had not known whether to cry or laugh in their circumstances. When they came down to the town and lived in a shanty with a tin roof and walls of reeds and mud, windows with thick plastic stretched over them instead of glass, she had said, 'Thank God we've got a roof.' It was then that his father had exploded for the first time: 'That's enough, woman! The more you give thanks, the worse off we are!'

Every cloud has a silver lining. Perhaps we saved our lives at the expense of losing Hevi before he was born. Perhaps the wheel of destiny turned in our favour. The writer helped and will help us further. A small shop selling knick-knacks, a small business in a pretty place by the sea . . . It could be carpets and rugs. Nowadays Kurdish kilims are in great demand, and foreigners in particular are snapping them up. Tourists and people with summer houses will come in the summer, and there will be plenty of sales. We will gradually build up the business. I won't let Zelal work. She can bring our children up, although she can be in the shop sometimes and check the accounts.

Carried away by his own dreams, he walks through the crowds with the smile on his face of a rather vacant child imagining a fairground. The writer *abi* had told them to keep a low profile, but this evening he did not feel like returning home straight away. That house is pleasant and comfortable, like the houses of rich people; but it is only pleasant with the one you love, pleasant with Zelal. Loneliness is bad even if you are in paradise. What use is beauty if you don't share it with the one you love?

Nothing would happen if he returned to the house late. No on was waiting for him. If Zelal were sitting at home watching out for him it would be different. Then he would have rushed back. I'll get back late. It's better anyway. The minibuses and buses will be less crowded. What's more, going up the slope in the dark will be safer. If there is anyone taking an interest in me it is better to shelter in the dark than be seen in broad daylight.

He strolled leisurely along the street that branched off from one of the city's main squares. Rows of shops selling smart clothes, women's clothes, men's shirts, trousers and suits . . . We must get Zelal some nice clothes when she's better. How they'll suit her. If she gets dressed up she'll look like a beauty queen! But wouldn't I get jealous of other men's eyes? Mahmut, you stupid twerp! Watch what you're thinking! Jealousy is all you need!

He passed in front of the kebab and *lahmacun* shops with their appetizing smells. The Dersim Kebab House, Urfa Grill, Munzur Kiosk, Komegene *Çiğköfte* House, the overpowering smell of roasted fatty meat . . . Amazing! Our food, smells and even our Kurdish names are taking over the capital. Kurds invaded the west long ago, but, look, they've even stormed the capital! He chuckled cheerfully, then pulled himself together. If anyone saw him they would think he had gone mad. He longed for a kebab. A spicy one, with plenty of onions, grilled tomatoes and peppers and a drink of *ayran*. He thought how long it was since he had eaten a kebab. As though you used to eat them every day! How many times did you eat a kebab at a shop, eh? In his childhood, when they were in the village, they used to eat meat. There would be animals they singled out for slaughter and sometimes an animal would become ill, a wolf would savage it or something else would happen, and they would have to kill it. His mother would roast it beautifully. There were no fresh vegetables, but onions would be fried in oil in a pan to go with the meat. And sometimes she would bury potatoes in the ashes of the hearth. All the children loved this.

He had been to a kebab shop twice in his life. The first time was when he was a child; those were the days when they had just moved from the village, when they were trying to get used to the hut of scraps at the edge of the stream. They used to call their hut 'rubbish house', not because they belittled it but because it was made from rubbish bins and materials collected from dumps. In those days, everyone in the house, apart from his mother, collected rubbish. In the morning before dawn the folk by the stream, whole families would hit the road; they would pour into the town centre, the wealthy districts and the neighbourhoods of civil servants. 'Well, I've had enough. I'm not coming to collect rubbish. This filthy work disgusts me,' said his big brother one day. His father had said nothing. He looked straight ahead and remained silent. When his mother nagged at him for not being tough with the lad he had said, 'It is offensive to a young man. It doesn't bother me or the youngsters, but a young man is ashamed of raking through rubbish.'

Didn't it bother the youngsters? It used to bother me. The rubbish smelt revolting, and I would tie a cloth over my nose and mouth. I was also afraid that someone from school would see me. It felt as though I was thieving. Two days after he had had his say and left home, my brother came back and told them that he was going to the mountains. My mother cried, and my father said in a feeble voice, 'Don't go, Son', but he did not entreat. Even if he had said, 'Stay, don't go', there was no alternative, no future for the boy he could offer other than the bins.

Mahmut owed his first kebab to this rubbish business. That day he had not gone off to work in the early hours of the morning. He had fallen into the deep sleep of a child and his mother had not had the heart to wake him. During the day as he was sifting through the rubbish in front of one of the kebab shops in the large market, the cooking smell suddenly overpowered the smell of rubbish. He had paused for a moment, put his sack on the ground, turned his nose towards the open door of the kebab shop and, with half-closed eyes, breathed in the inviting smell long and deeply. He was not especially hungry. His mother had fed him bread and onion that morning. But that smell! The smell could lead one astray, could drive one insane. Even if you had eaten ten loaves of bread you could not resist it. He heard a voice immediately behind him saying, 'Boy', and a hand touched his shoulder. Mahmut was frightened to death. Supposing the cops picked him up and took him away? When foreigners or high-level state visitors came to town they would pick up beggars, children selling tissues and people collecting rubbish in prominent public places and cart them off to the police station. He stood rooted to the spot with fear.

'Let's go and eat a kebab,' the man had said.

'No, umm, I don't want one,' he had murmured, ready to flee.

'Come on. Don't be afraid,' the man had persisted. 'When I was your age I used to love kebabs. We didn't have any money, so I couldn't buy them. I feel like one now – those damned kebabs do smell good. Come on. Don't be awkward.'

Finally he had had the courage to turn and look at the man. He was middle-aged, obviously a city-dweller; he spoke like one. He is lying not to upset me; he is lying so that I do not feel inferior. Mahmut had thought that the man did not look like somebody who had never eaten kebabs in his childhood through lack of money.

'Did you collect rubbish, too, in those days?' he had asked with childish logic to test the man.

'No, I didn't collect rubbish. I worked at other jobs. But I know the smell of kebabs,' he said smiling. And then without giving Mahmut the opportunity to argue he took him by the arm and pushed him inside.

Now Mahmut smiled to himself and went towards the door of the kebab shop in front of him. I'm damned if I won't have one! All right, I'm being careful with the money the writer left me. I'm keeping it for Zelal's convalescence. But surely I have the right to a single portion of kebab!

The second time his father had taken him to a kebab shop. It was when he had announced that he had passed the university examination. 'You deserve it! We'll go and have a kebab, father and son, and after that a baklava. When you become a doctor you'll take your mother and father, all of us, out for kebabs with your first salary,' his father had said. He remembers that he had made do with a single portion, not to make it too expensive. The money for the cramming course, the university entrance fees, clothes and a little spending money – even if he were to stay with acquaintances – was all to come from collecting rubbish, the work on building sites and quarries that his father found if he struck lucky when he waited every morning at the labourers' market, from the washing that his mother did and the cleaning job she had found at the town hall and the pittance he got from the hotel where he had worked nights while he was studying at school. And if the kebab money were to be added!

Whenever he thinks of that day he is cut to the quick. The joy of the success, the happiness and hope of being able to send his son to university on his father's tired face grown old before its time. My son will have a good career; my son won't go up the mountain; he will be a doctor; he will take care of sick people; he will earn money. The lightness in Mahmut's own heart of having made his father's dreams come true, the pride of having been a good son and the feeling of thinking he had managed to succeed. And then . . . He decided to eat the third kebab of his life. He turned with a decisive step towards the door of the shop.

This was a much smaller place, next to the Dersim Kebab House and the Urfa Kebab Shop, with a few tables – an unassuming place. He thought that small places like this would be more attentive as well as cheaper and was pleased. At the back, at a table near the grill two men were eating hastily without lifting their heads from their plates and without saying a word. He sat down at the table right by the entrance not to be choked by the fumes from the grill.

'Adana or Urfa?' asks the runt of a boy hovering around. He refrained from asking what the difference was. He said, 'I'll have an Adana and an *ayran* as well.

On one side was the heat of the fire and on the other the summer heat. Despite the rotating fan on the ceiling it was suffocating inside. The door was wide open, but it was as though flames came in from outside instead of a fresh breeze. Luckily the water in the plastic bottle that the waiter left on the table was ice cold. He filled two glasses one after the other and quaffed them thirstily. Refreshed by the cold water he calmed down and relaxed as he waited for his kebab. He was absorbed in watching the passers-by. Once Zelal was better and back on her feet they, too, would wander around arm in arm like this through the city. They would sit in a café, like those with tables on the pavement, in one of those crowded, smart places with flowerpots all around. They would eat ice cream, drink tea and chat light-heartedly.

The boy turned on the small television on the wall to the right-hand side of the door in the corner opposite his table. 'We'll get the results of the match. Those thugs have got it in for our team again. We've dropped from the league,' he said furiously. Mahmut was not interested in who had got it in for whom or who the thugs were.

When the boy brought the kebab the television was broadcasting national news. 'Breaking news: Separatist terror strikes our seaside towns. With the coming of the tourist season, terror has reached the sea. Three people died, two of them foreigners, and two people were seriously injured, while many were slightly hurt in the atrocious attack carried out using a remote-controlled bomb. We will continue to keep you up to date with information from our local correspondent. We are showing the first images, some blurred in parts and would ask you not to allow children to watch.'

Bodies with missing and severed limbs lying on the ground. Attempts had been made to blur the horror of the images – but were unable to hide them. The screams and the moans of the wounded. Blood spreading over the hot tarmac and splattered on the Mediterranean plants in the vicinity. People rushing around confused, helpless and horrified. A burning mini-bus . . . Blood, flames, blood, death, pain, blood, blood . . .

The kebab boy let forth another cry of 'Bastards. You should hand them over to the people, they would tear them to pieces in an instant. Oh, man! Oh, to be there now, I'd be after those bastards and then . . .'

Mahmut shuddered to the core. Despite the heat, a cold sweat broke out on his back and neck. He opened another shirt button. The television went on to foreign news. The attractive female broadcaster was relaying international stories with a set face that revealed her dimples. 'We are informed that following the suicide bombing yesterday in Iraq at a Shiite tomb, at least nineteen people were killed and many wounded in the bomb attack on a mosque where Sunnis were performing their midday prayers.' Immediately after that followed the news of a suicide bombing in Israel directed at a bus stop where small children were waiting after school: 'The latest news is that while three young pupils were killed instantly there are more than ten seriously wounded ... Hamas has claimed responsibility for the attack. In the Lebanon, too, there is no respite to the bloodshed. Last night the Lebanon was shaken by the news of a fresh assassination ...'

'Turn that thing off!' Mahmut shouted and was startled by his own voice.

One of the men from the table at the back said in support, 'We're fed up. too. For God's sake, turn it off!'

The boy threw in yet another 'Bastards!' to no one in particular. What's the world coming to, *abiler*? You just let me get hold of them! I'd show them no mercy! Just let the ones we have here swing, wipe them out. It doesn't matter whether they are terrorists or villagers. These bastards are all the same, *abi*.'

'That's enough,' said Mahmut, this time in a calm but firm voice. 'We're feeling depressed enough as it is. We don't want to listen to you in this heat.'

Realizing that his assistant had gone too far, the proprietor took the situation in hand. 'Shut up, you twerp! Stop blathering on. Everyone's had enough!'

Mahmut looked at the plate in front of him. The long *köfte* on the skewers, the onion and bean salad, the vermicelli pilaf all made him feel sick. He had no appetite. It was as though a rock was stuck in this throat and had blocked his gullet and windpipe. He filled another glass of water from the plastic bottle and sipped it. However much he tried, he wouldn't be able to eat it. So he was not meant to have the third kebab of his life. Just as he was about to call out to the boy, 'Give me the bill and I'll go', his eye caught on a man coming through the door.

He's either someone I know, or I'm mistaking him for someone I know. I think I've seen him recently. The cold sweat returned and spread all over his body. For some reason he remembered those two strangers waiting at the bus stop as he was going down to the road to go to the hospital. He trembled with the fear of a trapped animal.

In an instant the man scanned the kebab shop with his keen eyes. Then, without pausing, he walked straight towards Mahmut's table. He pulled out the chair opposite and sat down without asking.

'How are things, *heval*? How are things, Comrade Mazlum?' he asked like an old friend who has come across one of his comrades-in-arms years later.

His code name was Mazlum. A good name, unassuming and gentle. It hadn't even been two months since he had stopped being Mazlum and changed back to his own name, to being Mahmut. I had almost forgotten. People erase what they want to forget from their memories.

'You've mistaken me for someone else, *kardaş*,' he says. 'I'm not Mazlum. I'm Mahmut.' He tries to gain time, to work out who the hell this guy is.

'It doesn't matter. It's all the same to us whether you are Mazlum or Mahmut, as long as it's you.' He calls out to the waiter in a confident voice. 'Son! Give me one and a half portions of Urfa and a coke.' He looks at the plate in front of Mahmut. 'You haven't eaten. Have you lost your appetite?'

Mahmut remains silent. He cannot say: I've lost my appetite, the television robbed me of it and then you came and deposited yourself in front of me. He makes as though to get up. The man prevents him by putting his claw-like hand on his knee. *'Hele bise, me hin du-sê qise ne kirî ye, ma tu kûderê ve dicî?* Just you wait a minute. Where are you off to before we've even had a few words?'

It is then that Mahmut realizes that they've been talking Kurdish. As he knows his code name he must be from the organization. So they are after me. No, no! It can only be a coincidence. I wasn't important enough for them to send someone after me. They say that they don't send men after anyone. Isn't volunteering the principle in our job! All the same . . .

He pushes his fork around his plate so that his unease won't be detected. He takes a morsel and puts it in his mouth. The kebab has gone cold and the fat has congealed even in this heat. He feels as though he's going to be sick. Beliving that Allah will protect him, he asks, 'Where do we know each other from? Is it from school or somewhere? You're clearly from my part of the world.'

'Well, you could call it a kind of school.'

He senses that the man is playing with him like a cat plays with a mouse and that he is enjoying it. His anger begins to swell. 'I can't place you,' he says in a shrill, angry voice. 'It's obvious you've got the wrong person. I've got work to do. I haven't got time to mess around. If you'll excuse me . . . *Kardaş*, bring me the bill immediately!'

'Sit down,' says the man in a low voice. 'Don't play games.'

He has stretched one of his legs out straight under the table and is lightly pressing on Mahmut's foot. Mahmut notices that he is stroking the gun that is on a level with his right hip immediately above his other leg.

'What do you want from me?' Mahmut asks, this time in Turkish.

'One small job. If you pull it off without any trouble then you can live as you wish with your fiancée. You can go wherever you want. *Paşê ligel dergîstiya xwe tu çawa dixwezi tu jê wesa biji.*'

Mahmut freezes, right to the marrow. The man had said 'your fiancée'; so he knows everything. It isn't important that he knows his code name and that he ran away but that he knows about Zelal. So they had followed them. Who? If it were the work of the state . . . The state would be suspicious or they would have information. They would keep tabs on you and if you were someone important they would catch you. They wouldn't be interested in a girl. Was it the organization? Evidently the organization knows. The name Mazlum was not just a shot in the dark. Yet he is not really convinced that it could be the organization. Even though the *hevals* don't know one another, they would feel some affiliation. It was the stance, the way of sitting, a phrase, a tone of voice . . . There again, one cannot be a 100 per cent sure, a 100 per cent certain. In recent years there isn't the old unity in the troops.

'The leadership knew that you were confused, that you had a problem with focusing on what you were doing. If a person becomes confused it's only a matter of time before they go over to the other side. Your desertion wasn't unexpected.'

'I didn't run away. I was shot. I was wounded. My arm is still not right. I rolled down the slope wounded. I couldn't have gone back. If I had, I wouldn't have been able to find the *hevals* anyway. And no one came to look for me where I lay wounded.'

As soon as the words had left his mouth he knew that he had made a terrible mistake. He could have insisted that he was not Mazlum. Clearly the man hadn't recognized him at first hand. The other man waiting at the bus stop must be from the organization or an informer. I've landed myself in it – done a really stupid thing. And there is no way to undo it. The only thing to do is risk being shot and run for it.

'It's a good story, and perhaps it is partly true, but it's unconvincing. To tell the truth, in circumstances like these they wouldn't let a person live – you know that yourself. However, as far as we know, you did not turn yourself in to the authorities and you haven't informed. For that reason you have one last chance. It will be to your benefit to take it.'

I have one last chance. I had the chance to study and become a doctor. It did not work out. The mountains were a chance, and that didn't work out. Fleeing and establishing a new life with Zelal was a chance that didn't work out. Zelal being shot and meeting the writer was a chance, and apparently that didn't work out. Now I have one last chance.

'The last chance to prove yourself, a sort of rehabilitation. Rehabilitation not in words but in deeds. The leadership thinks that you are an element that can still be saved.'

'An element', eh? An element is for those whose names have been crossed out, for those who are no longer considered comrades; a word used for those who will be exterminated at the first opportunity. And they say an element can be saved!

At this moment he is in an ambush with all exits covered. Helpless and hopeless. He is overcome with exhaustion. He has not the strength to resist. He asks out of curiosity, 'How long have you been following me?'

'I don't know. they passed the job on to me. Someone was actually following the girl on a matter of honour. The girl's elder brother was from the mountain troops. He confessed. As you can appreciate, it's complicated. The organization is after you, the girl's brother is after her, and the state is after everyone. That's the story.'

'I don't want this any more,' says Mahmut without hope. 'I want to live quietly, far away from here. Say that I'm frightened, I'm soft then, not the man for the mountains. You said it yourself. I was neither informer, nor did I betray anyone. I just want to leave and go my own way. That's all.'

'No, it's not that simple. Entrance is free, but the exit costs. Didn't they tell you that at the beginning?'

Mahmut notices that the man is pointedly stroking the gun concealed in his pocket.

'When you talk about the beginning, what was said was different from what was done. And, what's more, the entrance was not free. The price was high. The price was a whole human life.'

If he were to get up suddenly, act quickly and throw the chair at the man, run out of the door and escape . . . Would he use the gun? There are people everywhere, the street in front of the kebab shop is crowded. Would he dare? With one last hope, to gain time and a little from curiosity he asks, 'What is it you want me to do?' He regrets it as soon as the words are out of his mouth. I've even started to bargain. He'll take advantage of that.

'It's a job you're no stranger to. A small explosion. There's hardly any risk. Remote-controlled.'

He looks at the man. Someone he has never seen but it's as though he knows him. No, he's not from the mountain; he's sure of that. From where? Mahmut cannot place him. Did he say 'a job you're no stranger to'? If the man had been really on the inside he would know that he was a stranger to this kind of job. What's more, is there a scarcity of troops for these sorts of town operations? Since when have these jobs been forced on anyone?

'I know the mountain,' he says. 'I've never done a town operation. What's more, the killing of innocent people is anathema to me. I fight only one to one.'

'Shut up!' says the man in a peremptory and hostile tone. 'You're bargaining like an out-of-work model who has been offered a job. This job will be done. It's the leadership's orders. The towns have been neglected recently because of this ceasefire business. There's been a ceasefire – and has anything resulted from this? The TC carries out operation after operation. Anyway, apart from those meddlesome intellectuals constantly publishing leaflets, there is no one who believes in ceasefires or peace. And from time to time we get those collaborating slimy bastards on the scene: a peaceful solution, burying our weapons and expressions of brotherhood . . . You have a ceasefire, and they come and bomb, they come and hunt you down in the caves like rabbits, an attempt to subdue and torment the people . . . Those mugs for peace get what they deserve.'

A small explosion . . . almost no risk . . . from a distance. Supposing they had proposed a suicide attack? I would have said no outright; I wouldn't do it.

The man continues as though he has read what is going through his mind. 'Look, the organization isn't asking you to do a suicide attack. It takes precautions to protect the lives of its troops. You press a button from a distance, a key on a mobile phone, and click. That's all.'

The images on the screen: dead, wounded, dead children, wounded children, women, men, young, old, dead . . . Scattered bodies, blown-off legs, arms . . . Blood, blood, blood . . . An organization that does not use suicide bombers but remote control to protect its troops. Troops' lives, leaders' lives, commanders' lives, people's lives . . . The writer's daughter-in-law's life of whom he said, 'We didn't even find all the scattered pieces' ... The life of his son who had been crippled and who had fled.

What have I done! What was I thinking? What was I calculating a second ago? Didn't it pass through my mind that they might have proposed a suicide attack? Didn't I weigh up the pros and cons? That means that I was ready to do the other; to press the button that the man talked about. In a suicide attack there is belief in the cause, there is self-sacrifice. A faith that is deep enough for you to sacrifice yourself, devotion at the risk of one's life. With a remote click you kill only others: the innocent. One more dead, one less dead, that is the whole difference; but that one life less or more is your own life, your very own life.

The waiter brings the other man's kebab.

'Give us tomato sauce and plenty of butter, eh,' says the man.

They remain silent until the boy brings the sauce. As he tries to pour hot sauce from the pan on the man's plate, some of it spills on the table. A stain of dark congealed blood spreads over the bare white Formica table. Mahmut has his eyes fixed on the blood. The stain grows and grows and covers the whole table, everywhere. It gushes from the screen of the television in the corner. It flows from the face of the man opposite. His feet touch the blood. It is rising. It comes up to his throat. He is drowning in blood ...

He regains consciousness with the man's voice. The waiter is bent over him, he pours cologne on his face and tries to get him to drink water. The water runs over Mahmut's face, his chest and wets his shirt. The mixture of the strong smells of sauce and cologne assails his nostrils. He feels sick.

'It's all right,' says the man in Turkish, 'my friend was not well anyway. Look, he couldn't even eat his kebab. And what with the heat. It's nothing. It's over. Just let him recover, and I'll take him home.'

Mahmut's chest is tight. He fixes his eyes on the top of the table. There is not even a tiny red stain on the table. There are just knife marks on the dirty white Formica, thin lines ... The waiter must have wiped the stain immediately. I had a nightmare. There is neither blood nor the stranger.

But the stranger is there, facing him. He is grinning or smiling, depending on how one interprets it. He is not teasing and not at all hostile as he says, 'Or can't you stand the sight of blood?'

Mahmut is silent. I thought I could stand it, but perhaps I can't now. Perhaps the man will give up. Perhaps he'll leave me and go. 'There's a lot of blood,' he says gathering all his strength. 'There's a lot of blood in the world. There's a lot of suffering. You're right. I can't stand it. Stop following me, whoever you are, stop following me. I'll disappear. I won't harm anyone. Neither the state, nor the organization, nor the *hevals* . . . I haven't done anything till now. You've seen that. I'm not a traitor.'

'Well, how soft you are! Why do they take people like you into the organization, especially into the mountain troops! Never mind, it's not my business. Pull yourself together a bit. Drink some water. Nobody is born a traitor. It's something they become. If you begin to question the cause, the leadership and, especially, the bloodshed, you are beyond hope. Blood gets shed; that's how it is. If you've recovered, let's go. We've been here too long. We've made a spectacle of ourselves.'

He doesn't have the strength to stand up and leans on the chair. The man is paying the bill in the corner. If his head weren't spinning, if he had the energy, he could run out of the door and mix with the crowd in seconds. But nevertheless he makes a move. He leans on the side of the door to stop himself falling to the ground. The man comes to the rescue and holds his arm like a friend or an elder brother.

'We'll go somewhere quiet where you can recover.'

He leans on the man as they walk, as they get into a taxi and as they enter a large park with a tea garden. His knees shake with each step as though all the blood in his veins has been drained. In his mind he goes through his three-term meagre medical repertoire. Tiredness, agitation, nerves; my blood pressure might have fallen. The wound seems to have healed, but there might be an internal infection, bleeding. Iron deficiency, anaemia, something in my brain: it could be all of these. And all this has happened for the sake of a kebab. I will never be able to eat one again.

In the tea garden surrounded by green plants they sit right next to the pool with a fountain in the middle. The man orders tea. 'Prepare some lemon and mint tea for my friend. For medicinal purposes. With plenty of mint and a lot of lemon. He isn't very well.'

Just look at the state I'm in; like a little boy who has been beaten and intimidated. I've thrown myself at my executioner's mercy, and I'm almost begging him for mercy! He slowly gets a grip on himself. He takes a sip of the lemon and mint. It does him good. 'The heat knocked me out,' he says. Then for some reason he lies. 'I had already eaten one portion of kebab. It must have been too much in this heat.'

'It was too much.'

Both of them know that it is the deadly reality behind this everyday idle talk that is too much.

'What was done to our people was also too much: The captivity, the tyranny was too much. If it weren't, why should so many people, young and old, women and men, take to the mountains? You wouldn't have gone, and neither would I. Who wants to die or kill? The war isn't over. It continues on every front. The organization needs you, and you need it. At least, so that you can clear your name in your own eyes. What does the leadership say? The honour of the organization is your honour. If you lose your honour then you become nothing, you lick the dust.'

The same old expressions that he knew by heart. Words that were pleasant to the ear, uplifting, that gave courage to and strengthened the militant. When said with conviction, they were words that ennobled a person and reminded them that they were human beings. It was all true, too. Why should so many people suddenly take to the mountains? Speeches, promises, guerrilla stories that had become legends . . . Were they all it took to pluck so many people from their homes, their families and their schools and drag them off to an adventure that would end in death?

All that the man had said was true. It was true but there was something shady in his speech. The words were in their proper place but something – what? – didn't seem right.

Mahmut keeps on stirring the tea in front of him. He listens to the tinkling of the teaspoon on the tea glass. There is no longer terror or fear, nor that cornered feeling inside him. There is a strange calmness, a deep sorrow and a strange regret that he feels – not for what he has done but for being alive.

'Find someone else for the attack. If necessary, I'll take to the mountains again. Besides, I have never witnessed these jobs done like this. How should I know who or what you are! Is this how orders for an attack come? I don't know.'

'So I need to show Sir an identity card. It's not that easy. It's as though Sir went up to the mountain pastures in the summer and came down when it took his fancy. Now let's talk straight. This is a chance given to you, an opportunity to live. The leadership is testing you one last time. There are volunteers in line to do this job, comrades, sound people waiting for orders, who have not betrayed their folk. In short, the decision is yours. You must know that the girl's life depends on your decision.'

Not to let it show that he is in a panic and trying to speak normally, he says, 'The girl has nothing to do with the organization.'

'Her brother picked up your trail. In other words, the girl is in our hands.'

'Even if her brother were an informer, he wouldn't touch Zelal. A man who has joined the organization, gone up the mountain would not bow to custom just because he had become an informer.'

'You are naïve, *heval*,' says the man with genuine pity in his voice and unexpected compassion. 'People don't discard beliefs and customs like changing a shirt. Customs and beliefs are instilled in us. Of course we love, but, by God, we still kill! And if the man has confessed, what does that mean? He will ingratiate himself with both the organization and the state to keep his life on an even keel. My last word: we'll stop the girl from being harmed if you make up your mind. We have a debt to settle between us. We traced you by trailing the girl with the help of her brother.'

Mahmut tries to work it out. What should he do? Appear to have accepted the job of carrying out the attack and try to smuggle Zelal away? How? Where to? Besides, are the men stupid? If you escape from one, the other will catch you. And if I did press the button, who is to say they'd release the girl alive? If the man carries out the honour killing, will I appeal to the police in my state? If I'm caught, what will happen to Zelal? Let's say I wasn't caught and that they didn't harm Zelal. How will we live without drowning in so much innocent blood? Oh, writer *abi*, writer *abi*! Why did you go and leave us? Why did we say to you, 'Go and look for the word in our homeland.' You will find the word and you'll write books, so what amid all that blood and all that suffering! You didn't realize that the word wasn't so distant. See, the word is here!

He keeps quiet. They both keep quiet. Another tea, and some more mint and lemon tea. In the pool in front of them goldfish are swimming around waving their tails. Mahmut is watching the goldfish, his mind completely blank. He remains silent.

'Is the girl really safe?' he asks a little later.

'If you carry out the job without any hitch you'll get the girl. Nothing should happen, but let us say there's a slip-up: if you tell us in advance who we should get in touch with we'll deliver her safe and sound to them.'

'Write the number down now somewhere. If something should happen to me you can let the writer Ömer Eren know.'

As soon as the number is written he realizes that he has made yet another tactical error, that he shouldn't involve the writer in this business. The man has done so much for us –and what am I doing for him in return? I'm embroiling him in this dirty business. I'm putting him at risk.

'What have you got to do with writers and people like that?'

'When we got into that trouble, when Zelal was shot at the coach station, he looked after us. He didn't ask who or what we were. He's just a decent man. I wouldn't want any harm to come to him. Anyway he's not around any more.'

The die is cast, he thinks. I've accepted the job. He feels a wrench when he remembers that it used to be called 'duty' not 'job'. If only I could believe that this was a duty that I willingly carried out as a sacrifice for the liberation of my people and its leaders. He becomes absorbed again with the fish undulating in the pool. They keep moving in so little water. They are prisoners, stuck where they are, helpless; but they don't know it. But I know. I know it all.

His mind feels numb. Like when a person loses a lot of blood and feels drained, his brain tingles agreeably. It is that sort of feeling, a state of drowsiness.

'Where and when is the job to be done?' he asks to put an end to the torment as quickly as possible.

The man holds out a mobile phone. It's small, the latest model, the type women use.

'You will be called on this phone. You will be told the place, the time and the details. The device is brand-new and the SIM card is, too. You must never use this phone either before or after the attack. When the job is done, destroy it. There is no need to panic. They won't be long in calling.'

His hand trembles as he takes the mobile and puts it in his pocket. Just like the moment he took delivery of his weapon and made his guerrilla pledge. With one difference: then it was from pride and excitement; now it is from fear.

He looks carefully at the man once more. He's familiar, very familiar, yet a stranger. He's evidently from the east. A Kurd but not someone he knows from the organization. He doesn't recognize him either from the camp, the mountain or from battle. In his mien and his attitude there is something foreign that doesn't belong to 'us'. If people were to ask, 'What is it?' he wouldn't be able to say. But he senses it.

'Why me? How can you trust me? Since when has the organization coerced elements that have fled the mountain into such action? Supposing I left this place and went straight to the police and told them everything.'

'You wouldn't, you couldn't do that. Everyone can inform, but you cannot, *heval*. Don't forget, the girl is in our hands. If you do anything underhand then we'll let the girl's brother loose on her. I have no idea whether the act has been forced on you or not, who gets it done in what fashion. I passed on the orders to you, that's all. Come on. Let's go. You go first.'

'The girl in your hands,' my Zelal. My woman. The one I love. The mother of the dead Hevi and the unborn Hope. The mountain sprite, the wood nymph in Mahmut's fairytale had not grown up with stories, was not besotted with a legend other than the legend of the mountains. 'The girl in your hands' knows numbers. She knows how to love and make love. She knows death and suffering. She longs for the sea she has never seen and does not know, and dreams of being united with that sea. 'The girl in your hands' waits for me in a hospital ward, in the bed beside the grumpy old woman, for visiting time tomorrow, for me to be with her so that she can cuddle up to me, speak her own language and lift her heaviness of heart. The girl in your hands . . .

He walked slowly out of the large park full of tea gardens, kiosks, pools and trees into the street. He had not altogether shaken off that strange state of numbness, the feeling of exhaustion. He was in no rush. Hurrying is for those who have people waiting for them, those who have work and those who have a destination to reach. He did not look back to see whether the man was following him. What was there left to be frightened of, to conceal? He should in fact be thinking what he was going to do, but he was thinking of Zelal. Of her body, her passion, her cleverness, the fiery way in which she offered herself, her snuggling to his breast like a baby. He thought about the fairytale life that they had had in the lea of the grove on the mountain. The tale of love that he never tired of telling himself which enthralled him anew with every telling.

'Let's stay here like this. Let's not leave the grove and go down the mountain ever,' Zelal had said one day. 'Let's live here for as long as we live. Like the first man and the first woman. Just the two of us, masters of our own destiny like the antelopes, rabbits and birds.'

'They would find us.'

'Let them. Let them find us. Let's live happily like this until they do.'

'It's all right at the moment, but when hunger pounds on the door and it gets cold . . .'

'Let it. What is the point of living a hundred years if you have a dull life in captivity, without love!'

'Why on earth should our love run dry, my woman? Why on earth should we be captive?'

'Isn't every day of our lives a gift anyway? If my father had not shown mercy and let me go, I would have been dead by now. If you had been shot in the head and not in your shoulder, you, too, would have been dead. What do we have to lose?'

That's how my love used to talk. Her words wrenched his insides. He knew that his woman was being ironic, that she was full of life and that she wanted to live and let live – not die.

'If anything happened to you what would become of our Hevi?' he would ask, to catch her weak spot.

They had believed in the miracle of Hevi. Hevi, like Jesus, was the son God had sent for peace on earth. They had no right to harm Hevi.

After that they had come down from the mountain. To raise Hevi without fear and to meet the sea. Then Hevi was shot. A stray bullet had killed God's peace envoy. And now . . .

Mahmut walked along the street that passed in front of the park rapt with emotion in the memories of their fairytale days.

The days were long; the first days of summer . . . Tired of the heat people had rushed out to the streets, the parks and the squares. Everywhere was crowded and lively. A flood of cars, buses and minibuses flowed down the wide avenue with a hum that numbed his brain and deafened his ears. Disoriented, aimlessly, pointlessly and without a destination, he walked down the wide pavement of the avenue not knowing which side of the unknown city he was in.

Young and old, children, men and women, women with and without headscarves; people holding hands, walking arm in arm, in groups and on their own passed by him. Young couples passed by; families passed by. Beggars, children selling tissues and chewing-gum, soldiers in uniform, smartly dressed gentlemen, youths in jeans, young girls with bare midriffs in tight trousers, veiled women of every age, poorly clothed and smartly dressed men and women people passed by. People from the capital city's shanty neighbourhoods, the poor working-class districts had sallied forth into the streets to take a breath of fresh air and enjoy themselves with a cone of ice cream, a toasted sandwich and a drink of *ayran*. Mahmut walked among them, with them. He walked in this crowd, feeling the security of being one of them and longing to be so. He tried not to think about what had happened, and he succeeded. He found distraction in looking at people and watching them. They were all different; all from another world. If one of them were to look at me and wonder, 'Who is he? What is he? What does he do?' would that person guess the fix I'm in? No, of course not. One cannot know a person from the outside. They cannot know what a person conceals within.

Mahmut strolled leisurely along the wide crowded pavement of the avenue. He came to a large square with a pool and fountain in the middle. The square was crowded and bustling. People were sitting on the benches around the large round pool and those who could not find a place sat at the edge of the pool or on the surrounding grass. Children had jumped into the shallow pool with cheerful screams, making a game out of avoiding the revolving jets of water. Mahmut sat at the edge of the pool and began to watch them. He took no notice of the droplets of water that occasionally reached him. The drops that fell on his neck, hair and shoulders cooled him down. He stopped himself from thinking about what had happened and what was going to happen. If he thought about it he would go crazy. He became engrossed with the fountain, the water and the children. In his imagination he brought Zelal and Hevi and sat them down beside him. He hugged them.

If I came here with Zelal we would embrace each other like that young couple sitting on the bench opposite and look at the water, children and people. We would buy ice cream and halva wafers. Zelal would be happy. Hevi would be with us. He would get into the pool like these children. His mother would be worried that he would fall in the water and get soaked. And perhaps some poor bloke like me, a lonely man, would watch and envy us, as I am doing now.

He grabs hold of the trouser suspenders of a little boy beside him leaning right over the pool to prevent the boy falling in. The little one frets and struggles. 'Let me go, *amca!* Stop it!' The child's father comes and thanks him and takes his son away from the pool, pulling him by the hand. How can the father know that I have a deadly weapon in my pocket. How can he know that tomorrow – tomorrow, perhaps now, here – that I am going to kill his child, his woman and him? How can he know that he has thanked Azrael?

Dusk has begun to fall. The square gradually empties. The coloured lights that illuminate the fountain come on. The drops of water fly about in the air and fall colourfully on those sitting at the edge of the pool. Against the backdrop of the sky that turns from a milky blue to indigo, from where he sits Mahmut can see Ankara Citadel. A huge flag waves over it. He feels the weight of the telephone that the man gave him in his shirt pocket. The telephone might ring at any moment. What if I turn it off or don't answer when it rings. 'The girl is in our hands!' 'The girl is in our hands!' How long have they been after us? And, more significantly, who are after us? Do they know that Zelal is in hospital? Or do they just know about Zelal and are bluffing? He has the feeling that they are approaching zero in the countdown. Six ... five ... four ... three ... two ...

I must call the writer *abi*. Why don't I do that? Is it because I've got him mixed up in this trouble? Oof! Mahmut's chest tightens as though it has been squeezed in a vice. He slowly dials Ömer Eren's number on the mobile that the latter had given him. He had said when he handed it over that Mahmut should call him if he were trouble. If I don't call him now when will I? When we're dead and gone? From the other world?

The phone is either off or out of range. There is no signal. It would be best to text a message. He'll get it when he switches on the phone. He keys in, 'SOS. We're in a tight spot. Urgent.'

A middle-aged man with a thin, sickly face comes over to the edge of the pool and squeezes in beside him. 'Could you make a little room for me, *kardaş*?'

Mahmut shudders. Is it one of them? Are they going to give the order in person and not by phone? He moves a little to one side to make room.

'It's evening, and it still hasn't cooled down,' says the man.

The voice is soft and friendly. There is no need to be frightened. He feels the need to talk to this man, to explain everything to him. If he can only talk to someone about it, share and confess so that he can be rid of guilt's deadly loneliness. 'Indeed it hasn't got any cooler, *kardaş*,' he says to continue the conversation.

'Where are you from? Because you look like a person from our region.'

'Which is is your region?' How keen our people are on finding a fellow citizen! He lies. 'I'm originally from Sivas.'

'From the city itself?'

'No, from Zara.'

Why did I dream up Zara? A trick of the memory! On the mountain there was a boy from Zara. He fell as a martyr in conflict later. He was so young, inexperienced, full of faith. How beautifully he described his homeland as we sat around the campfire.

'Even if we're not fellow citizens we're neighbours. I'm from Kemah.

And I always think, especially when the heat is really bad like this, why the hell did we leave and come here? Right now there must be a gentle breeze blowing there. Did you migrate here, too?'

'No, I came to study,' says Mahmut. As soon as he says this he feels so depressed he could cry. If only I had come to study. If only I hadn't been constantly suspended from school for singing Kurdish songs, for lighting a bonfire on the campus and jumping over it at Newroz, for being stubborn and telling the gendarme who teased me with his gun while checking identity cards at the crammer door, 'You've asked for my identity card three times before I've even got to the class door.' . . . Lies, empty dreams, how good they seem sometimes to a person's heart. What a refuge they are at times when a person can't cope with reality. 'I came to study.' What a neat phrase. Perhaps I should say 'I'm studying medicine. I've two years left before I become a doctor' and really make the most of it!

He decides against it. Such a dream, such a lie, seems too difficult to maintain – even for him. He remains silent, and so does the man. Realizing that their conversation is at an end the man says goodbye, gets up and walks off towards the road. Mahmut gazes after him. Who is he? What is he? What does he think? What are his worries, his anxieties? When I press a button, a key, and kill him, what will pass through his mind at the last minute?

That will not do. A man who is going to carry out a terrorist act must not think about before and after. Just like military service. A soldier doesn't think about an order; he doesn't argue about it. He just carries it out. A guerrilla does the same. War does not go with thinking. But I am not fighting, I've rejected war, I ran away. War had dreams and legends that kept the warrior alive. I ran away from them all. I ran away from the myths of the most beautiful young heroines, each one an Amazon, who washed their long black hair and their bullet wounds in crystal streams; from the legend of commanders, comrades, confidants in death, waving the flag of liberation with their last breath, at the moment of death, and who sacrificed themselves to bind the wounds of their soldiers, to save their comrades; from mountain tales, from heroic epics and from dreams of liberation and knights in shining armour. Those legends last for generations by being nurtured; to stay alive people take and give back strength to them. Our legends protect us from the painful thorns of reality, from the aridness of naked thought that kills enthusiasm. We feel protected by our myths and dreams. We are purified and ennobled by our legends and our epics. We measure ourselves against them and become heroes. Until the spell is broken.

He realizes that he has been sitting there like that for hours. If some-one were watching him they would be suspicious. He tries to get hold of the writer once more. His phone is still not responding. Night has fallen. A slight breeze has blown up. The force of the fountain has lessened. The water no longer spouts into the air and falls in great drops; it just trickles feebly. He must go home and try to reach the writer. He must find a way. Tomorrow morning early, before dawn, he must find a way to smuggle Zelal out of the hospital. I can't go home. I cannot spend the night all alone in that strange house. You are blowing this out of proportion, Mahmut, my son. You will just press a button, click! That's all. If you were a bus driver and you had an accident and the passengers died, it would be the same, wouldn't it? A button, a click – that's all. If you want to live in peace with your woman then happiness has to have a price.

Mahmut imagines being born in a different place at a different time. He used to think about this in his childhood, too. One day he had asked his teacher, 'If I hadn't been born in our village, if I had been born in a big city, for example, and if, for example, my dad had been a gendarme com-mander or a general, would I still have been me?' The teacher had laughed loudly, and had said with an endearment, 'You wouldn't, Mamudo. Then you would have been Mahmut the general's son. How do you think up such questions? You're a remarkable child!'

Who decides who will be born where and whose son you will be? Is it Allah? I thought Allah was just. I thought he was the one who spared and forgave? I was a remarkable child, true. I used to ask lots of questions. Didn't I take to the mountain because I asked questions? And, again, didn't I run away from the mountain because I did? And, now, am I not hesitating for the same reason? My religious-knowledge teacher used to say that God did not like those who asked questions. The organization doesn't like them either, although it tries to act as though it does. As the leadership emphasizes the importance of democracy and debate within the organization, it is encouraged, even provoked. But in a secret, sneaky corner of their consciousness those who ask questions are considered dangerous, their minds confused. The day will come when such people question the leadership and the cause itself. Those who ask questions lose their belief and their faith. The more they lose their belief, the more the questions will increase. The hand of those who ask questions will tremble. You see, my hand is trembling. When the signal to begin is given then it will tremble even more.

'The girl in your hands' is lying in a hospital bed. She lies there unprotected, helpless and quite alone; with no assurance or support other than me. And I have been sitting here at the edge of a pool talking to myself. I'm asking questions of life and death in terms of Zelal's life. If the man had come and said her life will be granted in return for yours, things would be easy. I don't even know how many lives it will cost for Zelal's life to be spared. When I press the button, the key or whatever, click . . . how many lives will be lost? Everything is easier when you don't see a victim in front of you, a person like yourself of flesh and blood. An air-force pilot, for example, who doesn't have the heart to squash an ant, who cannot smack a child, may drop a bomb on an entire city. I do not even know where they are going to plant the device. In a deserted place, at the most crowded point, in a shopping centre, the subway network? I don't know. I'm merely expected to go to the place they designate and press a key on this elegant pink ladies' phone. So easy, so simple. Isn't Zelal's life worth it? Isn't our Hevi worth it? Isn't leading a quiet, happy life for the rest of your days in a small seaside town worth it?

But if something should go wrong? It won't! Why should it?

Night really has fallen. The sky is navy, but the lights of the city obscure the stars. If you have ever lain on your back on moonless nights in the village or on the mountain and looked at the sky, stars fall on one like a torrent. At night Zelal and I would lie in each other's arms and watch the stars. Zelal used to say, 'Look, the evening star. As night advances and meets the morning, then it appears right on the other side. It becomes the morning star.'

'Where did you learn that?' I'd ask astonished.

She would answer, 'From my teacher at school', and I was surprised. The stars are difficult to distinguish from here, but he can see the evening star. It is the brightest one. He now knows that tomorrow before the day breaks it will be the morning star.

Just as he is about to get up from where he has been sitting, a little dog appears at his feet, a poodle with curly white fur. It has a red leather collar round its neck. Without being invited, it approaches and begins to sniff his feet and pull at his trouser leg. Standing on its hind legs and licking his hands, it wags its tail. Mahmut strokes the dog. He feels the heat of the animal, trembling with happiness and the softness of its curly fur under his hand. Warm, soft tears begin to trickle down his cheeks. He is surprised at them. I'm crying. I haven't cried for God knows how many years – although I did weep when they told me we had lost Hevi.

A young woman approaches him calling the dog's name. She scolds the puppy, gently, tenderly, like ticking off a child. 'I'm sorry, he's disturbed you. He's a good dog. He does it out of love and trust.'

'It doesn't matter. He didn't disturb me. I like dogs.'

He is afraid of the woman seeing his tears. He doesn't lift his head. He follows the young woman and her pet with his eyes as they slowly move away. The dog's vitality, the dog's heat, its tail wagging with happiness and high spirits . . . He scans the surroundings. Even though the square has become less crowded, it is still busy, animated. The vendors selling phosphorescent tops sparkling like fireflies in the semi-darkness, phosphorescent balls and flashing hairbands with butterflies for girls have taken the place of the sellers of halva wafers, the fortune-telling stands with rabbits and the children with trays hung round their necks selling all kinds of knick-knacks from lighters to biros.

A tiny little girl with a glittering phosphorescent crown on her head comes running to the edge of the pool. 'Look, *amca*, I'm a butterfly,' she says with delight and leans over the water. The phosphorescent band falls into the pool. Mahmut plunges in his arm, fishes the band out of the water and holds it out to the child. Her mother and father come storming over. As they drag the girl away by her arm Mahmut can hear them scolding her. 'Haven't we told you not to speak to strangers!'

True, very true. Children must not talk to strangers, they must not even go near them. There are deadly weapons in strangers' pockets. Especially those Kurds, Arabs, terrorists with their eastern faces! What does my face look like? He tries to look at himself from the outside. It's not frightening. A little eastern but not frightening. Since he has had his beard shaved, it could even be called soft-looking. I have a time bomb in my pocket. No one would be able to tell by looking at my face.

Looking at my face . . . Looking at his face . . . The face of the nightmarish man appears before his eyes. Since he first saw him, unconsciously he has been wondering where he has seen him before, and he realizes that this thought has been scratching away at his brain ever since the kebab shop. Zelal's face wanders around the most secret labyrinths of his memory and appears in all clarity in front of his eyes. Like photographs superimposed on one another, the face of the nightmarish man conceals Zelal's face. It becomes the negative of the photograph. He remembers Zelal's words: 'Our complexions were not similar. He was swarthy, but they used to liken me to my brother. My mother used to say, "Mesut is the Arab version of you."'

A little shriek like 'weeeee' or 'waaaaa' bursts from between his teeth. Traitor! *Xayin!*

Now he understands why the man seemed both familiar and a stranger; why, although he reminded him of the *hevals,* he cast an undefined cloud of suspicion that Mahmut could not put a name to and whose origin he could not explain. He was going to make me carry out this terrorist act. In addition to the 'martyr's funerals' and the suicide attacks in tourist areas there was to be a horrendous explosion in the capital! The golden link to be added to the chain of excuses and opportunities to swoop down on us . . . The inevitable rise of the informer, the greatest gift that he could have from his masters: a new face and perhaps a new life. Imagine! What is going on! Who gives the orders and who controls these operations? Who profits from bloodshed?

Mahmut is amazed but also relieved. Even if they traced us through Zelal, she was a means to trap me. Mesut *Abi* would not harm her. He could not. He was going to get me to do the job by saying the girl is in our hands. Well, we'll see . . .

He has another quick look around. No one is interested. Everyone is in their own world, living their own summer night's dream. He grasps the phone in the left pocket of his shirt with his right hand. The device is hidden in his palm. He dips his hand into the pool as though he is playing with the water. The phone slowly slips from it and sinks into the water. Tomorrow morning someone will see it and fish it out of the water. They will think that a woman sitting by the edge of the pool had dropped it.

He gets up and walks off with decisive steps. He stops a passing taxi and gives the name of the hospital. Security is tight at the main gate at this time of night. The door to the Accident and Emergency Department is always open. From there he will find a way to reach Zelal's floor. If that doesn't work, if they don't let him in, he'll curl up in a corner of the garden and wait until morning.

Either tonight or early tomorrow morning he will smuggle Zelal out. He will try to find the writer *abi*. After all he hasn't died. He has hasn't been buried, has he? Of course he will answer his phone. Let's say he doesn't. Let's say that they are once more totally alone in the world. They will take to the road again, dragging a whole lot of trouble behind them. They have no option. After that . . . There is no 'after that'; he doesn't know what will happen after that.

*

She awoke as though someone had prodded her. It was as though she had heard a familiar voice. A man's voice. Was it her father or her brother? Someone had called out. It wasn't Mahmut. She would recognize his voice immediately, and she wouldn't be startled by Mahmut's voice.

She tries to accustom her eyes to the darkness of the night. For some reason the night light next to the sick woman isn't on as usual. The room is in darkness. She must have dreamt it. She attempts to remember her dream.

It was a bad dream. In fact she has been having bad dreams for days. In her dream she was looking at the village from a high hill. It was night and it was dark. A dog had sunk its teeth into her skirt and was trying to pull at it, growling. Or was it a wolf rather than a dog? It was a savage, horrible creature. As she tried to chase the cur away she had fallen. She had seen the animal's huge jaws, its savage pointed teeth directly over her face, and she had tried to shout, but she had not been able to. She heard a noise from the direction of the village. Perhaps she had woken up to that sound.

Zelal searches the room with her eyes. The woman in the bed near the door is sleeping, snoring lightly. The door of the room is closed. The window right beside the bed has been left slightly open for air. She can see the sky from where she lies and the top branches of the mighty trees in the hospital garden. Dawn has not quite broken, but it is not far off. A faint red glow is rising from the east.

Since they moved her bed over to the window the evening before she is able to see the sky, the clouds, the stars and the birds that perch on the branches at the tops of the trees. Today, I will watch the birds and the clouds and pass the time until Mahmut arrives. What a good thing we changed our beds around. It is much more pleasant in front of the window; at least one can see the birds and the stars. She thinks about her elderly room-mate. The woman is breathing fitfully. What a cold, miserable cow she had been; then how suddenly she had changed. When she saw how frightened I was, she thawed out. Perhaps she was ashamed of how she had behaved. If a person has a conscience they feel another person's suffering. If they feel it once then they will find it difficult to do anything horrible. So the woman does have a conscience.

It's black in the village and on the mountain at this time of night. Adults threaten to leave naughty children out in the pitch-dark street. The redness of dawn heralds the end of fear. Here the city lights do not admit that darkest moment immediately before dawn.

She thinks about dawn on the mountain. Mahmut and I used to wake up cuddling up to one another. Listening to the sound of spring water, we used to wait for dawn to break. Our provisions had run out. There were just a few sugar cubes left. There was nothing to put in our mouths other than plants and the wild birds we caught, but what did we care? We made love as the dawn broke, the redness of sunrise fell on our glowing bodies. Each time we made love the child within me grew. It was as though he became one hundred children, one thousand children. We used to get hungry, and the child got hungry, too. We could no longer get provisions, bread and milk from the villages as before. Locals would quickly shut the door in our faces, either from fear or because they were fed up with us. They might even inform on one if one persisted too much. Nowhere was safe. Especially for us. Mahmut would go around looking for something to eat. I collected strawberries, plums, nettles, mallow and anything else that was edible. We used to light a small fire to cook the birds and little fish. After that we would wash at the spring. The water was like ice. It was good for both our hearts and our bodies. In my childhood I used to enjoy listening to fairy stories and telling them. Before a language was superimposed on my own and the two languages fought each other, the elderly woman storyteller in the village used to say that in time I would replace her. Perhaps I would have become a kind of female *dengbej*. I used to like fairytales because they were more glorious, happier than real life, because lovers would attain their desires, villains would be punished and good would win. I didn't need fairytales any longer. In our haven in the grove I was in the middle of the most beautiful one I had ever heard.

Zelal knew that fairytales could not last for ever. And that in real life one cannot attain one's desires and live happily ever after. But the couple's love was so powerful that the tale of the prince who had come to save the little Sultana who was fleeing from the wicked giants and monsters could not end badly.

She thought how much she loved her man. She felt Mahmut's love in her whole body, in her every limb, everywhere from the strands of her hair to her most intimate parts. She thought: Whatever the end was going to be it was good to have experienced this. To how many of his servants does God grant such a love! If I had not followed the black lamb that night up hill and down dale and left the village; if those men had not raped me; if Dad had been unable to spare his daughter, risk disobeying the code and secretly let me go, I would not have met Mahmut. Zelal was amazed at a person's fate. She blessed that night. She thanked Allah for what had happened to her.

Hope shone within her. Soon I shall recover and get out of this room. We will go towards the sea. I shall give birth to Hope.

She heard the door of the room open slowly. She looked towards the door trying to see who had turned up. She remembered that Nurse Eylem was on duty. She never neglected visiting all the patients on her wards when she was on night duty, whether they summoned her or not. She could tell not only a patient's physical state but also their state of mind just by looking into that person's eyes. She never asked what Mahmut was to me, who we were or what our troubles were. She did not speak much. However, she saw and listened with her heart, and she understood us.

In the redness of the breaking dawn, Zelal dimly saw the shadow in front of the door. It was not Nurse Eylem. It was a fairly tall well-built man. Then she heard a muffled sound. A gun, muted with a silencer or wrapped in cloth, went off. For a moment she thought that the noise had come from outside, from the hospital garden. Two more shots were fired. And then . . . the elderly woman's thin shrill scream. A commotion in front of the door. Shouts, swearing and another shot. The echo of footsteps – heavy boots – of someone running down the corridor. A familiar sound to her ears. A familiar face that disentangled itself from the darkness and slowly took shape, that forcibly recalled itself to her memory: *Kekê Mesûd*!..

Sirens, bustling, lights switched on one after the other. People on duty filling the room, doctors, nurses and the security guards that were too late.

She saw that it was Nurse Eylem lying on the floor. She heard the young woman say, moaning with pain, 'I'm not seriously wounded. He shot me in the leg.' She saw how the blood flowing from the head and chest of the elderly patient who lay on the bed in front of the door had stained the white sheets red. She watched them put Nurse Eylem on a stretcher. She observed how they had intended to wrap the dead patient in bloody sheets and carry her away but then gave in to those who argued against destroying the evidence. Instead, they eventually pushed the old woman still in bed into the corridor. Through the door, where both sides had been opened to allow the bed out, she saw people gathered, petrified with fear: she saw doctors, patients, carers and employees. Everything was dealt with as if Zelal had not been in the room, as though her bed was empty. The morning call to prayer rose from the loudspeakers of the nearby mosque. It must be half past five, she thought. The day is beginning. I'm alive. The old woman will not be able to see the sun, for she is no longer alive.

Zelal pulled the bedcover over herself and hid under the white sheets.

She wanted to merge with the white and vanish. Cleaners arrived with buckets and mops. She observed them through a slit she had made in the sheet in which she had wrapped herself. As they moved around her bed they commented to one another, 'That's some sleep! She hasn't stirred, even with all this commotion!' She made herself even smaller under the sheets. They are not going to leave me like this. In a while the police, the gendarmes, the security guards and the doctors will all come and question me, she thought. I'm deaf and dumb. I have become deaf and dumb. I've become a mute. No one will be able to get a word out of me.

She thought about her neighbour in the next bed. Had the poor woman had a premonition? Had she been horrible to me because somehow she knew that her death would be my responsibility? If she had not changed beds with me yesterday evening, I would be the one dead. She had not believed me when I said I had seen someone sinister at the door. She had said that it was normal for people to pop their heads round the door when it was ajar and for me not to worry. She did not believe me, but I did see a person: it was Mesut *Abi*. Death personified. He was in my nightmare, too. That was why I screamed in my sleep. I saw him. His face was the face of the Devil. It was the Devil I saw at the ward door disguised in the image of my Mesut *Abi* who used to bounce me on his knee, take me on his back to school when the Delice stream flooded and carry me over the water, who patted me, protected and watched over me calling me 'my sky-eyed sister with the gold-stranded hair', becoming as fierce as a lion if any of the village children so much as harmed a lock of my hair.

She had understood that the Devil had taken possession of her brother the day he came to the hamlet with the two evil men. His voice was not his own and neither were his looks nor his gait. The Devil had torn out his heart and taken it away. He had stolen Mesut's heart and entered his body. Her poor brother had become a devilish traitor.

Kekê Mesûd was unique. He was fearless and could be a somewhat brutal at times. He had such a way of wringing a hen's neck, putting a knife to the calf's throat that I was always frightened. But as far as my mother and I were concerned, he was an angel. He was loyal to his ancestry, to the customs. His uncles loved him, too. After the villages had signed up for the militia and my father had left the village and we had gone down to the hamlet, they had said that Mesut should stay in the village, but my father had not let him. He was just beginning to grow a beard when they took him.

Zelal remembers that night. The night they raided the village and filled the military vehicles with men amid shouted orders and oaths and took them away. They had left only her old grandfather who could not walk – although not before kicking him a few times to see that he really was disabled. They had taken her father and her Mesut *Abi* with the other men. Her father had returned three days later with swellings and bruises on his face. He was limping. He had not said much. He had told her, 'They maintained that we were aiding and abetting. Provisions will no longer be given to anyone who comes to the door, even if that person's my own son.' Shouting and crying, her mother had asked about Mesut. 'He'll be back in a few days. Don't bellow like that, woman, I told you he'll come, didn't I? What has the boy got to do with the mountain and the organization? They'll let him go. Don't worry!'

Her father was right: Mesut had returned to the village a few days later. He didn't look at all good. He had been beaten up. He had gone straight off the barn and crouched in a corner and had lain there for days without eating, drinking, speaking or communicating. He heard neither his mother's begging him to eat at least some soup, nor his father's words of advice and comfort. He was in shock. Who knows what they had done to the boy for him to lose his reason, they said, and they had even brought a *hodja* to say prayers over him – but in vain.

Then one morning I quietly came to him without anyone seeing me. I called to him, '*Kekê Mesûd.*' He didn't react. I asked him who had done this to him, so that I would know. He still remained silent. I wanted to stroke his face, but he pushed me away roughly. He had never pushed me, but this time he did.

He said, '*Kekê Mesûd* is dead.' His voice, his face, his behaviour – it had all changed. He really was dead. We never knew what they had done to him.

We asked others who returned to the village. 'For some reason they picked on him. They wanted to make him tell them where someone was, but he didn't. They threatened to do something to his mother and his sister, and then he gave in. They tortured him, too, because he gave in. They made him eat shit, we heard. And then they did the worst thing of all: they pushed a stick into him from behind. Nobody knows whether it's true or a rumour,' they said. What did my brother know that he could tell? He was only a village boy in the fields with the goats.

My father would always say that the teacher used to say, 'If you let him study he could be a university professor.' They had not let him study, and he had stayed in the village. Before that day I don't think he knew about the mountain and the organization or anything.

Then one day he left the barn. He said, 'I'm going to the mountains. Don't come looking for me.' Crying, my mother prepared some provisions. He did not take them. Towards the evening we saw him walking away towards the small town along the village road. He got smaller and smaller and disappeared behind the huge rocks. I think that Satan had entered him, not because he had confessed; but long before that day he had been released from the military post and returned to the village. Evil men had put the Devil in his head and into his body. The Devil had entered, but we had not realized it then.

The morning call to prayers had stopped. The day had long since dawned. Zelal lies hidden under the sheets. They had put a policeman in uniform on the door of the room. She sees this through her observation hole. A civilian and a young doctor friend of Nurse Eylem enter the room. The policeman salutes the doctor's companion. He must be someone important. The man is angry and reprimands everyone. He keeps shouting, 'You should not have moved the murdered woman's bed until it had been thoroughly investigated! Even the traces of blood have been wiped off!' His eye alight on the bed in which Zelal is lying.

'You should have moved this one to another room. Make a file on this one. We'll call on her for a statement. She is our only eyewitness.'

'This patient is a very young woman who was wounded by a stray bullet. They call it celebratory gunfire, you know. She lost her baby in the accident. She has not got over the shock yet. And then this incident on top of it. I really don't think she is in a condition to give a statement at the moment, sir.'

Zelal thinks the doctor is trying to protect her. After all he is Nurse Eylem's friend. They know about us, and they know that they have to protect us. Perhaps the writer had quietly said something to them.

'Of course it's your job to assess the patient's condition. But her statement should be taken as soon as possible.'

'We'll inform you in the shortest possible time as soon as she comes out of shock, sir.'

They approach the bed. The man slightly lifts the sheet that she has pulled over herself. He meets Zelal's huge pure-blue eyes and is surprised. 'She's very young, almost a child,' he says. 'Get well soon, my girl. When you are better, tell us what you saw. Don't be frightened. It's nothing to do with you. Trust in the state. We'll protect you. Don't be afraid!'

Zelal remains silent. She remains deaf and dumb. If they were to kill me I wouldn't open my mouth. I didn't see anything, and I didn't hear anything. Can one give a statement about a nightmare? I saw the Devil's face and blood. That's all. She looks at the man's face with vacant eyes.

The man avoids her glance. 'The poor thing really is in shock.'

Torrents of blood flow in front of Zelal's eyes. The Delicesu stream has turned into blood. Her Mesut *Abi* rolls into the river of blood as he carries her on his back. The springs of love on the mountain have become blood. Hevi is thrashing about in blood. The blood flowing from Mahmut's wound drips on the floor of the cave. The blood of the dead patient who took my place so that I wouldn't be afraid, so that I would sleep comfortably, transforms the white sheets into the red flag. Zelal feels sick, and her head is spinning. She wants to call the doctor who is about to leave the room. She would like him to give news to Mahmut, to tell him to escape. She trusts the young doctor. He is Nurse Eylem's friend. She calls out to him with all her might but no sound comes. She tries again. I don't want to play deaf and dumb any longer. I have things to say to the doctor. She shouts, 'Doctor *Abi*!' A croak comes out of her throat.

The young doctor conducting the stranger to the door hears the croak as he is about to go out and turns back. 'Is there something the matter?'

She nods. Yes, yes, yes . . . No sound emerges. There is no sound to give life to her voice.

With her finger she points to the ballpoint pen in the top pocket of the doctor's white gown. The doctor hesitates for a moment. He cannot understand what she wants. Zelal straightens up in bed and pulls the pen from his pocket as he leans over her. On a corner of the white sheet she writes in capital letters with one last effort, 'IT WAS MESUT ABI. MAHMUT MUST ESCAPE.' Then she slumps back on the bed.

The doctor checks out of the corner of his eye to see if anyone has witnessed this and then slowly gathers up the sheet. He folds it so that the writing cannot be viewed, crumples it and throws it under the bed. He shouts to the cleaner standing by the door, 'This patient's sheets are dirty. Please have them changed.'

He turns to Zelal and looks directly into her limpid blue, fathomless eyes. He nods as though to say, All right. He touches the girl's forehead with his fingers. 'Don't worry. You've been very frightened and made yourself dumb. It will pass after a while. It's better that you should carry on like this for now.' He winks at her with the smile of an accomplice.

Zelal holds the doctor's fingers which are on her forehead and brings them to her lips. She kisses them with respect and gratitude. A person can reach people, Mahmut had said one day. Do you see? They can.

She closes her eyes and relaxes. A little girl lies all alone, helpless and dumb in a strange hospital room, in a strange city, in a strange world. She does not even expect Mahmut any longer; Mahmut, her only support in the whole world. But she wants him to escape, not to come near her, to be caught or to put his life in jeopardy. She thinks of a fairytale. A fairytale in which enemies make peace, lovers reunite, death is timely and from old age, in which birth heralds life, streams and rivers flow deep blue and crystal clear and not the colour of blood, in which people hold out their hands to each other instead of shooting. She had said to the writer who had gone to look for the word, 'As you are a storyteller, tell me a story with a happy ending.' Had the writer *abi* been able to hear the faintly whispering voice? Had he been able to find the word he was looking for? Will he return bringing the word in his wake? Will he again be a godsend as he was that night at the coach station?

TEN

Cats Return to Their Homes

When she saw the man and the boy come through the hotel's revolving door Elif wanted to get up from her chair in the corner close to the reception desk and run over to them. She could not. She sank back into the chair. A whole night without a wink of sleep; a whole day wandering restlessly around the city, her hotel room being too confining; and now hours of tense waiting drinking endless cups of coffee and smoking endless cigarettes under the curious glances of the girl at the reception desk. And especially this last hour that, when Deniz said on the telephone, 'We're in Helsingør, we'll be there in an hour at the latest' seemed to her like a century.

Deniz was holding the boy's hand. The little blond boy who was just a tiny mite beside Deniz carried a large pack on his back that was almost as big as he was himself. As for Deniz's backpack it seemed just medium in size in comparison. She moved towards them, to hug and embrace them. This time she succeeded.

They must be tired. Who knows how they had got here. A long sea journey and then over land. Why didn't I think of sending a ticket straight away so that they could come directly by plane from Oslo to Bergen? Then they would have been here before evening and not be so tired. As she stands resting her head against her son's neck with her hand on Bjørn's head she is surprised at her weakness and exhaustion. If she could cry in loud sobs she would feel better. She cannot. She can only say, 'Miaow, miaowww . . .'

Finally she says, 'You are tired. And Bjørn must be dog-tired. Let's go straight to the room.'

She has already reserved their room. When asked for how long, she said she didn't know. She doesn't know. She hesitates to ask, to learn. She is afraid of the answer she will receive. The size of the packs on the backs of father and son looks promising. But still one never knows. One must not think about this now. It's not the right time. What is important at the moment is their being here, safe and sound.

As they take the key from reception, Bjørn prattles on, trying to tell her something. Deniz translates what the boy says. 'The Devil was angry with us. He burnt our house. He says that they don't want us there any more.'

'Don't worry, Bjørn. I'm angry at that devil, too. We'll burn his castle down. Then he can't stay on the island any longer. And I know very nice places where the Devil can't reach us. We'll go there all together.'

As they walk towards the lift Deniz translated to Bjørn briefly what Elif has said. She understands that he has not translated everything to the boy.

'Is there anywhere where the Devil cannot reach us, Mother? Do you really believe that? The unknown deserter had written, "The violence of the age will find you everywhere."' Deniz's voice, beyond being tired and daunted seems to have reached the end of the road. It is as though he is saying, 'Take the boy and me and do whatever you want. That's it from me. I give up. He has left the heavy burden of living on the ground, and it's as though he is saying, 'I cannot carry it any longer. Take it if you want or leave it on the ground.'

After Bjørn has wolfed down a couple of biscuits and gone to sleep and mother and son sit together with a glass of cognac each, he says, 'I would like to be stronger. I would like to be strong enough to enter the race and carry, not just my own, but the weight of the whole world. I would like not to need havens, calm harbours and be able to put out to stormy, wild seas. A person can drown in a glass of water. At least drowning at sea would have glory. You could say that I drowned with dignity.'

At first their conversation was hesitant, calculated and reserved. They were weighing each other up like adversaries, trying not to play into the other's hands and putting off the questions, not ready to listen to the answers. They were careful, lying in wait. It was as though there was a white piece of paper in front of them and an empty screen, and, with careful consideration, they were writing their shared fate on it. Every word they uttered was written on the report of their future in a way that could not be erased or changed. 'What happened on the island?' This question that Elif asked mustering all her courage seemed fleetingly to hang in the air.

As they cheerfully returned from the Big Fish competition, having caught a really big fish, they had first seen a distant red glow. If the horizon had reddened not in the east but in the west they would have ascribed it to the sunset, and they would have mused on the beauty of the purply red horizon. The fishermen who knew the seas and the skies of the island well were witnessing a miracle. The sun was setting both to the west and the east; the horizon was coloured red in both directions. Who said that word first? Did they whisper it? Did they shout it? Deniz cannot remember. He only remembers the word 'Fire!' And his own voice saying, 'The Gasthaus is burning.' Had he said it out loud? Had the others heard? He doesn't know.

They were a few miles away from the island and were approaching it from the north. It was not possible for the Gasthaus to be seen from where they were. But Deniz had understood with infallible instinct that it was the guesthouse which was on fire. Fisherman Jan said, 'That's the direction of the Gasthaus. There are just the rocks and your house. You're right!' He took the binoculars to see better. 'Yes, damn it! The Gasthaus is burning.'

Deniz continued his account. 'Then a strange but good thing happened. It was as though my brain emptied. I turned into a robot that saw everything but did not think or feel. I hid in the void of insensitivity and nonentity that the psychologist calls a black hole. It had happened to me a few times before. In times like those I became so unfeeling, unperturbed and calm that everyone was astonished. Once again I waited silently and calmly for us to reach the quay. The only thing I felt was Jan's hand was on my shoulder. There was only Bjørn on my mind.

'The festivities that had been cut short: all that remained was bewilderment, piles of empty bottles, nets decorated with fish and mermaids, abandoned stalls of junk food and beer, interrupted gaiety, silenced music, Bjørn's red car, people in their Sunday best . . . All had gathered at the square by the quay and were waiting for the boats returning from the Big Fish competition. Not to award a prize but to give news of the fire.

'Jan and I sprang from the boat together. Without running, without hurrying, I walked towards the crowd that had assembled in the square. I saw the island people not as individuals but a solid wall, as a dark stain darker than the twilight. They were not sympathetic. They were lined up there not to share the tragedy but to prevent the foreigner's curse. That's how it seemed to me. When we reached the end of the quay, with me in front and Jan immediately behind, a small yellow star slipped towards me from among the crowd. He jumped into my arms shouting, "Daddy!" Then I began to cry.'

'What about Grandmother and Grandfather?'

'There was no one at home when they set fire to the Gasthaus. They did it a few hours after you had left the island while everyone was swept up in the dancing, music and entertainment. You know that the door on the seaside was always left open. It wasn't difficult for them to enter. In any case they did not need to go inside to set fire to the house. The savage beasts: they even set fire to the kennel –without releasing Kurt's chain, not caring that he was burnt alive.'

'Was the house completely burnt out?'

'No, not entirely. The island has a very well-trained firefighting group. From time to time we all used to work there as volunteers. They arrived really swiftly. But, still, the north wing of the house was burnt, in other words, the room I used – you remember, the room of the old fugitive poet. The kitchen and the room you stayed in, the side by the sea, are still standing.'

'Did they find the arsonists? I was suspicious of those skinheads with motorbikes from the start.'

'They caught them. They just said, "We wanted to give the foreigner a lesson. We didn't think the fire would spread."'

'It's all because of me!' says Elif. 'If I hadn't come to the island, if I hadn't taken part in the festivities, if I hadn't shown off with Bjørn in the square, those foul bikers would not have been provoked and perhaps none of this would have happened. I've destroyed your last refuge, too. I didn't give you any peace there either.'

'Don't be silly, Mother. This has nothing to do with you. What is sad is that the evil seed has been sown even on that distant island. The islanders have learnt fear. They are wary now. When they begin to fear, people become hostile and cruel. So much has changed on the island within the past two to three days. The spell has vanished. Goodness and innocence have been defeated. The Devil has once more killed Princess Ulla. The last stronghold has fallen – but not because of you.'

Fearing the answer, she ventures to ask, 'Will you return to the island?'

'I didn't come here to return there. Perhaps if I were alone I might have gone back, but I can't sacrifice Bjørn. I wanted to prepare for him a safe haven without fear, hostility, tension and violence. I didn't succeed. I'm afraid you and my father were right. There is nowhere to take sanctuary. I imagine the owner of the Gasthaus, the old poet, eventually realized this, and that is why he put an end his life.'

Elif remembers the notebooks, the poems written in the old man's handwriting, the things Deniz had written and the disc of photographs in the drawer intended for Bjørn. They must all have been destroyed in the fire. She feels the weight in her heart of having seen and read them. She must share that weight with her son, otherwise it will be almost impossible to bear.

'I must tell you something. I looked through the notebooks that were lying on your desk. Forgive me. You know that even in your childhood I never did such a thing. I took care not to touch your private possessions. However, that day, before I left the island, as I passed your room the door was ajar. I went inside. What I really wanted was to be closer to you, to understand you better. I looked through the notebooks on your desk and read a few lines of your writing. There were the poems and the writings of the old poet. Then I was curious about the contents of your drawer. The Devil must have goaded me, as they say; it was that sort of impulse. I saw the photographs on disc; the photographs that you were going to show Bjørn when he grew up. It was as though those four photographs were the epitome of the fate and suffering of not only you but of all of us, of all mankind.'

There is an uneasy silence.

'They all burnt, and that's good,' says Deniz. 'One could not even take a step with the weight of that writing, those photographs. Nothing could be started again without them all being destroyed, erased. If only an arsonist had set fire to my memory. Now I think about it, I had no right to saddle Bjørn with that bloody burden. What a good thing they all burnt.'

He said 'taking a step'. He said 'starting again' . . . Elif keeps quiet, afraid of reflecting in her voice the selfish joy, cheerfulness and hope welling inside her. For a moment they look at the boy taking up the tiny space in the huge bed. He looks so small, so vulnerable that both are moved. They are seized with the desire to cover him and protect the little being from all the evils of the world. At the same moment, without knowing it, Deniz and Elif are both thinking of the same photograph. The image of the wounded, captive father with a black sack thrust over his head trying to protect his little son clutched to his bosom behind the barbed wire lodges itself in their eyes and their hearts.

'Mother, do you think that there is anything I can do in the world of people? I have to bring up Bjørn and get him educated. I'm responsible for him.'

Just as Elif is about to say, 'We'll bring him up and educate him together; we are all responsible for him . . .' She stops herself. She is afraid that it will hurt Deniz and undermine him.

'Of course there are things you can do. With all your skills and talents you can do anything. All you need is the will.'

'Today during the journey I was wondering what use I am. If I can't do anything else I can take photographs of food and table settings. Might there be such a job? Rather than taking photographs of atrocities and violence, taking pictures of food and decorated tables would much better.'

'The son of a friend of mine does that work. I heard from my friend that this is now a recognized branch of photography. It pays quite well, too.

'Yes, of course. I have to earn money.'

She cannot bear the capitulation in his voice, the acceptance of defeat, his bowing his head to routine. What sort of woman am I? And now I'm anguishing because my son is planning to return to a normal life and preparing to be a father who must earn his daily bread.

'Don't worry. Everything will sort itself out,' she says. 'You were right when you said that there isn't a place to take refuge. Even if there is no place left in the world it is always possible for a person to take refuge in themselves, in a deep, secret part inside them. When that is no longer possible then the world of man will have come to an end. Perhaps the last refuge is man's own heart, his own soil. Let's return home, Kitten. I, too, have missed home. Cats strive to return to their homes even if they are very far away. If they don't perish on the way, they return home sooner or later.'

He is lying on a bench in a corner of the hospital garden, out of sight. There is a heaviness like lead in his head that he has never known before, a vile nausea in his stomach and the sensation of heavy stones on his eyelids. He hears the disturbing sirens of ambulances and police cars. He doesn't know how and when he came here. He doesn't know where he is anyway. Perhaps he was shot and is lying in a ravine. It seems as though he been shot in the head, stomach and eyes. He struggles to get up, to get to his feet. His head is spinning, and he is sick, retching and gagging. After that he feels better. He revives a little with the smell of alcohol reaching his nose. He looks around in the half-light. He recognizes the hospital building. A few doctors and nurses in their white or green hospital gowns who have come off night duty pass by in the distance. It is then that Mahmut comes to his senses. 'What have I done!'

His first serious session of boozing, of inebriation. They say that it happens to every young person. It does not happen to us. People do not drink in our parts, neither in the town nor on the mountain. Especially now, in our state! Mahmut, you deserve every conceivable kind of trouble. You are a total arsehole. Did you think it was clever to get out of the taxi halfway and go into the first restaurant in the suburbs that served alcohol? You thought that you would distract the men, cover your tracks and make it more difficult for them to find the hospital. You thought that you would be protecting Zelal. Mahmut, you are an utter fool. You are a *çaş, çaş*! You are a complete idiot! It wasn't the first time you saw the rows of shops selling beer on the road to the hospital, the taverns looking like orderly cook shops. How many times had you passed in front of them? How many times had you taken a curious peek? So you had already thought about going inside. What in hell made you get out of the taxi and go into that tavern?

He utters a violent oath at himself, at life, the tavern, the mountain, the plain, fate, everyone and everything. *'Nizanim çi ji dîya bikim!'* Damn!

Had he wanted a drink? He did not know anything about drink to make him want one. He just wanted to relax a little. It was not going to be as easy to smuggle Zelal out of the hospital and bring her home as he had originally thought. You would have to avoid the grumpy neighbouring patient and the hospital staff and give the doctors and nurses in the corridor and the people on door duty the slip. You would have to find a taxi and help her into it. In the meantime Zelal needed to have some mobility and be able to walk, if only a little. Well, let us say we got into the taxi, it would be altogether reckless to drive straight back to the house they had been loaned. They would get out of the car earlier. The driver should not know where they were staying. After that he would carry Zelal in his arms. She is as light as a feather. What was her weight to him?

Thinking about all this had made him tense and he had wanted to relax, to gather his wits and to restore his strength. Moreover, if they are after me I would be able to spot them better while sitting and drinking inconspicuously.

Slumping down at a table at the far end, he had called 'Beer!' to the waiter. This was the drink he was most familiar with. And it was the one with the least alcohol, the most harmless. After the second beer the waiter had asked, 'Shall a give you a double vodka with it?' He had said yes, mainly to act normally and not to send the waiter back empty-handed. It also enabled him to stay a little longer. He had enjoyed it when he began to get slightly tipsy: he felt good; it had relaxed him. Obviously there was good reason for people to turn to the demon drink. He cannot remember when he left the place. And how he had reached the hospital and got through the garden gate? He had called at the Accident and Emergency Department entrance, and they had shown him the door to the Emergency Service, thinking from his state that he must be ill. He had wandered up and down the corridors for a while, probably trying to locate the stairs that went up to the ward where Zelal was lying. He had not been able to find them. Suddenly felt really bad and had rushed out into the garden – by which route he could not remember.

Now he is gradually coming round. His temples throb. His shirt is sticking to his body from sweat, and he stinks. He is disgusted by his own smell. He cannot quite see from where he is, but he notices a commotion, a bustle, at the hospital gate. The yellow flashing light of a police car passing through the main gate merges with the noise of sirens. What has happened? Who knows! What time is it? There was the call to prayers a little while ago; that means it's almost six. I'm late. I'm late for Zelal! Now everyone is awake. How will I take her out of hospital? How will I smuggle her away with all these police gathered at the door and amid all this activity?

He wants to wash his face and hold his head under cool water. On the mountain, when he and Zelal woke up to a new day, they would run to the spring. They would wash themselves clean in the cool water that flowed from between some rocks hidden in the bushes and trees. She would cup the water in her hands and transfer it into a sweet-smelling leaf or an alpine flower and drink it like that. They believed that the crystal water gushed from that rock just for them.

'I know this area well, this spring was not here before. The water bored through the rock for us, to quench our thirst, to bless our love and to purify us of our sins,' Mahmut used to say. He thought of himself as Ferhat, the valiant lover. They say that everything is most valuable in its rightful place. In the mountains, I was both Mazlum and Ferhat, I was Rüstemê Zal. In the mountains I was decent, strong and a hero. Who and what am I here? Am I a drunken mouse or a fugitive who hasn't the strength to protect his love or himself? A wretched Mahmut whose only support, only hope is some weird writer we know nothing about; who he is, what he is, where he is and whether he will return. Mahmut who lost himself to two beers and three vodkas on his way to save the one he loved.

One day when he came to visit Zelal and got lost in the labyrinth-like hospital corridors he had found himself two floors below the ground floor in a sort of garage or depot. He remembered that up some stairs there had been a door that opened out on to the garden. Immediately beside the door he had seen a tap used to water the garden and a garden hose. I must find that place.

I must have a wash, have a good drink of water and cool down. His body is burning like fire. I have a fever. I'm ill. He feels his pulse. Yes, I have a high temperature. He remembers his days at medical school. By now I could have been one of the new doctors at this hospital, swaggering around in my white coat; here to cure people's troubles and relieve their pain. He walks slowly to the back of the building. The hose is not there, but he finds the tap. He cups his hand under the water and drinks thirstily. The water that has absorbed the coolness of the night is good for both his heart and his head. He takes off his shirt and washes his neck and his arms. He feels better.

He can go up to Zelal's room now. Whatever has happened, there is pandemonium at the main door. One cannot enter from there. They won't let anyone in before visiting hours. He must try the door by the depot. He descends the dark narrow steps. The door is open. There is no one about. He will find C3 block in the end. If this doesn't work, he'll look for Nurse Eylem whom Zelal likes so much and ask her. He must reach Zelal before it's too late. I'm already too late. If I hadn't passed out like some dirty old drunk, she and I might now be in a taxi speeding away from here. He goes through the door. He moves ahead in the half-light to the wide corridor opposite. He begins to climb the first stairs that appear in front of him. If I go up two flights of steps I should reach the ground floor. And when I find the lift the rest is easy.

He passes through glass doors, dim corridors, other doors and more corridors. He goes up and down a few flights of steps. It had been like this the day they had taken Zelal out of intensive care and carried her to her room, when he first got lost among the wards looking for her room. He had felt as though he was in a nightmare from which he would shortly wake up screaming. The hospital was like a huge maze.

Expecting to emerge at the entrance, he realizes that he is in front of C3 block. It is very bright everywhere. Dawn has long since broken, and they have put on all the lights. There was an intense silence in the corridor. In front of Zelal's room there were a few men in uniform making notes. That was when Mahmut understood. He recalled what he had seen and heard in his drunken state, as he was sobering up. He leant against a wall so that he did not fall over. How come I didn't think of it? How come I didn't think that they would arrive before me and finish the job! The man had said, 'The girl is in our hands.' He had not believed him. He had thought he was calling his bluff. He had thought that if he really were the brother who had confessed he wouldn't have the heart to kill his own sister.

He walked towards Zelal's room. The men in the corridor stopped him before he reached the door.

'A relative of mine is here,' he said.

'Who is this relative? Show us your identity card.'

He takes it out. 'She's my wife,' he said. 'Her name's Zelal. She had an operation. She was in this room yesterday.'

The man paused for a moment not knowing whether to pity him or to grab him and take him away.

At that moment he didn't care about anything. They can shoot me, kill me or arrest me if they like! He lunged towards the room. It was completely empty. Neither Zelal's bed nor the one belonging to the elderly patient was there. The floor had evidently been wiped with disinfectant. It smelt strongly of Lysol.

'She was lying here on the bed in front of the door,' he whispered. 'I last saw her yesterday evening. She was fine. She was going to be discharged soon.'

'What relation did you say she was to you?'

'She's my woman, the mother of my unborn child. She's my Zelal.'

'Well, you'd better come along with us to the doctor's room where our chief is.'

'What's happened to her? Has someone done something to Zelal? Has her wound opened up again?'

'No, there's nothing the matter. Nothing. Just come with us.'

They passed through doors, corridors and stairs. One of the officers held him gently by the arm. Whether it was to prevent him from stumbling and falling or from escaping, he could not decide. He let himself walk beside them silently and unresisting. He didn't care if they took him away or locked him up. There was no longer any need to resist or run away. If there was no Zelal to protect, no life worth living, no children to be born, no seas to reach, what need was there to flee or to struggle?

He seemed to revive when he saw the familiar young doctor in the room to which they had taken him.

'He arrived at the door of the room where the crime took place, boss. We checked his identity. He had on his person an identity card with the name Mahmut Bozlak. He says that the woman named Zelal is his wife.'

'What were you doing here at this time of the morning? It's not visiting hours,' enquired the man they called their chief.

'I've always waited in the garden at night. And yesterday night I fell asleep outside. Then as day broke I heard noises and I became anxious.'

'Don't worry,' said the young doctor. 'Your patient is well.' Then he turned to the chief. 'I know this man. He really is the patient's husband. He has been here ever since she was admitted to hospital. The person responsible for the patient is the famous writer Ömer Eren. You probably know of him.'

'Sit down,' said the chief in a harsh voice used to giving orders. 'Your patient is well but in a state of shock. She cannot speak. We cannot get a statement from her. Perhaps you can help. Did you have any rivals or enemies? The elderly sick woman in the room was shot. But, if you ask me, she wasn't the real target.'

'We have no rivals or enemies,' said Mahmut firmly. He fell silent. He turned to the doctor. 'Can I see her?'

'We changed her room. It's better for now if no one knows which room she is in. Even you. Don't worry. She really is fine. She was very frightened. She went into shock. We are going to sedate her for a while so that she can recover. Anyway she's asleep now.'

'Please allow me to stay and wait here at the door. So that I can see her when she comes round. I'm in no state to go anywhere. I think I have a fever. I feel really bad.'

He felt like telling the doctor that he, too, had studied at medical school but restrained himself. If they should try to probe further into the shooting incident it would be best to play the role of hapless victim, the wretched ignorant, injured villager . . .

'Come with me,' said the young doctor. 'You really do look bad, I'll give you some medicine. May we go, sir?'

'Of course. Please do. The Hippocratic Oath requires one to look after patients. We'll just take a formal report. As you know this man we don't need him.'

They went into a room used as a depot for medicine and supplies next door.

'Our young patient – her name is Zelal, isn't it? – wanted me to deliver a coded message to you. It was "It was Mesut Abi. Mahmut must escape."'

His voice was mocking especially when he said 'coded', but he acted like a friend and accomplice.

'May I take her out of the hospital?' asked Mahmut.

'You can't take her out. She is not fit enough yet, and she is safe here now. We have taken major precautions. The hospital doesn't want a bad reputation. That poor elderly woman! They shot her instead of the girl. Who is Mesut?'

'He's her brother . . . You will keep this to yourself, won't you?'

'Yes, for sure.'

'It must be an honour killing. When I met Zelal she was running away from this code of honour. We ran away together. We thought we were safe here. So they found us. The poor old lady. What a terrible end! What a terrible fate! She died in Zelal's place.'

'She died, and Nurse Eylem was wounded. She is my fiancée. Violence is everywhere, and it always strikes the innocent. Take these pills straight away. You have a fever. There's no doubt you're ill. Go and answer the officer's questions. He's waiting inside. Give him a proper postal address if you have one, and find a safe place for yourself to rest up for a few days.'

'Thanks. You know, I studied medicine, too. Not for long; just three terms. I had to quit. I have a favour to ask. If anything goes wrong, please deliver Zelal to Ömer Eren. As you said, he is registered as responsible for her. Our situation's quite simple. In short, as Zelal and I were waiting at the coach station there was some shooting and she got hit by a stray bullet. The writer, who happened to be there, felt sorry for us and helped us. He brought her here and got her admitted to hospital – purely out of kindness. Right now we are in a mess. The only person we trust is Ömer Eren. He is out of the city at the moment, but he will return soon. I'll give you his phone number.'

'Fine. It's a deal. We haven't had this conversation. Don't tell anyone else about it. Things are complicated enough right now.' As they were about to leave the room, the doctor stopped and held his arm. 'I don't know who or what you are. It was the innocence of the girl that impressed me. It was the helpless, innocent trust she had in me. Sometimes I think innocence is the strongest weapon.'

The driver shouted, 'Zap Bridge!' as they passed in front of the crumbling abutments of the ruined bridge.

So it was the same driver as when he came. He recognized me and sent a greeting in his own way to the stranger who was interested in the old bridge. He did not even look at the ruins of the bridge that they had built years ago, carrying stones, mixing the sand and singing marches and folk songs and arguing all night long about revolutionary collaboration, the brotherhood of the people. In any case our bridge was not here. To make the driver happy he shouted 'Thanks' in a loud voice. The passengers on the bus did not understand what was going on and were not even interested.

What does it matter whether the Bridge of Brotherhood is here or thirty or forty kilometres further back when it has been destroyed? But, still, it warmed his heart that the young driver remembered it. A small victory won against the savage aggressiveness of forgetting. He leant his head against the window of the hot, stuffy bus with the broken air conditioning. Instead of looking at the view outside from the front seat of the bus progressing slowly along the rough road, he closed his eyes and looked into himself. Yet only a few weeks ago when he was coming – has it been a month? – he was looking outside trying not to miss a single detail as if to absorb all he saw. The yellow-grey of the earth, the precipitous rocky slopes, the beauty of the snowy peaks, the bends of the river, the abandoned hamlets and huts, the yellow daisies and the poppies blooming in the green grass, the soldiers mine-sweeping along the road, the forbidding gorges, the military fortifications, the men who stop and board the buses at crossroads to check identity cards, the weary passengers, the shabby cafés where they stop for a break, a wild flower that has blossomed among the rocks of an arid slope, the scraggy goats that climb the slopes leaping from rock to rock, the crags that the setting sun coloured red. He was trying to engrave, to imprint everything in his memory and in his heart.

He no longer wants to see and learn. He just wants to remember. Not immediately; recollection requires the healing power of time. But he wants to remember little by little for the rest of his life – however long that may be. He wants to make these recollections an essential part of himself. Everything is so fresh, so immediate and so poignant that it cannot possibly be a memory yet. He just tries to understand, accept and digest it.

I am returning on the bus in which I arrived. Is this coincidence, destiny or significant in some way? In a place where there are only two travel agencies perhaps this does not even warrant pondering. But, still, it niggles me. We are passing along the same road. Of course there is no other road. The mountains are the same mountains, the rivers, the valleys and the gorges are the same. We are stopped more times than when we came. We are searched with more suspicion, more roughly. We proceed along a mountain road with a ravine on one side, following the convoys of military vehicles heading for the border, the tanks and soldiers in combat gear, being stopped from time to time to give way to them; slowing down at checkpoints fortified with sandbags, barbed wire and machine-guns.

I'm returning along the roads I came along to the place I came from. To reach the starting point and complete the circle. When the circle has been completed I shall pause at that point and think about it. Why did I go all that way to reach the same point? I am not going to ask this question. That is because, when the road ends, the starting point will now be the destination. And I shall be the sum of all the roads I have left behind.

What was difficult was getting on the bus. He thought he could never do it. Now, with his head leaning against the window, his eyes almost closed and, having yielded to the drowsiness of relaxing after tension, his calmness and numbness almost turn into happiness . . .

They had not talked very much as he and Jiyan returned from the house in the village in the jeep driven by Diyar. All of them were tired from the long night they had spent. The three of them had eaten a simple supper on a large tray on the floor and they had not had a drink. Perhaps there was no alcohol in the country house; perhaps they had not wanted any, or it had not crossed their minds. Jiyan had made some herbal tea. She always drank this. Afterwards they had talked, about the country, the region, about the whole world, about everything; until very late, until daybreak. It was a good conversation. He was surprised that they had so much to talk about and share. He understood now, as they sat talking like old friends on cushions on the floor in the hall of the house and drinking herbal teas smelling of thyme, mint and linden, that the real words that were meant to be said and heard were crushed in the claws of his passion for Jiyan.

Talking to Jiyan like two old friends . . .

In fact, this was how it should have been from the time he came to town and first entered the chemist's shop. And so, what did you do, Ömer Eren? Why did you feel the need to create a theme for a novel? Why did you succumb to the appeal of your heroine? The source of the word was not in Jiyan's body, not in her unusual eastern beauty. It was other things that made her what she was. Later you gradually understood. But, still, it was the most beautiful feeling you have ever experienced. One of those few things that one can look back on with joy as one breathes one's last breath. That evening after looking at the *Hoca*'s books and handwritten notebooks, just as they were about to leave the room, Jiyan had stopped at the door and said, 'It's time for us to go. Not because the Commander said so, and someone wanted you to. But because there is nothing left for you to do here, because there are people waiting for you, and because every extra day that you spend here will gnaw away at all the good things that, in such a short time, we have enjoyed to the full.'

Thinking that she called him here today to say these things and to say goodbye Ömer had remained silent. She must have thought that it would be easier to sign the decree for our parting in this magical, mystical atmosphere or, rather, this 'sanctuary'.

He had only asked, 'What did our relationship mean to you?'

'I never thought about its meaning. Can love have a meaning? It was a passionate, exhilarating, unforgettable feeling that quenched the thirst in my heart and body. I'm happy I experienced it, and of course I'm a little sad. The sadness experienced after all good things that come to an end.'

'It does not have to end. You are the one who wants it to end, who doesn't allow me to speak, my woman.'

'You are right. I'm the one who wants it to end.'

'But why? If our parting makes you sad, why?'

'What did the fox say to the Little Prince? He would cry when he went, but he would always remember him because the wheat fields would remind him of the colour of his hair. You are the one who made me read *The Little Prince*, Ömer *Bey*, who made me love it. I understood that book deep in my heart. You know as the Little Prince returns to his distant planet he gives all the stars in the sky to the Pilot. All the stars would seem to laugh because he would be on one of them and because he would be laughing at his friend from there. Come on, let's play a game: when you return home and remember these parts you will see my face in everything to do with the east, and as you think about me trying to do something for people here you will feel what is happening here more deeply in your heart. Your interest in this land will overcome the political, conscientious, moral interest of the western intellectual and turn into a bond of passion, into feeling and love – in other words, what it should be. Like the Little Prince's laughing stars, I will have given you mountains and cliffs of love and the towns for which Jiyan's heart beats.'

'I don't want the land, mountains and towns. I want you. I want to hear Jiyan's heartbeats not those of the towns.'

'Jiyan's heart can only beat here. Jiyan is beautiful here, as long as she is distant and free. That is why you were interested in her, that's why you loved her. Because I belong here.' She stopped talking for a moment, played with the curls of her tousled hair and added, 'You told me that you had come to look for the word you had lost. I had not understood then, but now I do. You have found the word you were looking for. It has become easier now for you to leave here and go.'

Have I found it? How does she know that I've found the word?

'Are we now going to put a full stop like this to all we have experienced? Will it be like a passing fancy, just another relationship between woman and man? You said that I have found the word. I don't know yet. Even if I have, what good will that word be if it is not going to tell about you, to be told to you!'

'It won't just tell about me. It will tell about all of us. A word telling of one woman would be empty. Wasn't it emptiness that dragged you all this way! You said, "putting a full stop to what we have experienced". In my opinion what we experienced was a parenthesis. A parenthesis that explained our sentences, that rendered our sentences more meaningful and allowed them to be understood and broadened. We are not putting a stop; we are just closing the brackets.'

'I love you. I should like this parenthesis to continue to the end of the book.'

'I love you, too, very much. The brackets will close, but the narrative will carry on.'

The door of the room was open. They were discussing their lives as though they were speaking about what to eat, who was going to do the shopping and which books were going to be taken.

First they heard the sound of the dog and then footsteps.

'Diyar has arrived,' said Jiyan.

They closed the door slowly and went out.

'Activity is increasing. There seems to be preparation for a military operation. They want us to leave the area early tomorrow morning,' said Diyar without a trace of excitement. They discussed what time they would set off for the town the next day and the safety precautions that should be taken.

'I'm glad I came to this house one last time. Now we won't be able to return for a while,' said Jiyan. 'I have a strange feeling. We should not leave any of the private possessions, notebooks, anything that is of value to us, in the *Hoca*'s study here in case anything should happen to them.'

After that they began to argue about recent political developments concerning the region. They were heading towards bad times when it would be difficult even to talk about a peaceful solution. The different interests in the region, the different balances of power, the new difficulties brought about by the problem spilling beyond Turkey's borders extinguished hopes of a solution – or at least delayed it. Jiyan, with her passionate, emotional speech that had touched him the first moment he met her, believed that work schedules, current activities and plans should not be changed or postponed on the pretext of the emergency situation. She placed great importance on the act of shared mourning in which the families of martyrs and the families of those killed on the mountain – or at least their mothers – came together, and she advocated that this should be done at all costs.

'We have always put it off saying that it is not the right time or that the time has not come. Well, when will the time come for peace in this country? When, tell me!' she demanded angrily.

She had no intention of abandoning either the cultural festival that she had been working on for a year and that she had planned to the last detail or the women's project against landmines. She said, 'I shall try to do it even if I am left on my own.' And she added, 'They want us to give up, to get fed up and withdraw into our holes. We mustn't give them the opportunity.'

Ömer noticed lines of exhaustion on her face that he had never noticed before. He saw the shadow of sadness. She would keep on struggling like this. The lines and shadows would deepen on her lovely face. He would remember the book's parentheses. One of those brackets would be our love and our passion. Then one day the book would end. By itself, because the story had ended. Or – he shudders to think – a bullet, an unsolved murder, a treacherous mine, an insidious explosion . . . The book would fall to the ground before the story ended.

Late into the night, she had said, 'Diyar will show you your room. I want to go and collect the books, notebooks and my own private belongings together', and had left them.

Now, as he thinks about it, he cannot believe that such an ending can be real. In any case, he doesn't believe that there can be an ending with Jiyan. A beginning! Yes, it was a beginning. The beginning of a new word. Perhaps it was a sad very poignant word but a word that would find people's hearts and focus on the future.

When they passed under the arch over which was written 'One country, one language, one flag' and reached the town, Diyar stopped the jeep in front of the Yıldız hotel. They did not even get out of the car to say goodbye. Jiyan held out her hand, her graceful hand with the array of rings on her fingers. Ömer bent over and kissed the rings. 'Goodbye,' he said. 'Thank you for the notebooks that you have entrusted to me. I'm going to learn your language and read them.'

'See you.'

'See you.'

Now as he returns along the roads along which he had come he thinks about this. He keeps on saying 'See you' to himself.

The message box of his mobile is full to overflowing. It's as though he has forgotten the existence of his phone. It has been days since I turned the damned thing on. What would happen if I did not switch it on and threw this bloody device in the rubbish? I should have done it when I started on my journey in pursuit of a scream to look for the word. I should have burnt my bridges, but I could not.

Elif's message had come this morning: 'I still cannot reach you. I'm coming back with Deniz and Bjørn.'

There is not just one but five messages from Mahmut. The last one was sent towards dawn. 'SOS. We are in trouble.'

As for Jiyan's message it is very recent. 'You have found the word, so now be our voice.'

He ignores the other messages and phone calls.

As he collects together his few belongings in room 204 of the Yıldız Hotel he has a terrible fit of laughing.

He repeats the messages out loud, 'I'm coming back with Deniz and Bjørn ... SOS. We are in trouble ... Be our voice ...' And he laughs and laughs. He almost chokes and laughs until he cries. He cries and cries – in great sobs. In a hotel room in the most east of the east, in a town that waits with ears pricked to the distant sounds of fighting, to the Cobras flying and to the noise of tanks passing through the streets and heading for the mountains, Ömer Eren cries bitterly with his head in his hands.

Then he goes into the bathroom with the dripping tap and the toilet reservoir that does not work, and washes his face. He does not look in the mirror. He knows that he has a growth of beard and bags under his eyes. He dreads his appearance. He needs a painkiller and a strong drink. Should I drop in at the Hayat Chemist? What if a woman whose raven-black hair seems to have become entangled with her voice should say, 'Can I help you?' If we reshoot the film. If I play my part better this time. If I said to her, 'Your eyes are like a country. Your voice is the voice of these lands.'

He puts the notebook that Jiyan gave him in his bag. He sits on the bed and looks around to see if he has forgotten anything. He texts Elif and

Mahmut the same message: 'I'm coming now.' He does not reply to Jiyan. She does not expect a response. After casting a quick glance round the room, he goes down counting the stains on the maroon stair carpet. His coach is about to leave. He must hurry. If he is in time, he will catch the evening flight to Ankara. If he is in time he will reach Mahmut and Zelal. If he is in time, he will board the Istanbul plane. If he is in time he will find his lost son. If he is in time he will take up a new life. If he is in time . . .

The elderly hotel clerk has difficulty sorting out his bill. 'How many nights haven't you paid for? Were there any extras?' Then in a meek voice. 'You are going and leaving us, *begim*. You are right to leave. Things have started to get tricky again here. We had got used to you. Think of us.'

The cat Vırik is beside the door in its usual place and is licking itself with its face to the light. He strokes Vırik with the top of his foot as he goes out. For a moment he looks across towards the marketplace. He sees the Hayat Chemist shop. Vırik is happy with being stroked even if only with the toe of his shoe and rubs against the bottoms of Ömer's trousers.

The hotel clerk comes to the door to see him off. 'Wait. Let me call a car, *begim*. Don't walk all the way to the station.' He waves down a taxi waiting in front of the hotel.

He does not object. He must not wait. He must leave here immediately. There must not be any goodbyes. He must not be drawn to the voices of the sirens. Anyway the sounds heard in the town now are not the sound of sirens but of tanks.

The driver shouted 'Zap Bridge', pointing to the bridge of his imagination. Military convoys passed us by. We stopped and were stopped. Identity? Open your bag! Where have you come from? Where are you going? . . . Road closed, road open, the mountains are still beautiful, the earth is still that yellow-grey, and the Zap river keeps on flowing as usual.

I'm lucky; there is a place on the waiting list for the plane. I call Mahmut as soon as I land. He is waiting for me in the hospital garden. He tells me so much so quickly that I can only understand that they wanted to shoot Zelal but they shot someone else instead. I rush to the medical superintendent, I rush to the doctors, go to the police, see influential friends and go to the place where Mahmut is hiding . . . My mind is at home, on Deniz and Elif . . . I don't know where I'm going. I call Elif. I say, 'I've returned, but I have to stay in Ankara to deal with a very important matter. As soon as I have put things in order I'll be home.' I don't know how I will put things in order. Zelal looks at him with her limpid blue eyes. She'll get better. She has just got over the shock, says the doctor. I'll take you to the sea. Get well quickly, I say to her. I find a place for Mahmut to hide, somewhere safer. Don't know how I have done all this. I just know that I had to do it and that I'm responsible for their suffering.

One night a few days later I find myself again waiting for a bus in the Başkent coach terminal. I missed the last plane while trying to help Mahmut and Zelal. I cannot wait until tomorrow. I can't wait at all. I must set off immediately, tonight. I buy some cigarettes, a lighter and mineral water from the Başkent kiosk. I'm not drunk. My mind is clear, lucid. But I am tired. I have never been so tired in all my life, so tired that I could just fall down and sleep right there. Which platform does my bus leave from? Was it Platform 10? I walk in that direction so that I can get on the bus as quickly as possible and go to sleep.

The woman is there, in the same place once more. She is sitting on the bench in front of Platform 8 with the same straw hat on her head and the same light-coloured Capri trousers. This is something beyond a dream, a nightmare. Perhaps it is an illusion. The rightful rebellion of my nervous system. I don't change direction. I don't run away. I walk towards her.

'I'm not the one who escaped from the east. I wasn't among those people who were smuggled across the Danube. I didn't see the child either. The Hungarian bride had gone to look for the candlesticks. It's all a lie. I did not collaborate with them. Have you seen the child, sir?'

'No, I haven't seen him,' I say. I want the woman to talk and explain. I feel her years of suffering inside me.

'Where are we, sir?' she asks. 'They were going to send me to the west. The child was also going to come to me. What is this place? I've been waiting for the child for years. Have I come to the wrong place?'

'No you are in the right place,' I say. 'The child will come. All lost children will return.'

I want to embrace the woman and cry my heart out. For those who come from the east and west and lose their way; for the children who don't arrive, for the ships that could not be boarded, for dreams that cannot come true, for the youth one can't return to; for our days that go up in flames and for our past on whose ashes we walk heavily. I want to cry loudly for the mourning houses, the burnt villages, the lost children, the shot children, the unborn children, the unknown deserters and the unknown deserters of life.

*

I was looking for a word, I heard a voice.

I went far away in pursuit of a scream.

I did not know that the voice I heard was the voice of suffering born of violence. I learnt it.

I followed that voice. I found the word.

I now have a word to say.

THE IDLE YEARS
Orhan Kemal

978-0-7206-1310-0 • PB • 224pp • £11.95

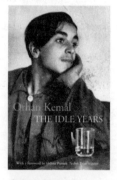

'Suffused though they are with the dark realities of poverty, Orhan Kemal's novels are celebrations of this other world. The optimism I find in them comes not from literature but from life itself.'
– Orhan Pamuk, from his foreword to this edition of *The Idle Years*

Orhan Kemal is one of Turkey's best-loved writers, with a standing akin to Dickens in England. *The Idle Years* is comprised of two semi-autobiographical novels, set in the 1920s and 1930s when Turkey was undergoing major social change. The unnamed narrator grows up in an affluent household in an Adana village with his brother, two sisters, mother and formidable father, a known political agitator, but the family are forced into exile on account of his activities. The boy develops into a rebellious and feckless teenager, reluctantly attempting to support his now impoverished family through menial work while resenting his father's stern attempts to control him. Eventually lack of money provokes him to set off for Istanbul to look for work. Before long he has developed into an alienated and self-conscious adolescent, and he soon has to make a humiliating return. The fact that his father is well born but notorious does not help him make his way in the world and things begin to look up only when he falls for a pretty young factory girl . . .

Peter Owen books can be purchased from:
Central Books, 99 Wallis Road, London E9 5LN, UK
Tel: +44 (0) 845 458 9911 Fax: + 44 (0) 845 458 9912
e-mail: orders@centralbooks.com

www.peterowen.com

Also published by Peter Owen

The Seven Churches
MILOŠ URBAN *(translated by Robert Russell)*
The Seven Churches is a bloody, atmospheric modern Gothic classic, a
bestseller in Czech, Spanish and German. Set in Prague's medieval
quarter, the narrator witnesses a series of mysterious murders,
triggering unsettling meetings with Gothic characters who appear to
be trying to reconstruct medieval Prague within the modern city.
PB / 978-0-7206-1311-7 / £8.99
'The Czech Republic's answer to Umberto Eco' – Radio Prague

Birdbrain
JOHANNA SINISALO *(translated by David Hackston)*
Birdbrain is a skilful portrait of the unquenchable desire of
Westerners for the pure and the primitive. A Finnish couple go on a
hiking trip in Australasia with only *Heart of Darkness* as reading
material. But what happens when nature starts to fight back?
PB / 978-0-7206-1343-8 / £9.99
'A sense of horror that will leave you troubled for weeks' – *Guardian*

Not Before Sundown
JOHANNA SINISALO *(translated by Herbert Lomas)*
In this award-winning bestseller, a gay photographer finds a young
troll and takes him home. It seems, however, that trolls
exude pheromones that have a profound aphrodisiac effect on all
those around them, and the troll becomes the interpreter of man's
darkest, most forbidden impulses.
PB / 978-0-7206-1350-6 / £9.99
'A punk version of *The Hobbit*' – *USA Today*

The Same River
JAAN KAPLINSKI *(translated by Susan Wilson)*
The Same River is the first novel by celebrated poet and essayist Jaan
Kaplinski. Semi-autobiographical, it describes a young man's life,
dominated by oriental studies, poetry and love, in Tartu, Soviet
Estonia, in the 1960s. But when he finds himself under investigation
for his relationship with an older poet, his life is changed for ever.
PB / 978-0-7206-1340-7 / £9.99
'A new light in the European galaxy' – *Independent*

SOME AUTHORS WE HAVE PUBLISHED

James Agee • Bella Akhmadulina • Tariq Ali • Kenneth Allsop
Alfred Andersch • Guillaume Apollinaire • Machado de Assis • Miguel Angel Asturias
Duke of Bedford • Oliver Bernard • Thomas Blackburn • Jane Bowles • Paul Bowles
Richard Bradford • Ilse, Countess von Bredow • Lenny Bruce • Finn Carling
Blaise Cendrars • Marc Chagall • Giorgio de Chirico •Uno Chiyo • Hugo Claus
Jean Cocteau • Albert Cohen • Colette • Ithell Colquhoun • Richard Corson
Benedetto Croce • Margaret Crosland • e.e. cummings • Stig Dalager • Salvador Dalí
Osamu Dazai • Anita Desai • Charles Dickens • Fabián Dobles • William Donaldson
Autran Dourado • Yuri Druzhnikov • Lawrence Durrell • Isabelle Eberhardt
Sergei Eisenstein • Shusaku Endo • Erté • Knut Faldbakken • Ida Fink
Wolfgang George Fischer • Nicholas Freeling • Philip Freund • Carlo Emilio Gadda
Rhea Galanaki • Salvador Garmendia • Michel Gauquelin • André Gide
Natalia Ginzburg • Jean Giono • Geoffrey Gorer • William Goyen • Julien Gracq
Sue Grafton • Robert Graves • Angela Green • Julien Green • George Grosz
Barbara Hardy • H.D. • Rayner Heppenstall • David Herbert • Gustaw Herling
Hermann Hesse • Shere Hite • Stewart Home • Abdullah Hussein
King Hussein of Jordan • Ruth Inglis • Grace Ingoldby • Yasushi Inoue
Hans Henny Jahnn • Karl Jaspers • Takeshi Kaiko • Jaan Kaplinski • Anna Kavan
Yasunuri Kawabata • Nikos Kazantzakis • Orhan Kemal • Christer Kihlman
James Kirkup • Paul Klee • James Laughlin • Patricia Laurent • Violette Leduc
Lee Seung-U • Vernon Lee • József Lengyel • Robert Liddell • Francisco García Lorca
Moura Lympany • Dacia Maraini • Marcel Marceau • André Maurois • Henri Michaux
Henry Miller • Miranda Miller • Marga Minco • Yukio Mishima • Quim Monzó
Margaret Morris • Angus Wolfe Murray • Atle Næss • Gérard de Nerval • Anaïs Nin
Yoko Ono • Uri Orlev • Wendy Owen • Arto Paasilinna • Marco Pallis • Oscar Parland
Boris Pasternak • Cesare Pavese • Milorad Pavic • Octavio Paz • Mervyn Peake
Carlos Pedretti • Dame Margery Perham • Graciliano Ramos • Jeremy Reed
Rodrigo Rey Rosa • Joseph Roth • Ken Russell • Marquis de Sade • Cora Sandel
George Santayana • May Sarton • Jean-Paul Sartre • Ferdinand de Saussure
Gerald Scarfe • Albert Schweitzer • George Bernard Shaw • Isaac Bashevis Singer
Patwant Singh • Edith Sitwell • Suzanne St Albans • Stevie Smith
C.P. Snow • Bengt Söderbergh • Vladimir Soloukhin • Natsume Soseki
Muriel Spark Gertrude Stein • Bram Stoker • August Strindberg
Rabindranath Tagore • Tambimuttu • Elisabeth Russell Taylor • Anne Tibble
Roland Topor • Miloš Urban • Anne Valery • Peter Vansittart • José J. Veiga
Tarjei Vesaas • Noel Virtue • Max Weber • Edith Wharton • William Carlos Williams
Phyllis Willmott • G. Peter Winnington • Monique Wittig • A.B. Yehoshua
Marguerite Young • Fakhar Zaman • Alexander Zinoviev • Emile Zola